Murder in Santa Barbara

Dean C. Ferraro

www.deancferraro.com

First edition, 2021.

Digital Biz Media

ISBN: 978-1-7378367-0-4 (Paperback)

ISBN: 978-1-7378367-2-8 (Hardback)

ISBN: 978-1-7378367-1-1 (eBook)

Acknowledgments

I want to give special thanks to my wife for her support and my children for their inspiration. I love you, and I could not have done this without you. Also, a special thanks to my wife for her professional, artistic sketch of the Santa Barbara Courthouse that was used as the focal point of the professional cover design, making it both unique and special.

Also, thank you to all my family and friends whose words of encouragement helped me cross the finish line. Not only have you supported my efforts to complete my lifelong dream, but you've also encouraged me to keep the ball rolling and the books coming.

Next, I would like to thank John Grisham, a fellow Ole Miss Law graduate. Your amazing storytelling drew me in from the first day I read one of your novels, ironically just a month before I started law school and roamed the same halls that you once strolled. While I can only dream of entertaining readers to a fraction of the extent to which you have, your courage to leave the practice of law to pursue your calling as a writer has inspired me to do the same. Hotty Toddy!

Finally, I would like to thank my readers. Without you, this book is just words on paper. Because of you, my writing has meaning. Because of you, my writing entertains, or so I aspire. To thank you further, I invite you to visit www.DeanCFerraro.com and sign up to join my email list. By doing so, you will receive a free audio version of the first chapter of *Murder in Santa Barbara*, along with updates and exclusive offers on the release of my third fiction novel, *The Grove Conspiracy.*

Chapter One

1

The marksman positioned himself on the rooftop of the charming local coffee shop. His laser-focused glare burned across the famed State Street in the coastal oasis of Santa Barbara. Although California wildfires were devastatingly common, no fire had ever raged like the one in him. He eyed his target. The clean-shaven, slick-hair-gelled, professionally dressed man sat at the patio table of Bayshore Cafe with whom appeared to be three other business executives, or so their attire would suggest.

The former college fraternity president appeared to be the alpha male at the table, monopolizing the group's conversation. He remained the sole focus of the rooftop stalker. Dressed in a navy-blue fifteen-hundred-dollar suit with polished loafers, life treated him well. With his coat hanging from the back of his chair, his shirt sleeves were folded up twice to cool him a bit from the summer heat. A designer watch flashed from his left wrist, flaunting his wealth. A power-red designer necktie completed his ensemble to wrap up his fashion statement, mirroring a model's portfolio cover photo.

The golden, blazing sun hovered over the wavy current of the Pacific Ocean, creating a majestic image that lived true to its nickname, "The American Riviera." What a blessed life, enjoying work in a charming, scenic town. What a blessed life, never wanting for money. What a blessed life, having your childhood dreams fall into place as easily as a preschool jigsaw puzzle. What a blessed life to call Santa Barbara home. Rage, envy, fury, and resentment. Without a doubt, these thoughts persisted. Given his past, what else could race through the rugged outsider's mind as he stared across the street, getting a glimpse of life on the other side of the tracks?

The well-to-do gentleman sat in the warm sun, smiling, laughing, joking, having no clue that his future lay in the hands of a stranger forty-five yards away. Fixated on his mark, the stranger's eyes bore a hole in the head of his target. He couldn't even blink. The hunter had envisioned the image of his prey, and the successful capitalist was a dead ringer. It was him. There was no mistaking it. Without a doubt, it was him.

The rooftop tracker looked to be in his late thirties or early forties, but his thick, overgrown beard, sprinkled with some early gray, visually aged him a bit. From the looks of his dense, jungly beard, if he wasn't going for a lumberjack look, he should have been. Because he nailed it. About six feet tall, he carried a slender frame, although somewhat muscular. The build of someone who spent most of his workdays doing outdoor physical labor. His dark tan and leathery skin complemented his manly physique. Construction worker, maybe; cement contractor, perhaps; armed forces, certainly. His left upper arm displayed the American flag draped over a silhouette of a bald eagle, advertising the same tattoo he shared proudly with his former Army unit. Awarded a Distinguished Marksmanship Badge during his service, he was nothing if not well-focused.

His past was tumultuous. With four tours in Iraq under his belt, he proved himself no stranger to violence and almost welcomed it when it played out on his terms. Disturbingly, his time at war held as some of the best days of the past twenty-five-plus years of his life. Less violent, and more of a sense of belonging.

He rested his elbows on the edge of the building and continued to stare. Watching every movement of the local resident with the precision of a world-class sharpshooter, he raised both hands slowly, tool in hand, visualizing taking the shot. Through the lens of his instrument, he locked-in to his prey. Concentration was crucial to accomplish the task at hand, and the trained Army vet followed the ritual he had engaged in countless times before: breathe, focus, aim, shoot.

Methodically taking slow, deep breaths, he focused. For years he searched tirelessly, struggled mightily, and lost hope repeatedly before reaching this point. He waited patiently for the right moment. And now, past regret, the moment had presented itself. The moment was here. The moment was now.

"BANG!" A loud, booming pop shook the salty air, echoing up State Street!

Jolting the man from his anchored state, the backfire of an old jalopy cried for help from the street below and snapped him out of his incomparable focus. The piece-of-junk clunker spat and puttered, struggling to make it up the slight incline of the touristy street. The '58 Edsel had flatlined and been jumped back to life more times than one could count and scared the bejesus out of passersby with every faux gunshot blasting from its defective exhaust system.

Back on course, the marksman regained his concentration, took a deep breath, and gathered his focus. He aimed carefully, once again narrowing in on his target. Breathe, focus, aim, shoot; he was three-quarters done. Then, with his right index finger positioned and steady, he took the shot, followed without delay by another shot.

In an instant, his mark hunched over the outdoor dining table. All the way stooped over; his forehead slammed on the edge of the table.

"Everything okay?" one of his table-side colleagues asked.

"Excuse me." The target reached forward, between his legs, and retrieved the white cloth napkin that had slipped from his lap. He returned to the upright position, lifted the napkin above the table like waving a white flag in surrender, and gave it a shake to display the source of his distraction; concurrently revealing a distinctive silver bracelet that he sported on his right wrist.

The damaged clasp of the chain loosened, and the bracelet clanked on the table. Before securing the fallen jewelry back on his wrist, he gently whipped the napkin clean and placed it on his lap. He chuckled at the disturbance he inadvertently had caused. Then, with his left hand, he returned the silver wristlet back to its natural habitat. The sun gleamed off its shiny metal tag that was personalized with a custom inscription, a sentiment he had never shared with a soul.

With the camera mode on display, and his phone in hand, the former military marksman took four more photos of the carefree thirty-something-year-old Armani suit-wearing traitor. He wanted to make sure. He needed to be certain. The observer zoomed in to the max and took two final shots: another of the turncoat's face and one of the silver bracelet.

The rooftop onlooker saved the photo shots in a newly created folder on his smartphone, labeled "Target X." It was him. He stared at the last photo, and confident in his military training, he trusted the old-school method of visual confirmation. From the eyes of the marksman, Target X's features made the Army vet as certain of the subject's identity as fingerprints and DNA ever could. Unmistakably, it was him.

A lost memory had turned into a faded memory. A faded memory had grown into a clearer memory. The clearer memory developed into a theory. The theory prompted an investigation. An investigation provoked a search. A search led to a place. The place led to a man. The man was Target X. And Target X was him. There was no mistaking it. It was him.

Chapter Two

2

J oshua Rizzetti was more than criminal defense attorneys could handle. Not even the best and brightest could match his courtroom litigation skills. Many tried, but all failed. And although Josh was still on the front end of his prosecutorial career with the Santa Barbara District Attorney's Office, his innate abilities seasoned him beyond his years.

Like most attorneys, his legal career did not start out as hoped. During his first stint as an attorney fresh out of law school, presented only with the common path of many young lawyers, he chose the road more traveled. An insurance defense law firm forced him into the pigeonhole of civil litigation. The United States' version of a sweatshop.

Associate attorney positions with insurance defense firms were the greatest in number, although seldom a top preference for any recent law school graduate or unemployed lawyer. In fact, those jobs presented the only choice for desperate, unproven lawyers. Well, choice may be too strong of a word. By attorney standards, the hours were brutal, and the pay was minimal. Who, in his or her right mind, would choose that? While entrenched in that grind, Josh joked with his non-attorney friends, "if I worked this many hours at a fast-food chain for minimum wage, I'd be making more money."

It didn't take long for Josh to realize he was not alone. In talking with other budding associates from various firms, Josh learned that all insurance defense law firms were the same, just with different surnames on the wall. Regardless of the firm's name, the conditions were indistinguishable. They required you to bill roughly one hundred forty hours per week, which meant, in truth, working two-hundred-seventy-two hours per week. "Wait," you say, "that math does not equate!" Correct, the math does not equate. Welcome to the life of a new associate at an insurance defense law firm.

The impossible hours rewarded by non-commensurate compensation were just a couple of the umpteen perks Josh enjoyed. An associate had to learn everything on his own because everybody else couldn't waste their time on non-billable stuff, like training the blockhead! This resulted in a vicious cycle of newbies spending non-billable time figuring out how to produce billable work. And a lawyer who was breathing and not billing was a liability, not an asset.

And a newsflash to the unburdened souls not blessed with the monstrous debt of a law school education; law schools don't teach the actual practice of law. Rather, they teach only the law itself, brainwashing students to think like a lawyer. But as to the practical application of the daily legal profession, Josh was on his own to figure that out.

And if all of that wasn't enough, there was more! That's right, associates reaped the benefits of more perks of the prestigious profession. Loaded with a hundred grand in debt, an ambitious associate arrived at the office before the partners, left the office after the partners, and if his billable work trailed, he'd better catch up and fast. Because if one was searching for work, that meant one was not billing. And if one was not billing, one was not making money for the firm. And if one was not making the firm money, then why the heck did they hire his lazy ass in the first place? If the law firm names were honest, instead of the likes of Smith, Jones, and Johnson, they would be more on the order of Bend, Dover, and Takit or Werk, Yurassoff, and Sukkit.

Josh devoted his time for two years with the firm Kissaway, Yurdreems, and Dye. Although that wasn't the legal name of the firm, Josh convinced himself that was the name on his paychecks. In point of fact, the receptionist at the law office answered the phone with the greeting "Wheatly, Marble and Rhye," so it's likely that was the correct name. Hearing her answer the phone only made Josh hungry and undoubtedly sparked happy daydreams of working at a bakery.

Oh yes, resembling the many insurance defense associates before him, Josh dreamed of doing something else. Anything else! And sadly, he experienced such regret awfully early in his legal career. So was the life of a rookie associate at an insurance defense law firm. A life of regret. A life of what could have been.

After two years of sweating in the heat at "The Bakery," the firm's local calling card, Josh got out of the kitchen. He applied, interviewed, and exuberantly accepted an offer of his dream job with the District Attorney's Office. It elated Josh to leave, but he remained grateful to the firm for giving him his first opportunity to bake . . . or was it practice law? Whatever it was, he was appreciative.

In giving notice to the firm's managing partner, Josh told him, "Mr. Marble, I have to tell you something. And I hope it doesn't get a *rise* out of you. The work here is becoming *stale*, and lately, I feel I'm just *loafing* around. I *knead* to work elsewhere before my career is *toast*. I'm taking a job as a Deputy District Attorney, as I know that's a *butter* fit for me. Don't be *sour, dough*. I'll speak *warmly* of this firm. It's the *yeast* I can do after all you've *done* for me."

Mr. Marble laughed so hard that tears ran down his eyes as he shook Josh's hand. The senior partner of "The Bakery" wished his blossoming associate good luck, knowing he had lost a good one. Mr. Marble was so impressed with his departing associate's cleverness, he printed, framed, and hung the parting words on his office wall. When word got out, Josh's resignation became legendary.

Josh set a high standard to live up to with his well-imagined, well-executed, and hilarious farewell to his previous employer. His unique exit plan, coupled with his well-respected reputation as an elite litigator, placed lofty hopes of Josh with his new employer. Happily, Josh was up to the task. Before long, he exceeded expectations.

Josh demonstrated himself as a natural courtroom litigator, seemingly born to argue and blessed with an unmatched ability to think on his feet. Tantamount to a master chess player, he was always several steps ahead of his competition. But what separated Josh from the pack went beyond his God-given talents, which translated seamlessly to litigation. It was his tireless, meticulous, borderline obsessive preparation that took his game to the next level.

***

A SIGN OF the times, metal detectors had become a part of daily life at courthouses across the country, and the peaceful coastal town of Santa Barbara was no exception. But this week was a little different. Given a glitch in the walk-through sensors in the stand-alone metal detectors, the court officers had been doing it in old-school style the past two days.

Deputy District Attorney Joshua Rizzetti spent most of the morning picking a jury. After wrapping up a few housekeeping matters, the presiding judge adjourned for lunch, with opening statements to begin after the break. On paper, the trial appeared to be an insignificant misdemeanor; and one that would settle one hundred out of one hundred times. But not this one.

The police had charged the four defendants each with the offense of Disturbing a Public Meeting. That crime was a misdemeanor offense punishable by up to six months in jail and a maximum fine of up to one thousand dollars. The group on trial was known as the *Formidable Foursome*. In short, they had attended a local city council meeting and created major chaos by imposing their will. Rather than follow the simple council protocols implemented to ensure peace, civility, and equal time for the attendees, they did things their way. As a result, pandemonium ensued.

A self-proclaimed civil rights activist group, the four defendants intentionally ignored the requisite step of getting placed on the city council meeting's agenda to be heard. Instead, they insisted on promoting their anti-police brutality message at the time and in the manner of their choosing. In classic form, they were an activist group that forced their message of "do as I say, not as I do."

Their anarchist activism, a form of *I don't have to live by the rules* approach, caused major disruption and a near riot at the meeting. It was only after the police drew their guns that peace restored itself. In recognition of their intentions, they charged the *Formidable Foursome* with Disturbing a Public Meeting.

The group's infamous ringleader, Clarence Irving, was an American activist, writer, and black anarchist. He also was a former member of the Black Puma Party and Active Citizens for Justice. Some recognized him as a Civil Rights Leader, although civil was never his modus operandi.

Twenty-one years earlier, Mr. Irving had hijacked a plane to Morocco to evade prosecution for allegedly trying to kill a KKK leader. His trial and felony conviction followed. However, despite being the first person ever to receive a life sentence for an aircraft hijacking under United States law, he only served fourteen years in prison.

Drawing the short straw, Josh was the lucky Deputy D.A. assigned to prosecute the *Formidable Foursome's* misdemeanor case. His experience equipped him to handle the related pressure, yet he wasn't too senior as to feel above going to trial on such a relatively minor case. Considering the infamy of Mr. Irving, the publicity surrounding the case was expected. The risk, however, was not.

During the weeks leading up to the trial, Josh had received several threats from all over the world, alleging that it was a racially motivated prosecution and demanding that he dismiss the case. Dreadfully, not all threats were merely strong words cowering behind the protection of a computer screen. Quite to the contrary, some were unpleasantly detailed death threats. So much so, the bomb squad screened all packages to the D.A.'s Office while the case was pending.

After in-depth discussions with his boss, they concluded that justice must prevail. Regardless of the intimidation, Josh was not to cave to the threats of violence. And so, they set the case for trial, and today was it.

Prior to the trial, Josh had alerted the presiding judge of the threats of violence surrounding the case. In response, the judge instructed the court officers to not only scan the trial bystanders with wands as they entered the courtroom but also to examine carefully the courtroom itself. True to their duties, the Sheriff's Deputies did just that.

After lunch, as everyone in the courtroom had settled, Deputy District Attorney Rizzetti stood up to make his opening statement. Prepared as always, the stage was set, and he was primed to perform. Josh buttoned the top button on his suit. He glided around the counsel's table and faced the jury, making eye contact with an elderly lady juror in the front row. But before the young prosecutor could say a word, one of the court officers swiftly approached the judge and whispered in his ear. The judge's jaw dropped, and his face turned pale as if he had seen a ghost!

"Counsel, can you approach the bench?" the judge beckoned.

Realizing that something was gravely wrong, the attorneys darted to the judge's bench, Josh almost at a gallop.

With no prelude, the judge dropped a bomb on the attorneys and spouted, "One of my court officers found bullets taped underneath a bench in the courtroom. Go to my chambers now!" In a flash, the judge disappeared from behind the bench.

Before Josh could change his diaper, screams of horror reverberated throughout the courtroom. In nothing flat, a gunshot boomed. The screaming escalated as panicked bystanders scattered faster than cockroaches searching for safety. The defense attorney, Lee Templeton, dove behind the podium centered twelve feet in front of the judge's bench. Deputy District Attorney Joshua Rizzetti dropped to the floor.

Chapter Three

3

The Boat Hut at Leadbetter Beach was the ideal respite for a lost soul. Nestled along the coast, it was a short walk up the beach from the Santa Barbara pier, on the north end of Shoreline Drive. Friday's happy hour truly made for several happy hours and hundreds of happy patrons, extending from 8 p.m. to close.

The oceanfront restaurant used the term happy hour loosely. Like other Santa Barbara eateries, The Boat Hut was heavy on the wallet, even with happy hour prices. In truth, the happy hour costs more closely resembled inflated menu prices for out-of-towners. But for locals, Friday evenings were a bargain. Offering a bountiful culinary variety, the happy hour menu included burgers, tacos, buffalo wings, chicken sliders, and more. And for seafood lovers, the surf options extended bite-size versions of select dinner menu dishes.

Well-designed, the glass-enclosed open-air dining area contemplated comfort and beauty. The dining patio covered nineteen hundred square feet to the side and back of the main building, highlighted by an unobstructed view of the Pacific Ocean. The orange glow of the outdoor heaters that were perfectly spaced throughout the outdoor patio tempered the cool ocean air. Aesthetically, the portable gas heaters complimented the orangish-yellow sunset blanket mother nature tucked in below the distant waves. Flattering the ambiance, a cobblestone gas fire pit provided added light and a profusion of heat to the open outdoor space.

The popular dining establishment was bursting at the seams. Outside the front door, a dozen people waited to be seated. Outdoors, patrons fully occupied the patio seating. The patio bar entertained several seated customers and those standing around its eight butt-warmed stools. With the crowd indulging in happy hour, the chatter level was boisterous, the mood was vibrant, and the music blared.

Nick Knowles leaned back in one of the solid wood Adirondack chairs that surrounded the firepit. He tasted the air, flavored by the smell of the out-of-this-world signature chowder fries. The famous appetizer eclipsed the mouth-watering world and entered the drooling stratosphere. They smothered the classic Old Bay Fries with homemade New England clam chowder and topped them with bacon, combining to create an enduring aroma. But, to the neglect of the delectable appetizer, Nick heavily favored the liquid diet. He started with two Blood Orange Margaritas, then progressed to his third IPA, while putting them away with the urgency of a hazed frat boy.

Although the firepit kept them warm, he seemed disinterested in the oceanic-style fries after just a couple of bites. Never letting his drink last long enough to become tepid, Nick consumed faster than his server could replenish. His fury was blazing at twice the temperature of the fire pit that warmed his legs, as he leaned back in his chair with his feet resting on the edge of the pit. Eight feet to his rear, a group of patrons ate and drank. Oblivious to his presence, Nick eavesdropped on their conversation.

Five patrons occupied the table in question: a beautiful young woman, one of Target X's lunchtime companions from earlier that day, two more sharply dressed, middle-aged men, and Target X. Despite Nick's effort, listening in on their conversation was no simple task. The thunderous music and jumbled chatter blended into a noisy mixture. The jumping joint appreciated its Fridays, and the buzz reflected that.

Nick struggled for some time, desperate to snoop in on the conversation to his rear; but his efforts proved futile. Absent sitting on the lap of his prey, overhearing enough to decipher the sum and substance of their dialogue was not going to happen. At this point, his ears strained less, his mind drifted further, and his mouth drank more.

From the distant look on his face, and in furtherance of his theory—a theory that once appeared unfathomable—it seemed natural that his life would play chronologically through his mind with the speed of a rewinding, vintage 8mm film reel. Nearly a lifetime, after countless years, the jigsaw puzzle that was his life was almost complete. A lifetime of loss. A lifetime of neglect. Riddled with struggle. Devastated by abuse. A lifetime of bouncing around like a pinball. What might have been? Finally, he supported his theory with visual evidence. It was him. There was no mistaking it. It definitely was him.

His waitress approached and snapped him out of a trance.

"Is there something wrong with your fries? If so, I can bring you something else." The soft-spoken waitress tried to comfort her patron, whose facial despair reflected that of someone lost and in emotional pain.

"No, thanks. But you can take them away. I'm just not hungry. But I will have another IPA. Thank you."

Nick downed two pale ales and three more IPAs over the next hour. Semi-unconscious in deep thought, he chugged away on autopilot. And not for the first time. Consuming a few too many was not a foreign concept to the retired Army Sergeant. And if ever it was justified, today was it. Neither the unspeakable events of wartime nor the years of childhood abuse ever evoked the rage he must have been feeling since scoping the enemy across State Street. Overcome with emotion, he continued to drink while periodically attempting to eavesdrop on the group of five seated at the table behind him. But his ability to listen decreased in direct disproportion to the increase in his blood alcohol content.

***

HE HAD FOLLOWED his mark after first setting eyes on him earlier that day as the affluent gentleman basked in the glow of State Street. After lunch on the patio, the marksman followed his target back to his workplace and patiently waited for him to finish the workday and leave the building. The overpriced—suit-wearing male model wannabe had the car to match the sumptuousness of his attire. He drove an Anthracite Blue metallic *Mercedes Benz* sedan. Having splurged one hundred and fifty thousand dollars for a car, subtlety clearly was not his strong suit. He was wealthy, and he wanted everyone to know it. Wealth meant power, and though he had plenty of both, he couldn't secure enough of either.

After leaving his workplace, the next stop was a drive-thru ATM at the American Riviera Bank and Trust on Anacapa Street. The stalker followed closely and was the next vehicle in line. Nick sported a baseball cap shoved down to his eyebrows and wore large, dark sunglasses that would've made every motorcycle cop jealous. With his large, lumberjack beard covering the lower half of his face, only the skin on his nose and a fraction of his lips were visible to the naked eye.

The luxury vehicle pulled away from the ATM and cautiously drove toward the bank's driveway exit with prudence common to the driver of an automobile priced higher than the average single-family home in middle America. The stalker-driven rental vehicle stopped at the ATM for authenticity but never lost sight of the *Mercedes*. Nick rolled down his window and waited, pretending to engage in a transaction to keep his cover.

After a significant delay, a receipt was discharged from the ATM. Playing the part of a customer, Nick grabbed the receipt and his eyes jumped to the balance. Not surprisingly, the withdrawal amount was huge. One thousand dollars! And the total balance had more digits than he had ever seen on an ATM receipt. In disgust, he crumbled it and tossed it on the passenger-side floorboard and followed on, concentrating on his mission.

The next stop was the parking area of the Santa Barbara Zoo. Roughly two-thirds full, cars sporadically spread throughout the entire lot, with just a few people exiting the local attraction and heading to their vehicles. The *Mercedes* parked at the far end of the parking lot, farthest from the zoo ticket booth at the entrance. Target X remained in his vehicle, windows rolled up and engine running. His tail parked two rows over and seven car lengths toward the zoo entrance, sandwiched between two small SUVs, waiting anxiously, and watching closely to see what was next.

Five minutes passed by without incident. The *Mercedes* sat there idling, polluting the beach air, although somewhat expected from such an entitled elitist. Was the rich man waiting for a female escort? Could he be waiting for a male escort? Was he purchasing drugs? Did this involve any kind of illegal activity, and hence the secrecy? At this point in his investigation, Nick Knowles had lots of questions and not enough answers.

Nick picked up his phone and took several photos. His pinched thumb and pointer finger pressed against the screen, then separated to zoom in on his target. In doing so, another vehicle rolled into his view. He snapped a quick photo and put the phone down to catch a broader look with his naked eyes.

The approaching vehicle was a black SUV with no identifiable logo and dark tinted windows, blocking any view of its occupants. From the size, shape, and style, it looked to be an eight-cylinders, three-row, eight-seater American-made SUV. Notably, it lacked a permanent license plate, having just the temporary paper license plate of a new automobile. And its most conspicuous feature, it was from the state of Nevada.

Creeping forward, the SUV pulled up face-to-face beside the *Mercedes.* About five inches away, the side view mirrors almost collided. The driver-side windows of both vehicles lowered simultaneously, and the SUV crawled to a stop. The vehicles themselves, along with their illegally dark tint, obstructed Nick's view and prevented him from seeing the face of the SUV driver. However, he could see body movement. He watched the SUV driver reach out the window and place a thick white envelope, maybe two inches deep, into the outstretched hands of Target X. A stack of cash, perhaps.

The SUV driver's hand was now empty, and it remained extended out the open window. Target X pulled his arm in, envelope in hand. After a six-second pause, his hand extended out his window and placed a small object, the size of a flash drive, in the open palm of the SUV driver. Tighter than a vice grip, the recipient clenched the object before retreating into his vehicle.

Not two seconds later, the driver-side windows rolled up in unison, and the *Mercedes* abruptly raced for the exit of the parking lot. What was with the cloak and dagger meeting in a semi-filled zoo parking lot? Who was in the SUV? What did the parties exchange? To keep a tail on his target, Nick had no time to answer questions. So off he went, trailing just beyond the shadow of the *Mercedes*.

The opulent status symbol turned left out of the zoo parking area and headed southeast on Ninos Drive toward Cabrillo Boulevard. The ocean view intersection crossed only a couple of football fields away from the zoo. Nick followed closely, but not too much. All of a sudden, the six-figure, four-wheel badge of wealth floored it as if engaged in a high-speed chase with the cops. In an instant, the ease of tailing the luxury sedan had passed. Unexpectedly, the bold maneuvers of the high-performance automobile, coupled with the audacity of its driver as he weaved in and out of lanes and passed vehicles as he raced up the coastline road, created a catch twenty-two for Nick. Torn between two choices, he needed to decide, and fast. Similar driving on his part would bring awareness to his tracking. Too complacent, and his target would slip away.

Fortunately for Nick, the tracked vehicle reached its destination before he lost sight of it. About to lose visual of his prey, Nick spotted Target X pulling into the parking area of a local oceanfront eatery. He did the same, keeping a strategic distance. The Boat Hut at Leadbetter Beach was a scenic restaurant that overlooked the Santa Barbara Harbor and its incomparable beauty. With its worldly view, a full house was a given; making it a cinch for Nick to stay on the down-low.

***

BY THE TIME he ordered his last drink, Nick's speech slurred repeatedly. Borderline intelligible, he asked the server for his check. Trained in drunk detection, and concerned with his level of inebriation, the waitress sent over the supervisor.

"Sir," the manager said as delicately as possible, to avoid triggering an angry drunk, which was not unheard of during happy hour. "Would you like us to arrange a ride for you?"

"I appreciate it. But I, I'm good. I'll walk to my motel from here. I think—I think it's just a few babablocks away."

The manager sighed at the unexpectedly polite response, having averted an ugly scene. "That's fine. If you change your mind, please just let us know. We'd be happy to call you an Uber."

"What? You'd be happy to call me a goober!"

"No sir. Uber! Lyft. You know, a ride."

"Oh! Thank you, sir, but don't worry," the tanked patron assured the manager, acknowledging his responsibility. "I won't be driving."

Intoxicated, infuriated, and inundated with emotions, Mr. Knowles wallowed in the warmth of the firepit. As the fire and his fury burned, the heat got to him. It was time to go. Abandoning his hope of snooping further on his target, Nick closed out his bill. He left a fairly generous tip to his server, clearly appreciating her service and delicate handling of the awkward situation he created.

Nick paid with his credit card. He had the cash to cover the bill and tip but certainly was not in a clear state of mind after his breakthrough that triggered a flood of emotions in his heart and alcohol in his blood.

With a rap sheet that included two prior DUIs, he should have known better than to pay with a credit card after drinking too much. Clearly, he wasn't thinking. And if he was thinking, it wasn't clearly. If he got behind the wheel and was pulled over, a credit card receipt yielded irrefutable, incriminating evidence that would nullify the classic defense of "I only had a couple of drinks."

Wandering toward the exit gate next to the parking lot, Nick was careful not to draw attention to himself. Undoubtedly, having put away enough alcohol to escalate his blood alcohol content well above the legal limit, a discreet and subtle exit mitigated the chance of an unpleasant situation getting worse. He trudged his way to the wrought iron gate that separated the outdoor dining area from the parking area. No good Samaritan tried to stop him. Thank God. The last thing he needed was to draw attention from his target. Not that his target had ever seen him. Nevertheless. To have years of investigation, digging, and searching all go down the toilet from a drunken binge would be agonizing. More devastating than the discovery that led to his search in the first place.

He opened the gate quietly, almost in slow motion, and closed it just the same. His eyes focused on his steps. He stumbled about four steps outside the exit gate when he tripped over the second of six flowerpots that outlined the walkway, leaving a pile of dirt in his wake. To his luck, or perhaps not, nobody saw him kiss the ground. The outside chatter and the ambient music of the restaurant drowned his noisy clumsiness. Struggling to get back on his feet, he placed the pot upright, with more of the soil spilling onto the concrete; and in a sweeping motion, dragged his right shoe like a broom to brush the soil closer to the pot's base.

He paused and gathered his thoughts. Where was his car parked? He scanned the area to look for clues. There were none. If only he had gone to *Disneyland*, he would've remembered parking next to Minnie or Pluto or some other memorable mutt to locate his vehicle. No such luck here. Perhaps they should have marked the lot with animated signs of fries, burgers, shrimp, and appetizers. On the other hand, that would only lead to drunks asking themselves, "did I order the calamari or park near the squid?"

He roamed the edge of the parking rows until he recognized his rental car. Surely, never had someone been so thankful for getting stuck with the last ride on the car rental lot, which in his case was an orange Subaru. He stumbled over to his automobile to grab his mobile phone, which in his scramble to follow Target X, he'd left in the car.

Luckily, he reached his car without falling over again, vomiting, or getting pancaked by a moving vehicle. Nick leaned against it in exhaustion. He shuffled through his pockets to recover his keys, then fiddled with his keys to spot the right key. He averted use of the keyless entry; perhaps in fear that his car might honk, beep, or make some other untimely, undesirable noise, and draw unwanted concern to the drunk getting in a vehicle, or perhaps because he was too plastered to figure it out.

The car being a rental, and given his intoxicated condition, he was in no position to recall if the unlock button triggered some type of loud noise or if it detonated a bomb. A bomb would have been a welcomed surprise, but God forbid he pressed the alarm button. Ninety-six seconds later, alas, the door was open. He plopped down in the driver's seat, reached into the center console, and pulled out his phone.

"Better make sure where the hell I'm going," he said aloud.

With his smartphone in hand, he struggled to search Google for directions from the restaurant to his motel to determine the shortest path as the crow flies, or more precisely, as the drunk walks. Orange Grove Inn, Grapefruit Tree Motel . . . it was some type of citrus fruit. That he was driving a car that looked like an orange and had been drinking Blood Orange Margaritas and Citrus IPAs added to his confusion. After several attempts at guessing an entire citrus grove in Florida, he landed on the right fruit, and thus his motel, the Lemon Orchard Inn.

He grabbed a double take at the directions. Was it really one point eight miles to his inn? Why did it seem like only a few blocks? Perhaps if he had spent more time walking around, and less time stalking, his sense of proximity would have been more accurate. After several days in Santa Barbara, it seems natural that he would have had a better layout of the land. But his focus and attention remained elsewhere. And understandably so. As for now, he looked too exhausted, too angry, and too inebriated to walk one point eight minutes, let alone one point eight miles. Given that, goober it was. Or was it Uber? Either way, he had the app downloaded on his phone.

He waited in his car for seventeen minutes. If the app was accurate, his ride should have arrived by now. What was taking so long? Did he screw up? Did he put in the wrong address? He checked again. The app initially had estimated a driver to arrive in six minutes. Finally, after twenty-two minutes, he received a message that the driver had a flat. A new driver would arrive in twenty-three minutes. "Really, twenty-three minutes?" Nick said out loud. "I can wander there in fifteen minutes."

Too impatient to wait, he canceled the rideshare. Again, he pulled up the directions on his smartphone. He stared at it for several seconds and dejectedly exhaled aloud, "One point eight miles. A long walk. A short drive."

Too tired to walk, he rolled the dice. After all, it was a super short drive, and if he traveled the side streets, he'd maintain a low profile. Up this street, over on that street, a few turns, and his head would hit the pillow in minutes . . . or so he must have thought when he inserted the key in the ignition and started his ride.

Chapter Four

4

TWENTY MINUTES LATER.

"Dispatch, this is Officer Rodriguez. We've got a leaving the scene of an accident at the intersection of Bath Street and Sola Street. We're gonna need forensics and another unit. Over."

"Derek, from the blood on the steering wheel, it looks like the driver hit it when the vehicle hit the light post. Enough to draw some blood, but not enough impact to deploy the airbag. The driver is probably still nearby." Officer Tom Wilkey pointed to the trail of possible blood drops leading away from the wreck while briefing his partner.

"Copy that, TW. I'll run the plates."

Officer Rodriguez ran the plates while Officer Wilkey continued to inspect the scene. TW, as he was called, picked up a wrinkled piece of paper on the floorboard of the vehicle and uncrumpled it with his hands. He looked at it. His eyebrows raised. Just then, his partner hollered out to him.

"TW. The vehicle came back as a rental. It came from Holiday Car Rental in Simi Valley, rented to Nicholas Knowles. There's no report of the car being stolen, so that's likely the identity of our driver."

"Good work, Derek. Let's get forensics out here to process the scene and collect the blood evidence. If it matches this Knowles fella, we've got our runner."

***

BLOOD DRIPPED FROM Nick's lacerated head, but he didn't have the energy to both walk and wipe the blood from his face, so walking took priority. He had stumbled back to his motel within ten minutes of his crash. With little to no time for an alcohol-saturated brain to think, he had to decide right away. If he reported the rental car stolen, it provided him with a viable alibi, but he had to hasten.

He washed the blood from his forehead. But before deciding what to do next, let alone act, the alcohol got the better of him. He crashed again, this time on the motel room bed. Fully dressed, and with shoes still on, he was out cold.

It didn't take long for the police to connect the dots. After learning the identity of the renter of the vehicle, they ran a credit card check under the same name. The recent card usage showed a security deposit for a hotel room in Santa Barbara. As simple as that, the police located the whereabouts of their primary suspect. Officers Wilkey and Rodriguez were on it.

Not two hours had gone by when Nick awoke to a knock on his motel room door.

"Hello. Open up!" Officer Wilkey pounded on the door three more times. "Santa Barbara Police."

Nick jumped up from the bed. He looked around the room, ready for an escape hatch to appear.

Officer Wilkey slugged the door a few more times, shaking half the inn. "This is the Santa Barbara Police," he repeated. "Open up."

With his only exit strategy being to plow past an officer-obstructed door, Nick reluctantly opened the door.

"Nicholas Knowles?" Office Rodriguez said.

The former military man showed his respect for the uniform. "Yes sir. What's wrong, officer?" he asked, playing ignorant.

"Mr. Knowles." Officer Wilkey extended his hand, pointing at the swirling red lights of the squad car that was parked at an angle, no more than ten feet in front of the inn room door. "We need to take you down to the station for questioning on a Leaving the Scene of an Accident." TW took a whiff and eyed the fully clothed but disheveled suspect, then added, "And possible DUI."

Chapter Five

5

For all he knew, it could be just a matter of time before his past caught up to him. For years, Target X operated on the unknown. Albeit possible, it was highly likely that he had nothing to worry about; for the one person who knew his secret had to be dead. Nonetheless, he left nothing to chance. Since day one, he had been taking steps to preserve his future and avoid the possibility of retribution; determined to dodge karma.

His threshold was limitless as to the actions he would take to protect himself from his past. A bribe here, a threat there, a bit of extortion where necessary, and creating loyal alliances whenever the opportunity presented itself. Once, he paid a techie wizard a small fortune for a hacking gig to alter key data in various databases. He even had a court clerk secured by his under-the-table payroll. Periodically and consistently, he checked into his days gone by for any new information or developments, operating based on the strategy of better to be safe than sorry.

For over twenty years he had been looking over his shoulder, terrified that revenge may tap on it when he least expected it. There had been nothing. But like a great white shark torpedoing itself from the deep to kill its unwary prey, a surprise attack could end his day at the beach in an instant. Thus, he needed to remain on high alert.

Despite his professional-GQ appearance, he was a wolf in sheep's clothing. Not a hint of fear could be detected in his outward appearance and demeanor. The slick-dressed mastermind exuded confidence in his day-to-day interactions with the public. Thanks to years of practice, he portrayed no visible evidence of the paranoia that lingered beneath the surface.

A few years prior, as his career and wealthy empire were on the rise, and the ceiling to his future nowhere in sight, he took yet another proactive step to insulate himself from the potential repercussions of the secret sins of his past.

An instrumental part of his plan was to be alerted if proof ever surfaced that warranted his paranoia. Although inconceivable, if scientific verification existed, an alert would warn him that the shark was in the water, hungry for a meal that could sustain it for life. If so, Target X's metaphorical surfing days could be numbered, especially if either he failed to escape the water in time, or discreetly remove the shark from the turbulent waters.

Target X had taken every step he thought of, to distance himself from his past. When his parents unexpectedly died in a car crash during his sophomore year in college, he raced to the courthouse to change his full legal name. To remove any traceable record of his past, he took it a step further and was successful in getting the proceeding closed to the public, with his former name kept under seal. Just like that, he was an unknown man with a limitless future.

With the benefits outweighing the risk, he had perjured himself in court as a means to an end. He successfully argued to the judge that his previous name placed him in danger of some less-than-credible creditors who had made substantial, private loans to his wealthy parents' business and who were now determined to collect on the less-traditional, compounded interest. Erring on the side of caution, the judge obliged. Lucky for Target X, no judge wants to be the one who denies a request resulting in the petitioner being found chained to a cinder block at the bottom of the Pacific.

Thanks to the generous inheritance from his wealthy parents, he possessed the means to transform his identity to another level. And rhinoplasty was the method. He was already self-conscious of his prominent nose after fracturing it during the vanity stage of his early teen years, and the timing was right, and the money was there. An alternative name, a newly restored honker, and the passing of time would give him a fresh start. And should he ever decide to return to the place of his youth, he could leave his former times behind him.

After another two and a half years of college, then additional years earning an advanced degree, trailed by five further years living away, he returned to the central coast. With the help of an altered snout and a new name, his transition back to life in Santa Barbara was harmonious. What's more, his original identity remained anonymous.

The next step for Target X was to shield himself from scientific tracing that might lead back to his true identity. Like everyone, his fingerprints and genetic blueprint distinguished him from the crowd. And although he couldn't change his blood and DNA, he could keep tabs on, and alter if necessary, the related databases. Accordingly, Target X secured an insider to notify him if relevant evidence ever entered the system. After all, forensic science proved successful in many criminal investigations and often was the most influencing factor in criminal convictions.

To cover all the bases, he hired a private investigator to dig and snoop at the regional laboratory for the Department of Forensic Services to uncover the most vulnerable employee. That agency was tasked with the responsibility of hosting the DNA records on file, and to which law enforcement compared their evidence. As such, gaining an inside source could prove invaluable. So, Target X's hired gun pried into the financials of all the employees, bringing one prime candidate to the forefront.

George Tyson was an unassuming, widowed lab tech in his mid-sixties. He would have retired two years earlier, but due to his financial instability, was forced to stay longer. Unfortunate circumstances altered his plan. Following his wife's two-year battle with cancer, exorbitant medical and funeral expenses left him broke. And besides being penniless, his age and submissive personality were clinching factors separating the senior member from his colleagues. That made him the perfect pawn.

George placed a phone call earlier that day. The recipient of the call had answered unwillingly when he recognized the number. Per Target X's order, only one reason for the call was acceptable. When George had spoken the magic words, a phrase the briber hoped he would never hear, "there's a hit", an immediate response would follow. But before crossing a point of no return, Target X needed to confirm the information with short notice. Years of speculation and preparation, and he had nothing to show for it. Suddenly, time was of the essence. He planned to verify the data that night.

Up to this point, the identification of the briber remained anonymous to George. Meetings were always in the dark, with a disguised, third-party middleman continually appearing on behalf of the mastermind. Payments arrived electronically, and from a shell corporation. And what commenced as a harmless, but lavish bribe, at once had George in fear of his safety. But now it was too late. He was in too deep to bail out without completion. And at this point, he was eager to complete his involvement and put this mistake behind him.

The odor in the lab room was unidentifiable, but present, nonetheless. Not rising to the level of a stench, and certainly not pleasant enough to classify as a fragrance, it unquestionably smelled like a lab. It scattered several workstations throughout the large room, designed to accommodate many lab rats. Wall to wall, surrounding the workstations, counter-height tables lined the workspace. Lab equipment was present all over, from test tubes to microscopes. And three large refrigerators against the far wall, enclosed with glass doors, were cluttered with blood samples and other specimens and concoctions. Finally, the lighting, bright as day during business hours, was dull and dreary after hours.

Other than a couple of mandatory OSHA and EEOC posters, and a traditional, boring, round clock, the Navajo White painted walls were naked. The simplicity of the clock on the wall was familiar, like the ever-present black and white eighteen-inch round clock that hung in elementary school classrooms everywhere. The hour on the clock approached 8:10 p.m., leaving the soon-to-be-retired lab technician as the only employee left in the building.

Oddly enough, this wasn't the first bribe opportunity presented to the docile lab rat. But it was the first and only one he ever considered accepting. With retirement looming and a regrettably neglected 401(k) that fell far short of sufficient, let alone ensuring financial security into his golden years, George Tyson had to do something, and fast. He was a desperate man. He took desperate action.

At first, simply accepting the payments wasn't a problem for George. After all, up to that point, he had done nothing wrong. He merely had been receiving money from a wealthy man, or at least that's what he kept telling himself. Now, regret masked his face. Now, its execution was mandated. The time had arrived for George to make good on his promise.

He sat on the swivel stool, shoulders stooped over the workstation, with his elbows weighing heavily on the lab countertop. He stared at the anonymous lab results with curiosity, shaking his head in disgust. The reports were identified by a combination of the last four digits of a Social Security Number and the person's date of birth. What had he done? Whose results were on the report? Who was he helping? Whatever it was, it was too late to turn back now.

The lab door crawled open, creaking like the entrance to a haunted house. Next, the sound of new, brightly polished designer leather shoes eerily squeaked as they crept up on the nervous lab conspirator. Ordinarily a law-abiding citizen to a fault, George never even thought of jaywalking on a side street with no traffic in sight. Suddenly, he found himself committing a felony, and not even knowing why or for whom. The squeaking cut short. The visitor stopped six inches shy of his pasty patsy.

George focused on the wall in front of him. A steady hand reached over his right shoulder. "Is that it?"

To avoid putting himself at further risk, George refused to look his co-conspirator in the face and thus was unable to identify his puppet master. He stared straight ahead at the pale wall that matched the hue of his terrified face. George said nothing as if it made him less culpable. His trembling hand lifted the two one-page stacked reports over his right shoulder. George's ticket to retirement plucked the reports from his sweaty fingertips.

"The last payment will be in your Cayman account by the end of business day tomorrow." Changing from matter of fact to a threatening tone, the next words breathed down the neck of the nervy technician like a winded gorilla. "And remember, I was never here."

When those crowning words fell upon George's neck, a warning hand reached over his left shoulder, dropping a photo in front of him. George held his breath and inched his head downward. When his eyes laid focus on the photograph, fear enveloped his entire body. It was a priceless photo of his daughter and two grandchildren smiling and playing in their front yard, yet it came with a huge price tag.

"Beautiful family you have," the voice whispered in his ear.

Like a homeless elf at the North Pole, the technician froze. The message-bearing hand, flattered by a pricey, gunmetal grey

Movado watch showcasing its signature crystal, edged back over his shoulder. George's eyes guardedly shadowed the hand from his periphery. He didn't breathe. And other than his bowels, he didn't move. If only he had worn adult diapers that day. He just sat there, nervously waiting for the presence behind him to disappear.

Finally, as the odor in the lab intensified to the level of a stench, the shrill of the designer leather shoes resumed and faded in the door's direction, then stopped. The door creaked and opened to the pitch-black hallway. And after a final three shoe squeaks sounded, the door slammed shut.

The terrified lab worker released his breath and more of his bowels.

Chapter Six

6

Joshua Rizzetti dragged his heavy feet along the dimly lit hallway of the Santa Barbara District Attorney's Office, toward his modest office. Not too far removed from the *Formidable Foursome* shooting that made national news, he still felt very weak-kneed when walking through the after-hours empty hallways of the District Attorney's Office. Any sudden loud noise and Josh was jumping out the window. Was it not for the lightning-quick reaction of Deputy Kyle Graham, the brave court officer who rose to the occasion, weak knees would have been the least of Josh's concern.

The one bullet hole embedded in the judge's bench, seven inches from where Josh stood, was the only physical damage stemming from that frightening day. Well, that and the disabling hole Deputy Graham put in the shooter's shoulder before slapping cuffs on the assailant. The emotional damage, however, told a different story. Such a traumatic event pounded an immeasurable mark on those in attendance. The fearless prosecutor was no exception.

Josh was the last one in the office laboring to organize his file for his next trial, once again a misdemeanor case against defense attorney Lee Templeton. He rarely needed to do much legal research before a DUI-Leaving the Scene of an Accident trial, but for this one, Josh felt compelled. Knowing he couldn't overprepare, he brushed up on a couple of legal issues to get ready for a pretrial motion to be argued the next day.

The fate of this criminal case hinged on the Defendant's motion in limine to exclude a DNA test, and with that, a motion to dismiss. Motion in limine comes from the Latin phrase meaning "at the start." In law, it means a motion heard outside the presence of a jury, and before a trial, in which one party requests the exclusion of particular evidence, or in less frequent circumstances, to get a pretrial ruling to allow for the inclusion of specific evidence at trial.

As to the facts of this case, it was not a typical misdemeanor case. Likewise, in terms of the evidence, the case had an unusual twist to it. If the motion was granted, even if the judge didn't toss the case, Josh would dismiss it on behalf of his client, the State of California. Why? Because excluding that specific evidence prevented Josh from being able to prove the defendant was the driver at the time of the one-vehicle accident. The motion was scheduled for argument the next morning, and if denied, the trial would follow that afternoon.

Absent a plea deal, a case of this nature typically took several months before proceeding to trial. But with an out-of-town defendant facing his third DUI, the defense pushed for an expedited trial and got it. Forty-eight days after the incident, the case progressed to trial in record time. To boot, a backlogged laboratory had delivered the lab results just a week earlier. The delay gave the defense little time to get the results, examine them and prepare any necessary motions. And whereas a motion in limine typically would be argued a few weeks before trial, the delayed results forced the potentially dispositive motion to be set on the same day as the trial.

If the motion went Josh's way, the trial was scheduled to start after the court's lunch recess. Josh anticipated that he would have the case in the jury's hands by 3:30 p.m., and a guilty verdict by 4 p.m. Given the unusual facts of this misdemeanor case, his estimate was a bit overly optimistic.

In five years at the D.A.'s Office, and having tried twenty-seven jury trials, and close to one hundred bench trials, Josh had lost only one case. And although he never spoke of it, his one loss was the direct result of a legal error made by the presiding judge. In a high-profile arson case, the judge had allowed the defense to call an "arson expert" to testify on behalf of the defendant. That wasn't the error. Having experts testify in an arson trial was not only common, but it was almost essential. However, it was not the allowance of the expert to testify on behalf of the defendant that was the error, it was permitting this particular "expert" to testify that constituted the error. Why? Because according to the legal standard required for one to testify as an expert, this person wasn't even remotely qualified.

In fact, under the legal standard, the defense's "arson expert" was no more qualified to testify than a firefly, and most certainly should not have been permitted to take the stand. Overruling Josh's objection, the judge let the so-called expert take the stand, wherein he fed some BS to the jury about how a stuffed animal in the storage attic spontaneously combusted and thereby started the blaze. His testimony was full of more crap than a ranch hand-less horse stable at an equestrian center. Nonetheless, the judge allowed it.

Left with a jury having been given the opportunity to give even minimal consideration to the "expert's" tall tale, possible doubt was created as to how the fire started, albeit far from the legally required reasonable doubt. But after locking twelve strangers in a room together for several days, what is reasonable? Answer—anything. And as luck would have it, the judge who had made that costly error, Judge Raymond Stricker, just happened to be the same judge presiding over this DUI-Leaving the Scene trial.

The case had originally been assigned to Judge Ricardo Munoz. However, just four days before trial, it got transferred to Judge Stricker when Judge Munoz took an unexpected leave of absence due to an illness in his family. But asserting his right to a speedy trial, the defendant refused to allow the trial to be continued. Consequently, the expedited trial date remained the on the calendar.

The silence in the air was deafening, other than the heavy steps of the young lawyer lugging through the hallowed halls. Josh was anxious to leave, walking with his head on a swivel. But he felt compelled to stay, at least until he reviewed his notes one more time.

Burning the midnight oil was a rarity for Josh, but occasionally had to be done. Generally, the workday of a Deputy D.A. was eight to five. But, when necessary, long hours came with the territory and the heavy responsibility of a prosecuting attorney.

The safety of the community was not taken lightly by Josh or any of his colleagues. True public servants, they did what was needed. Whatever. Whenever.

By way of example, Josh once tried a case in which he waited around the courthouse until 9:30 p.m. on a Friday night. If that wasn't enough, the case poured over to all-day Saturday for the jury to finish deliberating before they reached a verdict.

Similarly, Josh and his partner, Kendall, tried a case that lasted an entire week, including the weekend. The trial spilled into Saturday and Sunday because the judge didn't want to keep the sequestered jury from their families any longer than necessary. Fortunately for California prosecutors, such extreme measures were no longer allowed. A blessing in disguise, recent state budget cuts kept the courts on a strict schedule, with reduced hours. Along with that, the state permitted absolutely no overtime for the hourly court employees.

Despite his athletic build and borderline obsessive workout habits, the chiseled Deputy District Attorney was hitting the metaphorical wall. He plopped down heavily into his chair, opened his file, and pulled a manila folder from it labeled "Motion in Limine." After taking one last glance at the outline of his primary argument and supporting case law, he had enough. He knew it like the back of his hand. Any more work and he would pass out from exhaustion.

Nearly ready to head home for proper rest before the trial the next day, the weight of his eyelids overpowered his will to stay awake. Josh's head bobbed a few times before coming to rest on his chest. His final file review sapped him. If tired enough, Josh could fall asleep standing up like a tree trunk; so sleeping in a seated position was nothing.

But his rest was short-lived. About thirty seconds after his total exhaustion turned to catch Zzz, a ring as loud as a fire alarm awoke him, launching Josh out of his chair.

"What the?" He clutched his office phone in shock, then came to. "Hahahello. This is Joshua Rizzetti."

A soft, familiar voice spoke. "You need to get a life. I tried your cell, but it went straight to voicemail. Do you realize it's eight o'clock? What are you still doing at the office?"

"You know what I'm doing, Kristen. I told you yesterday; I have a trial tomorrow against your former colleague, Lee Templeton. The trial I'm not worried about, but there is also a pretrial motion in limine. I've been prepping for that. And I have to win that motion, otherwise, my entire case goes down the toilet."

"Got it," said the subtly sexy associate attorney. "And by the way, Lee wasn't really my colleague. I only interned at his firm the summer before my third year of law school."

After a slight pause, Kristen continued. "Josh, you whoop his butt every time you two go to trial. Heck, last time you had him on the ground before the trial even started." She thought twice after referencing the courtroom shooting. "Sorry. Too soon?"

"No, I'm good," Josh said. Still shaken up from literally dodging a bullet, he avoided exposing his vulnerability to Kristen. "I appreciate the attempt at humor."

"Attempt? Ouch!" Kristen giggled. "Aren't you overdoing it for a simple DUI case? You can try a DUI case in your sleep." Kristen waited for a response but then continued. "You know they elect District Attorneys? They're not promoted based on work ethic. So, this won't land you the corner office."

"As I said, I've been preparing for the motion in limine. But I'm wrapping it up as we speak," Josh replied defensively. "So, don't get your panties in a bunch."

"Panties?" Kristen snickered. "Who said I'm wearing any panties?"

"Huh?" Suddenly Josh was more alert.

Josh took a noticeable pause, letting his mind wander. Was there truth behind her statement? Was she serious? Was she flirting with him or messing with him? Or was she just giving him a hard time because he was such an over-achiever, focused to a fault? His attraction to the beautiful, dainty, and off-the-charts intelligent attorney was nothing new. But he never acted on it for fear of damaging her valued friendship.

"I'll call you tomorrow after my trial and we'll hit happy hour with the gang."

"Deal! See ya tomorrow. Good luck with your motion and your trial." Knowing that Josh rode his bike to work, she joked, "And don't get hit by a car on your way home."

"Ha-ha, very funny Kristen," said Josh. "I'll see you at happy hour after I school Templeton on the art of litigation." He laughed and hung up the receiver.

Joshua Rizzetti and Kristen Laney first met five years earlier at a Young Attorneys Association function. The national organization formed numerous branches throughout the country with a mission to help newer attorneys acclimate to the legal profession, both socially and professionally. In furtherance of their goal, the group hosted multiple functions throughout the year, and always with an open bar. The events encouraged camaraderie. The alcohol eased the pressure. On the flip side, mixing young lawyers with free alcohol inevitably proved to be a catalyst for calamity.

In keeping with that premise, the two young lawyers met under the most inauspicious circumstances. They accidentally backed into each other at the annual *Bar at the Beach Summer Shindig*. It started with Kristen spilling red wine all over her white blouse, prompting her to jump back, bumping Josh's backside. Josh tripped forward, dumping his beer on a judge. The judge then knocked a plate of finger foods with marinara sauce onto the only female partner from Kristen's firm, who just happened to be one of the mentors for the program. This prompted the partner to drop her dessert plate, which broke into pieces when it hit the ground, triggering a waiter to slip on the key lime pie that recently occupied the newly-shattered plate, and who then fell flat on his keister.

The embarrassment to Kristen and Josh was mutually assured destruction. But, once it was determined that no one was physically hurt and the initial shock from the comical series of events subsided, everyone broke out in hysterical laughter. The scene looked straight out of a *Three Stooges* movie. The "domino fiasco," as it infamously came to be known, became an instant classic and a legendary story that was retold at the inaugural lawyers' group event every year since that memorable meeting.

Josh glanced at his watch. It was 8:25 in the evening. He couldn't believe how time had vanished while reviewing his trial notebook. After several successful DUI trials, he wondered why he still prepared so diligently for each one. Although, deep down, he knew why. Preparation . . . it is all in the preparation.

He knew that to be the best attorney you had to be the most prepared attorney. He learned that philosophy early in his prosecutorial career from one of his mentors, John Jinnee, who was hands down the best trial lawyer Josh had ever seen. John once had a jury return a conviction without ever leaving the jury box. When the judge asked them to return to the jury room to deliberate, they all looked at each other, and nodded to the foreman, who then turned to the judge and said, "Judge, we find the defendant guilty on all counts."

Josh was extremely grateful, knowing that he had learned from the best. Mentored by the most talented litigation attorneys he had ever seen; his training was second to none. And that was saying something because he had litigated against countless attorneys. And after learning from the best, combined with his incomparable ability to convince anybody of anything, Josh developed into one of the best trial attorneys in the state, if not the country.

Since childhood, Josh displayed an absolute refusal to lose at anything. Sports announcers talk about the rare professional athlete that possesses the intangible "it" factor and simply knows how to win. Well, when it came to winning in the courtroom, that was Josh. He had the "it" factor. And thanks to his God-given gift that he methodically sharpened through his tireless work ethic; winning at trial turned into second nature.

But Josh's innate ability to win came with great responsibility and required the utmost integrity. For without integrity, he risked committing the ultimate wrong for a prosecutor, sending an innocent person to prison. To a prosecutor, a guilty person going free was far less egregious than an innocent person losing their freedom.

That being said, Josh held an ethical obligation to dismiss a case if the evidence indicated a defendant was not guilty of the crime. He was vigilant to comply, especially knowing that he otherwise easily could convict even the most innocent of defendants. When it came to convincing twelve neutral strangers of anything, Josh could convince a jury that the earth was flat. He was that persuasive. And while he was extremely vocal with self-confidence in other aspects of his life, Josh remained humble regarding his litigation prowess, further feeding his compulsion to over-prepare.

Once again, his head bobbed down a couple of times, nearly falling asleep in his place. His entire body jerked. He fought it, but without success. Then it hit him, and he fell asleep again, but only for a few minutes. Fortunately, his internal clock kicked in and woke him from his state of exhaustion. He knew he needed to leave immediately, for fear that the next time he woke up would be five minutes after his court appearance. "I gotta get home," he said to himself.

Josh opened his bottom desk drawer, where he kept his casual attire for the ride home. He summoned a burst of energy and went into action. He threw on shorts and sneakers, took off his dress shirt, leaving him with a plain-white T-shirt underneath, and slung his backpack over his right shoulder. Placing the box top on his file, he grabbed the banker's box that contained his entire file. Whether he would go through any of his files or not later that night remained to be seen; but he always brought his trial materials home the night before trial, just in case.

The spring-loaded door to his office slammed shut behind him as he struggled his way to the elevator. Despite only being on the second floor, he was too tired and overloaded to take the stairs. "Ding!" The door slid open, and he stepped into the elevator of the three-story Spanish-style office building. His right bicep flexed as a natural response to the motion of his arm extending so that his index finger could press the first-floor button.

Never skipping arms-day at the gym, the sleeves of his T-shirt were stretched to their limit. Although not comparable to the celebrity former governor of the Golden State in his prime, Josh was well put-together and worked hard to maintain his athletic physique. Weightlifting was the main stress relief from the day-to-day battle in the life of the young, but seasoned litigator.

His burst of energy faded, and fatigue sat in just as Josh locked the main office door behind him. He dragged himself over to the bike rack located about fifteen feet to the side of the entrance of the beige stucco, three-story office building. The rack was installed for his benefit. Although several employees of the D.A.'s office lived nearby, Josh was the only one dedicated enough to ride his bike to work practically every day. On sunny days, Josh diligently rode his peculiarly purple mountain bike to work. And on the American Riviera, almost every day was a sunny day.

His bike was distinctive, to say the least. Not only was it bright purple, making it incredibly unique in its own right, but it was also wallpapered with stickers. And not just any random stickers, but exclusively sports stickers. Big stickers, small stickers. All the professional football and baseball teams donned his rather expensive two-wheeler. It was a little tacky, and he knew it. But it accurately reflected who he was—the sports, not the tacky—and for that, he was not ashamed.

As overly demonstrated on his bike, Josh was a die-hard sports fanatic. To call him a fan would be a gigantic understatement. He was a fanatic through and through! He was the ideal "phone a friend" call for every contestant on *Who Wants to be a Millionaire* for any sports-related question. Sports and 1980s' music. And while he was in fact a master of most insignificant trivia, those were his main areas of expertise. "If only experts in those fields were needed in court," Josh often thought, being well-aware of the astronomical hourly fees charged by experts for court testimony. "I would quit the D.A.'s office, become a court expert, and become filthy rich." In short, he knew more about sports trivia and 1980s' music than Google.

On days when Josh knew he would be bringing a large workload home, one that he knew could not fit in his backpack, he towed a kids' bike trailer behind his mountain bike. With no child in tow, the idea seemed silly, and looked funny, but was actually brilliant. When his colleagues would laugh at his "bike train," as they jokingly called it, Josh would always respond with the same line—"If it can hold a kid, then why not heavy boxes?"

He unzipped the front mesh of his box hauler and gently tossed the dense box onto the seat. To ensure that the lid stayed on, and the contents remained in place, he secured the box with the seat belt. A click followed by a slight tug, and with his "baby" safely in place, he zipped closed the mesh cover to prepare the train to leave the station.

Josh removed the U-lock that secured his bike's front tire to the rack. Sliding the rubber-coated lock that surrounded his front forks, he admired the two college stickers worthy of a piece of metal on his preferred mode of transportation, with one on each fork: Cal Poly Pomona and Ole Miss, his college and law school alma maters, respectively. While most college graduates showed great pride in their alma maters, Josh was a walking advertisement for his. Clothing, hats, stickers, mugs, license plate frames, golf head covers, etc. You name it; he had it. He was a real-life advertisement for both the Broncos and Rebels alike.

Fortunately, the ride would be a short one. Josh lived just a handful of blocks over, on the opposite side of State Street. The weight from his backpack felt like he had the entire redwood forest of the West Coast crammed into his canvas bag. His muscles were tired, his shoulders were sore. Working his upper body at the gym the day before was a good idea at the time, but now, not so much. To ease the burden and lessen the pain, he removed his backpack from his shoulders, unzipped the bike trailer, placed it next to the box, and zipped closed the trailer. Without the trailer, the short trip would seem especially long with the weight of his trial on his back, both literally and figuratively. He boarded his bike, shifted all of his weight onto his right foot, pushed down on his pedal, and towed his mid-sized, fabric, mobile office along the sidewalk.

Josh cruised at a slow, but steady pace as he turned right up State Street. The traffic was unusually minor, even for a

Thursday evening. Josh lugged his way one more block up and prepared to turn left onto Cannon Perdido. Day after day he took the same route home, yet every time he glanced up at the street signs, he smiled at the reminder of the lyrical, Spanish names that adorned several streets in Santa Barbara. Definitely a city with a plan from day one, even little nuances like street names equally matched its Spanish architectural beauty.

Struggling to keep his eyes open, Josh continued to pedal his way home. One block from his home, he started his final turn. Halfway through his turn, a screeching noise pierced the air. A large, dark SUV appeared out of nowhere from his left. Josh glanced over his left shoulder and noticed that the headlights were off. The overhead streetlight illuminated his surroundings just enough for Josh to heed caution to the suspicious movements of the vehicle. The lightning-fast mental reflex of an elite litigator kicked in. But, before he could alter his course, the SUV came at him like a cannonball. With only a few seconds to react, Josh raced toward the curb in the hopes of jumping up the sidewalk. The barrier of the traffic light seemed to be his only hope of survival.

The wretched stench of burning rubber and smoke blanketed the intersection thicker than the morning marine layer. Josh squeezed his handlebars tighter than a boa constrictor and yanked them up, jumping his front tire up the curb of the sidewalk. He had no other choice than to commit to his only viable option for survival. Frantically trying to get his back tire up the curb, he sensed he was out of time. And his senses were as on target as the SUV that took aim at its bullseye. Just a few feet before Josh could reach the shield of the traffic light, the front bumper of the killer vehicle torpedoed into the bike trailer and rear tire of his mountain bike, launching Josh into the smoke-filled air. Except for his life flashing before his eyes, he couldn't see anything.

Disoriented and afraid, soaring through the dark night on a most unexpected and unpleasant flight and destined to end with a crash landing, he awaited sudden impact. His final destination arrived. Scratching, stabbing, and piercing Josh, the branches of the Chaparral Pea shrub defended themselves from his unexpected, nighttime arrival. With his momentum slowed by the bright pink flowering bush, Josh's upper body, guided by his head, slammed against a Big-Berried Manzanita tree and knocked him unconscious.

The black SUV stopped on a dime. Through the limousine-dark tinted windows, the driver paused as if to admire his work. The young man lay there, still, silent, lifeless. His snug, clean white T-shirt was now tie-died with blood. Once again, tires screeched. The homicidal maniac gunned his vehicle for a few seconds, aimed straight at his target.

Abruptly, he skidded to a halt, stopping twelve feet shy of his prey. The lethal motorist jumped out from his three-ton weapon and hurried to the bike trailer that was now mangled and flipped upside down. Remarkably, the contents of the trailer were relatively intact. Josh's diligence in securing his file had paid off, at least as far as his assailant was concerned. The box remained behind the seat belt, with the top in place.

Quickly and methodically, the hit man reached through the torn mesh and opened the box. Shuffling through the file, in a rush to locate the treasure of his hunt, he pulled several, meticulously labeled manila folders from the banker's box. Flipping through papers like a money counter fanning cash, he continued to toss aside document after document until he reached pay dirt. Finding his prize, he shoved the document into the leather tote bag that lapped over his shoulder and across his body. For good measure, to throw off the scent, he shoved some other random documents into his tote as well.

Multitasking to flee the scene undetected, he slid the tote bag down his right arm, grabbed it with his left hand with the speed and precision of a relay sprinter, and made a dash for the home stretch. In a sprint, the thieving attacker raced back to his SUV.

With the door still open and the engine running, he threw the tote onto the passenger's seat and hopped into the driver's seat to make his getaway. In a rush to disappear before being spotted, the assailant nearly snapped the column gear shaft jamming it into drive. Then, dropping the hammer on the accelerator, the vehicle rushed from the scene, and deep into the night, leaving the young lawyer phenom for dead.

Chapter Seven

7

E ven by upscale Santa Barbara standards, the private law firm office space of Bonds and Paine, PLLC was posh. Impression was important. A firm that presented a high-end image attracted high-end clients. And with a practice concentrated on corporate law and wills and trusts, the firm benefited from a wealthy clientele.

Lee Templeton was a Junior Partner with the firm, although he specialized in criminal law. Ironically, he benefited from a poor client base. The polar opposite practice areas of the firm and Lee made for strange bedfellows. But the latter was an exceptional attorney, so the firm was fine with it. Lee possessed a strong passion for criminal law and relished spending most of his time in court as opposed to the endless paperwork of the firm's predominant practice areas. Moreover, his roots in the firm grew deeper than just as an employee.

Luther Paine, one of the founding partners of the reputable Santa Barbara law firm, was a lifelong friend of Lee's father. As did firm co-founder Franklin Bonds, Luther had a genuine passion for criminal law. However, when they started their firm, they set their desire aside and opted for the money in corporate law and estate planning. But, when Lee graduated from law school, Mr. Paine delighted in offering his childhood friend's talented son an Associate position with his firm and welcomed Lee to pursue his passion for law representing the dark side.

The elegant office space occupied just shy of thirty-two hundred square feet on the third floor, overlooking the heart of Santa Barbara on the legendary State Street. Founded in 1982, the firm had a prime spot on the famed retail street. Below the law office, the building and its adjacent structures accommodated several boutique shops and a few fancy restaurants with elevated prices and mediocre food.

To the casual observer, the pulse of Santa Barbara seemed unaffected by the floundering economy. In less than a two-mile strip, the renowned thoroughfare housed more than one hundred restaurants and retail shops, satisfying even the finickiest shoppers. During summer and on weekends, the tree-lined State Street remained a popular appeal for tourists, drawing thousands of visitors.

The moderate weather and timeless Spanish architecture highlighted the attraction of this California treasure. With its breathtaking beaches lined by inland mountains, the small coastal city known as the American Riviera lured folks worldwide. Shopping attracted the rich. Surf attracted the young. Sunshine attracted everyone. Santa Barbara had it all.

The Junior Partner leaned back in his black leather, high-back executive chair, kicked his feet up on his contemporary urban office desk, and took a deep sigh. Only slight muttering echoed from the sparse evening crowd on the street below. Lee's eyes wandered across his large office, scanning over his degrees that were a testament to his educational and professional accomplishments. Given his relatively modest upbringing, the self-made professional took pride in his achievements. Not only was he the first in his family to receive a college degree, but he also earned a law degree for good measure.

Lee's office was partially lit by a banker's lamp on the far-right corner of his desk and enhanced by the streetlights that peaked through the partly closed three-inch wood blinds hanging over two large windows. The back wall opposite the windows overlooking State Street stood as a shrine to his educational accomplishments. Centered on the wall hung his prized possession, his UCLA Law degree. His bachelor's degree from Cal State Long Beach, aka "The Beach," flanked his law diploma along with his licenses to practice in the State and Federal Courts of California.

He studied his notes for his motion in limine one last time before loading his file into a banker's box. Like most diligent attorneys, Lee usually brought his respective file home the night before a trial, even if he had no intention of reviewing his case again that evening. He moaned, struggling to lift the box from the floor. It was unusually heavy for a DUI-Leaving the Scene trial, but it made him feel weak, nonetheless. In his defense, pun aside, this was not a typical DUI trial.

With one arm scooping the underside of the box, the other reached for his briefcase and headed for the door. Except for Lee, the office had been unoccupied since 7:07 p.m. He had spent almost three hours in total silence holed up in his office preparing for trial. A blessing for any litigation attorney, he accomplished much more when the phones weren't ringing, and the office was empty.

"The cleaning crew should be coming in soon," Lee mumbled to himself. In a rush to get home, he bumped into the door jamb on his way out of his office, causing him to fumble, and nearly drop the heavy box.

"Whew! That was close. The last thing I need to do is drop everything," he said aloud in relief. Lee tended to talk to himself when he was alone in the office. Taken to an extreme, he practiced his opening and closing statements aloud in front of a framed mirror that hung beside his office door.

The stairwell was on the other end of the law firm opposite Lee's office. He strained to make his way to the exit door, flipped off the hallway light with his elbow, again almost dropping everything, and backed into the doorway entering the dimly lit stairwell.

For a building occupied by attorneys, it was ironic that the stairs were so poorly lit, likely to the degree of civil negligence. It was a lawsuit waiting to happen. And although the law firm knew better than to unnecessarily expose itself to such liability, nothing had been done about it thus far. Perhaps it was because a skylight at the top of the stairwell provided plenty of additional light during the daytime. But at night, the few densely lit lights were far from enough.

Lee was determined to make it down the stairs and to the parking lot without having to rest. Rip off the band-aid. That was his approach. Painful but quick.

His left shoe hit the second stair when the door slammed shut behind him. But before his right foot left the ground, a one-inch thick, three-foot-long iron pipe pounded his head with the force of a Bronx Bomber crushing a fastball over the heart of the plate. The banker's box jetted into the air and papers and folders flew everywhere like frightened crows dispersing from a tree. Lee launched forward from the violent blow behind him. His body tumbled around and then crashed head-first on the bottom step before settling on the landing between floors, knocking him unconscious immediately.

A dark shadow hurried down the stairs and hovered over the body. Two hands, protected with black leather gloves, reached down. With quick and precise force, the left hand gripping the chin and the right hand tugging the back of the head to his right, a disgustingly loud snap echoed throughout the stairwell. Just as quickly, the gloves dropped Lee's head like a watermelon, sounding a heavy thump on the stairs.

Papers and file folders were scattered all over the steps and covered half the stairway landing. The force in the night pulled a pocket-size flashlight from his coat, twisted it on, and bit down on it with his crooked front teeth. The assailant sifted through the mess with a definite purpose. After glancing over several documents, he picked up a green sheet of paper, paused, and read carefully. "This is it," he whispered. He grabbed several other documents, so as not to draw attention to one specific document missing from the file, folded the papers, and once again shoved them into his tote bag and raced down the stairs.

The late middle-aged assailant, dressed from head to toe in black attire and breathing heavily through his dark ski mask, reached the bottom of the stairwell. Clearly out of shape, he panted like an old dog chasing tennis balls in the park. He slowly cracked the emergency exit door and removed the paper clip he had used to jam the bolt latch open, a trick of the trade he learned to prevent the beeping mechanism from activating when he opened the door.

Earlier that evening, the experienced henchman had strategically inserted the paper clip shortly after the last person had left the building, so as not to alert Templeton when he entered the building. It worked. His three visits to the office complex the prior week to surveil the building and construct his plan had paid off. He got what he needed, and the risk of any attorney-client-protected secrets being revealed was eliminated as swiftly as the dead man in the stairwell.

He peaked out to make sure the coast was clear. His pale, grayish-colored eyes looked left, then looked right. Clear. Gently closing the door, he scurried one block over and two blocks down to the corner of Chapala and Anapamu Streets where his vehicle was parked. He jumped in his black SUV, and with the headlights off, drove away slowly.

Chapter Eight

8

The room was pitch black. As the hour approached midnight, the wealthy socialite unbuttoned his top shirt button, loosened his solid, teal blue chic tie, removed his silver cuff links, and rolled up his sleeves just below his elbows. Closing his eyes, he leaned back in his high-back, ergonomic, brown suede executive chair. Dressed to the nines, but with his suit coat off, he took a deep breath.

His office was eerily quiet. The singing of the subdued crickets drifted through the open window into the tranquil office. The slight breeze off the Pacific Ocean was somewhat cool in early fall, providing needed relief on hot days. He took another deep breath and stared out the window into the peaceful night. Looking lost in thought, the smell of the ocean air likely triggered memories of simpler, younger days.

How long had it been? Could he even recall the last time he wasn't looking over his shoulder? Twenty, twenty-five years, give or take. The more ambitious he became, the faster the years passed. And most recently, on his rapid journey toward greater pursuits, his train teetered on the brink of going off the rails. No one could see it, but he felt it. How could he not? After all, he was lingering in his dark office in the middle of the night, waiting on a call that was unimaginable just a short time ago.

He sat and waited in near silence and total darkness. No one else had been in the building for hours. Anxiously he sat. Impatiently he waited. Like a stiff corpse, he did not move.

The vibration of the burner phone shook the old-school flip phone to the end of the hand-carved mahogany desk. Just as it was about to go over the edge, as was he, his hand grabbed it.

The irritated, intimidating voice spoke first. "Well?" He leaned back in his office chair, waiting for a response.

"It's done," a scratchy voice said matter-of-factly. It was the sound of a voice that had smoked thousands of packs of cigarettes over the course of thirty-plus years, seemingly a carton every thirty minutes.

Eagerly, the master shifted to the edge of his chair. "Did you get what I need?"

Sitting under a massive shade tree, leaning back against the old gazebo in Alameda Park, just east of State Street, the chain smoker spoke in that poisoned voice common to battle-scared chain smokers from the Marlboro Man era. "Yes."

"Are you sure?" Clearly frustrated, and secretly panicked, the dominant figure needed to be certain.

"I told you," said the raspy voice. "It's done."

"I just want to be sure." He loosened his tie some more, another two inches below the base of his neck. "The devil is in the details."

"The devil is on the other end." The ballsy lackey coughed, wheezing as he exhaled; symptomatic of chronic bronchitis if he was lucky, lung cancer if he was not.

"Don't you forget that."

"How can I, with you constantly reminding me?"

Pulling the chain on the desk lamp, in the now faintly lit office, the impatient voice asked, "Were there any problems?"

"None."

"Are you sure?"

Annoyed, the smoker countered, "This isn't my first rodeo!"

"Hey smart guy, don't forget who's paying you."

"Speaking of payment—"

Commanding in his deepest, most powerful voice, the alpha male presumptively interrupted his hired hand. "We have a deal! Don't you push your luck."

"Don't you forget what I know," he said smugly, lighting up a cigarette under the dark sky.

"Don't you forget who I am!"

Beep. The flip phone slammed shut. Then silence.

Chapter Nine

9

Kristen had been sitting by Josh's bedside all night, after rushing to Village Hospital a few minutes before midnight, when she received a call from Officer Tom Wilkey of the Santa Barbara Police Department. Officer Wilkey also happened to be part of their happy hour hangout group when he was off duty, and one of Josh's closest friends. His partner and closest friends called him TW for short, or T-dub for shorter.

"You look like you got hit by a bus. How are you feeling?" Kristen said, leaning against Josh's hospital bed, adjusting the tubes tangled around his left arm.

"Actually, it was an SUV, but tomayto tomahto," said Josh. "I feel like I have one foot in the grave and the other on a banana peel." The beaten patient grunted, pointing at his right leg encased in a hard cast up to his knee. It hung from a stirrup. "I either severely injured my leg or I'm getting prepped to give birth."

"At least you haven't lost your sense of humor," Kristen said. "Does this mean you are going to flake on happy hour tonight?"

she joked rhetorically to ease the obvious pain of her legal pal and best friend. "When I told you not to get hit by a car, I guess I should've made it obvious that I meant it literally. What the heck happened?"

The youthfully spirited Deputy District Attorney was off his game, feeling groggy from the pain medication. He struggled to keep his eyes open. Despite being knocked out for the entire evening, he longed for at least ten more hours of sleep. He certainly needed it. Josh had taken a serious pounding. He sustained a broken fibula, two broken ribs, a concussion, several contusions on his arms, legs, and face, and had a golf ball-sized bump on his forehead for good measure.

"I'm not sure if it's the medication or the egg on my forehead talking, but I believe I was intentionally targeted."

"I think you hit your head on the tree too hard," Kristen said. "TW was on routine patrol last night. He and his partner were headed over to SB Munch Shack for a late-night snack and they spotted a mangled, but very recognizable, purple mountain bike. With no one in sight and no reports of an accident, TW figured you were the victim of a hit and run. Who would've imagined? T-dub's healthy appetite saved your life!"

Kristen walked up to the side table beside Josh's bed and adjusted the vase of flowers she brought for him. She hoped it would brighten the atmosphere of the otherwise depressing hospital room. "Why in the world would anyone intentionally try to mow you down with a vehicle? You are one of the most well-liked people I know. Even people who don't like you, still kinda like you. Did you convict an innocent person who got paroled recently?"

"Not that I'm aware."

Josh lowered his eyebrows as he stared out the window of the recently remodeled Village Hospital. He played back the prior night. Much of it remained foggy because of the effects of the medication. Nonetheless, Josh racked his brain. Why would someone try to hurt him? Or kill him?

He recounted the previous evening when he awoke in the middle of the night, soaked in sweat, from what he thought was a nightmare. In it, he saw the eyes of the driver staring him down as the car flew toward him. Now, with new information in hand, he realized it wasn't a nightmare, it was his genuine recollection of the horrendous incident.

As Josh pondered, a slender, strikingly beautiful doctor entered the room. Her champagne blonde hair and smoldering brown eyes were only outdone by her swimsuit model-like figure, whose shape could not be hidden by her formfitting white coat. She smelled as good as she looked. Kristen shifted with discomfort in her chair as Josh's eyes widened at the sight of his gorgeous doctor, who looked to be in her early thirties.

His pain disappeared as his mind wandered further. This stunning young lady visibly missed her calling. Supermodels make even more money than doctors. In fact, way more! Didn't she know that? What the heck was she thinking?

"Don't worry, I clean up nicely." The eligible bachelor laughed flirtatiously. "So, what's the verdict Doctorrrrr?"

Josh stared at her full, kissable lips as she replied, "Doctor Overman."

"Hmm," he said. "Doctor Overman. Interesting name." Continuing to flirt, he gave her a grin.

Few would have the onions, or the confidence, to flirt with such a striking, intelligent, accomplished professional. Few could pull it off. But Josh could. He could flirt with the best of them. But that's where it ended, as historically he had a lousy track record with relationships.

Josh was a good guy; some might say a goody-two-shoes. And inevitably, the ladies he'd fall for ultimately got lured away by the bad boy type, and that was something Josh couldn't fake even if he tried. After getting dumped, he'd console himself with a reminder of the cliché that there was plenty of fish in the sea. But even with fresh bait, a fisherman still had to troll for the right fish if he hoped to catch one.

Slowly, subtly shaking her head, she lowered it, trying to hide her smile. The doctor grabbed Josh's medical chart at the end of his bed, glanced it over, then looked at her patient's hanging leg. "I think you should plead no contest. And a word of medical advice. Never play chicken with a car while riding a bike."

She continued with a little legal humor to match her patient's wit. She tapped her pen on the medical chart, like a judge's gavel on the bench. "Your sentence is two weeks of strict bed rest, followed by six to eight weeks of light, transitional activities, along with a lifetime ban from the Tour de France."

The doctor glanced at Kristen, who looked annoyed by the verbal foreplay. "All kidding aside, you'll live. You took a violent hit, but I don't think there is any permanent damage. You must either be in great shape or you're extremely lucky. Or more likely, a lot of both. According to the police report, given the distance you flew from the estimated point of impact to your landing point, it's a miracle you're alive!"

"I guess the gym finally paid off," said Josh, immodestly flexing his impressive right bicep.

"We want to keep you one more night for observation, just to be safe. Maybe two, if your sense of humor doesn't improve." Dr. Overman held up two fingers. "But seriously, you should be good to go by tomorrow morning."

"No rush, Doctor. I like the view from my room." Josh continued with his flirtatious banter, passively glancing out his room window but failing at his attempted subtlety. While the view of the trees and charming neighborhood around Village Hospital was pleasing, both ladies knew what he meant. The doctor looked flattered; Kristen looked pissed. "Thank you, Doctor."

As she walked toward the door, Josh couldn't help but peer out of the corner of his eye to admire the doctor's professional white coat that accentuated, rather than hid, her supermodel physique.

With the door closing behind the doctor, Kristen disrupted Josh's mental drift. "Keep it in your pants Rizzetti."

Josh smiled at his best friend. "Do I detect a hint of jealousy?"

"Don't you wish, Casanova? I just don't like to see you making a fool of yourself. And something about her doesn't sit well with me."

"Hmm. Yep. Like I said, jealousy."

"No, it's not that. I don't know what it is. Call it a gut feeling. But go ahead, call it whatever you want to make yourself feel better."

"I did. I called it jealousy." Josh winced in pain and shook his head. "But unfortunately, it doesn't make me feel better."

For the past couple of years, Kristen had become increasingly possessive of Josh's attention because of her unexpressed, intimate feelings for him. Feelings that had progressed with time. Sadly, for both of them, she shared the same flawed rationalization as the subject of her desire. She too internalized her feelings toward Josh to avoid jeopardizing their friendship. Unfortunately for both of them, analysis paralysis triumphed.

Panicked, a massive shock wave jolted Josh's body, causing his upper torso to launch forward like a slingshot "Oh my gosh, my court hearing!"

Just as Josh's mind caught up with the present, a young man entered the room. "Dude, is this your not-so-subtle way of getting out of our bet and trying to snap your four-game racquetball losing streak? One more loss and you owe me fifty bucks bro."

"Hey Tyler, what's the status of my hearing? Did someone from the office cover it for me? How did it go? Did the judge deny it? Did it get continued . . ." Josh continued to fire away questions about his scheduled hearing and trial against Lee Templeton until Tyler interrupted.

Raising his right hand, Tyler said, "Slow down, Josh! Don't worry, it's not even eight yet." With the maturity of someone twice his age, the twenty-one-year-old Runner said in a calming voice, "Kendall will cover your hearing."

Tyler had been working summers as a Runner at the D.A.'s office since he was sixteen and only five-foot-seven, running memos, letters, evidence boxes, and the like to and from the various law offices around town. Now going into his senior year at UC Santa Barbara and towering at a lean six-foot-five, he still enjoyed the low stress, high physical activity, and camaraderie of working at the D.A.'s Office, full-time in summer and part-time during the school year. Even more so, the six-foot-one Deputy D.A. was like an older, albeit shorter, sibling and mentor to the athletic, versatile Criminal Justice student.

"First of all, how are you, bro?" Tyler walked up to his bed-ridden faux-brother and gave him a fist bump.

Over the past couple of years, Josh and Tyler spent a lot of time together, even outside of the office, including weekly games of racquetball. Tyler kept his mentor feeling younger, and their regular weekly duel was the main source of Josh's cardio. Treadmill, stair master, aerobics, or God forbid running; forget about it. The buff Deputy D.A. loved the weights but hated doing cardio, so racquetball gave him the workout his heart needed, without the boredom that his mind dreaded. As were Kristen and TW, Tyler was one of five regulars in Josh's happy hour group.

Pointing to his leg dangling in the stirrup, Josh responded with a chuckle, "I feel like I got hit by a truck, but I'll be ending your winning streak by week's end!"

Josh's lighthearted response didn't get a reaction from Tyler. None. Not a smile, not a smirk, not even a twitch. He just stared at Josh, with a total loss for words.

Kristen's eyes widened like a deer in headlights, recognizing that something else was wrong. "What is it, Tyler? I haven't seen you this serious since the Sandbar raised its happy hour prices."

Not knowing what to say, or how to say it, Tyler blurted out, "Lee Templeton is dead!"

"What?!" Josh and Kristen reacted in unison.

"Around the same time of your," Tyler raised his arms and hands, putting up air quotes, "accident last night, Mr. Templeton was murdered in his office."

Josh and Kristen shouted simultaneously, "Murdered?!"

"The cleaning crew at his office building found him at the bottom of the stairwell after eleven o'clock last night, with his trial box scattered all around him," Tyler said. "According to the medical examiner, the cause of death was a broken neck, and her preliminary report labeled it a homicide."

Like clockwork, Josh and Kristen again spoke as one. "Why does she think it was a homicide?"

"He could have broken his neck falling down the stairs," added Josh.

Tyler went on. "The coroner said that Mr. Templeton also sustained blunt force trauma to the back of his head, consistent with being struck from behind by a hard object."

"Also, there was redness around his chin, as if someone had snapped his neck." Tyler continued in more detail, having the advantage of working for the office that was the first to know all the intricate details of every major crime in the County. And long before anything hit the *Santa Barbara Daily Press*.

Josh and Kristen immediately gazed at each other like they were reading each other's minds and confirming Josh's suspicion that his violent game of tag with the SUV was not just an accident, but rather attempted murder. And Josh was *it*!

Chapter Ten

10

Kendall Jackson was the most senior Deputy D.A. for the Santa Barbara District Attorney's Office, and not to be confused with the winery by the same name. He was also Joshua's partner. The court-bound prosecutor entered the foyer from the hallway on his way out of the building and toward the Courthouse.

"Good morning boss," he greeted the District Attorney where two hallways met, as he too was leaving the office building.

"Good morning Kendall. You know how much that bugs me when you call me that. Anyway, I'm headed over to the hospital to check on Josh. Are you headed to court right now?"

William Tell, the second-term elected District Attorney, had the utmost confidence in Kendall, who also held the title of Executive Deputy District Attorney. Not only did they have in common sharing famous names, William and Kendall joined the District Attorney's Office as rookie Deputy D.A.'s the same year, some twenty-five years earlier. Having gone through the trenches together, their mutual respect and trust were second to none. A lifetime ago, they were each other's best man at their respective weddings, godfathers to the other's firstborn, and true friends long before the Facebook era.

"Got it covered, Bill. I'll reach out to you after the hearing and give you an updated status. I'll be requesting a continuance, and I'm certain the judge will grant it. Shannon scheduled a brainstorming meeting with all of our attorneys and investigators for 1:30 p.m. this afternoon. Since it's Friday, no one has court this afternoon. We'll see if we can make any sense of this."

"Thanks, Kendall. Good luck."

"Thanks. Give my best to Josh and let him know I'll visit him this afternoon."

***

DESIGNED IN THE Spanish-Colonial style, and completed in 1929, the Santa Barbara Courthouse was a sight to behold. Even as a fully operational building, the Anacapa Street landmark remained one of the most magnificent, iconic public buildings in the United States. The red Spanish tile roof, distinctive arches, and four-faced clock tower with a panoramic view of the Santa Barbara coastline and surrounding mountains made it one of the most recognized buildings in the country. As the Empire State Building symbolized New York and the Golden Gate Bridge signified San Francisco, the elegant Spanish courthouse embodied Santa Barbara.

The open-aired hallways were unique to the architectural masterpiece. Only year-round mild, sunny weather could make such hallways workable for a public building and the American Riviera had it. Over the course of the year, the local temperature typically varied from forty-two to seventy-seven degrees Fahrenheit, with an average of only eighteen inches of annual rainfall, well below the national average and providing a climate ideal for its unique layout.

The main courthouse property covered an entire city block. Nestled between Anacapa and Santa Barbara Streets on the Southwest and Northeast ends, and Anapamu and East Figueroa Streets on the Northwest and Southeast ends, respectively, the timeless structure occupied only a small portion of the property. The building's placement was of a reverse-block-lettered "J" shape on the massive grounds, with the rest being adorned with plush, green grass and colorful flower gardens. Not many, if any, courthouse properties could lay claim to being the chosen venue for summer concerts, garden weddings, and local festivities; but this one did and in spectacular fashion!

The front of the courthouse was just a few minutes' walk from the District Attorney's Office. From the back side of the courthouse, the D.A.'s Office was just across Santa Barbara Street. One of the rewards of being a Deputy District Attorney in Santa Barbara County was embracing the short, but incomparable everyday walk from the office to the courthouse. Albeit short-lived, the unique walk to start one's workday was unparalleled. And for the court-assigned Deputy D.A.s, an average of fifty to seventy-five percent of the workday was spent in the courtroom, making the days fly by.

Kendall opened the massive wooden door to Department Three. The courtroom was virtually empty, with a couple of local attorneys snapping briefcases closed, and heading out of the courtroom. Most matters were scheduled on the calendar for 8:30 a.m., and Judge Stricker liked to keep a light docket on Fridays. The judge had scheduled the motion in limine hearing for 10:15 a.m., figuring that everything else on the docket would be done.

Judge Stricker preferred to schedule any potentially dispositive motions as the last hearings of the day, and today was no different. However, scheduling a trial for a Friday afternoon was most certainly different. But given the court's tight calendar, the addition of a transferred case, and the need for an expedited trial date, the choices were limited.

Mark Patterson was sitting at the defendant's counsel table, with his client seated to his left. He whispered something to his client, who then stood up and walked out of the courtroom.

Mark was one of the newest associates to Bonds and Pain, PLLC, but was a seasoned attorney nonetheless. Going into his eleventh year of practice, he had spent the better part of his career with a larger firm down in the San Fernando Valley, south of Santa Barbara. Having been with his new firm for just over three months, he didn't have the opportunity to get to know Lee very well. Taking that into account, Franklin Bonds probably sent Mark to cover the hearing, knowing that almost certainly he was the least emotionally affected in an office that was devastated by the tragedy stricken upon them early that morning.

Kendall walked slowly up the center aisle and opened the swinging wooden gate to the bar. A familiar, yet undefined term to most people outside of the legal community, the bar is the railing or partition that separates the general public from those involved in the trial or hearing of a case, such as the judge, lawyers, jury, clerk, and court officers. Like everything else associated with the Santa Barbara Courthouse, even the bar was nicer than every other courtroom most attorneys had ever seen. The dark, rich mahogany pony wall, elegantly trimmed with intricate detail, was a carpenter's delight.

Gently placing his left hand on Mark's right shoulder, Kendall spoke softly. "I'm so sorry about Lee. Our entire office sends our thoughts and prayers."

"Thank you, Kendall. The entire thing is so surreal. How is Josh?" News of this magnitude traveled instantly in the relatively small legal community.

"He's really banged up, but fortunately he should be fine in the long run."

"So, Kendall, I'm sure you're thinking what I'm thinking." He paused, glanced around the mostly empty courtroom, and took a deep breath. "What happened to Lee and Josh on the eve of this hearing has got to be more than a coincidence, right?"

Mark was spot on, and they both knew it. But as if acknowledging Mark's assumption out loud would make it more real, Kendall simply nodded once.

"Just a heads-up Mark, I am going to request a short continuance. Maybe sixty to ninety days."

"Of course," Mark said. "I don't think Judge Stricker will expect either of us to be up to speed on this case in such short order. And I'm certainly not willing to open myself up to an ineffective assistance of counsel claim, given the fact that I've had only thirty minutes to skim through the file. I've explained that to Mr. Knowles. He understands."

"Good morning, Mary Kay. Good morning, Deputy Graham." Kendall greeted the judge's clerk and the court officer respectively and sat at the counsel's table designated for the prosecutors. He pulled out his canary-colored notepad and his black ink ballpoint pen. Appearing as if a million thoughts raced through his head, he stared at the empty judge's chair as he waited for Judge Stricker to take the bench.

"How's Mr. Rizzetti?" Mary Kay asked Kendall. The normally shy clerk was very fond of Josh, as were all the single, female clerks at the courthouse. Josh had a special knack for making everyone feel equal, mainly because that is truly what he believed; and his consideration was well-recognized and widely appreciated.

"All things considered, he is doing well."

Over the next ten minutes, a few reporters and a news camera person entered the back of the courtroom. Just as the cameraman finished adjusting his tripod, the court officer roared.

"All rise! The Honorable Judge Robert Stricker presiding."

Judge Stricker, draped in his traditional black robe, entered from the hidden door behind his chair. He pulled out the chair from under the bench and sat.

"Please be seated." Judge Stricker extended his left arm and grabbed the file folder handed to him by his clerk. "Thank you, Mary Kay."

He opened the file, glanced at the first page, then turned to the yellow tab placed on one of the many pages that comprised the half-inch thick, pale blue folder.

"We're here on a Motion in Limine in the case of *State of California v. Nicholas Knowles*. Counsel, please state your appearances."

"Kendall Jackson present for the State."

"Mark Patterson present for the Defendant, Nicholas Knowles. My client, Mr. Knowles, is in the hallway, Your Honor. I told him his presence for this motion likely would not be necessary. Also, I figured Your Honor would want to discuss some housekeeping matters first given the recent, tragic events of last night."

"Your Honor, may we approach the bench," Kendall requested.

"No need counselor. I think I know why, and I am one step ahead of you. I see we have some interested, but non-essential visitors in the courtroom. Given the shocking events of last night, I'm anticipating that the State wishes to have this hearing closed to the public, as an ongoing investigation is likely underway."

"Thank you, Your Honor," Kendall said, accompanied by a nod.

"Deputy, can you kindly escort our friends from the press to the hallway until the conclusion of this hearing? Thank you."

"Mr. Jackson, do you still wish for counsel to approach?"

"No, Your Honor. You read my mind. Thank you."

"Mr. Patterson?"

"No thank you, Your Honor."

"I'll give each of you a chance to be heard, but I think I can expedite things if I speak first. Obviously, I am aware of the terrible events of last night. And Mr. Patterson, my condolences to your entire firm. Mr. Templeton was a fine member of this community. While I am sure both you and Mr. Jackson are well-capable to handle this hearing, and depending on the outcome of the hearing, to proceed with the trial right away, there is clearly more at stake here. Given the gravity of the situation, the yet-to-be-discovered factors involved, and the emotional circumstances of what has transpired, I propose that the hearing and trial be continued for at least forty-five days out."

Turning to the defense attorney, the judge said, "Mr. Patterson, obviously your client is out on bond, correct?"

"Yes, Your Honor, he is."

"Counsel, are we all in agreement?"

Mr. Patterson looked over to the empty chair beside him, then looked to the judge.

"Your Honor, of course I'll have to confirm with my client. But I'm confident that the defense agrees. If not, I will inform the Court and the State."

"Deputy District Attorney Jackson?"

"Yes, Your Honor, the State agrees."

Judge Stricker, turning to his clerk, "Mary Kay, please get with counsel on agreeable dates for both the motion in limine and the trial that fit into our calendar. Thank you."

"Court adjourned."

"Counsel, can I see you both in my chambers?" Judge Stricker commanded but in the form of a question. He then pushed his chair forward, turned, and exited the courtroom.

Walking through the back hallway that ran parallel to the length of the building, along which all the judge's offices were situated, Kendall held open the door to Judge Stricker's office for Mark. The judge was seated behind his ornate mahogany desk. It was an exquisite piece of furniture, clearly too fancy to be state-financed. Typical of most judges, there was nothing in excess on his desk, unless one considered superfluous the hand-carved letter box that decorated the front corner of his desk, and which famously always sat empty.

The letter box had been given to his honor by his now late grandfather the day Judge Stricker graduated from law school. A former judge himself, his mentor died just two months after his graduation ceremony. The one-of-a-kind box was made by the judge's grandfather and father some fifty years earlier, and the sentimental recipient felt that nothing ever was important enough to distract from its classic craftsmanship. It also continued to symbolize the emptiness the judge felt since his grandfather's passing over a decade prior, or so he expressed to those who asked about it.

With his robe hung neatly on the wooden coat rack five feet to the right of his desk, the judge leaned back in his pricey suede executive chair. He had ditched the government-issued office chair and splurged on a high-end, business chair to customize his office. And why not? He could afford it.

Judge Stricker was a sharp dresser. While all the judges at the Santa Barbara Courthouse dressed professionally, with business suits the norm, Judge Stricker kicked it up a notch. Designer suits, designer shirts, designer shoes, designer ties, cuff links, and expensive watches. If the local Superior Court judges were a corporation, and appearances established its hierarchy, Judge Stricker would be the CEO. Judges made a decent salary, but not that much. Unlike the other local judges, Judge Stricker came from wealth and was flashy with his inheritance. His grandfather and parents always told him to dress for success; and since it worked for them, who was he to prove otherwise?

Judge Stricker's grandfather undoubtedly would have been proud of his accomplishments, especially now that he was being seriously considered for a federal appointment with the Ninth Circuit Court of Appeals. A lifetime appointment on the federal bench was Judge Stricker's goal since the day he decided to follow in his grandfather's footsteps and attend law school. And to be considered for such a prestigious position on the bench in one's late thirties was unheard of and had the judge talking of sitting for the nation's top court one day. Late thirties, Circuit Court of Appeals. Late forties/early fifties, U.S. Supreme Court. Early sixties, Chief Justice. He was determined to make his dream board a reality, to transform it from two-dimensional to three-dimensional, and willing to do whatever he needed to make it happen.

Kendall extended his right open palm toward the guest chairs opposite the judge's desk. "Should we sit Your Honor?"

"Not necessary gentlemen, I'll be brief. I just wanted to make sure we are all on the same page with this case. Clearly, there may be more to this case than anyone knows at this point. That being said, I think we all need to be flexible with bringing this case to resolution. Why don't we set this case for a Case Management Conference about thirty days out, to see where everything stands? Depending on where we are at that time, we can readdress the motion and trial dates if necessary. Get with Mary Kay to schedule a CMC that works with your schedules."

Both attorneys agreed in harmony, "Yes, Your Honor."

"Thank you, gentleman." Perching his reading glasses on the tip of his perfectly shaped nose, shifting his focus to his computer screen, and reaching for his mouse, Judge Stricker dismissed counsel. "That's all."

Chapter Eleven

11

Josh's two bedrooms, one-and-a-half bathrooms cottage was hidden at the back end of a long-but-narrow lot, shaded by several Jacaranda trees that produced breathtaking purple blossoms during spring. A short, stonewashed brick walkway that flowed from the driveway, between a tiny, perfectly groomed lawn, and two yellow rose bushes, led to the front door. Just to the right of the wood-stained, heavy craftsmen-style door sat two swivel patio chairs, and the smallest side table ever crafted. If the Lilliputians made furniture, this table was their signature piece.

Josh cherished getting up at the crack of dawn every Saturday and Sunday morning, coffee brewing courtesy of auto brew, cutting a generous piece of a raspberry-cream cheese Danish that covered the entire plate, and enjoying his continental breakfast relaxing in his modest front yard. Like clockwork, every weekend, around 5:15 a.m., the Saturday and Sunday editions of the *Santa Barbara Daily Press* thumped at the end of the long driveway that ran alongside the front house and stopped just shy of Josh's one-car garage in the back of the subdivided lot.

His weekend morning snack plate consumed every inch of the table, as Josh would lean back in one of his surprisingly super-comfy patio chairs and read the morning paper. While reading, Josh favored the old-school method. He preferred reading the newspaper the way it was meant to be read—shaking the oddly large, flimsy paper as his fingers turned black with irksome ink that never completely dried. But this Saturday morning, his newspaper was still set in his driveway, wholly untouched.

This particular Saturday, sleep in a hospital bed usurped his ritual. Well, not so much as sleep as it was pseudo-sleep. To classify whatever he had as sleep would be a gross overstatement. It was more akin to what one calls the rest one gets when nurses and doctors pop in and out, poking, prodding, checking charts, adjusting drip medication, or just being friendly. That's what he got.

As the clock approached 9:45 a.m., Dr. Overman entered the room. The heart-stopping supermodel and the flirtatious prosecutor exchanged repartee before the doctor released her spirited patient.

"Do you have a ride home?" the doctor asked, with a hint of jealousy, at least through the ears of the confident Deputy D.A. "Is your girlfriend picking you up?"

"Oh, no, she's not my girlfr—I'm mean, uh, um yes, I have—Yes, I have a ride," Josh stuttered as if the doctor might ask him out.

"You must have the jurors eating out of your hands," she jeered, mocking his verbal stumbling.

Josh chose not to respond. He only smiled.

Twenty years earlier, that statement would've crushed Josh. Today, it served as a reminder to him that no matter what hand you're dealt, you're never out of the game unless you quit.

Born with a speech impediment, Josh had spent one evening a week for much of his childhood in speech therapy, struggling to overcome it. For years, kids had mocked him, even his closest friends. But Josh stayed the course. And not only did he conquer his speech disorder, but he also now shined in a profession in which one's ability to communicate effectively was paramount.

"Here's your prescription for the pain medication," the doctor said. "Call me if anything seems wrong. Until next time." She smiled at Josh, and before he could reply, she was out the door.

"Did she just give me a wink?" Josh dreamed out loud. "Was she asking me to ask her out? Noooo . . . or was she?"

Disturbing his euphoric fantasizing, a white-haired nurse trailing a wheelchair squeezed through the door. It banged against the door jamb, adding to the countless dings in the doorway. Her name tag read "Nedra, R.N."

"Ready to get outta here, Mr. Rizzetti?"

"Yes ma'am."

"Good. We're ready to be rid of you." The feisty nurse was too funny for words. She had Josh in stitches the moment she had checked on him after he first regained consciousness. Blessed with a dry sense of humor, and a spunky personality, it was evident that she was the go-to nurse for the crusty old male patients whenever a kick in the butt was deserved. Firm, yet caring. Professional, yet the salt of the earth.

With both hands cupped under Josh's heavily coated leg, she gently raised it. Josh pushed both hands down firmly on the mattress, supporting the weight of his upper body. His triceps flexed. Clearly the arms of a man who compulsively did dips of five sets of twenty reps, five times a week. He shifted his body perpendicular to the bed while the nurse slowly swung his leg around to the floor. A little more synchronized maneuvering and the two had Josh comfortably in the chair.

After dinging the door jamb some more for good measure, Nurse Nedra rolled Josh down the long hallway. The white walls seemed excessively bright, perhaps because of the lack of patients or medical personnel roaming the corridor. A page came over the loudspeaker calling for Dr. Overman; likely a male patient requesting a sponge bath, or so Josh suspected. As they passed the third-floor nurses' station, three smitten nurses smiled and waved at the popular patient. Josh wasn't a hundred years old, and he had fewer wrinkles than a Chinese Shar-Pei, so those factors alone made him a sight for a nurse's sore eyes. And the fact that he could wipe his own butt made him a God in their eyes.

"Thank you all for taking good care of me." He smiled back, adding a playful wink.

"Come back soon," said the cute, rookie nurse, who was admonished there and then with a gentle swat from the supervisor beside her.

Just as Josh and Nurse Nedra approached the end of the hallway, about eight feet in front of the elevator doors, the bell rang. "Ding." The door opened. Nedra waited for the elevator occupant to exit, as both her hands gripped Josh's wheelchair, ready to push forward.

The runway model, displaying the latest fashion in all-white medical professional attire, stepped out and extended her left arm to hold the elevator door for her patient. Her hands appeared damp, so perhaps a patient did score a sponge bath. Lucky old Shar-Pei.

"You finally got enough of our gourmet food?" Dr. Overman joked, continuing with her subtle flirtation.

"Actually, the breakfast burrito here is delicious!" Flirting aside, Josh was serious. He found it to be surprisingly good, even by "real" restaurant standards. "However, I will miss the view from my room."

The two exchanged smiles as Nurse Nedra pushed Josh into the elevator. "Thank you, Doctor." The door closed.

"Keep it in your pants young man," Nurse Nedra scolded. Hearing the familiar comment, Josh chuckled. The nurse didn't. The flirtatious attorney slouched over, ready to crawl into the doghouse when the spunky nurse eased the tension. "I'm just messing with you. Heck, that doctor has every male in Santa Barbara jumping in front of buses hoping to get treated by her. And half the females!"

The two roared with laughter.

Josh watched the numbers countdown, and a few seconds later, the number one lit up. "Ding," the elevator sounded, and the doors opened. Taking a step forward, ready to enter the elevator, his friend stopped, with a quick inhale of pleasant surprise.

"Perfect timing." Kristen lit up, happy to see her best friend out of the grips of the depressing hospital bed, and his leg no longer suspended in midair. "Are they discharging you, or kicking you out?"

"I think we all know the answer to that," Nurse Nedra kidded.

Kristen turned, and the three proceeded beyond the main desk, adjacent to the lobby, and toward the main entrance. Although no more words were said, the vibe flowing between Kristen and Josh was different, but in a good way. From her ear-to-ear smile, Kristen was visibly grateful that Josh was alive. And as for Josh, after narrowly escaping death, he had a new appreciation for the gift of life, and more importantly, his best friend. With no family in the area, she indeed was a blessing and one that he swore to himself, as he rested immobile in his hospital bed the night before, to never take for granted.

Upon exiting Village Hospital, the intuitive nurse lifted her right hand from the chair handle, and with an open palm, raised it, motioning to Kristen, assuming she wished to do the honors to her vehicle. Kristen nodded, then obliged.

They headed southwest down Pueblo Street; and still, no words were spoken. Nurse Nedra trailed about five yards behind to give the two friends a little privacy, although only silence was shared. They entered the parking structure and still no words were spoken. Kristen adjusted the front passenger's seat of her *Mercedes C300*, extended it all the way back, and still, no words were spoken. Josh slid onto the sleek, shiny black leather seat and the deafening quietness persisted. Still, not a word.

Nurse Nedra pulled the wheelchair away from the car. She spoke, breaking the silence. "Get better soon, Mr. Rizzetti."

"Please, it's Josh. And thank you for everything, Ms. Nedra. You're the best!" The nurse walked off with a smile, rolling the wheelchair in front of her.

Without saying a word to each other, Kristen started her car and drove off. Her passenger sat quietly for the ride home. He lived so close to the hospital; he could have walked home—if he could walk. The drive was short. No words were said, not one. Certainly, at no time in history had two attorneys gone so long without saying a word. Josh thought of checking the *Guinness World Records* website when he got home because this had to be some sort of record.

The shiny black *Mercedes*, spotless on the inside, pulled into the narrow driveway, cruising slowly to the end, and parked a few feet from the single-car garage. Kristen got out of her car, reached into the back seat, grabbed the crutches she purchased for her friend earlier that morning, closed the door, and walked around to the front passenger door. Meanwhile, Josh had opened the door, and with the cast in hand, struggled to get his broken leg out the door. With her right hip pushing up against the door, Kristen gently supported his leg and rested it on the ground.

No words were spoken. They were shattering the world record. No one would believe that such an occurrence was possible; two attorneys went several minutes without talking. It was a judge's dream.

Kristen leaned forward, almost face to face with Josh. They could feel each other's breath. They paused. Kristen stared. Josh imagined. Thoughts played through Josh's mind at the speed of light, as they often did.

Normally, Josh's brain processed information and thoughts at the speed of a computer microprocessor. To most, it couldn't be explained in terms that could be understood. Josh likened it to having the ability to eloquently present to a jury the world's best closing argument while simultaneously solving a complex math equation in one's head. If one could do that, she understood how his brain functioned.

This time, however, his thoughts were different. His thoughts encouraged immediate action. Life was uncertain. Life was a gift. Today was a gift. Kristen was a gift. Amidst the ocean of thoughts racing through his genius brain was a quote he remembered from one of his closest and smartest high school friends—women have choices, men only have chances. It stuck with him all these years. And no statement was ever truer than this statement, on this day, at this moment.

Here it was. Right before him. Josh's chance. No time to analyze, just act. "Carpe diem. Seize the day," said Josh in his head. "Seize the moment."

Within a couple of seconds, Josh processed all his thoughts and emotions and was eager to act. But then, a fraction of a millisecond before he leaned in for a kiss—thee kiss—Kristen grabbed his left hand and swung his arm over her shoulder to help him out of the car.

"Are you frickin' kidding me?" Josh thought. "I missed my chance. Where's the rewind button? Do I get a do-over? Where's my mulligan?" His thoughts refused to accept the reality of the squandered moment. But he had wasted it, and he knew it. He blew it. He missed it. He missed his chance.

The beautiful, caring, selfless, cerebral attorney guided Josh down his short walkway, past the patio chairs, and into his charming cottage. The doctor had instructed him to rest in a bed that day. Kristen led him to his bed, pulled back the covers, and hoisted his broken leg onto the bed. Remarkably familiar with Josh's place, she walked to the kitchen, opened the cabinet right of the sink, and grabbed his favorite water bottle. "Go Rebs!" written on the side, she filled the aluminum-lined, twenty-four-ounce, red, white, and blue bottle with water from the fridge.

Being a grown man, Kristen often teased Josh because he had so many Ole Miss items in his house. "You could open a Rebel Gift Shop here," she'd tell him. Defending his law school alma mater, he'd explain, "Once you experience The Grove on a fall Saturday afternoon, you will understand."

Lightheartedly, imitating her best southern accent, "But y'all always lose," she would humorously but accurately respond.

"We may lose the game, but we never lose the party," again referencing The Grove in his final argument. "The State rests."

"You've never taken me, so I guess I'll never know," she'd retort.

Home of the most famed and revered college football tailgating atmosphere in the country, The Grove was an influential factor in Josh choosing Ole Miss Law over thirteen other law schools to which he had applied. The Grove offers a ten-acre park-like atmosphere, adorned with over one hundred and fifty trees of fifty different species, naturally shading the center of the beautiful University of Mississippi campus. Aside from the peaceful refuge or picturesque gathering place it provides during the school day, it comes to life at the crack of dawn before every Ole Miss home football game. As Josh would explain it, "The Grove experience is one of those rare things in life that, no matter how much people hype it, the real thing will never disappoint, and most often, considerably outshine the buildup."

"Here you go." Kristen set the water bottle on Josh's granite-topped, wrought iron base nightstand. "Can I get you anything else?"

"Happy hour!"

"That shipped sailed last night."

"You mean you all went without me?" Josh asked.

"You know, you're not always the life of the party. We all have a life outside of you, ya know," she said, misrepresenting the facts. In truth, the happy hour gang did meet up the previous night, as they did every Friday night. This time, however, there was a lot less drinking, and mostly deliberating. What could they do to find out what happened? What if this was not a one-time event? Did somebody want Josh dead? Could something like this happen again?

"Apparently not," Josh said, emphasizing the last word with disappointment.

"Cheer up Rizzetti. Fortunately for you, life does go on."

"Unless you need anything else," she said, "I have a hair appointment today."

"I'm good." He paused, reached over to his bottle of water, and raised it like a wine glass. "Hey Laney," as he often called her, "thank you. Seriously, I don't know what I'd do without you."

"Don't forget that next time you shop for my birthday present." They both laughed as she walked out of the room.

A few seconds later, Josh heard his front door shut. The car in his driveway started up. He barely could hear the music coming from Kristen's car through his closed bedroom window positioned at the front of his house. Her Michael Bublé CD tenderly sang over the purr of the German engine.

"How fitting," Josh ruminated out loud, torturing himself over the near-perfect, but botched, opportunity. "When will she be next to me? Tell me, when, when, when?" he sang to himself. Michael Bublé, he was not. Kristen's car quietly pulled away. Along with the song, the sound of the engine faded, as did Josh's hope for romance.

Needing rest, Josh wanted a distraction to fall asleep before he immersed himself in frustration and regret. Otherwise, thinking would lead to worrying, worrying to regret, regret to insomnia. A podcast or music usually did the trick. Focusing on his preferred relaxation-inducing-genre would keep his mind from thinking, enabling him to fall asleep more quickly and easily.

"Alexa," Josh said to his AI speaker. "Play smooth jazz radio."

Eyes glued shut, twisting to find the least uncomfortable position, a flashback raced through his mind. Josh could see and feel himself flying through the air again. Just before he struck the tree and was out cold . . . he was out cold!

Chapter Twelve

12

It was a cool, crispy Saturday evening. As fall began, the weather began its minor shift favoring coolish autumn, at least as much as Central California experienced any change of the four seasons. Winter, spring, summer, and fall. More like hot, hotter, too hot, and not as hot. Fortunately for Santa Barbarites, the cool ocean breeze coupled with a gorgeous sunset over the Pacific offered a much-needed reprieve from the heat. Other than a few patchy clouds, the sky was blue for miles, providing for a spectacular orangish-yellow sunset as the sun inched beyond the massive ocean.

Once a year in October, on the Saturday before Columbus Day, the County of Santa Barbara put on a black-tie event on the sands of Cabrillo Beach. Large white tents outlined with strings of white lights temporarily replaced the beach volleyball nets. Underneath, the classy tents covered a portable wood parquet dance floor, a classic jazz band, and a food spread to-die-for. Guests dressed to the nines. The atmosphere was opulent, the amenities lavish.

Given its popularity, the annual gala spared no expense. The Santa Barbara Business Association financed the effort. Initially, they envisioned honoring and thanking local elected officials, officers, and judges for their service to the community. But, over the years, it grew into the "Event of the Year." Illustrative of its growth, even some world-famous celebrities who owned first or second homes in Santa Barbara or neighboring Montecito graced the local civic leaders with their presence. That alone made the gala a must-attend event.

Most of the white tablecloth-covered tables were available for open seating. However, various tables contained labels with name cards for the honored guests. As the gala grew every year, reserved seating provided the only guarantee of a seat. And if one wished to indulge in the buffet of shrimp, lobster, and a variety of local, fresh seafood catches, not to mention an array of signature appetizers from the top local restaurants, having a place to sit and eat was imperative.

Each table had seating for ten people. Table three was one of the tables designated for certain guests of honor. Including "and Guest" the table labels read as follows: Mayor Paul S. Dosteel III, Judge H.C. Nielsen, District Attorney William Tell, Council Member Ella Caballo, and Winston T. Reeves, Santa Barbara County Board of Supervisors Member.

After practicing law for twenty-six years prior, Judge Nielsen had announced his retirement effective the end of the year after serving eighteen years as a Superior Court Judge. Council Member Elicia Caballo, whose ancestors were among the founding families in Santa Barbara, was in her second term on the city council. She, not unlike many others at the gala, was very wealthy, in large part due to the fruits of her husband's real estate business enterprise. Of course, it was no secret that her husband was born with a silver spoon in his mouth and that his lucrative business ventures got a jump start from his parents' wealth.

Of the group, Mayor Dosteel stood out as the only member at the table unaccompanied by a spouse. He was a bachelor, married to his political career, only leaving himself enough additional time for one affair; that of his various business endeavors, most of which were exceptionally profitable. The youngest mayor in Santa Barbara history, he took office in his early thirties. Now in his mid-to-late thirties, he was ambitious, successful, and wealthy. Driven by the rush of power, his aspirations extended far beyond City Hall on the Central California coast. Sacramento, definitely. 1600 Pennsylvania Avenue, perhaps.

Like some other affluent locals, including two other men at his table, his wealth came courtesy of his rich, deceased parents. But then again, that was a common theme for so many of the local business and community leaders—old money.

"Hello Stella, Hello Bill." The sharply dressed, young politician pulled out the chair next to the District Attorney's wife.

"How is Mr. Rizzetti doing?" asked the mayor as he sat down.

"He was released from the hospital today. He'll be on bed rest for a while, but he'll be back in court again in no time. You know Josh."

"Yes sir. He's about as tough as they come." As the head of the city, the mayor was well-aware of the formidable Deputy D.A. and his vital contribution to the safety of the sunny, coastal getaway by ensuring that the violent criminals resided on the losing end of the metal bars.

After exchanging pleasantries with the other guests at their table, the assertive politician dominated much of the conversation at the table. A true politician, he was a real talker. And like a great politician, he was good at engaging others to talk about themselves, making him appear more likable. It was an old trick, but it still worked. It got him elected, then re-elected, so why change it?

The night sky grew darker. The ocean breeze blew stronger. The food table became sparse. The open bar's tip jar began to overflow. And when no one was looking, the savvy bartender would grab a wad and shove it in his pocket, making room for the rich guests to tip more. Couples danced and rested. The band's genre decelerated from traditional jazz to smooth jazz, then from smooth jazz to soft jazz. The occupants of table three came and went, mingling with the crowd, and enjoying the amenities.

Council Member Caballo's husband, Anthony, owned a successful real estate development company in the area. Responsible for some of the larger developments in the county, La Compra Plaza was his biggest accomplishment. The largest social precinct for dining, shopping, and entertainment, the open-air mall on Upper State Street was a premier destination for both locals and tourists alike. Many of his larger real estate developments were funded predominantly by Winston Reeves, a multi-billionaire entrepreneur and close friend of Mr. Caballo.

Having met his wife at a political fundraiser when she first ran for office, Anthony had become golfing buddies and more with the mayor and Winston Reeves. Although the owner of a private company, Anthony's office was located in the Town

Hall, in the same building as his wife, creating a win-win for everybody. The city contracted numerous projects with Anthony's real estate development company and had open office space available that it needed to lease out for additional revenue. In exchange for being able to work in the same building as his wife, and the convenience of working in the government building that housed the city departments with whom he conducted much of his business, Anthony was willing to pay top dollar.

At least once a month, Anthony, Mayor Dosteel, and Winston were part of a very distinguished golf foursome, which included Judge Raymond Stricker as the fourth, and who enjoyed rotating through the breathtaking, exclusive golf courses the golden coast had to offer. All four were proud members of the Shoreline Bay Yacht Club and the American Riviera Country Club and were a familiar foursome on all the other high-priced, local links.

The group's inception came about when they all were seated at the same table at Councilwoman Caballo's fundraiser about six months prior to her first election into office. Initially, with none of them being more than an acquaintance of the others, small chitchat progressed into deep conversation, revealing uncanny similarities among them. There was no shortage of common interests, and by the time the evening was over, they learned that their similarities were astonishing: same age, career driven, no kids, deceased parents, inherited wealth, high ambition, community involvement, and love of golf. Heck, they even looked alike: around six feet tall, dark brown hair, and brown eyes, and all were relatively handsome.

From that day forward, a bond was forged. And it wasn't just golf. They drank together, played cards together, and even vacationed together. And the relationship extended beyond social. Anthony Caballo and Judge Stricker contributed to the mayor's campaign, Mayor Dosteel and the judge contributed to Anthony's wife's campaign, Anthony and the mayor contributed to the judge's campaign, and super-wealthy Winston contributed to all three.

The table conversation focused on politics and business, which was not surprising given the fact that everyone at the table lived and breathed one, the other, or both. The lengthiest topic revolved around a local business deal, worth hundreds of millions to billions of dollars, and would have national implications if all the pieces to the puzzle fell into place. Other than Bill and his wife, all the guests seated at table three had a dog in that fight, with the size of their investments ranging from a terrier to a St. Bernard.

During a momentary lull from the business talk, Bill turned to Anthony, "Did you hear about the break-in at Dr. Durbin's office earlier this week?"

"Susan, his receptionist, mentioned it to me the other day when I called in to schedule a follow-up appointment. Fortunately, they don't think anything was taken. Just made a mess. Since nothing of value was missing, I wonder what that was about?"

"It was likely a junkie looking for some prescription meds for a fix," Bill said. "That's typically the motive behind that type of break-in. Probably couldn't find a quick fix and took off before the police could arrive."

Mayor Dosteel chimed in, "You both go to Dr. Durbin as well?"

"This town gets smaller every day," the mayor continued. "I started going to him last year. Great guy. Cold hands, cough cough," he chuckled, "but a warm personality."

"I don't know an adult male in Santa Barbara who hasn't been to Doc Durbin at one time or another." Bill grinned as he gestured to Judge Nielsen, seeing as how His Honor had referred Bill to the reputable physician a couple of decades earlier. "Every male on the bench is a patient of his."

"So Bill, any idea what's behind Thursday night's tragedy?" Judge Nielsen asked, adjusting his bifocals with a pinch of his right forefinger and thumb.

"We're going through our files with a fine-toothed comb, and Bonds and Paine's office is doing the same. We're trying to determine exactly what was taken, and then we will try to figure out why? As you know, I can't say much more than that. For the most part, we're still in the dark."

Councilwoman Caballo interjected. "Any red flags with the defendant on the DUI case?" Being a fifth-generation Santa Barbarite, and a third cousin by marriage to Franklin Bonds, the conservative Council Member took a particular personal interest.

"None that we know of," Bill said. "He's not from around here. It seems that he was up here visiting. As I'm sure you read in the *Daily Press*, he had a few too many at The Boat Hut at Leadbetter Beach, and apparently thought he was okay to make the short drive to the motel where he was staying. His car struck a light pole. He wasn't at the scene when the officers arrived, so the defense filed a motion to exclude some important evidence. That was set to be heard in the morning, with the trial to follow—yesterday afternoon. You know the rest."

The D.A. took his position very seriously, as he should. He was responsive to their questions, while at the same time being careful not to disclose anything he couldn't. He basically repeated what had been documented in the local newspaper. Everyone at the table understood and respected that.

**

TABLE EIGHT WAS an open seating table but was claimed by one of the junior partners of Bonds and Paine shortly after the event started. Once a member of the highly respected firm sat at the table, no one outside of the firm even attempted to sit there, mostly out of respect for what the members of the close-knit firm were going through. It wasn't every day that a thirty-something-year-old colleague was brutally murdered, and in their office building no less. And in a town that averaged about one murder a year, if that, the unexplained fatality was all the more devastating.

As table eight filled, the occupants avoided talking about the pink elephant in the room. They ate, they drank, they sat. No one danced. No one mingled beyond their table. For a group that spent the better part of their lives with each other, common to most private law firms, not much was said. Simply, they were in shock. Complete, total, overwhelming, tragic shock.

Mayor Dosteel, Anthony Caballo, and Winston Reeves ran into Judge Stricker on their way to the bar to gather refueling libations for the guests at table three. Judge Stricker said he was on his way to give his condolences to the devastated workmates seated at table eight. The trio from table three agreed to join him. The distinguished gentlemen approached the attending members from Bonds and Paine.

"Excuse us. Luther, Franklin," Judge Stricker took the lead, "we just wanted to extend our condolences to you and your law firm. Lee was an excellent attorney and a very fine young man." His three mates nodded.

"Thank you, gentlemen," Franklin spoke for the two senior partners. Handshakes and nods were exchanged. Judge Stricker continued with a little small talk with the named partners, followed by bits of awkward silence. The mayor, Anthony, and Winston moved on to express their sorrow to the rest of the firm members at the grief-stricken table. With the ice now broken, several members of the community were lining up to give their sympathies.

Franklin Bonds leaned over to his partner and whispered.

"Luther, before I forget, we need to schedule a meeting next week and put together a committee to look into Lee's case, and his death. There's got to be something in the file that could give us an idea as to why."

"Agreed Franklin. There has to be some link, and we need to find out what that is, otherwise, somebody else might—" Shaking his head and then looking down, Luther stopped, not wanting to say the unthinkable.

Chapter Thirteen

13

"**K**nock, knock, knock."

Josh heard a noise in his head, uncertain if he was dreaming or not. He rolled over to his right side. A sharp pain hit him like a wrecking ball. Regardless of his position, he couldn't shake the Iron Mike Tyson body blows to his ribs.

"Knock, knock, knock." There it was again.

"Housekeeping!" a disguised, high-pitched voice pronounced.

"Alexa, stop," Josh commanded. The music stopped. He opened his eyes, grimacing, struggling to get upright.

"Room service!" This time, a voice spoke with less accent and more familiarity.

"Coming!" Josh hollered. He let out a big moan, reaching for his crutches that were leaned up against the foot of his bed.

Now silent, and kidding aside, the voice coming from the front door waited patiently.

Resting his underarms on the hard padding, supporting his weight, Josh hunched over his crutches and made his way to the front door. What usually took a few seconds seemed to take forever as he struggled to reach for the door. Forty-seven days later, he made it. Groaning in excruciating pain, he opened the front door.

"Did I wake you up?" Flaunting her long, perfect eyelashes, Kristen greeted him. She stood there awkwardly, with both hands behind her back.

"What time is it?" the groggy voice said, oblivious to how many hours, or days, he slept in a comatose state.

"You mean, what hour is it?"

Josh crinkled his eyebrows and tilted his head to the right. "Huh?"

"It's happy hour!" Kristen smiled, pulling a six-pack of Apricot Blonde Ale from behind her back with her left hand.

"I don't mean to sound ungrateful," said Josh. "But truth be told, I'm starving!" He grinned, although worried he came across like an ingrate.

With the quick slide of hand of a magician, her right hand swung around from her backside for the reveal. "Two bean and cheese burritos, extra cheese, extra hot sauce!"

"You're the best!" Josh said with surprise, but not surprised.

"Thank you. But the beer is all you." Crutches in hand, he stepped back to yield for his friend to pass and pointed to the six-pack. "I can't drink alcohol with my meds."

A deep, authoritative voice of sarcasm emerged from the walkway. "No cat litter, Columbo!"

"Good thing I'm the investigator, and you're the prosecutor." Officer Tom Wilkey approached with a bounce in his step, a six-pack of alcohol-free beer in one hand, and a twelve-pack of

State Street Brewery IPA in the other. "Do you think I'm gonna drink this non-alcoholic swill? No thank you. The unleaded fuel is for you. The high-octane IPA is for me and the rest of the gang." He turned back to the other two members of the happy hour gang trailing behind him.

Presents in hand, Kristen squeezed by Josh, grazing her chest across him as she crossed the entryway. Josh leaned toward the doorway, happy to see more of his friends coming from his driveway. Catching up with TW, Tyler and Jen McClure shuffled up the walkway with their hands full of food and beverages.

"Since you missed happy hour last night, we thought we'd bring it to you tonight!" Jen lifted a sealed, plasticware container. "I even brought some of my famous deep-fried pickles that you love so much."

A former Deputy District Attorney of three years, Jen refashioned her career a year earlier, becoming the first female City Manager in Santa Barbara history. She stood five feet nine inches tall, crowned with straight, dirty-blonde hair draped just below her lean shoulders. At thirty-six years of age, she was the senior member of the happy hour group and their grounding force.

Jen's unique, high-pitched voice, with a thick southern drawl, lulled strangers into a gross misconception of her level of intelligence. She was as sharp as a *Ginsu* knife! From the moment the City Council got a glimpse of her intellect, administrative acumen, and good judgment, complimented by her genuine passion for serving their coastal community, a unanimous appointment ensued. With her legal career now behind her, she had finally found a practical use for another one of her degrees; one that for years had been gathering dust as a mere wall ornament—a master's degree in Public Administration from the University of North Carolina at Chapel Hill.

A native southerner, Jen grew up in the small town of Booneville, Mississippi, about seventy miles northeast of Oxford, home of the University of Mississippi. Coincidentally, like Josh's law school years, she spent her childhood fall Saturdays tailgating in The Grove. Unfortunately, fate dealt her a rough deck, and the lifelong Rebel fan wasn't able to attend Ole Miss.

The summer before her senior year in high school, Jen's father passed away, prompting her mother to move Jen and her younger sister closer to the maternal side of the family in Fayetteville, North Carolina. To stay close to her mother, Jen chose to attend college at the University of North Carolina at Wilmington, where she grew to love the beach. And after graduating with a bachelor's degree in Political Science, she went on to graduate school at UNC-Chapel Hill. Next, still apparently not getting enough from the academic world, the professional student headed to law school at Duke University.

Having gone from UNCW to UNC to Duke, Josh loved to tease Jen by asking her, "Is there a university in North Carolina that you didn't attend?" And to add to the jovial jabbing of his friend, Josh had insisted that she get another degree from Appalachian State. "Why?" Jen had asked. "It only makes sense," Josh had joked. "You're from Booneville, which is out in the boondocks in Mississippi. And apparently, Appalachian State is the only college in North Carolina that you haven't attended, which ironically happens to be located in Boone, North Carolina."

Jen placed her container that housed her much-loved fried pickles on Josh's coffee table. Tyler loaded up the fridge with enough beer to accommodate a frat party, while TW filled three bowls with chips, salsa, and mixed nuts respectively.

The kitchen and great room were essentially one sizable room, separated by a substantial, granite top island. Kristen and Jen sat on the short section of the L-shaped sectional couch, adjacent to Josh's tan-colored, microfiber recliner, discussing Kristen's salon treatment earlier that day. Kristen sat closest to Josh.

On the opposite side of the coffee table from the sectional, and next to Josh's recliner, was a light gray and navy-blue striped accent chair. The stripes were about two inches wide, giving the room a hint of a nautical look. With his recliner fully extended, elevating his sore and beaten legs, Josh couldn't help but smile, relishing Jen's fried pickles, appreciating his exceptional friends, and enjoying the sweet life.

"*La dolce vita*," he thought, his mind thinking in Italian.

Josh's modest, but homey abode was like a second home to the close-knit group. It also served as their default home base during football season, making good use of his seventy-inch high-definition TV that blanketed one of the great room walls. Josh had an open-door policy with his friends. "Mi casa es su casa," he would repeatedly remind them. As long as it was the weekend, any and all were welcome to just drop in, unannounced. Having grown up with neighbors that were more like family, unquestionably Josh was more comfortable with pop-ins than most.

Tyler handed out drinks to the group, as TW placed the snacks on the rustic knotty-pine chest that doubled as a coffee table. Before the two servers could take a seat, there was a knock at the front door. Stunned, they all looked around at each other, as though they were taking inventory. Who could be at the door? Everyone was present. With confusion lingering in the air like incense, TW curiously approached the door.

Opening the door with a hint of trepidation, TW's jaw dropped at the sight of the attractiveness that graced the other side of the threshold.

"Helloooo, how may I help you?" He struggled to even sputter.

"Hello. I'm looking for Joshua Rizzetti. Is this the correct residence?"

Amazed and confused by his friend's unexpected visitor, he gathered his composure. "Yes, it is. May I tell him who's here?"

"Doctor Ashley Overman. I treated Mr. Rizzetti at the ER."

"Oh. Okay. Hello Doctor. My name is Tom. My friends call me TW or T-dub. You can call me anytime. I mean, you can call me either. Please, come in."

The astonishing doctor stepped into Josh's entryway, which opened to the great room, making her strikingly visible to the entire gang. Skin-tight denim jeans clung to every luscious curve of her lower body. If one could lift his eyes from that heavenly sight, he would've noticed a white long-sleeve button-down blouse on her top half. Needless to say, she could've been wearing shoulder pads and a football jersey, and the three men wouldn't have had a clue. The facial expressions in the room varied immensely: Jen—curious; Tyler—impressed; Josh—intrigued; TW—drooling; and Kristen—concerned, bummed, and undoubtedly, jealous.

"I thought house calls were a thing of the past." Halfway through her sentence, Kristen tried to catch herself and grab her spoken words in midair; but her heart took control of her mouth before she could stop.

"Hello Doctor. I'd get up, but you all don't want to hear a grown man scream like a schoolgirl."

"I'm sorry, Mr. Rizzetti. I don't mean to interrupt your party."

"No apology necessary. To what do I owe the pleasure? Is my medical bill past due already?"

She laughed, appreciating the humor at the expense of greedy hospitals and their grossly inflated, borderline criminal billing practices. And as if her perfect face and eye-popping figure weren't enough to turn heads, Dr. Overman's beauty extended to her adorable laugh as well. Kristen looked as if she wanted to puke.

"After our exchange of witty banter at the hospital, I was worried you might think that I was minimizing the seriousness of your injuries. That certainly was not my intent. I just wanted to clear the air and let you know that I'm here to help. So, if you have any questions, or need anything, please don't hesitate to let me know."

"I could use a sponge bath," Josh thought to himself. Oh, how he hoped he didn't say that out loud. But since Kristen didn't kick him, he was fairly certain the thought stayed confined in his head. When the dirt in his mind cleared, he said, "I appreciate that. But don't worry, I didn't doubt your professionalism. I'm an expert judge of character. It's an occupational requirement for a Deputy D.A."

"Well, everyone, I'm sorry to barge in and interrupt. Enjoy your evening." With a polite wave to the group, the considerate physician turned toward the door.

"Please, join us." TW took the liberty to say what he knew Josh and Tyler were thinking.

"Thank you, but I don't want to impose."

"It's no imposition," Josh said. "Please, get comfortable and Tyler can get you a drink, assuming you're not on-call." The host peered out the corner of his eyes, engaging his peripheral vision to monitor Kristen's reaction. She sat quietly.

Tyler stood up and motioned to the fridge, to get the okay from the lovely doctor if she had clearance to drink. Plainly struggling not to gawk at the blonde's apricots, he asked, "Apricot Blonde Ale?"

She responded with a smile and a nod, "Please. Thank you."

Kristen extended her right hand, palm up, directed toward the only empty seat, which unfortunately was the accent chair, nearest Josh. "Please, Doctor, have a seat."

"Ashley, please," the doctor insisted.

"So, Doc. As a cop, I spend my fair share of time at the hospital. I've never seen you around. And trust me, I'd remember if I had," TW complimented. "Are you new to town?"

"As a matter of fact, I am." She smiled at his flattery. "I just moved here about eight months ago."

"Did you get transferred to Village Hospital from another hospital?" Kristen asked.

"I don't work there full time," Dr. Overman said. "I recently started filling in part-time because they're currently short-staffed. I also have a small private practice with a partner in Goleta, not far from UC Santa Barbara, in the complex across the street from the largest shopping center."

"Oh, I've seen your place. It's on the corner, next to a pharmacy, right?" Tyler asked.

"That's incredible! Yes, that's it. And the pharmacy next door is part of our practice as well."

"Oh yeah, that's right," Josh interjected. "Tyler and I eat at that burrito place next door to the pharmacy once a week after we play racquetball."

"Burrito Dynamite," said the doctor.

Tyler rubbed his stomach and licked his lips. "Yes, Burrito Dynamite," he said. "Perfect name for that place, because of the double meaning. The burritos taste great going down. But later on, kaboom! Serious detonation!"

"Tyler, please," Jen scolded. "Come on. Not in front of our guest."

Shrugging his shoulders, Tyler uttered, "Sorry."

"No worries," the doctor said. "That's actually pretty funny. And you're right, the food is great! And the couple that own the place are a hoot. Bruno Dias is hilarious. He's super-witty, and kind of a goofball. And his wife Shelley runs a tight ship and keeps her husband in line. She's clearly the manager of the place. Together, they're more entertaining than a sitcom. And they've got two amazing kids. Both in college. Super-bright, like off the charts."

"Wow!" Josh said. "I thought Tyler and I ate there a lot."

TW chuckled, then took a quick swig. "So, how did you end up in Santa Barbara?"

"My partner and I went to med school together, and he's got family in the area. In fact, his great-uncle was the former owner of a chunk of land that got bought out for that new resort development up the coast."

"Oh yeah, Heaven's Vista," said TW. "Like the filthy rich need more options around here."

"So, Ashley, what type of medicine do you practice?" Jen asked.

"General practice. We focus on elderly people." The doctor reached forward and set down her drink. "We've implemented a type of concierge medical practice, making house calls to those who have trouble getting out of the house, and those in senior care facilities. My partner and I alternate between treating patients in-office and making house calls."

"Oh, kinda like that T.V. show a while back, *Royal Pains*," Josh, the television show aficionado, blurted out. "The main character was a concierge doctor in The Hamptons. That's a great niche for this area."

Kristen leaned over and whispered to Josh, "Brown nose."

Tyler chuckled. "She's not going to prescribe you more pain killers for kissing her butt." Undoubtedly, his mind shifted from kaboom to the doctor's caboose.

For the next fifteen minutes, the group asked questions of Dr. Overman, making her feel comfortable and included. Another twenty plus minutes passed with the group engaged in pedestrian conversation, avoiding any personal topics that might make the doctor feel too much like an outsider.

The happy hour gang made the newcomer feel welcome and at home. Consistent with their personalities, each individual was courteous and empathetic of others. Those common characteristics of the group were part of the reason why they became so close, almost like family. That, and their collective love of good beer at a good price.

They continued to participate in small talk, ranging from the two new microbreweries that had recently opened on State Street, to the new Citrus IPA at their favorite watering hole, to the new lion exhibit at the Santa Barbara Zoo, to the never-ending road construction on Upper State Street, to the ostentatious resort coming in that would simply cause more congestion. Heaven's Vista—yeah, right! More like Hellish Traffic. Sprinkled in, they shared with Dr. Overman the best hole-in-the-wall eating establishments in the area, including some that didn't cause a butt explosion.

Throughout their conversation, Josh and the doctor would catch themselves looking at one another and smiling. Jen and Tyler dominated much of the small talk, oblivious to the "privileged" looks exchanged between the doctor and her patient. To Kristen and TW, this did not go unnoticed. For Kristen, jealousy heightened her awareness. For T-dub, besides ogling at the hotness of the runway model doctor, it was an occupational habit.

"So that sizzling, young City Clerk asked me out," Tyler said to Jen.

"Wonderful, young stud," the City Manager said. "That's all I need is you corrupting my staff."

"Hey, she asked me out. I can't help it if the ladies find me irresistible."

"Gees, Tyler," Kristen interjected, shaking her head. "You're starting to sound like Josh. He's corrupting you, now you're going to corrupt the city clerks. Where does the corruption end?"

They all laughed, in part from watching Tyler choke down food as if he hadn't eaten all week. TW wasn't far behind. And while normally Josh would have given the two a run for their money, like part of his case file after the hit and run, his insatiable appetite was missing.

"So, what's up with her driving a brand new, convertible *BMW*?" Tyler asked. "Not that I mind going out with a lady of means, but since when does that position pay so well?"

"Now I know why our city taxes are so high," Josh said.

"Didn't you know?" Jen said. "It was a gift to her from her uncle."

Dr. Overman's comfort level rose. "Who's her uncle?"

"Believe it or not," Josh chimed in, "the Honorable Judge Robert Stricker."

Dr. Overman's raised her perfectly waxed eyebrows. "I assume judges make decent money, but I didn't know they got paid that well."

"They don't." TW leaned back and clasped his hands behind his head, flexing his well-trained biceps in a shameless effort to impress the ravishing newcomer. "Judge Stricker comes from money."

"And he has his hands in various business ventures as well," Kristen added. "You know, the rich get richer."

"Speaking of money," the officer exclaimed. "I'm one step closer to getting a major pay bump." He snuck in a chug of the local IPA chilling his right hand, waiting for a response.

"You mean you passed?" Josh gave a thumbs up to his pal.

"Yep!"

"Congratulations, T-dub!" With a fried-pickled-filled mouth, Tyler high-fived TW. Some food remnants sprayed Jen in the face. Normally, a comment in the nature of "Say it, don't spray it" or "I made the food for y'all. You don't have to return it to me" would have followed. But Jen didn't want to embarrass Tyler in front of their guest, so unlike his chomped food, she kept it to herself.

"Jack it up." Josh raised his non-alcoholic, watered-down beer bottle. "Raise your drinks in salute to future Detective Tom Wilkey. Congrats, my friend. You've earned it!"

With bottles raised and glass clanking, an amalgamation of congratulations was directed, mumbled, and slurred to the rising officer. In the celebration, an ounce of liquid spouted from Ashley's bottle and wet Josh's good leg.

"Oops." She immediately brushed her hand across his leg, as if that would dry it.

"Oh, I'm so sorry," the doctor added.

"Tyler cut off the good doctor." TW laughed at his own comment.

Kristen leered at the doctor, then at Josh's leg. The heat from her glare could've dried his shorts, and perhaps burned the doctor's hand in the process. Strictly as collateral damage, of course.

There was a slight pause in the conversation. A few hands reached for snacks, the others took a guzzle, and all talking had ceased. For the first time since Josh's guests had arrived, there was total silence.

Abruptly, TW blurted out, "So, when are we going to address the pink elephant in the room?"

Instantaneously, Josh and Kristen looked at each other, then at Ashley. Totally shocked, Josh seemed rattled, thinking TW, and perhaps the entire happy hour group finally had detected the romantic vibe between him and Kristen. The look on Kristen's face reflected the same. And now T-dub had broken the silence, let the cat out of the bag, and opened Pandora's box. After a few seconds of awkward silence, but for what felt like minutes to the host, like the sweat glands on Josh's forehead, the stillness was broken.

TW answered his own question with a question. "Are we going to try to figure out why someone killed Lee Templeton and tried to kill Josh, or what?"

Josh and Kristen took a collective sigh of relief. They both noticed, but nobody else did.

"Well, here's what we know so far," Tyler pronounced.

As somewhat of a Mr. Do-It-All at the District Attorney's office, Tyler had consistent interaction with everyone in the office, and more frequent contact with offices around town while running files, letters, and the like back and forth. He continued speaking, laying out all the facts that he could think of that were most definitely related to the tragic circumstances of the past week.

The group dug deep. Discussing every feasible scenario they could conceive, leaving no stone unturned. Other than the *State v. Knowles* case, what other cases were Josh prosecuting in which

Lee represented the defendant? Were there any links between the cases? What about the *Formidable Foursome*? Were there any former clients that Lee represented, and Josh prosecuted, that recently got paroled? Was there any unusual evidence in the Leaving the Scene-DUI case that raised any red flags? Was there anything missing from Lee's file that was in his possession when he was murdered in the stairwell? Was Lee's firm involved in any controversial cases, criminal or otherwise? The newly formed think tank covered the gamut, looking for something, for anything, to give them a clue as to why this happened and to determine if Josh might still be in danger.

Regardless of the theories they pursued, all but one path led to a dead end. There had to be something pertaining to the *State v. Knowles* case that was behind this. Lee's murder and Josh's "accident" could not have been a coincidence. They all agreed that this recurring link had the most merit.

"There's obviously more to that case than appears on the surface," Jen said.

"But what?" TW asked. "What is it?"

"That is the sixty-four-thousand-dollar question. I almost just 'Died In Your Arms,'" said Josh, cleverly referencing the famous old game show and the Cutting Crew's one hit wonder in one swoop.

Josh was an avid fan of most things old-school, and everything eighties. His particular passions were playing and watching sports, classic television shows and 1980s' music. If an opportunity to reference an eighties' hit presented itself, especially one-hit wonders, Josh rarely missed it. His friends mocked him for it, but were amused and impressed by it, nonetheless.

Showing off her knowledge of her best friend in front of the new, ridiculously attractive female guest, Kristen jumped in. "We've got to figure this out soon, before 'Another One Bites the Dust.'"

Josh looked Kristen in the eyes and gave a nod. "Touché." She responded with a wink.

Chapter Fourteen

14

The early morning sun rose above the horizon, warming up the cool autumn air. A few morning clouds that scattered throughout the pale blue sky looked like a picture straight out of a postcard. Morning dew dampened the newspaper that still lay at the end of Josh's walkway, waiting to be picked up and read. It was out of the ordinary for the paper to stay undisturbed for so long, now approaching two hours past its typical "wake up" time.

Josh awoke lying flat on his back. Strictly a side sleeper, his discomfort prompted him to reposition himself constantly in the middle of the night, hoping to find the least uncomfortable position. Despite such a short period, he realized how to position his body in a manner so as to produce the least amount of pain. He opened his eyes, surprised to see much more daylight than he was accustomed to when he awoke. Not yet ready to endure the pain that awaited him, he avoided turning to his side and lay still.

"Alexa, what time is it?"

"The time is seven twenty-seven a.m. Have a great morning," responded the virtual assistant AI companion.

Josh's first thought was to jump out of bed. After all, he never slept this late. Then, with a sudden pinching sensation in his leg followed by excruciating soreness in his ribs, it reminded him of why he lay sedentary in bed. That his friends didn't leave until after midnight was partially to blame as well. Determined to get things back to normal, if possible, he felt compelled to get out of bed. But with nothing on his calendar other than watching NFL football, he was in no rush.

Moving a tad quicker than the day before, Josh still endured considerable pain. He struggled to get himself upright, with his legs resting on the floor and him seated at the side of his medium-firm, memory foam mattress. A firmer mattress would have made it much easier for him to navigate his way out of bed. An adjustable bed frame—even better. While ifs and buts crossed his mind, he made peace with his current situation. The fit go-getter refused to fall victim to his circumstances. He had neither the time nor the luxury to wallow in self-pity. It happened, he survived it, and now he stayed focused to find out who was behind it and why. Until he did, the pain would persist, and the risk would remain.

Josh performed his morning ritual in the restroom but skipped taking a shower. He needed to keep his cast dry, so he figured he could wrap his leg in plastic and take a bath later that night. He labored to throw on a pair of cargo shorts and an Ole Miss T-shirt. Removing a Denver Broncos cap from his hat rack in the corner of his room, he cringed in pain as he lifted his arms and placed it on his head. His stomach growled knowing it was past its feeding time. Josh hobbled back to the end of his bed to grab his crutches and teetered his way into the kitchen.

Moving at a snail's pace, and before he could grab coffee from the cabinet, he heard a knock at his door. He wasn't expecting anyone this early. With NFL football starting later on in the day, perhaps his friends might come by, but not this early. Maybe it was the gorgeous doctor, he thought. Maybe she wanted to come by hoping that she could catch him alone. He had to keep his cast dry, but a sponge bath right now would do just fine. Clearly Dr. Overman's pop-in the night before was more than a professional house call, or so Josh wished.

Two more knocks sent him back to reality.

The famous eighties' lyrics of Men at Work played in his head, as Josh sang to himself.

Four more knocks.

The song continued to play in his head until he realized they weren't going to go away.

"Coming," Josh hollered, swinging from his crutches like a monkey, working his way toward the door. "Who is it?"

"Housekeeping," a terribly fake accented voice responded.

Josh laughed and opened the door.

"Good morning sunshine," Kristen greeted him with her chipper smile.

Josh looked at his wrist, but his watch wasn't there. "Hey. What are you doing here so early?" he said, sounding a little too surprised.

"Great to see you too, Oscar."

"Ha. I get it. The grouch. Funny." Josh smiled. "I'm sorry. Good morning. I didn't mean it like that. I'm just surprised to see anyone here this early."

"No worries. I hope I'm not bothering you. I know how rare it is for you to sleep past six. I just thought I'd bring you a breakfast burrito. I figured you could use a little more substance than your traditional raspberry Danish and coffee. But, seeing as your paper was still in the walkway, I'm guessing you haven't even had that yet."

With her left hand, Kristen handed Josh a brown bag that smelled like heaven—or bacon. Same difference. And with her right hand, she held up his newspaper.

"You know me so well," Josh said, stepping aside to welcome Kristen in. "And you certainly treat me better than I deserve."

Kristen puttered in, waving the bacon-scented bag by Josh's nose as she moved past him. "True and true!" She giggled.

Josh closed the door behind Kristen. He ambulated his way behind her and the two sat down on his couch, side by side. Josh extended his leg to the side of his coffee table chest, placed the bag on it, reached in, and pulled out an enormous breakfast burrito. Eggs, bacon, potatoes, peppers, grilled onions, chorizo, diced avocados, and salsa, all wrapped tightly in an oversized sundried tomato flour tortilla. The appetizing aroma told Josh's stomach that relief was on its way.

Before either could say another word, Josh went to town on his surprise breakfast, throwing caution to the wind for what the onions had in store for him. With each bite, he moaned in pleasure. If Kristen didn't know him better, she might have thought he was moaning in pain from his injuries. Instead, she just laughed. His moans of pleasure were all too familiar to her, although not in the way they both secretly hoped. Sadly, although she had heard those moans from him countless times, it was always triggered by mouth-watering food.

Josh came up for air from his food. "I'm sorry. I'm being rude and selfish," Josh muttered, screening his burrito-stuffed mouth to show some semblance of manners. "Can I make you some coffee?"

"You enjoy your gluttony," Kristen said. "I'll make the coffee."

Kristen walked over to the kitchen. She opened up the brick red, farm-style tin that housed the coffee, adjacent to a stainless-steel coffee maker. The smell of Juan Franciscan Vanilla Nut ground coffee overpowered the breakfast burrito scent. Kristen had introduced it to Josh last Christmas, and now he swore by it. The aroma was unmistakable, the taste was delightful. Within seconds, she had everything done and the coffee was brewing.

Her familiarity with Josh's place, and everything in it, was second to none, including Josh. On average, she was at his place at least twice a week for the past couple of years. You name it, she was part of it. Decorating, painting, organizing, gardening. She enjoyed helping and loved the company even more.

Kristen waited for the coffee to finish brewing. After three beeps, she poured a cup for each of them, followed by some French Vanilla creamer. A quick stir, then she traipsed to the coffee table and set the coffee mugs down in front of her companion.

Kristen scooted around the table and sat back down next to Josh, with her hip pressing up against his side. He smiled, enjoying their closeness. She leaned forward, reaching for the paper. Kristen picked up the front page, pulling it from the other sections. While opening the fold, a white index card fell from it and dropped to the floor.

Thinking nothing of it, Kristen picked up the blank card and tossed it on the table. The card flipped before landing flat next to the rest of the newspaper. What appeared to be a handwritten message, in black marker, drew their attention.

Josh set down what little remained of his burrito. He picked up the card. At the same time, Kristen placed her section of the newspaper on her lap and reached over to pick up her coffee mug.

Pausing to swallow the baseball expanding in his throat, Josh read aloud, "Drop the case, or else . . . accidents happen."

Kristen went limp, dropping her mug. Coffee spilled at their feet, but neither even seemed to notice. The frightened friend trembled; her jaw dropped. Unable to speak, she just stared at Josh. His eyes remained glued to the note, afraid to look at his friend. The reality of the danger he was in had risen to a new level and looking at the panic in her eyes merely would make it sink in further. For the first time since the "domino fiasco," he did not want to look at her.

Now clearly with a target on his back, he denied showing his fear and declined to make eye contact with his terrified mate, for it only would intensify her anxiety. In a similar fashion, he denied releasing the build-up in his gut, but it only intensified his discomfort.

He refrained until he couldn't hold back anymore. Josh lifted his heavy eyes from the note, slowly turned his head, and made the mistake of making eye contact. He lifted his heavy leg from the couch, slowly twisted his torso, and made the mistake of leaning forward.

Kristen broke her silence. "Oh my God!"

Josh broke wind.

Chapter Fifteen

15

Weekday mornings at the District Attorney's Office were typically chaotic, especially for the Deputy District Attorneys. Catching up with the new arrests over the evening, they ordinarily handled arraignments first thing before moving on to the scheduled matters on the courts' dockets. This particular November weekday was calmer than usual because it was Veteran's Day, a court holiday. With the courts closed, it meant most judges were chunking divots on the golf course by 7 a.m. and guzzling cocktails on the Nineteenth Hole before noon. For the District Attorney's Office staff, their boss gave them the choice to take a paid holiday or work and get an extra paid vacation day of their choosing. With no court responsibilities for the day, the Deputy District Attorneys who came in that day were in their offices, reviewing files, or in the break room, telling courtroom war stories, devouring doughnuts, and drowning in coffee.

For the District Attorney himself, it started no differently from any other day. When you reached his level, the work was mostly administrative and political. Earlier in his career, as a Deputy D.A. in the trenches, he paid his dues. Now, an elected official, he enjoyed the benefits of being more of a figurehead—lunch with City Council members, golf with State Senators, mixers with community leaders.

Except for trying the high-profile cases, District Attorney William Tell had little direct involvement with the day-to-day prosecution of the county's criminal cases. His office operated like a well-oiled machine. Owing to his staff, it was well-organized and highly systematized. And his team of Deputy DAs was exceptional in handling the day-to-day business of getting cases through the criminal justice system and putting bad guys behind bars.

As soon as he got the call from Josh about the threatening note, D.A. Tell directed his secretary, Shannon, to set up an emergency meeting of a select group of local leaders as quickly as possible. Josh appeared shaken. And coming from a young man who was fearless, the District Attorney realized he needed to be proactive. The D.A. had Shannon email the members of a group known as the Santa Barbara Emergency Council to schedule an emergency meeting on the first day on which they all would be available. Turns out, that was a month out, on Veteran's Day.

The group, comprised of an assortment of local community leaders, formed nearly five years earlier in response to a massive fire in the area. The blaze devastated the town and led to the evacuation of the entire population, and the destruction of hundreds of homes. Sadly, it wasn't the first time. And since potentially disastrous fires had become so prevalent in the drought-stricken region, the committee established itself to discuss fires specifically, but its scope had morphed to include any emergencies. Each year, a new member or two would join the council as others retired, but their focus remained constant.

The mission statement explained the primary duty of the emergency council, "to proactively address any potential crisis to mitigate the likelihood of an emergency response whenever workable." In a nutshell, to err on the side of caution. Although vague in giving direction, its purpose was clear. The council sought to address problems at its inception, with an aim to prevent crises.

In light of the recent tragedy, the need for a meeting was imminent. With one attorney having been murdered and a Deputy District Attorney nearly killed, the urgency was there. And now, the surviving target had received a threat. Such extreme violence in the span of a couple of hours was unprecedented in the otherwise peaceful town. And with recent acts of calculated violence, perhaps politically motivated, the threat level to the local citizenry remained uncertain. Consequently, the meeting was warranted.

At first, William was reluctant to convene the council. He already had two previously scheduled meetings with some prominent people for later that morning and would have to squeeze the Emergency Council meeting into his schedule. In sync with the primary duty of the Council, he erred on the side of caution and scheduled the meeting despite his busy calendar.

His 9:30 a.m. meeting with wealthy philanthropist Winston Reeves had been on his calendar for months and was a vital step to finalize a top priority of the District Attorney. Funded largely by the multi-billionaire, the District Attorney's Office was sponsoring and facilitating a youth program called *GO MAD*, an acronym for "Go Out and Make a Difference." It was a community outreach program aimed at educating elementary and middle school students on crime prevention through volunteer programs for youth. Since Reeves too was a member of the Emergency Council, the timing worked well.

Assembling the Emergency Council turned out to be the right decision by District Attorney Tell, as was verified when Shannon reported back to her boss upon the completion of her task. A few days after Shannon finalized a meeting date for the Council members, Judge Rupert Haley, the head presiding judge in charge of all Santa Barbara County Superior Court judges, called William and informed him that Judge Stricker reported receiving an intimidating note in his mailbox. Terribly similar to Josh's note, it threatened "Dismiss the Knowles case, or else . . . accidents happen."

The emergency conference was set for 8 a.m. sharp. All had arrived early. William sat at the head of the lengthy conference table that was the center focal point of the District Attorney's Office library. With his canary legal pad resting on the table in front of him, and his custom Cross pen in hand ready to take notes, William called the meeting to order. The nine other members of the Emergency Council, plus one, sat on both sides of him, with four members to his left, plus Judge Stricker, and five members to his right. Judge Stricker insisted that he come with Judge Haley since he was the recipient of a threat as well as the presiding judge over the case that had an apparent link to the unexplained violence.

Starting clockwise from his left, and going around the large, oval conference table, the group included the following: Jen McClure, City Manager; Judge Haley; Dr. Shawn Taggart, Chief of Staff at Village Hospital; Mayor Paul Dosteel III; Judge Robert Stricker; Anthony Caballo, President of the Santa Barbara Business Association; Fire Chief Francisco Loma; Ted Trimble, retired former Mayor of Santa Barbara for twenty years; Ed Conerly, retired Santa Barbara Sheriff; and Randall Price, civil engineer-turned-owner of the *Santa Barbara Daily Press*.

They went around the room, giving each member a chance to ask questions, make suggestions or pose theories. No mysteries were solved, but at least everyone was up to speed. No one could later claim that further harm could have been avoided if they had been in the loop. This mitigated the typical finger-pointing or blaming, and most importantly for District Attorney Tell, it served as a CYA.

Something unusual was happening in their town, and they needed to raise the level of awareness. With little to go on, feedback and input from various sources with a vast spectrum of expertise certainly couldn't hurt any. It was a shot in the dark, but what could it hurt? With everyone on high alert, perhaps they could uncover a vital clue that would shed some light on the mysterious acts of violence in the otherwise safe, tranquil beachfront town.

Well, hope springs eternal. The meeting was over by 9:14 a.m. The result—no answers, more questions.

***

BY 9:19 A.M., the Santa Barbara Emergency Council had dispersed and left the office, save for the District Attorney and Winston Reeves, who had stuck around for their meeting. District Attorney Tell excused himself for a few minutes and went to his office to check his messages.

One of the secretaries brought Winston a fresh cup of coffee and a doughnut as he texted various business contacts from around the world. A man with his success, locally and internationally, didn't achieve such massive wealth from inheritance alone. He made the most of every minute, doing the next deal, making the extra buck, accumulating more wealth, and with it, more power.

Winston Reeves owned more property in Santa Barbara County than any other private individual. Adding to his vast portfolio, his companies owned quite a bit as well. He was also responsible for the development of several significant buildings in the city, ones that he funded and many of which Anthony Caballo's company built. Among the most prominent, Winston owned the tallest building in Santa Barbara, The Grandiose.

The Grandiose was built in the 1920s but was severely damaged over the years by numerous earthquakes. Originally built as the tallest building in the city at one hundred and ten feet tall, it was surpassed by the Santa Barbara Courthouse a few years later. The courthouse stood at one hundred and fourteen feet, edging slightly over its contemporary, where it held the top position for decades. Shortly after Winston bought The Grandiose building, he renovated it structurally and architecturally, and in the process bumped its height up to one hundred and twenty-four feet, reinstating it as the tallest building around.

With its height and prime location, The Grandiose's view overlooking State Street, down to the pier, and across the Pacific, made Winston's ideally situated office building the envy of every socialite in the county.

The large building supplied more space than Winston needed for the staff of his primary holding company, so he generously donated the first floor to be used as a community theater and rented out four floors to several local government departments, including the County Board of Supervisors, of which he was a member. Taking advantage of a unique municipal code, by renting out certain minimum square footage for governmental use, his historic structure qualified as a government building for purposes of various codes, thus it received special benefits and certain tax exemptions.

As part of the *GO MAD* program of which he was meeting with the District Attorney that morning, The Grandiose's theater was the designated venue for a performance to be presented by the youth members in the program.

Winston relaxed at the conference table. Taking a rare break, he put down his phone, took a sip of coffee, and waited for the District Attorney who had not yet returned for their meeting. He set down his cup when one of the two doors to the office library opened, and a staff member entered.

"Oh, I'm sorry," Josh said. "Good morning Mr. Reeves. I thought the Emergency Council meeting was over."

"It is. I have another meeting with your boss in a few minutes." He peeked at his designer watch.

"That's a beautiful watch," Josh said, before regaining focus. "Well, my apologies. I just came in to do some quick research . . . the old-fashioned way."

"I'm sorry?"

Josh pointed to the wall-to-wall shelving littered with legal publications. "You know, books. Old-school."

"Oh, yes. Of course." He glanced down and responded to a text message, then at Josh. "So how is your recovery coming along?"

"Fine. I'm getting there. Thank you for asking."

"So, I gather you won't be able to ride your bike for a while. With so many narrow streets, some one way, some two way, you've got to be careful cycling around here. Like the saying goes—"

Just then, District Attorney Tell marched in, slightly out of breath. "I'm sorry to keep you waiting Winston. I had an urgent issue that needed to be addressed. You now have my undivided attention. Joshua, can you please excuse us and close the door behind you?"

"Yes sir."

"Good day Mr. Rizzetti," said Winston.

"Have a nice day, Mr. Reeves."

Chapter Sixteen

16

He sat at his office desk; suit coat unbuttoned. Even in the office, his commitment to dressing impeccably was compulsive. The coolness of the late morning air had faded, and the central air chilled the sparsely populated workplace on the exceptionally warm November day. He looked at the black sunray-brushed dial of his stainless-steel *TAG Heuer Monaco* watch. Designer watches were his thing, tardiness was not. His visitor was scheduled to arrive in ten minutes and, although it was common for his expected guest to come by the office, in this instance, discreetness was essential.

It was an official holiday, and his secretary was the only other person in the office that day. A brunette lady in her early sixties, widowed for three years and with no children, she had worked for him since day one, since the day her boss stood several rungs lower on the social ladder. With no children, and living alone since her husband's passing, her coworkers were her only family. Staying after office hours was not a problem. She welcomed keeping busy and enjoyed being around others. Going the extra mile for her boss was not a burden, but welcomed, and tending to his extra-curricular endeavors was not uncommon. Picking up his dry cleaning, ordering new ties, planning office parties . . . no task was too menial to his loyal employee.

Beyond his everyday job, he was a man of wealth who wore many hats. Angel investor, silent partner, entrepreneur, and philanthropist. Being so diversified required assistance, so his secretary's dedication and flexibility proved vital. And although officially she was an office employee on a defined salary, her boss paid her extra, under-the-table compensation, appreciating her services. The extra cash was kept on the down-low, known only to the two of them. If made public, his reputation could be irreparably damaged, as his perceived integrity was the corner-stone of his success.

Although a paid holiday, the rest of the staff opted to receive a bonus vacation day by attending an all-day workplace sensitivity seminar. Thus, it was a suitable time for the covert meeting. To ensure privacy, the secretive boss needed to distract his secretary for the next twenty minutes or so. Since she wore many hats for him, preoccupying her was easy to do.

The boss leaned across his desk and pressed the intercom button on his office phone. "I need to get more files over to Perricone, Pocino, and Salvatore for that major investment pro-ject I mentioned to you. I gathered the requested information from my records at home and put them in the conference room, but I haven't had time to separate all of my records recently, so various documents are mixed together. Can you organize that information into categorized files, put them in a banker's box, and take it over to their office when you step out for lunch?

They're sending a Runner from their office to pick it up, but I want you to accompany him to confirm they get it."

"Yes, sir," his secretary said. "I'll get on it right now."

"Thank you. There's also an envelope in the front of the files. A little something extra for you to show my gratitude for your loyalty and going the extra mile."

"Thank you, sir."

He closed the curtains over the two windows behind his office desk, darkening his office substantially, save for his desk lamp that provided enough light to keep one from banging a shin on a piece of furniture. With the curtains open, the natural light coming in made use of the overhead lights practically unnecessary. With the blinds shut and the blackout drapes closed, the room got as dark as the ocean floor.

***

SEVENTEEN MINUTES LATER, there was a gentle tap on his office door.

"Come in."

The visitor entered the office, quietly closed the door behind him, and walked toward his collaborator.

"What the hell?" Tapping his six-thousand-dollar watch. "What took you so long? We scheduled this meeting for a specific time for a reason."

With a deep exhale, the latecomer caught his breath. "I was having trouble getting away from work."

"What are you talking about? You're the boss. Don't you control your own time?" He rose from his office chair, walked around his desk, and pulled a canvas bag from the bottom drawer of his executive wood credenza, embellished with elegant crown molding details, positioned against the wall. "Did you come in the back door with the key I gave you as I said?"

"Yes, of course. Do you have the money?" the visitor said, pointing to the bag in his cohort's hand. "We gotta be quick."

"Hey, you're the one who's late, not me."

Handing over a small duffle bag, stuffed to capacity, the payer said, "Here's half of it."

Unzipping the bag, the recipient looked down, then up. "Half?" he replied, sounding pissed.

The payer threw both hands in the air. "Well, the deed is not fully done," he said. "Once completed, and without arousing suspicion, you'll get the other half."

"Well, I have to be discreet about this, ya know," said the payee, almost apologetically. He shook his head, disappointed in himself. "I can't believe I let you talk me into doing this."

"I didn't have to talk you into it. The money did. I knew it would. Everybody has a price."

"Regardless. I still can't believe I'm doing this." He looked down, dipping his head in shame, and squirmed toward the door. Before walking out, he turned and said, "And it's not like I need the extra cash."

"We're cut from the same cloth. We all want more. So, we do what we have to do, to get where we want to go. Remember, what got you here, won't get you there."

"Thanks, Confucius. But the only way I'm going to get there is by getting myself outta here." Money bag in hand, he hustled out of the office.

Chapter Seventeen

17

The law firm of Perricone, Pocino, and Salvatore rolled off the tongue like something straight out of *The Godfather*. A firm of twelve attorneys, they specialized in all aspects of business law. Contracts, entity formations, mergers and acquisitions, real estate leasing and purchases, patent and trademarks, and securities law were at the core of this high-priced boutique firm. The firm's small size was a stark contrast to the big business they handled. The small-town firm had a big reputation across the state of California. Besides their local client base, lucrative businesses in the Bay Area, Silicon Valley, Los Angeles, and San Diego comprised their client list.

Kristen Laney had been with the firm for nearly five years. In a practice area of law dominated by older men, she was an up-and-coming star in the business law world. Having finished at the top of her law school class at Cornell, which she attributed to her extraordinary memory, her options were endless when she graduated. Wall Street firms, Silicon Valley firms, you name them; they recruited the Ivy League phenom.

To the amazement of everyone, Kristen took a low-paying job with Central Coast Legal Services after graduation. Crazy as it seemed to outsiders, she chose a career in law intending to serve people in need. She had a soft spot for those who did not have adequate financial resources to get help. And growing up in the coastal town of Santa Maria, north of Santa Barbara and just south of San Luis Obispo, she returned to her Central California coastal roots.

Having grown up in a family of below-modest means, Kristen had an unrelenting passion for helping those less fortunate. Working for legal services, she did just that. And while other attorneys there worked thirty-five to forty hours per week, she sweated sixty.

Finally, after three years of burning the midnight oil serving the indigent through Legal Services, she had her fill of community service from the labor perspective. But, while her legal career may have shifted from serving the poor to helping the rich get richer, her giving nature did not. Next, she turned her legal efforts to representing the wealthy, which made her wealthy. Accordingly, this enabled Kristen to donate a quarter of her income to charities, which she did annually without hesitation.

As a rule, the atmosphere at the firm was very formal, save for less formality at the end of the week. Fridays were fairly laid back, especially for a high-end firm for whom about ninety-nine percent of their clients consisted of one-percenters. The modern trend with law firms had developed into allowing business casual all the time, except for court appearances, depositions, and initial client meetings, in which formal business attire was a must. But Perricone, Pocino, and Salvatore were old school.

Business suits Monday through Thursday, even if your entire day was going to be spent holed up in a corner at the law library researching mind-numbing legal precedent or falling asleep to the tax code.

In fact, it was only in the last year that Kristen and a couple of other senior associates were able to persuade the partners into permitting business casual attire on Fridays. Well, it might not have been their persuasion so much as it was the Johnnie Walker Blue Label Blended Scotch Whiskey that they left on the respective desks of each of the three named Senior Partners, coincidentally on the morning of the Partner meeting in which that topic was on their agenda. In turn, the partners happily rewarded their prized Associates for thinking outside the box. The support staff was even more grateful to the associates, as it awarded them casual-casual Fridays. That condition was "non-negotiable," Kristen politely had told the partners, emphasizing the importance of their staff, and consistent with her innate nature to fight for the underrepresented.

And speaking of being holed-up in the law library, today Kristen was doing just that. The hour approached two in the afternoon and Kristen moved on to the next set of boxes. She searched diligently through papers scattered across the firm's library conference table.

The quiet atmosphere, coupled with the extra-large workspace, provided the ideal environment for an attorney engaged in the tedious act of document review. Unfettered space and silence were the optimal factors necessary to go through thousands of documents effectively and efficiently. The three boxes on the table were just the tip of the iceberg. The fourteen

additional boxes stacked two high and seven across in the corner behind Kristen were waiting in line to be reviewed with a
fine-toothed comb by the top Senior Associate of Perricone,
Pocino, and Salvatore.

Her eyes were burning, her vision blurring. She lowered her
head and closed her eyes, desperate for some brief relief from the
monotony. Just a few minutes was all she needed to re-energize.
But as usual, no such luck, at least not of the kind she was
seeking.

"Psst. Psst." A faint whisper sounded over Kristen's right
shoulder.

A look of minor annoyance crossed Kristen's face, as she
turned to see who was interrupting her.

Annoyance turned to sudden delight when her eyes spotted
her visitor. "What are you doing here?"

Leaning over his crutches, Josh responded, "Did you forget
we had plans for lunch?"

"I'm so sorry. I did! I completely forgot. I have been buried in
document review all day and I totally lost track of everything. I
am so sorry," Kristen said contritely. "I don't think I have time
to go out for lunch. I've got too much to review and I need to
get this done ASAP. Can I get a rain check?"

"No," Josh said.

"What? Really?" Kristen's voice faded with disappointment.

"So, you have time for a nap, but not for your best friend?"

"No, it's not that, I um—"

"Relax," Josh interrupted. "I can do one better." He grinned,
lifting a large, handled brown paper bag with his left hand, as his

underarms supported his weight. "How about I bring lunch to you?"

"Are you serious?"

"I figured you'd be buried in work all day today. When we talked on the phone last night, in passing, you mentioned some doc review, legal research, and due diligence for a major business deal you are working on, or something like that. I expected that mind-numbing work might have you drowning in papers all day, with little time to breathe, let alone eat. So, I hedged my bet and picked up meatball sandwiches with extra provolone from Lombardo's Deli on my way here. Am I the man, or what?"

"Oh, thank God! I am starving! And how fitting—my Italian friend bringing Italian food to my Italian law firm." Kristen giggled at her own joke and Josh smiled. He pulled out the chair beside her. "And it's Lombardo's. My favorite! Our favorite. Heck, everybody's favorite!"

Setting the bag of food on the table, he rested his crutches against the side of it. Kristen cleared some space for them to eat. Reaching into the bag, and pulling out a bonus surprise, Josh continued with the theme that Kristen astutely pointed out. "And don't forget the Italian cannolis."

"You *are* the man! And I won the lottery without even buying a ticket!" Kristen said, gracefully stroking her left hand on Josh's right knee.

Josh inelegantly flinched a bit, and forestalling her flirtation, slid a sandwich from heaven in front of Kristen and placed one in front of him. He lightened the awkwardness with humor. "You won a lotto scratcher, not the *Powerball*! Now, *mangiare amica*!"

From the bottom of what appeared to be one of those magic bags, where an endless number of objects keep coming out, Josh pulled out even more. Two bottles of *Pellegrino* and some napkins followed. Josh placed them on the table in front of them and the two beamed with delight.

"And of course, Italian water," Josh spoke with his best Italian accent, bouncing his right palm off his forehead.

The deli foods from Lombardo's were legendary in the coastal beach area. Generosa Lombardo, and her daughter Micaela, learned their craft from Generosa's grandparents, who were renowned chefs in the old country before immigrating to the United States. The deli's tagline, *Sandwiches from Heaven: Made with the freshest ingredients and the most love*, was famous throughout Santa Barbara, Ventura, and San Luis Obispo counties, courtesy of a catchy jingle in their local commercials. What was launched from a humble homemade shack in Hollywood Beach in Oxnard, had expanded into eight locations, with the southernmost deli in Thousand Oaks and the northernmost in San Luis Obispo, including two midpoint locations in Santa Barbara.

Lombardo's became so popular that two generations of locals bombarded Micaela with requests to open a fancy, fine dining Italian restaurant in Oxnard, not far from the location of the original sandwich shack. The shortage of quality formal dining in the area made it a simple decision. Succumbing to the overwhelming and flattering demand, she opened La Vita é Bella in the charming ambiance of Heritage Square in downtown Oxnard, thirty-eight miles down the coast from Santa Barbara.

Overnight, it became the go-to classy Italian dining spot in the area. If you tried the Grilled Onion Chowder, you'd never order soup at another restaurant again. And the Portobello Florentine . . . fuhgettaboutit! Josh took Kristen there once, after which Kristen delighted that the food was phenomenal, and the owner made her feel like *uno di famiglia*—one of the family. Josh's mouth concurred emphatically while his stomach eagerly anticipated their return.

But even after being spoiled by the discerning palate dishes perfected by the Lombardos at La Vita é Bella, it by no means diminished his love of their deli's masterful meatball sandwich. The smell of fresh meatballs and homemade marinara sauce covered with provolone cheese was to Josh like the sound of a bell to Pavlov's dog. Like Joey Chestnut taking to a *Nathan's* hot dog on the Fourth of July, Josh shoved the sandwich in his mouth, engulfing a huge bite before he had time to drool.

The two sat quietly as they enjoyed their food. Sitting side by side, they stared out through the thirty-foot glass wall that separated the library from the main hallway of the firm. Except for the front desk receptionist, a few secretaries, and a couple of attorneys, most of the firm was out of the office for lunch or otherwise.

The two continued to go to town on one of the most popular sandwiches in the region. It was one of those food items that kept people quiet, and focused on the task at hand, which was relishing every bite! In what seemed like seconds, Josh regrettably took his last bite, with Kristen only about halfway done. Every time Josh finished a Lombardo's meatball sandwich, he wished he had taken more time to enjoy it rather than devour it. But when it came to any type of Italian sandwich, Josh's self-control was weak; and when it came to Lombardo's meatball sandwich, it went out the window as quickly as the meatballs went down his gut. As he wiped the marinara sauce from his mouth, chin, cheek, and nose, he watched two men walk down the hallway, past the library's glass wall.

"Was that who I think it is walking with Mr. Perricone?"

"Probably," Kristen mumbled, covering her full mouth with her hand.

"He was at my office this morning, along with the entire Santa Barbara Emergency Council. My boss scheduled a special meeting at our office, trying to make heads or tails of that dreadful Thursday night. Do you know what he's doing here?"

"I'm not at liberty to say." She pointed to all the boxes around them. "But you'd be surprised at how many locals have a lot riding on the resort project."

"Interesting. A lot of locals, huh? Learn something new every day."

"Your work has you so entrenched in the gutter you forget there is another side to the law as well."

"Oh yes, Robin Leach," Josh mocked, while fancying the opportunity for a reference to the 1980s' popular TV show. "You get to engage in the *Lifestyles of the Rich and Famous*."

"I'm guessing you're making another one of your eighties' plugs?" Kristen responded, unfamiliar with Josh's reference.

"Oh, my dear Kristen. You need to watch more television."

"I watch enough. It just so happens that I watch shows from this century, Grandpa!" A slight snorting sound came from Kristen as she laughed at her own joke.

"Adorable!" Josh chuckled. He loved her perfect imperfections.

Kristen quickly diverted attention from her snort. "Don't you have to get back for afternoon court?"

"No court today. Courts are closed. It's Veteran's Day. And to celebrate, the gang's meeting for happy hour tonight."

"The charmed life of a government employee," Kristen said. She loved to tease him. "Is there a holiday that you don't get off?"

Raising his eyebrows, Josh looked at Kristen with a grin. After hearing out loud what she had said, Kristen smirked and shook her head with faux repulsion.

"Well, ya know—" Josh started, paused briefly, then passed on crushing the giant golf ball Kristen had teed up for him. Maybe she'd appreciate his restraint from making a crude comment at such an obvious opportunity. He capitalized on scoring some points and bit his tongue. "I don't have today off. Just no court today. But, like you, I do have a ton of work to do back at the office."

Kristen snickered. "*Gimme a Break, Matlock*," she said. "Thanks for lunch, but some of us are 'Working for a Living.' I've got to make a *Quantum Leap* to get through all these boxes because 'I Still Haven't Found What I'm Looking For.'"

"If you don't 'Beat it,' I'll never make it to happy hour tonight," Kristen continued. She was on a roll throwing out the eighties' references. "I'll probably be late as it is, and 'I Can't Go for That, (No Can Do).'"

"Well played, counselor." After a cerebral pause, Josh beamed. "I counted seven 1980s' references there. 'Time After

Time' you 'Take My Breath Away.' Well, I've gotta get back to work too. Otherwise, they'll think I'm *Moonlighting*."

"Touche."

Josh scooted his chair back and reached for his crutches. Full after consuming every crumb of his heavenly sandwich and cannoli, he had a tough time getting upright. He felt ten pounds heavier. He grimaced in pain; and aided by his bruising crutches, hobbled toward the library exit. Rolling would've been easier, Josh thought.

In a pathetic attempt to imitate the 1980s' Scottish rock band Simple Minds, Josh's terrible singing voice revealed itself. 'Don't You (Forget About Me).' I'll see ya tonight."

"Thanks again for lunch. I may have eaten my whole sandwich, but 'I'm Saving All My Love for You.'"

With his back turned to Kristen, Josh left the library. He couldn't help but smile and wonder at Kristen's final 1980s' reference. Whitney Houston. Interesting song choice, he thought. Did she intentionally pick a song with love in it, or was that the only one she could think of on the fly? He allowed his mind to meander through the possibilities, simultaneously distracting him from the pain of lumbering his damaged body toward the exit.

Lost in his own head, Josh took a left turn down the long hallway, choosing a shortcut. There was an exit door at the far end of the hallway that did not require walking through the firm's lobby area to leave the office, and Josh preferred the discreetness in using that egress. Everybody at the firm knew Kristen and Josh were close. He just didn't want his friend to be the water cooler talk-of-the-day. Like a pendulum, Josh swung himself down the tranquil hallway.

Josh was repeatedly impressed with the elegance of Kristen's law firm. Walking with his head down, he noticed that even the carpet at the affluent law firm put the modest District Attorney's office to shame. Wainscoting made of dark cherry wood lined the walls of the spacious firm, with expensive artwork displayed above the chair rail throughout the hallways. The size of the office was disproportionately large for the number of people it employed. Josh felt as if he was walking down a runway. A fancy, posh runway. As he neared closer to the exit, he walked adjacent to Mr. Perricone's substantial, corner office. The office door was closed, but clearly not soundproof.

Josh walked by the office and heard voices, and not of the friendliest tones. He tried not to listen as he quietly worked his way toward the exit, but the client's angry voice was too loud, only a tad muffled behind the closed door. Josh's pace increased with his anxiety.

"I don't want to hear about problems. Only solutions! I have too much invested in this! Am I clear?"

Josh's face cringed. Inadvertently hearing part of a privileged conversation between an attorney and his client was bad enough, making Josh feel very uneasy. Hearing a client talk to an attorney that way, especially when he knew them both, made him exceptionally tense. If he was seen, even though just innocently passing by, overwhelming awkwardness would persist indefinitely.

Not wanting to draw any attention to his presence, Josh engaged in stealth mode, at least to the extent to which he could in light of his physical limitations. Normally a fast walker, he presently did not have such capability. He could not seem to scoot fast enough no matter how hard he tried or how fast he moved. He felt like a cartoon character whose legs were moving quickly yet whose body remained in place.

To avoid the thumping, he lifted his crutches and tenderly dragged his cast along the Berber carpeting. Unexpectedly, he heard a startling noise. It sounded like someone had grabbed the door handle inside Mr. Perricone's office. Josh stopped. He froze every inch of his body, save for his eyes that peered at the door. Then, realizing that standing still, especially in that location, was the worst thing he could do, he proceeded in the direction of the exit. Quickly but quietly, he raced for the "escape" door.

Mr. Perricone's office door opened. After about six inches, it stopped. More words echoed from his office and down the hallway as Josh scampered to outrun the heated remarks.

Triumphantly, he reached the finish line without being seen. He extended his left hand for the door handle tentatively. He slowly and silently lowered the bar handle. The door latch sounded with a "click." To Josh, it resonated as loud as a snapping beetle. In reality, it couldn't be heard from ten feet away, and certainly not through a well-insulated wall or a crack in a doorway sixty-plus feet away. Though still in a panic, he delicately opened the side door and stepped out. Just as gingerly, he closed it.

At once, he kicked it into high gear, which with crutches, was only second gear. But it was the best he could do in his current condition. So, second gear at maximum RPMs it was. Almost clear from potential detection, he descended the stairwell with urgency until he reached the bottom. He exited the building, relieved that his flight was kept under the radar, and he was freed from risky air space.

Josh was astounded to hear anyone talk to Mr. Perricone with such assertiveness, let alone rage. One of the most successful and respected attorneys in Santa Barbara, Saladino Perricone was like the Godfather of attorneys, and not simply because he was Italian. More so because he was revered in the legal and business communities. And his reputation was earned and well-deserved.

Born in the small town of Palermo located in the southern part of Sicily, Mr. Perricone's family moved to the United States when he was eight years old. Growing up, his family was extremely poor. "I needed binoculars to see the poverty line when I looked up," he liked to say. He worked his way through college and law school, by painting houses on weekends and working at a convenience store at night. Declining the easier route of taking a lucrative associate position with a big firm after graduation, he hung his own shingle and launched his firm with virtually nothing. Beginning with one room in which he shared space with a part-time accountant, he transformed it into a top-tier firm that clients now begged to put on retainer.

Mr. Perricone always took a particular liking to Josh, whose great grandparents just happened to be from the same small town in Italy, before they journeyed to the United States. It also didn't hurt that Josh would bring him a dozen homemade cannolis when the urge struck.

Likewise, Josh was very fond of Mr. Perricone; telling him he reminded Josh of his deceased great uncle, a benevolent family man who also started with very little and amassed a business empire. Saladino Perricone liked to joke with Josh, "Son, your last name would look good on our wall," as if their reception desk needed another Mafia-like name hovering over it. Josh could just picture it on the wall, with a tagline to boot; for example, *Perricone, Pocino, Salvatore, and Rizzetti- Contract Attorneys. We'll Make You an Offer You Can't Refuse.* Better yet, they could open a scuba diving business together; namely, *Perricone, Pocino, Salvatore, and Rizzetti- We'll Take You Swimming with the Fishes.* He insisted that Josh call him Sal, but Josh couldn't bring himself to such informality.

***

ANXIOUS TO GET her work done, or at least make as much progress as super-humanly possible, Kristen plunged back into the records and financial documents. The nature of this matter was too complex, and the financial stakes too high, for any other associate to be tasked with the responsibility that was bestowed upon Kristen. While the other associates in the firm were top-notch, Kristen was exceptional—the crème de la crème. And there was absolutely no margin for error on this project. The economic outlays of the investors were substantial, and the environmental implications were global. Most importantly, the political repercussions were local in that the core group of players was among the Santa Barbara elite, pouring in local money for local development, but for worldwide enjoyment and out-of-this-world profits.

Kristen meticulously flipped through the miscellaneous papers that she had stacked on the conference table. She had moved on to a new set of boxes, and a different investor. "Investor C" was written in black marker across the side of the box in which she was currently entangled. She was labeling each box with alphabetical anonymity, so as to ensure confidentiality, maintain privilege, and avoid improper disclosure to just any passersby roaming their office, who would not be privy to these attorney-client relationships.

Her task was three-fold; to organize, analyze and synthesize. Each box represented a key investor. Within the respective boxes were the financials, business holdings, business affiliations, relationships, and the like of the partners in the venture. While remaining detached and professional, Kristen couldn't help but raise an eyebrow at the amount of wealth of this particular financier. The prosperity of the parties engaged in this venture was no secret to anyone who lived in Santa Barbara, but the enormity of many would have surprised most.

"Wow! That's a lot of money!" Kristen said aloud, as her index finger scrolled across the financial statement.

Ready to move on to the next manila file folder, Kristen paused. She rubbed her fingers on the folder. Something felt wrong. It was unusually thick. She rubbed her right thumb, pointer, and middle fingers back and forth on the folder until it partly separated. Another manila folder was stuck to the back of the "Financial Statements" folder.

The folder tab was blank; it had not been labeled. She pulled it from behind the front folder and opened it. There weren't many pieces of paper in the folder, so it was understandable it could have gone unnoticed. First, she gave them a cursory look to see what they were. It appeared to be nothing more than some random medical records.

"Not sure these are supposed to be in here," she said to herself. "But Sal told me to review everything in the investors' files, so—"

She labeled the tab with a red marker: "Misc. Documents/Med docs." Next, like with all the files, Kristen fastidiously examined all five pages. Nothing appearing noteworthy, or even relevant to the business venture, she moved on to the next file.

The nuts and bolts of this deal centered on a major real estate development with multiple investors. Several acres of undeveloped coastal land that had been held up in litigation for years over environmental concerns were now cleared for commercial development. It meant a massive payday for the current property owner of a portion of the designated land, not to mention the hundreds of millions of dollars in profits on the back end for the group of investors.

With a coalition of venture capitalists pooling their resources together, the legal services of Perricone, Pocino, and Salvatore were retained to assemble, orchestrate, and navigate the alliance, establish the primary business entity and any necessary holding companies, and handle all the real estate, legal and business logistics. The magnitude of development translated to an abundance of billable work for the firm, and with that being the case, Kristen was assigned to head the legal team working on it.

**

ALTHOUGH JUST A few blocks away from Kristen's office, Josh caught a ride-share service back to his office. Even though it was his second full week back at work, he was still under the doctor's orders to rest as much as possible. So, needlessly walking a few extra blocks with his crutches would have been frowned upon by the gorgeous Dr. Overman.

District Attorney Tell had Josh on desk duty since his return, to slowly acclimate him back into his work routine. Normally, that would have involved getting the files for his upcoming trials and organizing them for trial prep: putting exhibits together and in chronological order of intended submission into evidence; creating witness lists; reviewing evidence to determine if any pretrial motions were merited; outlining questions for direct testimony, and outlining cross-examination for anticipated testimony of opposing witnesses. The list was extensive, the importance was invaluable.

However, today Josh was tasked with examining the file of *State v. Knowles*. But not in the nature of trial preparation. Today, he was instructed to make a list of anything and everything that he could ascertain was missing from his file. An associate with the firm of Bonds and Paine had performed a similar task with Lee Templeton's file while disclosing no confidential or privileged information. A list of missing items was provided to the District Attorney's Office for comparison.

Josh knew his file, soup to nuts, like the back of his hand. He already had prepared this case for trial, which meant he knew it backward and forward. His familiarity with the contents of the file was like that of parents' knowledge of their newborn child. Every freckle, every birthmark, every bump, the tone of skin color, what should be present and what shouldn't.

On the canary-colored legal pad on his desk, Josh created an outline of the documents that should be contained in the various folders and the various folders that should be contained in the entire box. Next, he expanded the outline to include any specifics or idiosyncrasies that each particular file should contain. For instance, a case of this nature, wherein he needed blood evidence to identify the driver, would contain a folder labeled "Scientific Evidence," whereas an embezzlement case would have a folder labeled "Financial Records" to trace the inception and breakdown of missing funds.

He finished one complete go-through and found six things missing. He concluded a second go-through and noticed two more things unaccounted for. The nature of the missing contents was part subjective and part objective. The subjective items that were nowhere to be found were some of his random notes, as well as two outlines of his witness's examination.

As he compared the substance of his notepad to the list provided by Bonds and Paine, only one thing in common jumped out. It was objective in nature and vital to the case. Without it, Josh had no case. But what struck Josh as odd was not that the particular document was missing, it was that it could easily be replaced by requesting another copy of it from its source.

Josh wrote the name of the missing document on his notepad and stared at it, waiting for the answer to jump from the page. No such luck. He stared some more. Nothing.

Josh once again wrote down the name of the missing document on his notepad, this time with an exclamation point. But that didn't seem to help. He repeated that three times. Still nothing. Next, in a whisper, he said it aloud to himself. Surprisingly, that didn't seem to work either. Nada, zilch, niente.

Ballpoint in hand, he stared blankly toward the wall. He pondered. Other than his thumb on the end of his ballpoint pen, nothing clicked. Then, shifting his focus back to his legal pad, he wrote a giant question mark over his notes, circling the period at the base of the question mark continuously, until he put a hole in the paper.

"Why would this be worth killing for?"

Chapter Eighteen

18

It had been well over a month since the break-in at Dr. Durbin's office. The initial unease of the staff members had faded to a minimal level, almost completely forgotten. To date, nothing of monetary value was determined to be missing. Assuming the break-in was nothing more than a junkie looking for a quick fix was a practical premise, and the conclusion of the Santa Barbara Police Department Report had settled on that theory.

The medical office was located on Upper State Street, one mile north of the hustle and bustle of the retail hub. Although it was an older, single-story building, it maintained the Spanish-style Santa Barbara charm. And while its architecture was timeless, the security system obviously was outdated. So, in light of the recent burglary, Dr. Durbin's office scheduled new locks and a modern security system for installation later that week. It was the soonest date available. And while Dr. Durbin wasn't thrilled with the delay, he had no choice, as the security company was backed-up and couldn't schedule the installation any sooner.

The value of the assets in the office was not the chief concern. Although it housed expensive medical equipment, the demand on the street for those items was in effect nonexistent. The primary concern was patient confidentiality. It was the security of the patient records that posed the greatest risk. Dr. Durbin emphasized integrity and flourished on his reputation. The vulnerability of his extensive patient records was now in question. And with a patient list that had grown as significantly and consistently as the local housing market, anything less than the best security was intolerable.

The eight-by-ten-foot exam room was at the end of the hallway. A male patient sat on the cold vinyl exam bench in the center of the small room. He had been waiting about fifteen minutes, or about enough time to read the posters on the wall explaining how to lower one's cholesterol, the importance of annual prostate exams, and the dangers of not protecting one's skin with sunscreen.

The doorknob turned just as the patient was going to check his emails on his phone. A familiar voice spoke before he could see the doctor, shielded by the portable screen that prevented patients from being seen from the hallway whenever the door opened.

They added portable screens after an uncomfortable but comical incident. A delivery lady, bringing fresh supplies into the office, saw a prominent patient with his drawers down, head turned, and coughing when an untimely nurse opened the exam room door. Sadly for the patient, the delivery package contained tongue depressors. And just as the nurse opened the door, the delivery lady had stopped in the hallway in front of the door, turned to the office manager, and asked, "What do you want me to do with these small thin sticks?"

Dr. Durbin entered the room and greeted his patient, "Good morning, sir." He released the door behind him and walked around the screen. The door slammed shut causing the patient to flinch.

"Good morning, Doc," the patient said, straightening his posture.

The two gentlemen shook hands.

"How are you doing today?" the doctor asked.

"I don't know, you tell me," sneered the patient.

Lifting his head up from the medical chart secured to the clipboard in his left hand, the silver-haired doctor, who sported a pseudo-handlebar mustache, delivered the news of his patient's most recent test. "The good news is your bad cholesterol levels are down."

"Good news?" the patient replied with a question, with a hint of worry in his voice. "Does this mean you have bad news as well?"

"Well, I wouldn't say bad news. As you know, we sent your blood off for some standard tests. You know, CBC, cholesterol, and the like. All of which look good." The doctor handed his patient a copy. "But of course, in addition to the most recent tests, your medical file in our office contained some other test results. Of course, I'm referring to the ones you requested previously. And I know the importance of those results to you in order for you to find some answers to your family's medical history."

Growing impatient at the painfully drawn-out explanation that still told him nothing substantive, the patient spoke. "Yes. Of course! And?"

"Well, the recent test results are all here. However, the previous blood test results were not in your file. Unfortunately, as a result of the recent break-in, some files were tossed and scattered all over the place. Some of your records may have been misfiled when we put the office back in order. My assistants are looking for your missing test results as we speak. If we don't find them, we'll have the lab send us another copy."

"So, the burglar may have stolen a copy of part of my medical file?"

"No," the doctor reassured. "Well, I mean it's possible but highly unlikely. It's not like a junkie would have any interest in medical records. Yours or anyone else's for that matter. And yours wasn't the only file that had some documents missing. So, as I said, they were probably misfiled. It's really nothing to worry about, but I needed to tell you, nonetheless. My apologies."

"I understand doctor," the patient said calmly, although his facial expression reflected hints of fear and panic. He shifted his butt on the exam table, causing the sanitary paper cover to crinkle. "I believe you gave me a copy when those results first came in. I'm sure it's with my files at home. But please, keep me posted on the status of your office copies."

"Certainly," said the accomplished doctor. "I'm sure it will turn up once my staff gets through all of our patient files. Also, to further put your mind at ease, we're making more upgrades around here. In addition to having a new security system installed, we've ordered new filing cabinets with the most secure, up-to-date locking system."

"Unfortunately, future security measures can't undo this recent burglary, can it?"

The good doctor was taken aback. Such a tone had never been used on him by this patient. It wasn't his fault some druggie was hunting for a fix, and his office was at the wrong place at the wrong time. At the same time, engaging in an argumentative conversation with his affluent patient only would make a bad situation worse. So, with his tail between his legs, Dr. Durbin took the high road. "You are correct. Unfortunately, it cannot."

Chapter Nineteen

19

The firm of Bonds and Paine had withdrawn as counsel for Nicholas Knowles in the case of *State v. Knowles*. With an apparent link between that case and the death of their young criminal defense attorney, as well as the fear of a looming threat that could hinder their vigorous defense of their client, they needed out. They no longer wanted to touch the case with a ten-foot pole, even if their client had been willing to waive in writing all conflicts of interest.

Nick had retained new counsel a couple of weeks prior. Still wet behind the ears, his new defense counsel was barely two years out of law school and had just hung up his own shingle. And for a green attorney on his own for the first time, a paying client was essentially impossible to turn down, especially for a young husband with a pregnant wife and a two-year-old child to feed.

For Brandon Knight, the pay was too good to skip. By adding Nicholas Knowles to his client list, he brought his paying client total up from zero to one. Yes, he had other clients, but not one had paid him a dime yet. He had heard so many excuses from his other clients why they needed a couple more weeks to pay their invoices; he was positive he'd never get paid. Broken-down car, family medical emergency, loan shark threatening to break legs . . . he had heard every justification, bar none. For once, he had a client who could, and indeed did, pay the initial retainer.

They had set the Case Management Conference on the court's calendar, and tomorrow was it. This meant the motion in limine and the trial date would be quick to follow. The criminal defendant had to act pronto. Nick had been gathering pieces of the puzzle for years, piecemeal clarifying a great deal, but not enough to get the full picture. At least not yet.

After the Case Management Conference, a more definitive clock would start ticking. If convicted of a third offense DUI, Nick was facing a minimum of one hundred twenty days of jail time. But it wasn't the possibility of jail time that prompted his urgency, it was the extended time away from bringing his plan to fruition. His target could hide proof. His target could alter incriminating evidence. In the worst-case scenario, his target could flee. And given his target's infinite resources, fleeing equated to vanishing forever.

It had taken Nick six years to reach this point. Six years of quitting good jobs to chase down dead-end leads. Six years of driving from Podunk to the boonies only to find nothing. Six long, demoralizing years before he located the whereabouts of his target. And now, after well-over two thousand soul-crushing days, finally he tracked him down and he wasn't going to let him get away now that he found him. But thanks to Nick's drunken bender that led to a fender bender, he was on the verge of going back to square one, or at least square one and a half if he got locked up.

Despite diligent efforts to stay below the radar, the occurrences of the past month made it evident that his target was, at most, on to him, and at the very least, suspicious enough to justify eliminating risks. His lawyer was murdered. The prosecutor was being targeted. Evidence was missing. This chain of events seemed beyond coincidental, and more in the realm of proactive, intentional conduct.

The former military man had developed many skills during his time in the Army. Not only did he master the skills for which he was professionally trained to carry out his duties while deployed; but simultaneously he became a sponge, absorbing all the skills and knowledge he could from his fellow soldiers. From information gathering to surveillance techniques, he learned from the best and put it to the best use he could think of—revenge.

It was in his last four years of active service that his memory gained clarity. Until then, doctors could not explain to him why his past, and more specifically the years from age twelve and younger, was a total blank. All that was known was that he had sustained a serious head injury at age twelve, resulting in total retrograde amnesia. The specific circumstances of that injury were only known to the extent of the truth and veracity of the man who allegedly found him, a Navy Veteran.

According to his rescuer, on August 9, 1996, the retired military medic brought him to the Ventura County Department of Children and Family Services, claiming he had found the injured child near his home. He was unconscious on the side of a secluded, private road, heavily bruised and bleeding extensively. With adequate medical facilities over an hour away, and able and equipped to treat the boy, the rescuer felt it imperative to the boy's health to bring him home to provide with him life-saving medical treatment. When the boy awoke, he had complete retrograde amnesia. The good Samaritan did not see any reports of the missing child, so he assumed he was a foster care runaway, and thought it best to get the boy stable before returning him back into "the system" that likely was responsible for dumping, figuratively and perhaps literally, the left-for-dead boy in the first place. When the good Samaritan dropped the boy off at the Department of Children and Family Services, sure enough, his hunch was correct in that the boy had been reported as a runaway a couple of weeks prior.

Meanwhile, during the investigation that had ensued immediately after the pre-teen disappeared from his foster home, his foster siblings had reported physical abuse in the home. Consequently, the twelve-year-old boy was placed in a new, different foster home. New, but so much like the old. Different, but so much of the same. For the next six years, he bounced from home to home; the next home ostensibly worse than the one before. When describing his childhood to his closest friends in the service, he maintained that he was grateful for his amnesia, because "if the first twelve years in foster care were even half as bad as the last six, memory loss was a blessing."

***

NICK SAT INTENTLY at his motel room desk and took a bite of a submarine sandwich he had picked up earlier when he went to purchase the daily edition of the *Santa Barbara*

Daily Press. Papers were stacked and spread across most of his workspace, with just a hint of oak visible underneath the years of evidence he had accumulated. Newspaper clippings, county records, Secretary of State filings, photos, notes, miscellaneous documents, and a recently obtained medical record. Some of the items he had reviewed hundreds of times, other items just recently had been added to his arsenal.

He moved around the pieces of the puzzle as if to shed more light on his target, mapping the road from his prey's past and speculating on the dealings of his present. As much as he knew about his target, it appeared only to be the tip of the iceberg.

Fatigued after three straight hours of staring at the same photos, rearranging records, and organizing documents, he secured his evidence in a locked briefcase and placed the briefcase under his clothes that were neatly folded, military-style, in the dresser drawer that propped the motel television.

Within minutes, he was fast asleep on the soft, lumpy mattress. The blaring television of the deaf motel guest in the room next door didn't bother him. The pounding on the ceiling from the kids up above jumping on the bed did not faze him. The loud music from the teenagers parked in the motel parking lot did not wake him. He was out cold.

Four hours later, the raucous disturbances had ceased, but Nick's comatose state had not. And if the noisy disruptions from earlier couldn't wake him, then the fiddling at the door didn't stand a chance.

A metal instrument clinked and clanked a little, fidgeting inside the door handle. A five-star hotel, this was not, and it had a dated lock and key system to prove it. Gaining entry for a seasoned pro was a walk in the park. In less than thirty seconds, the door crept open, while the sleepy guest remained undisturbed. The snoring from the bed drowned any squeaks or creaks that might have followed. The intruder quietly closed the door and tip-toed toward the far bed of the small, two double-bed motel room.

The plan was simple, or at least simple for a hired hit man. Go in, smother his face with chloroform, inject him with enough drugs to kill a large horse, transfer his prints to the syringe, leave some more drugs lying around, wipe the chloroform residue from his mouth, grab the evidence and get out.

The hired gun hovered over his next victim for several seconds and then prepared for the next step. He had to disable his mark. Weaponized cloth in hand, he firmly stifled Nick's mouth waiting for the inhalation to incapacitate his victim. A reasonably foreseen brief struggle followed as the victim awoke to the suffocating fabric cloth that had been saturated with the sweet-smelling solvent. But what should have ended there, did not. And what ensued next could not reasonably have been expected.

Just as quickly as any victim would have been knocked unconscious from the heavy, volatile liquid, the military vet's instincts kicked into high gear, and he propelled into action. Nick's fist crushed his assailant's face before he could flinch, thrusting him back onto the adjacent double bed, closest to the door.

"Shit!" the goon cried out, blood gushing from his broken nose.

Nick popped up from his bed faster than a whack-a-mole and was ready for combat.

In an instant, the quiet motel room transformed into an Octagon, and a championship bout followed. Broken lamps, a corded telephone now cordless, a dresser tipped over, and a shattered television on the floor. The assailant was holding his own but fading, taking three blows to everyone that he could dish out. Ultimately, he proved no match for the trained combatant. But for the words of the interfering motel manager, the assailant would have been found dead on the motel room floor.

After a few minutes of glass breaking, furniture falling, and bodies slamming into the walls, and over the chaos consuming the once-quiet Room 108, the motel manager yelled from the parking lot. Waking whatever sleepy-head guests that remained in dreamland, he hollered, "The police are on their way."

Like a rat to a flashing light, the aggressor scuttled away, out the door and down the dark street. In a full sprint, but slowed from a fierce beating, he reached his vehicle parked a block away, quickly entered it, and discreetly drove away with the escalating sound of sirens approaching the motel.

***

THE NEXT MORNING.

The courtroom was cleared. Other than the court's staff, it was only Joshua Rizzetti for the State of California, Brandon Knight, attorney for Defendant Nicholas Knowles, and his beaten client. The persistent members of the press tried subtly to enter the courtroom but were immediately escorted out by the court officer, Deputy Graham. They waited in the open-air hallway of the historic courthouse, wishing for a scoop that potentially could make its own history.

Never in the bygone times of this safe, affluent, pristine coastal town had such a series of related violent events occurred. And from all indications, it wasn't over. The attack and attempted murder of the defendant less than twelve hours earlier strongly suggested more violence and tragedy were likely, if not imminent. After all, attempts on the lives of three people had endeavored, yet only one was successful. Was the culprit going to make further attempts to eliminate Josh and the defendant until successful? Did the dangerous architect behind this mysterious sequence of events have more people on his hit list? If so, who else was at risk? The questions were many, the answers were few.

"All rise!" Deputy Graham bellowed. "The Honorable Judge Robert Stricker presiding."

Judge Stricker entered from behind the bench. "Please be seated," he said, taking his seat.

"We're here for a Case Management Conference in the case of *State v. Nicholas Knowles*. Counsel, please state your appearances."

"Joshua Rizzetti present for the State."

"Brandon Knight on behalf of Defendant Nicholas Knowles, who is also present."

The judge took a long, hard look at the defendant, who sat next to his green attorney with his head down. It was the defendant's first time before Judge Stricker, after a random reassignment of Judge Munoz's cases shortly before the case's original trial date. But undoubtedly, from the violence surrounding this otherwise victimless case, this wasn't just any other case and, likewise, this wasn't just any other defendant.

"I'll give each of you a chance to be heard, but I think I can expedite things if I speak first," Judge Stricker said. "I've just been made aware of the tragic event of last night. Sadly, I'm starting to sound like a broken record in this case. First, Mr. Knowles, how are you?"

Mr. Knowles looked at his attorney, getting clearance to respond. With his head down, he stared at the table in front of him. "Fine, Judge. I've been to war, so I've seen worse days."

"I'm glad to hear you're fine." Judge Stricker opened the Court's file, then continued. "And while combat is expected in war, it certainly shouldn't be expected in this peaceful town . . . unless you've done something wherein you anticipate it."

"I'm sorry to interrupt Your Honor," Attorney Knight interjected, pulling a piece of paper from his briefcase. "Before we continue. This morning I filed a motion in the Clerk's Office. I filed a Motion to Be Relieved as Counsel, as well as a Declaration in support thereof."

"In case a copy of that has not made it to your file yet, here is a copy." Attorney Knight handed the documents to Deputy Graham, who walked over and handed it to the judge. "I've provided a copy to Deputy District Attorney Rizzetti. He said he has no objection, and my client has consented."

"While I can't say that I'm surprised, can you state the basis of your motion for the record," Judge Stricker said.

"My wife is making me." Attorney Knight injected some levity, getting a slight chuckle from the few spectators present in the courtroom. "In all seriousness, Your Honor. I have a pregnant wife and a two-year-old child at home. And given the tragic murder of Mr. Templeton, and the attacks on Mr. Rizzetti and Mr. Knowles, not to mention the threats, I have legitimate concerns for my safety, and possibly that of my family, if I continue to represent Mr. Knowles. In light of that, I respectfully request that this Court grant my motion. Thank you, Your Honor."

The judge turned to the Deputy District Attorney. "Mr. Rizzetti?"

"The State has no objection, Your Honor."

"This Court finds that sufficient grounds exist for Defense Counsel's Motion to Be Relieved as Counsel and hereby grants said motion," Judge Stricker ruled. "We'll continue the CMC to be heard in fourteen days to allow Mr. Knowles time to retain counsel and get him or her up to speed. Court adjourned." The sound of wood pounding wood echoed in the courtroom from the unnecessary hammer of his gavel, serving no purpose other than dramatic effect.

Mr. Knight shook his now former client's hand, wished him luck, and bolted out of the courtroom, wasting no time to rid himself of the case and the dark cloud that overshadowed it.

"Mr. Rizzetti and Mr. Knowles, I'd like to see you both in my chambers please." The judge motioned his left index finger toward the hallway.

Josh tossed his pen in this briefcase and stood. Mr. Knowles placed sunglasses on his face to cover his matching shiners and waited for Josh to take the lead. The two complied and promptly headed down the back hallway to Judge Stricker's office. A court officer was standing guard outside the judge's door. He gave a nod to the judge's visitors, signaling permission to go inside. When they entered the judge's chambers, Judge Stricker was already relaxed in his executive high-back chair behind his desk, as if he sprinted to his office.

Mr. Knowles was following Josh the entire time but stopped as soon as they were two steps into the judge's chambers. This wasn't Josh's first rodeo, so he knew he needn't wait for an invitation to sit. Mr. Knowles, on the other hand, appeared unwilling and kept his distance near the door; facing it at a ninety-degree angle, staring straight at the door.

"Mr. Knowles," the judge said. "You are welcome to take a seat."

"I'm fine your honor. Thank you. After last night, I prefer not to have my back to the door."

"Suit yourself. But my chambers might be the safest place in Santa Barbara right now. After all that's taken place in connection with your case, my office is being guarded like Fort Knox."

The defendant continued to keep his head down and his hands in his pockets, as if either ashamed or avoiding eye contact with the wealthy judge.

"Mr. Knowles, why do you look familiar to me? Have we met before?"

"Not that I remember, Your Honor. This is my first time in Santa Barbara."

The judge opened his mouth to respond, but before a word could come out, his phone buzzed.

He pressed the intercom button. "Yes?"

An older, female voice on the other end spoke. "Judge, I'm sorry to interrupt, but that call you were expecting is on line two."

"Thank you. I'll take it." Judge Stricker picked up the handset with his right hand, pointed his index finger up from the receiver as if to indicate "just one second" to Josh, pressed line two and turned the back of his chair to his guests. He mumbled, whispered and gave short, one and two-word responses in a cryptic manner.

Nick turned his head in a scanning motion, looking around the judge's lavish office. Super nice digs for a modestly compensated state court judge. The judge continued to whisper and mumble for a little over a minute, giving Nick enough time to look around the room. He pulled his hands from his pockets and lifted a plaque displayed on the bookcase beside him that read: "Hole in One, Central Coast Country Club . . . Hole #8, 170 yards, 5 Iron." He placed it back on the shelf before gluing his eyes back to the door and away from the judge. Judge Stricker abruptly spun his chair around, tossed the receiver on the base and took a deep breath to gather his composure.

"I didn't want this on the record," the judge explained. "I know it's not my place to say, but I feel it's worth saying. Mr. Rizzetti, in light of the threshold evidence that you need to proceed with this case, and that which is the subject of the motion in limine, clearly this case is not a slam dunk by any means. That being said, and given the collateral damage this case has inflicted, I'm trusting that the State is engaging in a cost-benefit analysis to determine whether it's best to pursue this case further."

"Of course, Your Honor." With his mouth, Josh agreed in part. In his mind, he reflected on the only loss of his legal career and was thinking more along the lines of responding something akin to "You're right Judge, it's not your place to say. Perhaps you should spend a little more time researching the requirements of allowing someone to testify as an expert in court, and a little less time telling me how to do my job." Not in the mood to be held in contempt, fined and jailed, he refrained.

"Thank you, gentlemen. You're excused."

"Good day Your Honor." Nick was out the door before Josh could walk away from his chair.

In the courtroom, the judge's clerk, was focused on her computer screen and entering her notes into the system. Deputy Graham leaned against the wood-paneled pony wall that separated Mary Kay from defendant counsel's table, positioned closest to her workspace, and was bragging about his daughter's athletic prowess at a volleyball tournament that past weekend. Mary Kay half-listened, more focused on making accurate entries over polite conversation.

Josh sat at counsel's table that was designated for the prosecution for criminal matters, and plaintiff's counsel in civil proceedings. He placed his notepad and manila file that housed his motion notes and supporting case law into the larger, brown expandable file that rested next to his briefcase. Mr. Knowles approached hesitantly.

"Mr. Rizzetti," he said apologetically. He exhaled. "I'm sorry to bother you, but can we talk for a minute?"

"Mr. Knowles," Josh said. "You shouldn't talk to me without counsel present."

"I understand. But technically, right now I am representing myself."

"In a sense, yes. But you haven't represented to the Court that you would like to represent yourself. You are just in between attorneys. So, I don't feel comfortable talking to you."

"I understand," Mr. Knowles said. "So, how about this? You don't have to talk to me, you can just overhear what I say as I talk out loud."

Josh looked up at the defendant with a slight grin. He paused, then nodded.

"And let's be realistic," Mr. Knowles said. "Unless I can find an attorney with a death wish, I'm not going to be able to find anyone to represent me."

Josh interrupted. "If that's true, I'm sure the Court can appoint a Public Defender to represent you."

"Regardless, I don't think I'm willing to put anyone else at risk. So, I may just tell the judge I want to represent myself."

"Mr. Knowles, I'm not going to beat around the bush. My gut tells me that you might have some information that could shed some valuable light on what's going on." Josh looked him in the eyes and raised his eyebrows. "If that's the case, and you are not involved in whatever is behind all of this mess, I'd be happy to discuss a lesser charge. From the looks of your black eyes and swollen nose, I'd say you already got more than your fair share of punishment last night."

"I appreciate the offer. I do. I'm lucky that my case was assigned to someone as fair as you." Mr. Knowles gave a quick nod, then flipped a coin he had removed from a special slot in his wallet pulled from his pants pocket. "But I'm not in a position to do that just yet."

"What's that?" Josh pointed to the coin.

"It's a silver dollar from the year I was born," he explained. "I keep one in my wallet at all times. It's supposed to bring good luck."

"With the luck you've had lately, you might want to upgrade to a two-dollar bill. It looks like inflation is taking its toll on your luck."

"Good point," Nick said with a speck of laughter.

Judge Stricker re-entered the courtroom, glanced over to Josh then locked in on Mr. Knowles, and walked in the direction of his clerk.

Mr. Knowles looked intensely at the Deputy D.A. and spoke abruptly, "I'll be in touch sir, but I—" In mid-sentence, he rushed toward the door and, in an instant, vanished behind the massive, ornate wooden door.

Already curious from the semi-cryptic conversation with the defendant, his sudden exit at the sight of the judge raised even more intrigue in the hardened prosecutor. What Josh ordinarily would've brushed off as coincidental, the progressively mysterious case now had him on heightened alert. He had seen his fair share of defendants intimidated by a judge, but this seemed different.

Josh sat and pondered for a minute. But before his thoughts could lead him anywhere productive, he remembered that he still needed something before heading back to his office. He stood and approached Mary Kay. Deputy Graham had taken a break from his story, and the judge had returned to ask his clerk Mary Kay a question.

She pointed to something on her computer screen and responded softly to the judge, "Yes, Your Honor. Here it is. It was filed at the same time."

"Thank you, Mary Kay." Judge Stricker turned and walked back toward his hidden door behind his seat. Whatever brought him back into the courtroom must have been resolved, because he was leaving as quickly as he had appeared.

"Oh, Your Honor. Speaking of, don't forget that this weekend is the Annual Central Coast Blood Drive. With your rare blood type—" Mary Kay paused, then said, "Well, you know."

Two years earlier, Judge Stricker's court was the venue for a high-profile civil trial in which the parents of a thirteen-year-old girl had sued a large corporation for the wrongful death of their child after the company's delivery driver ran a red light, striking their teenage child who had been crossing the street. The critically injured girl suffered substantial blood loss before being rushed to the hospital. In need of a transfusion, the hospital didn't have enough blood due to a short supply of her rare blood type. Tragically, by the time the hospital received a new supply, it was too late, and the young girl died.

After the conclusion of the heart-breaking trial that resulted in a multi-million-dollar verdict in favor of the victim's parents, all the court employees under Judge Stricker's supervision decided to donate blood at the annual blood drive. Most notably, in light of having the same rare blood type as the young victim, Judge Striker made a solemn promise to donate every year.

Turning back to Mary Kay, the judge nodded to acknowledge his clerk, then disappeared behind the hidden door.

"I'm sorry to bother you, Mary Kay," Josh said. "But do you mind if I take a look at the Court's file on this case? I need to check on a report attached to my response to a motion."

"Not at all." She stopped typing and handed him the Court's file. "Here you go."

"Thank you."

Josh flipped through the file. Documents appeared chronologically, with the most recent at the top. Attorney Knight's motion was on top. Then the minutes from the previous court hearing. Next, BINGO! Josh's Response to Defendant's Motion in Limine. His response was four pages long, and the report had been attached as an exhibit to the response at the time of his filing. He flipped through the four pages of his responsive document. It was all there. He flipped over the final page, to view the attached exhibit. The next page—no exhibit . . . no report. Rather, it was Mr. Templeton's reply in opposition to Josh's response, and out of order.

"Hmm," Josh mumbled.

He double-checked, to make sure that pages weren't stuck together. No luck. He continued to flip pages, going through the entire file. Nothing. He repeated this process again. Still nothing.

"Mary Kay." He held the file open to the page taking up the space of the absent report and showed it to her. "The report attached as an exhibit to my responsive pleading isn't in here. And I'm positive I attached it before it was filed. The report was also attached to Lee's motion, and it's not in here either."

Josh handed the file to the judge's clerk. She flipped through the file. And then again. She put the file down and vigorously typed a mile-a-minute on her keyboard.

"I'm certain it was in the file." She pointed to her screen. "And look here. Here's an entry from when it was filed. And it indicates that a report was attached as Exhibit A to your response."

"Okay," Josh said. "So where is it?"

"Good question. I don't know. It should be in here. Can't you just file another copy of the report?" Mary Kay asked.

"I wish I could," Josh said, understandably dejected. "But it went missing from my file the night I learned my bike can fly. And the copies were missing from Mr. Templeton's file after he was killed."

"That's odd," Mary Kay said. "What about getting a copy from the lab?"

"I tried. Believe it or not, their hard copy disappeared, and their digital record is gone."

"Gone. What do you mean, gone?"

"Apparently it was erased from their system."

"What?" Mary Kay shook her head in disbelief. "That can't be a coincidence. Right?"

"Who has access to your file?" Josh asked with suspicion.

"Once a case is assigned to a judge, it's usually just the judge and his or her clerk." Mary Kay paused and swallowed the lump growing in her throat. "So, since the time it got transferred to our courtroom, Judge Stricker and me. It's possible one of the clerks downstairs could have gone through it to file something, but not likely. Usually, any new filings in our pending cases get placed in my inbox, and I file them."

Unnerved, Mary Kay continued. "Last time I flipped through the entire file; I know it was in there."

Josh stared facing the jury box, silent and deep in thought.

"Do you think that means something?" Deputy Graham interposed.

"I'm not sure if that gives me any answers or just more questions." Josh rushed to the counsel's table, grabbed his briefcase and file, and strode to the exit. "You all have a nice day."

And before they could reciprocate, Josh was out the door.

Chapter Twenty

20

It was 5:30 p.m. on Friday night, and the happy hour group was meeting at one of their traditional watering holes. But this night differed from most Friday nights. The group was minus two. Josh and Kristen prearranged to go out to dinner unaccompanied by the happy hour gang and somewhere else. Although not a first, the two exclusively had not enjoyed dinner in a few months. Now and then, the best friends found it consoling to openly vent to a fellow attorney about work frustrations, with which only they could empathize. They liked to call it their "Misery Loves Company Night Out," and one was long overdue.

Kristen was a big sushi fan. And it being her turn to pick, she couldn't pass up the opportunity to choose her favorite restaurant, Sushi Tsunami. Smack dab in the middle of the hustle and bustle of downtown, tucked away in the cozy Paseo Nuevo open-air corridor of shops and restaurants that sprouted off of State Street, the location was prime, and the food was amazing. And while the restaurant was within reasonable walking distance to both of their offices, Kristen insisted on chauffeuring her wounded companion until they cleared him to ride his bike or drive a car.

Josh stood outside his office building, waiting for his friend. He took a deep breath and consumed the crisp ocean air. He eyeballed the cars driving by, paying little attention to most. It was the high-priced luxury vehicles that caught his attention, and more so, the black SUVs. Since his bike-launch date, the once ignored large black SUVs now grabbed his attention, and justifiably merited being noticed. Josh found his newly formed concern to be exhausting, as they were everywhere. Similar to when you never see a specific vehicle model until you buy it, and then suddenly it's everywhere. Well, that's how Josh now felt about large black SUVs.

He heard laughter across the street and looked over to see what was so funny. He observed two teenage boys playing catch with a football in the open grass area of the courthouse property. Josh took a moment to take in the artistry of the courthouse landscaping that surrounded them and then refocused back on the boys. He eagle-eyed them. One boy had a cannon for an arm and kept yelling for his friend to go deeper. He chucked the ball to his friend, sometimes on a dime, sometimes over his head. Reminiscing on his youth and his love for playing catch with a football, Josh watched blissfully. He, too, had a cannon for an arm.

Josh looked at his watch. Kristen would arrive any minute. He redirected his attention to the teenage future NFL star quarterback and his buddy across the street. "Go deep!" the future first-round draft pick hollered and launched a torpedo, well beyond his friend's outstretched arms, landing on the sidewalk that lined Santa Barbara Street. Josh followed the ball with his eyes, admiring the tight spiral, until it came to a rest, five yards from a large, black SUV that was stopped curbside.

Understandably, the SUV drew Josh's attention. A distance off, Josh could see that the driver was doing something on his phone, and then looked up in the direction of Josh, then back down to his phone. Josh quivered instinctively, then shook it off. For a brief second, it gave him the creeps. Fortunately, before he could dwell on it, or create paranoia out of thin air, Kristen pulled up in front of him.

Josh opened the passenger door to Kristen's *Mercedes*, tossed his crutches on the back seat, and got in.

"Hey Josh. You okay? You look like you just saw a ghost."

Josh wiggled his head. "Hey. Uh, I'm fine. Just hungry." His seat belt clicked.

Kristen pulled away from the curb and cruised slowly up the street. She turned left at the end of the block, southwest on Anapamu Street in the direction of State Street. Still haunted by his past, Josh peered over his left shoulder to check on the SUV. It appeared to stop in the same place, but possibly edging forward. Josh pointed his head forward, gathered his composure, and thought better of it. He was letting his imagination get the best of him, and he refused to be a victim again. He snapped out of it and began chatting with his friend.

When they arrived at Sushi Tsunami, their table was waiting. Kristen planned in advance, having reserved a table for the two of them. She couldn't afford to risk a long wait, one that could give Josh a lame reason to request they dine elsewhere. Josh liked sushi, but it was never his top choice; so Kristen prepared accordingly. And though Josh was always several steps ahead of everyone, Kristen was always one step ahead of Josh.

The weather was perfect, so she requested an outside front patio table to enjoy the cool, ocean air, mixed with the comforting warmth of the commercial patio heaters. Josh loved to eat outdoors, so that was a plus. Good drinks, great food, splendid company, and people-watching. What could be better?

Unlike Kristen, who was open to trying any and all sushi, Josh was persnickety. Most certainly not a connoisseur of raw seafood, Josh left nothing to chance and insisted that Kristen order for him. She knew what he liked and disliked, and he trusted her unquestioningly, and not just with sushi.

The lovely young hostess commented on what a cute couple they made. They immediately corrected her, then looked at each other and smiled. She seated them closest to a heater, and in between a table for four and a table for two. The table of four consisted of two couples, all in their late thirties. They were laughing and drinking like they hadn't been out in years. From the looks of it, likely they had young kids at home who were being half-watched by a teenage babysitter glued to her phone, texting her friends, while they took the limited opportunity for adult conversation and tying one on. If their constant laughter was any indication, the fear of leaving their children with a preoccupied teen faded with each drink. The table for two was vacant but given the Friday night frenzy, not likely for long.

Josh politely pulled the chair nearest the heater and motioned for Kristen to oblige, which she did. He took the other chair directly opposite the small table, just outside the limited reach of the propane-produced heat. The mixed temperature of the heated outdoors suited them perfectly. He knew she hated to be cold, and she knew he hated to be hot.

As Josh scooted in his chair, another hostess escorted a single man to the adjacent table for two, where the man briefly stood glancing around like he was looking for someone. Perhaps waiting for a friend. Perhaps waiting on a date. Perhaps being stood up. It was too early to tell.

"Can I put in drink requests for you?" their hostess offered.

Kristen looked at Josh. "The usual?"

"Sure."

Kristen turned to the hostess. "I'll have a glass of Pinot Noir and he'll have a bottle of your most popular Japanese beer, please. Thank you."

"I'll put that in, and your waitress will be with you shortly. Enjoy."

They made small talk for several minutes, just to unwind. Current events, weather, sports, and commenting on passersby were popular topics. Rarely did they jump right into work, and the inevitable venting. After a long, rigorous work week, some chill time was warranted. But once their drinks arrived, all bets were off.

A young, female waitress stopped at their table, balancing several drinks atop a food tray.

"I'm Madison and I'll be your waitress. Here you go." She placed their drinks on the table and continued to balance the others on her tray. "I'll give you a few minutes, and then I'll be back to take your order."

"Thank you," the two said in harmony. Madison smiled, nodded, and walked away.

Kristen took a sip and Josh took a swig.

"Ladies first." Josh could tell that Kristen had something weighing heavily on her mind, so he deferred to his friend.

"What do you know about Ponzi schemes?"

"Ponzi. Hmm. Well, the role was played by Henry Winkler on the show *Happy Days*, which ran from 1974 to 1984." Josh laughed.

"Hilarious, Mr. Television," she said. "But seriously, what do you know?"

Josh perked up, extremely curious as to where this was headed. "Well, in its most basic form, it's a type of fraud that entices investors with high returns, and then pays those high returns with funds from the more recent investors; and the cycle begins. You know, like a rob Peter to pay Paul business model."

"Do you think you would be able to recognize a Ponzi scheme with some minimal evidence?"

"Why? Are you offering me a business opportunity?" Josh joked and lifted his lager for a chug.

"Yeah, right! I'm offering a Deputy District Attorney to get in on a Ponzi scheme," she pronounced. "If that was the case, I'd save myself a little time and a lot in attorney's fees, and just go straight to the jail and lock the cell door behind me."

On the verge of spitting out his drink, Josh quickly grabbed his napkin and put it over his mouth. He struggled to keep from busting up. He held up his hand, begging Kristen not to say anything else funny. He was on the brink of spraying his friend with Japanese beer, and he knew she preferred wine with her sushi.

And while the drought-ridden Santa Barbara could use the showers, fortunately for Kristen, Josh refrained from the man-made kind. Finally, after several seconds, he was able to contain himself without incident. When it became clear that he had successfully swallowed his beer, they both broke out, laughing hysterically.

The table of four was yapping and drinking so much, the frenetic laughter didn't faze them. The solo man looked over at Josh and Kristen and definitely noticed the hysteria. At times, it appeared like the loner was talking to himself. Clearly, his drink and sushi weren't providing him with the same vibrant company as the guests around him. Josh observed as much, and briefly felt sorry for him, but continued to laugh uncontrollably.

Their laughter subsided and their waitress approached. Kristen placed their order, choosing a variety of items palatable to Josh's taste buds, and a few new menu items just for her. The waitress stepped away and their conversation continued.

"Okay." Josh sighed. "In answer to your question, as a trained and experienced prosecutor, I certainly hope that I would be able to recognize a Ponzi scheme from a little evidence."

"I'm assuming this isn't just coming out of left field," Josh said. "And from the look on your face, and with this being vent-time, I'm presuming this has to do with work. That being said, I know there's a lot you can't tell me. So, let me ask you this. What can you tell me?"

"Well, let's just say this." Kristen was careful not to disclose any confidential client information. "You know that big project that I've been working on?"

Josh leaned in, anxious to hear more. "Yes."

"I came across a series of business records that simply don't add up. So, I went through them several more times, hoping to explain some discrepancies, and hopefully eliminate the red flags. But I couldn't."

"Did you talk to Mr. Perricone about it?"

"Sí, Señor," Kristen spoke Spanish and occasionally liked to keep her skills polished. But given Josh's limited Spanish familiarity, she stuck to the basics with him.

"And what did he say?"

"It was kind of odd." Kristen paused, looked around, and then leaned in, speaking softly. "From his reaction, he seemed shocked. But not in the sense of being shocked by my observation in and of itself. More along the lines of shock I found something that he was aware of. He even looked a little scared."

"That has the makings of a classic, law school ethics exam question. You know, where you have a client that may be engaged in ongoing criminal activity or committed some crime in the past. And you have to determine whether and when it's permissible to disclose attorney-client privileged information and when it's not. Since my client is always the State of California, admittedly I'm rusty on those rules. If I recall correctly, the exception to the privilege applies when a client is planning to perpetrate fraud. But I don't need to tell you that. You're the one with the perfect memory."

"That's exactly what this seems like, a law school ethics exam," Kristen agreed.

"I do remember one thing very vividly. Even when I knew those rules cold, there is such an enormous gray area when applying them to the facts of one of those ethical-dilemma-scenarios."

"Truer words have never been spoken, my friend," Kristen said. "And therein lies my problem."

"Is there anything I can do to help?"

"Unfortunately, not for now, but thank you for offering. However, once I figure this out, and if it is criminal, and if I can or must disclose it, then I'm sure my prosecuting abogado amigo can be of the greatest help."

"If ifs and buts were candies and nuts—" Josh paused.

Kristen interjected, "We'd both choose an easier profession."

"Truer words have never been spoken, my friend," Josh echoed. They smiled and laughed.

Their waitress came over and placed their food plates on the table. Josh was starving but politely waited for Kristen to help herself first. Being the selfless person that she was and with chopsticks in hand, for every sushi roll she placed on her plate, she placed one on Josh's. Meanwhile, Josh pinched a huge lump of wasabi with his chopsticks and plopped it in his mini dipping bowl, followed it with some soy sauce, and mixed them vigorously with his chopsticks. No amount of wasabi was ever too much for Josh. If a large amount made his nostrils burn, he didn't have enough. If his nostrils caught on fire, then he hit the mark.

The two began to eat. Kristen ingested her food, Josh scarfed his. She commented on how wonderful everything tasted and Josh's stuffed cheeks agreed with a nod. In a futile effort, she offered him to sample the new menu items that she raved about, but Josh stuck with the staple items Kristen ordered for him: California Rolls, Spider Rolls, Spicy Tuna Rolls, and Shrimp Tempura Rolls.

Their waitress drifted over to check on them. "How is everything? Can I get you anything else?"

Kristen swallowed. "Everything is wonderful! Thank you."

"Madison, the California Rolls are delicious. The Shrimp Tempura Rolls are fresh. The Spicy Tuna Rolls are zesty, and the Spider Rolls are fantastic. But also can we get some Tootsie Rolls please?" He kept a straight face and allowed for an awkward pause. His eyes locked into hers, waiting for an answer that he knew wasn't coming.

The waitress looked panicked and at a total loss as to how to respond. Was her customer serious? He sure sounded like it and he most certainly looked like it. The wrong response could drastically affect her tip.

Josh let the awkward silence linger, knowing that Kristen would come to the waitress's rescue.

"Ignore him, Madison. He's just kidding," Kristen said, tossing a life vest and relieving the flustered waitress from her discomfort. "Can you please bring him another beer? Maybe then he'll behave, or better yet, pass out."

"Of course. I'll be right back with that." She shuffled away.

"Okay, Deputy District Attorney Rizzetti," Kristen said. "You have the floor."

"So, you know the motion in limine in the Knowles Leaving the Scene case?"

"The one that got Lee killed and almost got you killed. Yeah, I vaguely remember something about that." She grinned, sarcasm dripping from her chin.

"Well get this. When I got hit by that SUV, some of the documents from my file were taken, including the report that was an exhibit to my response to the motion in limine. And when Lee was murdered, God rest his soul, documents from his file were taken, including the report that was an exhibit to his motion. So, I contacted the lab that did the tests and issued the report, and their physical report is missing, and their digital record has been erased."

"Oh, my gosh!" Kristen dropped the sushi roll from the grips of her chopsticks, prompting a splash landing in her soy sauce bowl.

Josh's voice escalated. "That's not all!" He then lowered his voice and spoke again. "I went through the court's file so that I could request a copy of the report from them, and the exhibit to the pleadings was missing. The judge's clerk then checked their computer system, and the pleading entries reflected the motion, and my response were filed with the attached exhibit."

"Wow!" Kristen edged forward in her chair. "So maybe now we're getting somewhere with this. Although, I don't know if that provides any answers, or just raises more questions."

"That's exactly what I said. Great minds—"

"So, the report," she said "what exactly did it contain? If you can tell me."

"Sure, I can. I filed it, so it's public record." Josh leaned forward and whispered, just in case any lonely guests or first daters were lacking in good conversation and searching for something better. "It contained results from a blood test, matching blood from the unoccupied vehicle at the scene to that of the defendant."

"So, by blood, you mean DNA, blood type, either or both?"

"Both actually. Obviously, the DNA is the clincher, but it's standard for the lab results to include blood type as well."

"Sounds like the defendant would have the biggest motive to make sure that the evidence linking him to the scene disappeared."

"Ordinarily, I'd agree with you one-hundred percent." Josh leaned forward, with his gut pressed against the table, and whispered loudly. "But get this. Someone broke into his motel room last night and tried to kill him. Fortunately, his military training kicked in and he staved off his attacker. But he took a good beating."

"Could he have staged that to divert attention away from him?"

"I thought that too. But my instincts tell me otherwise. My gut tells me that he knows more about all of this than we do, but he's not the evil engineer. He's involved in some other way. I just don't know how." Josh paused. "Yet!"

The two stared at each other, both deep in thought. Simultaneously, they guzzled a drink. Their synchronization was eerie. Whether it was taking a drink, saying the same thing at the same time, coughing, or even sneezing; oftentimes their simultaneous action meshed into true harmony. "Great minds," Josh loved to say.

"Nancy Drew. Let's solve this mystery another day. For now, let's enjoy the rest of our dinner and drinks. We deserve it." Josh raised his bottle and extended his arm to toast. Kristen followed suit.

"Jack it up!" Josh smiled and his eyes watered while he reflected on the story behind the phrase.

Josh's father's name was Jack, and he was a man of many talents. Fix a car, build an outdoor kitchen, athletic, engaging, and he could cook like nobody's business; not to mention being a fine-wine enthusiast. A blessed man of countless friends and a loving family, he had passed away unexpectedly a couple of years earlier. In the spirit of what his dad would have wanted, a Country Club party replaced a memorial service, with food, family, friends, and drinks. The whole nine yards.

At the Celebration of Life gathering, with a microphone in hand, Josh addressed the hundreds in attendance, including people from every phase of his dad's life. From grade school classmates to recently made cigar buddies, Jack's reach was far and wide.

In addressing the crowd, Josh revealed his thoughts of how he had often reflected on his dad's name, and how challenging, at times, it must have been for his father because of all the negative connotations associated with his name. The list was long: you don't know jack shit; jackass; jack something up; carjacking; jack around; and more. He had the crowd smiling and laughing, distracting many from the grief inside. And like a captivated jury, the room hung on his every word, inserting themselves into his story, eager to see where it would lead them.

Then, as all talented storytellers do, he redirected the feelings of his audience, sending them on a roller coaster of emotions. Josh enlightened everyone of the good in the name Jack and reminded them of a famous, positive connotation that was befitting of his dad's versatility, Jack-of-all-trades. He then urged them to start using Jack in a more positive light and made a pronouncement that would become timeless. From that day forward, they would start a new, upbeat reference to the name Jack. Instead of saying "cheers," or "salute" as the Italians say when they toast, they would say "Jack it up!" in tribute to his father and the positive impact he had on the lives of everyone present.

"We love you Dad." Josh had raised his wine glass, and fighting back his tears, toasted the assemblage of family and friends, "Jack it up!" Glasses raised, the beaming crowd reciprocated, "Jack it up!"

There wasn't a dry eye in the house. And within a few days, a video of Josh's speech went viral; and the positive reference to his dad's name, as well as his dad, was forever memorialized. Taken a step further, a park bench was donated to the city of Carmel-by-the-Sea, California, where Jack would hang out with his cigar buddies, have a stogie, and discuss life. A memorial plaque, centered on the top slat of the wooden bench, paid tribute with the words: "'JACK IT UP!' In Loving Memory of Jack Rizzetti."

"Jack it up!" With a tear rolling down her cheek, Kristen smiled.

***

KRISTEN'S CAR WAS parked a couple of blocks from the restaurant, on Canon Perdido. She was parked on a one-way street while contributing to one of Santa Barbara's biggest money-makers, parking meters. Her dinnertime estimate was almost spot on, as about thirty minutes remained on her meter. The two walked gingerly down State Street, enjoying their time together, and the vibrant atmosphere of the famed thorough-fare on a Friday night.

Their stroll led them down to the cross-section at the end of State Street and Cabrillo Boulevard, and across the street to the pier, Stearns Wharf. The nearly half-mile-long structure had withstood the test of time, being the oldest working wooden wharf in the state of California. They considered stopping for coffee and dessert at one of the pier's restaurants but decided otherwise when they agreed they were both too stuffed. Instead, they leaned against the weathered wooden rail, overlooking the massive Pacific, enjoying the cool air, stunning view, and price-less company.

After fifteen minutes of reveling in nature's incomparable views from the historic wharf, they strolled back up the famous, palm tree-lined street several blocks until they reached Canon Perdido and continued in the direction of where Kristen's car was parked. Josh's usual speed-walking was being slowed by his injuries, and that suited Kristen just fine. She liked to take her time whenever they wandered around downtown and had told Josh more than once, "What's your hurry?" But tonight, she had no need. He couldn't speed-walk if he tried.

They sauntered another block, with her car now in sight, parked across the street, about midway down the next block. They continued another thirty yards, almost reaching Kristen's car which was parked directly across the street. They looked both ways, up and down the dimly lit street. No moving traffic was in sight, so they headed toward her car, crossing in the middle of the block. Josh separated a couple of steps ahead, moving toward the back of her car to walk around to the passenger's side. About two-thirds across the street and six feet from her door, Kristen reached into her purse to grab her keys. She pulled them out, but in fidgeting for her car remote, they slipped from her fingers and dropped to the ground. She squatted down and reached for her key chain, causing her purse to slide down her shoulder.

Now positioned directly behind her left taillight, Josh heard the jingle of Kristen's keys hitting the ground and turned to look at her. But before his eyes caught sight of his best friend, a disturbance looming in the background rerouted his attention. Suddenly, out of reach of the faintly lit streetlights, and out of the darkness beyond her, Josh saw bright headlights rapidly approaching Kristen, nearly blinding his vision. Tires screaming, the dark SUV zoomed toward his distracted companion, who was now a sitting duck in the crouching position. Twenty yards from striking his best friend, the SUV's headlights shut off.

"Kristen, look out!" Josh yelled and motioned to save her.

Kristen screamed and dove for her life, headfirst, aimed straight at her car.

Josh's mind was willing, but his body was weak. Before he could take another step toward Kristen, a racing bullet had other plans for him.

"Bang!" A gunshot boomed, knocking Josh back and plummeting to the ground. His head forcefully thumped the edge of the curb and, in a flash, knocked him out cold.

Kristen was midair, with her head an inch from crashing against her driver's side door, when the SUV struck her right foot as it zoomed past her. Her head slammed into the door like a bowling ball pounding the one standing pin completing a spare, then her body dropped to the ground like an anchor.

Minutes earlier, the jubilant young lady was floating up State Street. Now, with blood pooling beneath her concussed head, her stationary body posed dead in the roadway.

Their "Misery Loves Company Night Out" unexpectedly took on a new, darker meaning as they both laid motionless on the asphalt, knocked unconscious, bleeding in the street, and pounding on death's door.

Chapter
Twenty-One

21

"WHO SHOT J.R.?" The front-page headline of the *Santa Barbara Daily Press* couldn't pass up using the iconic catchphrase that encapsulated a distressing, yet fitting caption for the 1980s' obsessed prosecutor. The article read in part:

> Yesterday evening, Deputy District Attorney Joshua Rizzetti was shot in a drive-by shooting on Canon Perdido, a couple of blocks off of State Street in downtown Santa Barbara. He was walking with his friend and fellow attorney Kristen Laney at the time of the incident. It is believed that the vehicle responsible for the drive-by shooting of Mr. Rizzetti then struck Ms. Laney while she crossed the street and apparently attempted to jump to safety. Fortunately, near-

by pedestrians, who were just around the block, heard the tires screech, followed by a gunshot. In response, they rushed to the scene, presumably saving one life, and hopefully two.

The Santa Barbara Police Department is investigating the incident. They assume there's a correlation to the heartbreaking events of last month. In October, on the Thursday evening before Columbus Day, Deputy District Attorney Rizzetti was struck by a black SUV while riding his bike. On that same evening, Attorney Lee Templeton was tragically murdered in his office building. The two attorneys were opposing counsel on a case set for trial the following day. Among multiple injuries he sustained last month, Mr. Rizzetti was recovering from a broken leg that necessitated him walking with crutches.

Despite the horror of yesterday evening, Mr. Rizzetti was fortunate to survive. According to police, the bullet ricocheted off of his crutches, changing the trajectory of the bullet, and giving him only a minor wound to his midsection. But also, he incurred a head contusion and concussion when his head struck the curb as he fell to the ground after being shot. Paramedics transported him to Village Hospital and Mr. Rizzetti is expected to make a full physical recovery.

Ms. Laney was not as lucky. Besides sustaining a broken foot, most likely from being struck by the hit-and-run vehicle, she incurred a serious head injury while seemingly diving to safety. First responders rushed her to Village Hospital, where doctors had to place her in a medically induced coma to protect her brain from swelling because of the forceful head injury.

According to Dr. Shawn Taggart, Chief of Staff, their goal is to reduce the pressure and swelling, which cuts off blood flow to the brain and can kill healthy brain tissue. "The key here," explained Dr. Taggart, "is to protect her brain from secondary injury, which can prove more damaging than the initial injury."

The recent sequence of violent acts is foreign to Santa Barbara and has local officials and residents more than alarmed. . . .

***

JOSH OPENED HIS eyes, looking straight at the dreary white wall that was becoming way too familiar. The clock showed 6:50 a.m. At first disoriented, it took him only a few seconds to remember where he was and what had happened. The horror of the earlier evening caught up with him in a flash. He abruptly sat up in his hospital bed in a panic and winced in pain, thanks to the bullet wound that punctured one of the beers in his six-pack abs.

"Kristen!" His complexion turned white as a ghost. The last thing he remembered seeing was a large SUV zooming straight toward his best friend. Where was she? Did she get hit? Was she okay? Was she alive?

Tears rolled from his eyes at the thought of losing his friend. They spent countless hours together every week. They had hundreds and hundreds of meals together. They had thousands and thousands of conversations with each other. And not once did he confess to her how he felt. He knew that she knew he cared for her deeply. But how deeply, he never expressed to her. And why? Because he didn't want to ruin their friendship. How lame that excuse seemed at this moment. In retrospect, he thought, a friendship as strong as theirs could sustain anything. Well . . . anything except death.

What if she did get struck by the SUV? What if she wasn't okay? What if she was seriously injured? What if she was—?

The opening of the hospital room door rescued him from his thoughts. Dr. Overman entered the room, as stunning as ever. But this time, he didn't notice her beauty. This time, he didn't notice her model-like figure. This time, he saw nothing other than someone who should have answers to his questions.

"Good morning, Mr. Rizzetti. Looks like you're trying to earn frequent-flyer miles here. You sustained a—"

Josh blurted out, "How is she?"

Josh interrupted the doctor before she could give him a prognosis. He was in no mood to joke. He was in no mood to flirt. He couldn't care less about his condition.

"Well—" The doctor paused.

"Is she alive?" Josh held his breath and his face turned whiter than the bed sheets.

Dr. Overman raised the medical chart to her heart and nodded. "She's alive," she whispered. She hesitated, then shook her head. "But not in the best of shape."

"What do you mean? Why?" Josh shrieked, fearful of the response. "What happened? Did the SUV hit her?"

He had so many questions but was looking for just one answer. He wanted to hear that she would be fine. Unfortunately, that's not what he got.

"Right now, she's unconscious. We had to place her in a medically induced coma for precautionary reasons."

Loud enough to wake the unconscious, Josh hollered, "Coma?!"

"It's to reduce the pressure and swelling of her brain. From where her body was found in the street, next to her car, it seems that she may have jumped toward it, head-first, and sustained severe head trauma both from her car door and the asphalt."

"So, the SUV didn't hit her?"

"This is the first I'm hearing about an SUV. From talking to one of the investigating officers, he said that witnesses heard tires screech and then a gunshot from around the corner of where the two of you were found. They rushed over and found the two of you laying on the ground, next to a *Mercedes*. The back of your head was up against the sidewalk, bleeding from apparently striking the curb. Her head was almost underneath her door, also bleeding. And you were both unconscious."

"Yeah. An SUV came flying toward us from down the street. I was behind Kristen's parked car, walking to the passenger door. She was almost to the driver's door when it sounded like she dropped her keys. I looked over at her after I heard a jingle noise. She squatted down to pick them up, and that's when I saw an SUV appear out of nowhere from down the street, and it had floored it and was bolting straight toward Kristen. I yelled to her to look out, and she took a nosedive toward her car. Almost simultaneously, someone from the SUV shot at me. I fell down, and the next thing I know, I'm waking up in what's become my second bedroom."

"That could explain it," Dr. Overman said.

Josh, peeked with curiosity, wrinkled his brow. "Explain what?"

"Your friend also sustained a broken foot," the doctor explained. "It's possible that the SUV struck her foot while she was in midair, diving to her car. Some bones in her foot are shattered. That's certainly consistent with being struck from the force of a fast-moving vehicle."

"When can I see her? When can you take her out of the coma? Is she going to have any permanent injuries? Is she—"

Dr. Overman held up her hand. "Slow down Josh. I know you have a lot of questions. Doctor Taggart is her treating physician. I'll get him in here shortly and you can ask him your questions. He'll be more than happy to answer all he can. He's our Chief of Staff, and he's as good as they come. So, rest assured, Kristen's in the best hands possible."

"Thank you." Josh took a deep sigh.

"Don't forget, we still have to take care of you as well. You sustained your second concussion in as many months. So please, sit tight and I'll see to it that Doctor Taggart comes by as soon as he's available." She looked down at his medical chart and made a note of something, then looked at her patient. "As for now, one of the investigating officers has been waiting outside to talk to you about what happened. Are you up for talking to him right now? If so, I can send him in."

"Of course. Please, send him in. Thank you, Doctor."

Dr. Overman left the room. Less than thirty seconds later, a uniformed officer entered Joshua's hospital room, with a notepad in his left hand and a pen in his right. He was thirty, tall and thin. He walked up to the right side of Josh's bed and introduced himself.

"Good morning Mr. Rizzetti. I'm Officer Brian Brownstone with the Santa Barbara Police Department."

"Good morning officer," Josh said, tilting his head slightly and extending his right hand for a handshake. "Brownstone? As in retired Police Chief Bob Brownstone?

"Yes," the officer said. "He's my father."

"A family of blue bloods. He must be proud that you followed in his footsteps."

"I'm fourth-generation cop. So, not much of a choice."

"We all have choices," Josh said.

"Oh, don't get me wrong. I love it." Officer Brownstone smiled. "Well, I know you need some rest, so I'll get right to it. So, if you don't mind, I just need to get the details of what happened last night. Why don't you give me a summary, and then I'll follow up with some specific questions?"

"By all means," Josh said.

Josh continued on, paraphrasing what he had told Dr. Overman about the details from the previous night. Dinner, Drinks. Conversation. A short walk. An SUV barreling toward his friend. A gunshot. And once again, a hospital bed.

"Did you get a look at who was in the SUV?" Officer Brownstone asked.

Josh closed his eyes and tried to visualize the SUV coming toward them. It was dark, the windows were tinted, and his attention immediately shifted to Kristen. Suddenly, he couldn't clear his mind. He just kept seeing the big SUV speeding toward Kristen. No gunshot. No falling to the ground. Just his friend in the street, with a fifty-eight-hundred-pound lethal weapon aimed straight toward her. He opened his eyes in a sweat.

"No," Josh said. "It was too dark for me to get a look at who was in it, how many people were in it, the license place . . . I've got nothing."

"Did you notice anything unusual leading up to it? Anything strange? Anyone strange? Anything that seemed out of the ordinary?"

Josh grabbed the bed remote and pressed a button, raising the bed to a more comfortable, upright position. He closed his eyes again and pressed a button in his mind, rewinding it to a more reflective state. He paused, pinched his lower lip with his free hand, then released it.

"Well, now that you mention it," Josh said. "I'm not sure this is noteworthy, but there was a gentleman sitting at the table next to us at dinner. He was alone, and a few times it looked to me like he was talking to himself. I didn't think anything of it and kinda felt sorry for him. It's probably nothing."

"Maybe," Officer Brownstone said. "Maybe not. Can you describe him?"

"Not really. At least not know. I'll have to think about it."

"Okay. That could be important. You never know." The young officer wrote some notes in his notebook. "Anything else?"

"Not that I can think of right now."

"Okay." Officer Brownstone finished his notes and closed his notebook. "So, in the past month you've been hit by an SUV and you've been shot, yet you're still alive. You look like you're in pretty good shape, and you must be to survive all of that. I'm guessing you played some football when you were in school."

"Yep." Josh nodded his head. "I played defensive back in high school and, when I got bigger and stronger in college, I played linebacker. College was a club team, thanks to the massive California budget cuts, but we played legit Division Two programs. You?"

"I played wide receiver in high school. What I lacked in size, I made up for in speed. Our quarterback had a rocket launcher for an arm, even got a D-One scholarship, so we passed a lot."

"Football!" Josh clapped his hands once and pointed at the officer. "That's right! I forgot about that."

"Forgot about what?"

"When I was standing outside my office waiting for Kristen to pick me up before dinner, I saw a couple of kids playing catch with a football on the courthouse lawn."

"Okay. And?" The officer anxiously waited for the nexus.

"There was a dark SUV across the street from me. It was parked, but someone was in it. I think the dude was watching me. And after Kristen picked me up and we turned up the street, I could've sworn that the SUV started edging forward."

"Did it look like the same SUV that came after you and your friend last night?" Officer Brownstone opened his notebook again and began jotting down more notes.

"It certainly could have been. It was a large, dark SUV with super-dark tinted windows. Just like the one that tried to take us out."

"This is good. We might be getting somewhere." The officer closed his notebook, placed his pen in his uniform shirt pocket, and handed Josh a card. "I'm going to let you get some rest. A clear mind could help you give a description of the loner at the restaurant or remember more details about the suspicious SUV you noticed yesterday. Please give me a call after you get some rest."

"Also," Officer Brownstone continued, "we're going to keep a uniformed officer outside of Kristen's room just to be safe. And, of course, yours as well."

"Good idea," said Josh. "Thank you, sir."

Officer Brownstone walked toward the door and opened it. He paused and turned his head and looked at Josh with sympathy. "Oh yeah, one more thing, Mr. Rizzetti," he said. "I hope your friend gets well soon."

Josh tipped his head. "Thank you. Me too."

The officer left the room, leaving Josh alone with his thoughts. He stared outside the window, watching the effects of the ocean breeze that culminated with branches swaying, leaves falling and his mind wandering.

Going over the facts with the officer had provided Josh with a brief distraction from his biggest worry, Kristen. And before he could think about her further, seemingly another distraction walked in, or so he hoped. Unfortunately, this distraction was a false positive, in that it was Dr. Taggart, who was there for the sole purpose of talking about the subject from which Josh needed the diversion.

"Good morning, Mr. Rizzetti. My name is Doctor Shawn Taggart," he said formally. "I'm one of the physicians treating your friend, Ms. Laney."

The hospital chief of staff stood about six feet two inches tall, with mostly salted hair, still a headful but sporting a crew cut. Black-rimmed eyeglasses rested on the bridge of his nose, with bi-focal lenses for the middle-aged.

"Good morning, Doctor Taggart." Josh said no more. For a man who, minutes prior, had a thousand questions about Kristen's condition, he now was afraid to ask any. He just sat there in silence, staring at the doctor, in physical and emotional pain.

As a criminal prosecutor, Josh was a master at reading faces, expressions, body language, and demeanor. It was an invaluable asset in his line of work, being able to read lying, hostile witnesses and self-serving, pathological defendants. Countless times he was grateful for having such an astute gift. But for the first time, in terms of his ability to read people, he wished he was illiterate.

Chapter Twenty-Two

22

J osh spent Saturday laying in a hospital bed, with nurses coming in and out of his room every twenty minutes. He enjoyed the attention and was grateful for them doing their jobs, nonetheless, he struggled to stay awake. Walking seven steps to the restroom was a chore. They explained to him that constant attention to him was a precaution since he had sustained his second concussion in as many months. He got that, but they could explain it all day long, and it still didn't change the fact that he felt exasperated from sleep deprivation.

How many times had he heard a medical professional remark that rest is the best medicine? How ironic, considering they never let him get any. And here he was, getting no rest but feeling fine, and Kristen was getting endless rest but in critical condition.

By Sunday Josh was told his condition was stable, and they gave him the choice to be released that afternoon. He struggled with it at first, not wanting to leave Kristen and feeling guilty that he was abandoning his best friend in her time of need. But the hospital staff assured him there was nothing he could do for her other than pray, and that they would notify him at once if her condition changed. Against his strong desire to stay, he returned home later that day and crashed on his couch before his front door slammed shut behind him.

Monday morning rolled around in a flash, and once again Josh was back on desk duty. This go around, he was more than happy to numb his butt cheeks, rather than the alternative, which was moping around his house, panicked about Kristen. Better boring desk work than worrying himself sick and missing more work. His boss demanded that he take at least a week off, but Josh insisted on coming into the office. District Attorney Tell caved in, knowing it was a losing battle. Josh previously had missed a couple of weeks of work after getting struck by the SUV a month prior. And for someone who hadn't missed a day of work in over five years, his recent absence was enough for his lifetime.

Given his condition, Josh was under doctor's orders not to ride his bike to work for a while, and not to drive while taking his medication. With no other choice, the battered prosecutor caught a ride share at sunrise and arrived bright and early, beating everyone into the office. The sooner he could surround himself with colleagues, the better, as the distraction was his only solace.

He had a massive stack of his cases on his desk, set for potential settlement in court that day, and he was writing offers for Kendall to present to the defense attorneys on behalf of the State of California. Kendall was a pro's pro and didn't need the help, but Josh refused to lay the extra burden on his partner's shoulders. It was the least Josh could do. Kendall had his own cases to handle and would labor in court twice as long if he had to evaluate Josh's cases on the fly.

Josh was plugging away for about thirty minutes before his workmates began to trickle in. One by one, as his coworkers walked down the hallway, a head poked into his office saying, "How are you doing?"

Each time, his response was the same, "Fine, thank you. How are you?" But he wasn't fine. Physically, he'd survive. Emotionally, he was crushed.

Nine people had popped in, yet not one had asked about Kristen. Undoubtedly, it wasn't from lack of concern, for they all knew and loved her. More likely, they refrained from inquiring so as not to upset Josh, well aware that she meant the world to him. He had been through so much in the past month, with fresh wounds replacing the old ones, and now his best friend was fighting for her life. Why add to his pain?

Kendall was the tenth person to stop by Josh's office, but the first to enter it. The cozy office covered a ten-by-twelve-foot space. It was brightened by the natural light that entered the glass window that covered the width of the room, from chair rail to ceiling, on the back end behind Josh's desk and office chair. To the right of his desk, a five-shelf mahogany bookcase pressed against the tan wall. To the left of his desk, his degrees and professional certificates adorned a good portion of the wall. Josh's office was simple, yet functional. Spending most of his time in court, that's all he needed.

Kendall sat down at one of the two beige client chairs on the opposite side of Josh and faced the desk front. "How are you doing partner?"

"Just my typical weekend. Knocked unconscious one day, woke up in the hospital the next. You?"

Kendall paused to read his courtroom companion, whom he knew so well. Josh appeared dead serious, but Kendall knew better. He waited for what was to come next.

Kendall looked his partner in the eyes for one . . . two . . . three. And with the flip of a switch, Josh smiled and laughed, and Kendall laughed with him. Josh appreciated the value of levity and laughter and pulled it out of his back pocket whenever a situation became too serious and required it. Kendall knew it, and Josh knew that Kendall knew. Kendall smiled, happy to see his colleague relieved of some pain, even if just for a minute.

"I was just making polite conversation with you," Kendall said. "I really couldn't give a rat's behind about how you're doing? You just cause me more work." Kendall shifted from laughter to sincerity. "What I really want to know is, how is Kristen?"

Josh's laughter stopped and his smile vanished. "She's still in a coma in the ICU." He paused, fighting back tears.

"Her condition really hasn't changed since Friday night," Josh said, shaking his head. "I'm going to visit her during lunch today, and hopefully get a positive update."

"Anything I can do for you, please, let me know. Laura and I have her in our thoughts and prayers, my friend."

"I really appreciate that, Kendall," Josh said. "You're lucky to have someone like Laura. And I'm sure Kristen knows you're both praying for her."

"Don't sell yourself short, Joshua. Kristen is lucky to have someone like you. The question is, when are you going to let her know the reciprocal is true? I can't help but think of your friend's quote that you've mentioned a few times—women have choices, men only have chances. I don't want you to learn after it's too late, that any chance you're given might be the last chance you ever get."

Kendall stood up, walked to the doorway, stopped, and turned. "So, when are you going to take your chance and let her know what she really means to you? And you and I both know that it's more than friends."

Josh sat at his desk, completely silent and confused. Confused as to whether the question was rhetorical and more confused as to the answer.

"I'll come by on my way to court and pick up your files." Kendall patted the doorjamb, turned and drifted down the hallway.

Chapter Twenty-Three

23

TW and Jen stood at the reception window in the lobby of the District Attorney's Office, making small talk with the receptionist, Tammy, while they waited for their friends. Josh and Tyler were summoned over the loudspeaker to join up with their friends to visit Kristen during their lunchtime.

"So, Tammy," Jen said. "I understand congratulations are in order. I heard you got engaged."

"Thank you." Tammy placed her left hand on the countertop to show off her ring.

"Yes, congrats Tammy." TW reached up with his right hand, and gently lifted Tammy's left hand to get a closer look at the ring and expressed his admiration. "Wow, that's impressive."

"Very nice," Jen concurred. "I'm somewhat of a jewelry snob, so I'd say your fiancé is a keeper."

The three chuckled.

TW released Tammy's hand and leaned his lower right arm on the counter, causing a clanking noise.

"Officer Wilkey, that's a neat bracelet you got there," Tammy said.

"Thanks. It's my military dog tag. I had a jeweler turn it into a bracelet after my honorable discharge from the Army following my combat injury."

"What a nice idea," Tammy said. "It's funny. Someone lost a somewhat similar silver chain bracelet here not too long ago. Our cleaning crew found it one evening on the floor underneath our library conference table. I think the clasp was broken. It was a unique piece of jewelry and looked to be expensive. Definitely not something you'd wanna lose."

"Really?" Jen asked. "Do you know whose it was? I'm always in the market for unique jewelry. I'd love to ask the owner what jeweler made it."

"I don't know. We had so many outsiders in and out that day, you would've thought we were serving Double-Doubles. The next afternoon, the owner sent over some gopher to pick it up. But someone else was covering the front desk for me when it was picked up."

"Mine's not worth much monetarily," TW said, at the same time Josh and Tyler came puttering through the door separating the office hallway from the lobby. "But sentimentally, I couldn't put a price on it. It reminds me to be grateful for every day that I'm given."

"Speaking of," Josh said, popping out with Tyler from behind the hallway door that opened to the office's waiting area. "Shall we go check on our friend?"

***

FOUR OUT OF five of the happy hour gang sat patiently in the hospital lobby, waiting on the latest news touching on their favorite member. As soon as they arrived, they fished for a taste of news while they awaited the doctor. But, since none of them were family, the tight-lipped cyborg at the nurse's desk wasn't comfortable providing them any information . . . literally nothing.

Making a stressful event worse, the nurse was downright rude about it. She merely told them she could page Dr. Taggart, and he could decide what could and could not be disclosed to them, "but you don't have a right to know anything about her condition," she snapped. She was probably on the final end of a twenty-four-hour shift because her unpleasant tone and attitude left a lot to be desired. If not, and she had just started her shift, she was in the wrong line of work.

Knowing that an ongoing criminal investigation was at stake, Dr. Taggart wouldn't take long to greet his patient's closest friends, two of whom were law enforcement personally involved in the investigation. He received the page, dropped the paper-work he was reviewing in his office, and headed toward the lobby.

Quietly, the four anxious pals sat on the cold, boring chairs. The cool vinyl material was perhaps intentional, symbolic of the frigid chill that accompanied all bad news. The combined stress of his three amigos was pale in comparison to what Josh was feeling. For this was not the first time doctors had placed Kristen in a medically induced coma, but only Josh knew that. Having once felt privileged to know such a private aspect of his friend's life, he now carried the burden.

When Kristen was about ten weeks old, her single-parent mother woke up one morning to find that her baby girl had stopped breathing. She would later learn that her beautiful newborn girl had suffered a cardiac arrest. When the paramedics arrived, they shocked Kristen with a defibrillator and injected her with adrenaline to stabilize her heartbeat. Upon her admission to the hospital, doctors placed Kristen into a medically induced coma to protect her brain from further damage.

After subjecting the strong, young infant to several tests, they learned she had a cardiac fibroma—a tumor that blocked the blood flow to her fighting heart. The tumor was nearly two inches wide, which was enormous in comparison to her tiny heart. Only an extremely expensive surgery—one that would bankrupt her mother forever—could save the life of the precious child. Word traveled quickly in their supportive town, and donations came flowing in, but unfortunately, it was only a fraction of the enormous cost the surgery would entail.

With nothing but the health of her child in mind, Kristen's mom authorized the surgery, knowing full well that she would spend the rest of her life trying to pay the bill. Then, befitting of Kristen Grace Laney's middle name, and through the grace of God, two miracles followed: Kristen's surgery was a colossal success, and an anonymous donor generously paid the remainder of the hospital bill.

The day Kristen shared this private moment with Joshua, a unique bond was formed between the two. And from that day forward, he truly appreciated how special her heart was and better understood why she was so eager to help those in need.

Today, Josh's chair felt warm to him, like someone had been sitting in it for hours just before he arrived. He stared at the floor, almost afraid to look up. For if he saw Dr. Taggart coming, there was a real possibility of terrible news. No Dr. Taggart meant no news. And after all, no news is good news. Immersed in his denial, his head weighed heavy with his eyes glued to the Spanish floor tile. Finally, as if feeling a presence approaching him, Josh dared to look up.

Dr. Taggart appeared from down the hallway, making his way into Josh's sight. He sauntered in the distance, and as he got closer, he appeared to walk slower. For what seemed like hours, Josh locked his eyes on the doctor, moving in slow-motion. The closer the doctor got, the slower time moved, and the warmer Josh's chair felt. Then, in a flash, like a flame under his butt, Josh popped up.

"Here he comes," Josh blurted to his companions.

They all stood and turned toward the doctor, who finished taxiing the runway and had finally reached his destination.

Josh was terrified to look the doctor in the eyes, highly cognizant that his people reading skills worked on autopilot. If the news was bad, Josh undoubtedly did not want to think about it before he heard it, on the one percent chance he read the doctor wrong.

Mercifully for the happy hour gang, Dr. Taggart did not let the anxiety linger. Not leaving a second for the fearsome foursome to become the fearful foursome, he spoke quickly. "She's out of a coma and resting comfortably."

The group remained speechless. The news was joyously welcomed, but they still held their collective breath, waiting for some more specifics to ease their concern.

"After such a forceful impact to her head, she's fortunate to be alive. She's still critical, but her condition is improving." Dr. Taggart managed a slight smile and the gang breathed.

"Oh, thank God," Jen wailed, loud enough to prompt everyone in sight to turn their heads. A cranky nurse standing at the nurse's station, gossiping with the nurse who refused to tell them anything, gave Jen a nasty look; like a librarian staring down a noisy group of teenagers working in their study group. She, too, must have been on the tail end of a very long shift.

Overcome with elation, Jen turned to Josh and gave him a tight bear hug. TW slapped Tyler so hard with a high five that it almost knocked him over, while Josh's eyes watered, and Jen cried with joy.

"For now, we have her on a ventilator, to ensure that she gets a proper amount of oxygen to her heart and brain. Unfortunately, she can't have any visitors at this time," Dr. Taggart said. "But you are all welcome to come back tomorrow during visiting hours for a brief visit."

Before the happy hour gang could thank the doctor, a female voice resonated over the loudspeaker, "Attention, Doctor Taggart, we have an emergency. Doctor Taggart, please report to Room 127 immediately. Again, Doctor Taggart, please report to Room 127, we have a code blue! I repeat, we have a code blue in Room 127!"

Josh fell to his chair that had turned bitter cold, muffled his mouth with his hands, and screamed at the top of his lungs, "Nooooo!"

The doctor, who just minutes earlier so nonchalantly eased up the hallway to comfort his patient's friends, set a world record in a sprint down the hallway to Room 127—Kristen's room.

Chapter
Twenty-Four

24

The view from the stunning Spanish Colonial Revival home, nestled in the hills on Puesta Del Sol and overlooking the Santa Barbara coast, was a sight to behold. Built in 1947, and having recently undergone a substantial and immaculate upgrade, the gorgeous showcase home rested on three lovely, pastoral acres of gardens, walking paths, and mature trees. Its divine renovation involved painstaking attention to detail and significant expense by its current owners.

The strong yet refined presence of this world-class hacienda extended well beyond the structure itself. The little details boosted it over the top. A high-strength, galvanized steel security gate anchored the driveway with sharp embellished tips and powder coated to prevent rust. That led to a spacious motor court, capped by a four-car garage, and a walkway to the custom wrought iron entryway, protecting a majestic glass door.

Beige stucco walls, richly stained woods, and masterfully choreographed custom and ambient lighting created an ambiance of casual, unpretentious luxury and refinement. Stunning mountain and ocean views, and that of the grounds, graced several rooms, courtesy of a profusion of large windows and French doors at every bend. Its three terraces magnified the sweeping ocean views from the Channel Islands to Campus Point. Its two large stone-paved patios and two courtyards enhanced further the outdoor mystique. Collectively, they offered the ideal venue for entertaining in the American Riviera's Mediterranean climate and coveted indoor-outdoor lifestyle.

With the newspaper in hand, the former debutante sipped her coffee, leaning forward in her patio chair. Absorbing the morning sun, she sat on the patio just off the living room, which offered a secluded sanctuary that rivaled the outdoors of a five-star resort. Her eyes fixated on the newspaper, with a glare stronger than that of the late-July California sun.

The July 27, 1996 edition of the *Santa Barbara Daily Press* front-page headline read "OLYMPIC PARK BOMBING IN ATLANTA" in giant, bold, all caps font. She continued to read the article that read:

> Early reports indicate that early this morning, around 12:58 a.m. Eastern Time, a security guard spotted an unattended green backpack beneath a light and sound tower at Centennial Olympic Park, the designated town square of the '96 Atlanta Games. He at once alerted Georgia Bureau of Investigation officers. Nine minutes later, a

911 call from a nearby phone booth told dis-
patchers: "There is a bomb in Centennial Park.
You have thirty minutes." At 1.15 a.m., a team
of security officers began clearing the area. The
contents of the backpack, believed to be one or
more pipe bombs, detonated nearly ten minutes
later before all spectators were removed. . . .

"Good morning, Mom," said the pre-teen boy, taking a seat next to his mother. "Mom, Mom!"

She did not respond.

"Mom, Mom!"

Finally, separating herself from the article, she responded, "Yes. Oh, good morning son."

"Is everything okay?"

"No! Look!" she said, holding up the front page of the newspaper for her son to read.

"Oh my gosh! I was watching the Olympics last night until I fell asleep. Any deaths?"

"At least two people that they know of. And countless people injured."

"That's horrible!" he said, shaking his head. "Did they catch who did it?"

"Not yet."

After a brief pause, he spoke again. "Where's Dad?"

"At the Country Club. He had an early tee time. He wanted to wake you up to join him, but I told him to let you sleep. You were up pretty late last night, watching TV, so I thought you could use the sleep."

"Bummer! I was looking forward to hitting the links and getting some exercise. I was glued to the couch for so long yesterday, watching the Olympics, that my legs fell asleep. I think I'll go for a bike ride after breakfast, and maybe meet Logan later for some tennis at the Club."

"Good idea, Tim. Just because you're on summer break, doesn't mean you shouldn't stay active. A bike ride and some tennis with your friend will do you some good. Rosie's in the kitchen right now. You can have her whip you up an omelet before you go."

The twelve-year-old youngster was mature beyond his years. Ambitious, intelligent, and highly focused, his thought process was different from that of his contemporaries. That made it difficult for him to make friends. He had a few close friends, but virtually no "casual" friends. A fly on the wall would say he was more comfortable talking to adults, rather than to kids his own age. His bright future appeared certain and growing up privileged undoubtedly did not hinder its likelihood.

As an icebreaker when meeting kids his own age, he liked to show off the battle scar that ran about two inches down the right side of his neck, just behind his ear. He considered it a combat wound after his surfboard fin sliced him a year earlier, just two months after taking up surfing. A top plastic surgeon, flown in from the Bay area, seamed him together with an even one hundred closely-knit stitches, sewing with fastidious precision to minimize the scar.

His slim build did not accurately reflect his insatiable appetite, likely due to the elevated activity he maintained that was surpassed only by the metabolism of a twelve-year-old boy.

He scarfed down a Denver omelet, three pieces of sourdough toast, five pieces of bacon, a sliced avocado, and a bowl of fruit; eager to hit the road. An avid cyclist, he preferred to ride almost everywhere, rather than have his parents chauffeur him around town. The effects of being an introverted only child, his twenty-one speed *Bianchi Super G* resembled a sibling joined to his hip. Any reason he could find to air out his over-priced racing bike, he took it.

Racing to the garage, leaving no time to digest, he lifted his bike from the large, space-saving hook that housed his two-thousand-eighty-dollar, two-wheel, labor-intensive mode of transportation. Tripped out to the extreme, it contained all the bells and whistles, including a backlit dual speedometer designed for a Harley Davidson. The over-the-top accessory proved useful when the aspiring professional cyclist modeled the time trials of the Tour de France.

Snugly strapping his helmet over his headphones, Tim buckled the chin strap under his pointy jaw, glancing down to admire his Team USA cycling attire, embellished with a yellow jersey, signifying the stage winner of the world's premier cycling race. Pulling his cycling gloves comfortably down both hands, he tightened the Velcro firmly around his left wrist. Then, using his left hand, he loosely secured the Velcro over his special bracelet that had forever decorated his right wrist. The thick silver chain bracelet had been purchased when he was an infant and given to him by his parents for his eighth birthday. Similar to an ID bracelet, a thin, rectangular metal plate joined the chain, with a custom engraving from his parents on the underside. The gift remained a permanent fixture on his wrist for four-plus years, only being removed briefly a couple of times to add a few new links along the way to accommodate his growth.

Fully geared up, Tim was primed and ready to go. He popped Hootie and the Blowfish into his Discman, strapped it securely around his svelte, but bloated waist, and rocketed down the meandering driveway.

In route to the American Riviera Golf and Tennis Club, riding conditions were ideal. Warm, approaching hot, but cooled by the overgrown trees that provided a picturesque canopy over Mission Canyon Road, a slight ocean breeze made the temperature near perfect. With his feet secured to the spiked pedals, emulating the cycling legends of the Tour, he raced atop the narrow, windy road, cutting turns like navigating laps of the Champs-Élysées.

Traffic on the way to the club was non-existent this time of day. The ardent golf and tennis players flooded the links and courts early in the morning to avoid the midday heat. The strictly social members loaded the bar in the early afternoon to take advantage of the midday drink specials. This left the late morning on the quiet roadway to offer the idyllic stage for the enthusiastic cyclist.

Mountain Drive was quickly approaching. A razor-sharp left turn, measuring twenty degrees at most, would direct him straight to the country club. The youthful rider's thin but muscular legs stopped pedaling before he shifted his weight to his left, preparing to make the turn at a maximum speed, one he had made a hundred times before. He focused ahead as far as the eye could see, which was minimized by several, full-size, wild shrubs that lined the corner of the intersecting streets. Nature's obstruction limited the range of visibility to roughly ten to fifteen yards in either direction. With a slight squeeze to his rear brake, he entered the turn. The speedometer on his bike reduced . . . twenty-nine miles per hour, twenty-eight mph, twenty- seven mph, zero mph!

A heavy thump of metal on metal thundered up and down the secluded streets!

"What the hell?" yelled the white-knuckled driver, instinctively forcing all of his weight into the floorboard under his right foot. The quick flash of an image prior to the heart-stopping impact did not give him near enough warning to stop in time. The aged white, *Ford Econoline E-150* tires blistered to a screeching stop!

Clearly, in a state of complete shock, the driver of the vehicle pulled to the right to a small dirt clearing on the side of the road. Panicking, the frightened driver jumped from the driver's seat, placed his right knee on the front passenger's seat, and jiggled the jammed door in a frenzy, struggling to free himself to examine the scene. Lowering his right shoulder, he lunged at the door, decisively forcing it open and propelling him to the ground, face first into the dirt.

Hopping to his feet as he spat dirt from his mouth, he swiped down his front side, dusting the dirt from his uniform polo shirt that displayed the name "Carl" across his left pectoral. He immediately went to see what could have been on the losing end of the violent impact. The dent to the front right metal bumper was noticeable, but not to the extent of what caught his attention as he looked beyond the clearing and into the flowering bushes. Protruding from a California Lilac was the front portion of a bike frame, headed by an "L" shaped front rim, and what appeared to be the lower half of a leg wedged in a mangled bike frame.

The fifty-two-year-old man rushed to get a closer look. His worst fear came to a realization. His van had struck a bicycle rider, and a child at that.

Immediately, his instincts kicked in. First, he checked for a pulse. With complete disregard for his body, he forced himself into the bushes, getting scratched, poked, and clawed in the process. Then, when within reach of what looked to be an unconscious young boy, Carl reached out his right hand, placing his index and middle finger to the side of the windpipe of the victim. With his fingers over the carotid artery, the world stood still. The world fell silent. Holding his breath, he focused and waited for a sign of life.

"Oh!" he sighed, exhaling in relief. "Thank God!" he rejoiced aloud upon locating a pulse.

To his advantage, the young cyclist had been struck by a skilled, former Navy medic. Understanding that the victim likely had broken something, his experience told him that moving the injured boy without the assistance of a helper and the proper equipment could be dangerous. Removing himself from the shrubbery, the veteran rushed back to his van to call 911.

Carl stopped when he reached his van, motioning to open the door. Placing his right hand on the rusted, chrome passenger door handle, he hesitated. He released his hand from the handle, walked around the van, and sized up the damage to the front of his vehicle. He stared up the empty road, then looked over to where the victim lay. He paused and thought. He had a major decision to make, and he had to make it quickly.

Tilting his head in deliberation, he looked to his left, directing his sight to the side of his van. The logo on the sliding door read "Quick Rescue Plumbing." He reflected on his situation and the predicament in which he found himself. What now?

The salt and peppered-haired, retired military medic-turned-plumber had been dishonorably discharged from the Navy in his forties after he began experiencing periodic, unexplained seizures. What later was diagnosed as epilepsy, remained a mystery for a long time.

After surgery, and struggling with various medications, his epileptic seizures finally seemed under control, but only after a significant traumatic incident that further altered his life.

Four-plus years earlier, everything changed. On the one day that Carl had failed to take his medication, he was involved in an automobile accident that severely injured the other driver, leaving her paralyzed from the waist down. After a prolonged civil lawsuit, resulting in his insurance company settling for a hefty sum, a criminal prosecution ensued charging him with criminal negligence.

Accepting a plea deal, as a strict condition of his probation, Carl was allowed to drive only to and from work and only while on his medication. And for four years, he was meticulous in complying. But all of his diligent efforts to stay on track could be undone with one mistake, and today he had made it.

Earlier that morning, he received a call from Coastal Plumbing Company, a plumbing company that was under contract with the American Riviera Country Club, giving them exclusive rights to handle the club's plumbing needs. Quick Rescue Plumbing served as an independent contractor plumbing service and would assist Coastal Plumbing Company with any emergency plumbing work needed at the exclusive golf and tennis club if all their employees were on other plumbing assignments.

The emergency call came to the Ojai-based plumber around 9:45 a.m. that morning. If he could get to the exclusive club within the hour, the job was his. With no traffic, he knew he could be there in about forty-two minutes. Given his recent reduction in workload, he needed to take the job, so the last-minute request to him was a no-brainer. But in a rush to get out the door and on his way, he had forgotten to take his anti-seizure medication.

He stood there assessing his circumstances. Would this constitute a violation of the terms of his probation? If he reported this accident, regardless of fault, he could be brought before the court for violation of his probation, have his suspended sentence revoked, and face serving prison time.

***

THE ABUSED WORK van, now more beaten than before, sputtered down the dirt driveway. Rolling up to the modest two-bedroom home, hidden in the rolling hills of Ojai, it came to a complete stop in front of a one-car garage door. The retired medic's secluded property was a welcomed oasis for a military vet. Fronted with a half-size football field of overgrown bushes and mature trees, the shrubbery rendered the cabin invisible from the street. The isolated environment mitigated the paranoia that spawned from the panic-stricken situation. But make no mistake about it, even for a man who had been to war, this was a panic-stricken situation.

Carl shifted to his right, and slowly looked over his right shoulder, as if he moved slowly enough the boy miraculously would not be there. No such luck. The unconscious boy was no longer a victim of a hit-and-run accident, he now was an abducted child. But the probationer couldn't concern himself with that crime at this moment. His instincts and humanity were solely focused on treating the child back to health. Once the boy was stable, Carl could cross the next bridge and deal with the consequences.

He ducked his head, shuffling inside toward the back of the van, opening the sliding side door on his way. Gently placing his arms under the slender victim, he lifted the limp boy and swiftly headed into his house to provide him immediate medical treatment, and hopefully save the boy's life, and Carl's hide.

Chapter Twenty-Five

25

The northbound Coastline bus exited Highway 101 at Pleasant Valley Road/Santa Rosa Road as it entered the charming town of Camarillo, California. The quiet, mid-to-upper income community, known for having "the best weather on Earth" and miles of strawberry fields, sat roughly forty-five miles south of Santa Barbara. Nearly fifty yards to the right of the freeway exit, on the southwest side of Santa Rosa Road, was his stop.

A thin young boy, age twelve going on thirty, stood anticipating the next stop, firmly gripping the crossbar with his right hand. The brakes squeaked with the piercing sound of fingernails on a chalkboard, and the bus came to an abrupt halt in front of the covered bus stop bench.

"Thank you," the anxious traveler mumbled to the driver, who triggered the door to swing open.

"Stay safe young man."

Plodding off the last step, with an overstuffed backpack slung over his right shoulder, he exited the bus. Glancing up from the sidewalk, much to his relief, he spotted a McDonald's restaurant next to the bus stop. He was starving. His caloric intake had been minimal the past seventy-two hours, and his energy tank teetered in the red, a pinch above empty.

It had been three days since the juvenile ran away from his foster home, marking the fourth time that the pre-teen pinball escaped the instability and abuse conferred upon the young pawn in "the system." This time, he stood determined to make a permanent break. This time, he had a plan.

Named Craig Bauer at birth, they promptly changed his last name to that of his first foster parents, Pearson, to give the infant a clean slate. He was the poster child for the stereotypical version of a foster child. His most recent home had been with a family in Pacoima. Although well-disguised, Pacoima was the poorest city in the San Fernando Valley, with a poverty level above eighteen percent.

But it wasn't the poverty that prompted his flight from "The Valley." Despite having lived in countless foster homes, this last one had been the worst. His foster mother was addicted to painkillers and daytime television, and his foster father was an unemployed, abusive alcoholic. Woefully, *The Jerry Springer Show* ingrained in his head was a welcome diversion from his real life. Although his foster parents housed four other younger foster children, being the oldest meant the male tweener earned him the role of the lead punching bag.

Moving past eighteen months with his most recent family, he couldn't endure it any longer. He developed a plan and made his escape at the first opportunity.

His plan, although developed on a whim, was to seek help from his former foster parents. From the ages of eight to ten and a half, the unlucky boy caught what looked as if to be his only break. During that period, he had lived with a foster family, the Perez family, in Northridge. Mr. Perez was employed as a delivery driver for an animal food supply company, distributing products as far south as the Los Angeles Zoo, and as far north as the Santa Barbara Zoo. Mrs. Perez, caring for a steady stream of foster children, worked full-time as a homemaker.

A devout Catholic family, they provided Craig with a stable and loving home. Although nothing spectacular, he was properly fed, sufficiently clothed, and generally cared for in the manner in which a child should be. And for the first time in his life, he was actually happy, having won the foster child lottery. But just when it seemed that his life finally had taken a turn for the better, the rug was yanked out from under him.

Mr. Perez's mother, who lived in Ventura, an hour-plus up the California coast, suddenly had fallen ill and needed constant care. Dropping everything, including their foster children, the foster couple moved to Ventura within three weeks of breaking the news to the heartbroken boy, whom they had grown to love. He was devastated.

The Perez couple tried to cushion the blow. As if it were any consolation because they were familiar with his turbulent past, they had assured him they would be there for him if he needed it. Regrettably, because of the short notice, Child Services dumped him with the less-than-ideal foster family in Pacoima, from whom he now eagerly fled.

Now, day four of his quest for sanctuary—however brief it might last—the quickly maturing runaway had made his way up the coast, stopping in Camarillo to get some food and then catch the next bus heading up north to Ventura.

Mustering enough strength to replenish his inner fuel tank, Craig dragged himself down the sidewalk, around the drive-thru lane, to the front of the golden arches. He pressed his hands firmly on his head, patting his hair, then tugged on the bottom of his grungy T-shirt, in a feeble attempt to clean up his appearance.

Standing near the entrance door, he paused briefly, looking around at his surroundings as if being followed. Just then, he noticed a police car enter the opposite end of the small strip center that was anchored by the McDonald's. Quickly, he ducked into the fast-food chain.

The mid-morning hour had the restaurant near empty. An old man sat in the far corner, a newspaper in hand, and a steamy coffee on his table. The table closest to the entrance was occupied by a middle-aged couple, sitting opposite each other, laughing at something said by the husband.

"Good morning. What can we get for you?" The twenty-something-year-old employee lowered her brow, as though curious as to why the boy looked like he had slept in his clothes.

Too hungry and worn to even say hello, Craig replied, "I'd like two sausage biscuits, an order of hash browns, and a cup of water."

"That'll be three dollars and twenty-seven cents."

Pulling his left fist from his wrinkled jeans pocket, the transient boy opened his palm, counted out three $1 bills, dropped the crumbled papers to the counter, and mumbled under his breath, "Three."

Then, reaching into his right pocket, he pulled out a handful of change and shuffled through it until he found a quarter and two pennies. In a louder, clearer voice, he counted as he placed the three coins on the counter, "Twenty-five, twenty-six, twenty-seven."

Another employee, bored yet eager to do something during the slow business hour, overheard the order and had it on a tray and ready to go before the cashier could finish putting the money in the register. Placing the tray on the counter in front of the boy, he said, "Here you go. Have a nice day!"

"Thank you." Starving and anxious to eat, the boy raced to a seat beside a window, farthest from the entrance, and with a direct view of a thirty-two-inch television strapped to a mounted shelf on the wall in the far-left corner of the dining area.

Within seconds, one sausage biscuit disappeared. In large part due to extreme hunger, and partially the taste of freedom, surely fast food never tasted so good. However, as if recognizing that it might be his only meal of the day, he slowed down to take a bite of his hash browns. Chewing his potato patty, the low but audible volume of the television drew his attention.

The news anchor spoke. "Three days into the investigation of the Olympic Park bombing authorities are still searching for answers. Tonight, on News at Six, we hope to have further updates on this tragic event that forever may define the '96 Summer Olympics."

In shock from what he was just learning, having been on the lamb since the horrific act of domestic terrorism, Craig's eyes remained glued to the television. However, the jolt of that news paled in comparison to the unimaginable shock of the news that followed.

The news anchor continued. "In further news, Santa Barbara Police continue to investigate the hit-and-run disappearance of a twelve-year-old boy, who has been missing for more than seventy-two hours. On the morning of Saturday, July twenty-seventh, the young boy went for a bike ride in the hills near the American Riviera Country Club. His damaged bicycle was found in the bushes off the road, about a mile from the club, but the child remains missing. If you have seen this boy or have any information pertaining to his whereabouts or this incident, please call the designated hotline number below immediately."

The boy's jaw dropped in complete disbelief! His eyes widened in a manner defying human physiology, resembling the likeness of a fictional offspring of Marty Feldman and Betty Davis. Clear as day, on the television screen in front of him, he saw the most shocking portrait imaginable. It was a picture of himself! But not a photo he remembered ever being taken. Why? How in the world was that possible?

Continuing to stare, for what seemed like minutes, his focus gradually shifted to the broader picture on the television. It was only then that he noticed the freshly pressed, baby blue, button-down, collared shirt worn by the boy. That was definitely not a shirt that Craig ever had the privilege of wearing. Was the photograph altered . . . or could it be his doppelgänger?

He continued to stare vacuously through the monitor when finally, the mid-morning news program broke for a commercial break. Panicked and in shock, he quickly scanned the room to make sure that none of the patrons were attentive to the television. To his relief, they still looked to be engaged in their initial activities.

With his self-preservation instincts kicking in, Craig discreetly reached to his right to unzip his backpack and plopped beside him in the booth. Shoved atop his traveling storage unit, he grabbed his dirty, faded Dodgers baseball cap and shoved it as far down his head as it would go as if trying to bust the seams. And although the wear and tear of the hat made it appear as though it actually had been worn by the great Sandy Koufax, it served the purpose of partially concealing his face.

Staring out the window and into the distance, concurrently eating on autopilot, his mind wandered. In disbelief of what he had seen, he didn't know what to think. In the wonderment of the situation, he didn't know what to do.

An enterprising McDonald's crew prepared in expectation of the ensuing lunch crowd. The aroma of a fresh basket of greasy McDonald's fries filled the air. The identifiable fragrance of the classic scent floated under the nose of the bewildered adolescent. Processing this familiar scent, his olfactory bulb connecting the amygdala and hippocampus areas of the brain instantaneously triggered a hazy, almost forgotten memory; miraculously shedding clarity on the otherwise inexplicable previous five minutes.

While Craig had lived with the Perez family, the generous couple treated the kids to a Happy Meal every Friday evening when they behaved well during the week. With all three foster children being under the age of eleven, this proved to be an effective incentive to promote their good behavior. With the rare combination of being with a loving family and receiving treats for good behavior, needless to say, most Fridays ended with happy kids eating Happy Meals. Exposed to the scent of McDonald's fries almost once a week for two plus years, it was almost synonymous with the smell of oxygen to Craig.

One Happy-Meal-treated Friday night, when Craig was nine years old, he woke up around midnight from one of his recurring nightmares. As he lay in bed, waiting to doze back to sleep, he overheard his foster parents talking about a young child, the identity of whom he was unaware. And with them being foster parents, they had seen many kids come in and out their front door; so the possibilities were endless. Seconds before he was totally asleep, Craig heard Mrs. Perez say something along the lines of, ". . . the odds of *having* a completely identical doppelgänger are one in a hundred and something, but the chance of *seeing* yours is like one in a trillion. I can't believe you saw a child at the zoo that looks identical to him." Almost simultaneously hearing that, he was fast asleep. When he awoke the next morning, almost certain that he had dreamt it and not heard it, there was no reason for it to cross his mind again—until now!

Could it be that the vague memory of what he may have heard was in fact reality, and not a dream? If so, was he the boy of whom Mr. Perez had seen an exact copy? More pointedly, was the missing boy on the television his doppelgänger? Undoubtedly, anyone faced with these circumstances would have such questions.

With the lunch crowd likely minutes away from swamping McDonald's, Craig had to get out of the restaurant. Assuming the story had been running the past few days, the risk of being recognized was great. He needed to avoid crowds. He needed to find a library to see if he could dig up some evidence to shed more light on this potentially life-altering discovery.

He shoved the remainder of his food down his throat like a garbage disposal. Crumbling up his trash, he tossed it in the trash receptacle behind his booth and placed the food tray on top. Craig rushed to the front counter and asked the cashier for directions to the nearest library. The helpful employee happily obliged, reassuring the clearly anxious patron that it was only a couple of miles away, at most.

With fuel in his tank, the transient-turned-investigator eager-ly began his trek to the Camarillo Library, with the prospect of a discovery that would rival that of Columbus in the eyes of the re-energized youngster. "Up Santa Rosa, left on Flynn, right on Adolfo, left on Upland. Up Santa Rosa, left on Flynn, right on Adolfo, left on Upland." He repeated out loud the directions as he speed-walked along the wavy sidewalk shaded by beautiful, mature trees. The peaceful, serene town was a pleasant change from the chaos of "The Valley"; providing a nurturing atmosphere for his mind to contemplate what his past might have been if he had grown up with a wealthy Santa Barbara family.

Craig's forty-five-minute walk seemed to fly by in a matter of minutes. Deeply engaged in thought, the unexpected sight of the library took him by surprise. Were it not for the sign in front that identified the building, he would have walked right past it. The gorgeous Spanish-style architecture of the massive build-ing was incomparable to any library or public building he had ever seen. From appearance alone, it looked like the building was brand new. The magnificent structure and pristine land-scape of weed-free, thick green grass and freshly planted flowers surrounding the library more strongly resembled that of The Ritz-Carlton than a library. The premises screamed "Welcome! Please, come in and learn!"

With his mouth wide open from astonishment, Craig walked through the courtyard that led to the library entrance. As if the building was not spectacular enough, he paused to admire the convenience of a snack store adjacent to the main doors as he approached the entry to this palace. Clearly, they thought of everything when they built this library.

"Man, I could live here!" he said himself, walking through the sliding glass doors and into the cool temperature of this bastion of knowledge.

The foyer opened to a large, wooden reference desk cen-tered as the focal point about fifteen yards into the grand en-trance. Immediately to his right, was a rack of newspapers and brochures. The newspapers were encased in those oddly spliced "newspaper sticks" that, although peculiar, served their purpose of keeping each newspaper together while also supporting it to hang well-organized from a wooden rack.

Craig approached the newspapers with anticipation. The television news coverage mentioned the boy missing for a few days. Given the recency of the accident, and because the boy was still missing, the likelihood of newspaper coverage of this story was high. With his head tilted seventy degrees to read the names of the publications more easily, he reached for the one that read *Ventura County Times*. His right hand gripped the stick. Just as he lifted it from the holder, the newspaper above and behind it caught his attention—*Santa Barbara Daily Press*. Reflexive in nature, he dropped his first selection and quickly snatched the Santa Barbara newspaper.

Looking like a hiker with his backpack resting on his traps, fully secured through his arms and hanging from his slender frame, he carried the wood stick draped with a newspaper. He discreetly walked by the reference desk. Fortunately for the delinquent boy keeping a low profile, the librarian sat preoccupied at the front desk. Talking on the phone to a patron while staring at her computer screen and typing away, she was oblivious to the shabby visitor that tiptoed by her. A pink elephant could've stomped by, and she wouldn't so much as blinked.

The main floor was separated into a couple of sections. To the right was a large entrance to another enormous room, with the words "Children's Books" tastefully painted above the arched entryway. To the left was a grand staircase that led to the massive second floor that was visible beyond the ornate railing. The upper level was fronted by a panoramic balcony that extended beyond the width of the main floor reference desk area that it overlooked.

Craig softly walked between some bookcases to the far end of the library, finding a secluded cubicle tucked away in a corner beyond the first portion of the Nonfiction section. Other than visible to an older gentleman who was buried in the pages of the *Ventura County Times* and dozing off while lounging in a paisley-patterned accent armchair about twenty-five feet away, Craig was completely out of sight.

Slouching as if his backpack had been increasing in weight as the day went on, Craig removed his heavy knapsack from his achy shoulders and placed it on the floor, to his left, leaning up against a wall. Setting the newspaper on the desktop of the solid wood cubicle, he sat his sore, bony butt on the hard, wooden chair. Being mostly on foot the past several days, his leg muscles were throbbing.

Starting with the front page, the eager boy scanned his eyes across the *Santa Barbara Daily Press*. Turning page-by-page, his nervous eyes thoroughly searched each page, looking for a headline containing words similar to "Santa Barbara Boy" or "Missing Boy."

Each time he flipped to the next page he shook his head in disappointment, with his hope of learning more about the missing boy fading with each turn. Page four, nothing. Page five, nothing. Page six, nothing. He needed more information! The news clip on the TV was just a teaser . . . the cliffhanger at the end of a television show season that left him hanging and longing for more. Analogous to the suspense that "Who Shot J.R.?" created to the generation before him, anxiously waiting to find out how the storyline would end.

The discouraged youngster got through the entire front section of the newspaper without seeing anything remotely related to his search. Disheartened, but still determined, he moved on to the next section of the paper. With his enthusiasm dwindling with every turn of a page, the dirty ink feeling on his fingertips progressed from noticeable to annoying. His weary eyes examined above the fold of page B-1. Once again, nothing. Redirecting his focus to the bottom of the first page of the "Local" section, the story headline jumped off the page and punched him in the face like heavyweight boxing champ Mike Tyson on Frank Bruno five months prior! "SEARCH CONTINUES FOR MISSING BOY."

Instantly rejuvenated, his slouched-over posture perked up. Scooting his sore posterior to the edge of his seat, he radically altered his body language. And greater than the extent to which the headlines changed his posture, the article that followed would drastically change his life. He quickly looked around with the paranoia of someone getting ready to engage in some forbidden, criminal activity. Now entirely focused, he peered into the newspaper and read every word . . . slowly, carefully. It read as follows:

SEARCH CONTINUES FOR MISSING BOY

Santa Barbara authorities continue their search for a twelve-year-old boy who went missing on Saturday, July 27, 1996. A search party of local volunteers is assisting police in hopes of finding the young boy, while his family and friends pray that he is alive and safe.

Detective Bob Brownstone of the SBPD is leading the investigation of the hit-and-run disappearance of the twelve-year-old Santa Barbara boy, who now has been missing for more than seventy-two hours.

In the mid-morning of Saturday, July 27th, the young boy went for a bicycle ride in the hills near the American Riviera Golf and Tennis Club. According to his mother, her son was going to meet a friend at the country club to play tennis. After the young boy was a couple of hours late, the friend called his home to find out why he never showed up. It was then that his mother feared that something was wrong.

The worried mother drove the route that her son would have taken to go to the country club. About one mile from the club, she noticed what appeared to be fresh skid marks and a broken piece of plastic of what looked to be a headlight cover. She immediately contacted the police, whereby they met her at the area where she had found the possibly related evidence. It was near there that the police noticed fresh skid marks on the road and found the missing boy's damaged bicycle nearby in the bushes, just off the roadway. In addition, blood on the scene was tested and the blood type matched that of her son.

The missing boy's parents, Steven and Sandra Schafer agreed to release the information about their only child in hopes that it will help in the investigation. A prominent Santa Barbara family, Steven is the Founder and CEO of H&J Industries, a successful industrial equipment supplier located in the northern part of town, near the border of Santa Barbara and Goleta.

Their preteen boy has been identified as Timothy Schafer; twelve years old; five feet five inches tall; approximately one-hundred twenty pounds. He was riding a twenty-one-speed Bianchi Super G road bike and was wearing black cycling shorts and a bright yellow cycling jersey at the time of his disappearance.

A hotline has been set up to assist with the investigation. If you have seen this boy or have any information pertaining to his whereabouts or this incident, please call the designated hotline number immediately - (805) 555-HELP. The Schafer

family is offering a one-million-dollar reward to
anyone who provides credible information that
leads to the return of their son.

Craig sat there, frozen in shock, with the demeanor you
would expect from someone who had finally imagined that his
entire life could have been utterly different and considerably
better, rather than buried under the neglect of a misfit toy.
His eyes burned through the paper, with laser-like focus, but
no longer looking at the actual words on the paper. Instead,
he stared blankly into the space that was occupied by the paper. He saw nothing. He heard nothing. To say that he looked
stunned would be more of an understatement than to say the
Grand Canyon was a small ditch in the middle of the desert. His
breathing slowed to a near stop. His body remained completely
still, with less motion than a mannequin.

Suddenly, akin to a boxer's reaction when a corner man
dumps a bucket of smelling salts under his nose, a jerking reflex
energized the incapacitated youngster from his statuesque state.
His posture now fully upright, uncontrollably he blurted aloud,
"That's it!"

"Shh-shh's" echoed from nearby but fell upon deaf ears. Fixated on his revelation, he ignored the shh-shers, tore out the
article, and began the plan of a lifetime, or possibly two.

Chapter Twenty-Six

26

T he Coastline bus pulled into the Santa Barbara Bus Depot just after 10:05 a.m. on the morning of Thursday, August 1, 1996. With new information, Craig had a new idea. He skipped the exit in Ventura, ditching his original plan before he stepped foot on the bus. Putting his new plan into action, he continued his venture an additional thirty miles up the coast to the American Riviera—Santa Barbara.

His initial plan to seek his former foster parents for help blew away in the gusty winds of Camarillo analogous to the breezy dust obscuring its acres of strawberry fields. All the better, as that plan could only be a temporary fix, even on its best day. Most certainly, after the dust settled, his former foster parents would feel obligated to return him back into the foster care system. So, whatever help they could offer him, it would have been short-lived at best. Fortuitously, the newspaper article folded away in his pocket triggered a more long-term plan, and if executed properly, perhaps a permanent solution. Whatever the risk, the conceivable reward could far outweigh it.

The bus depot took up half of the block on the southwest corner of State Street and West Montecito Street, directly adjacent to the bridge that unintentionally provided the gateway up the famed State Street and carried the track that escorted the Gold Coast Train up the California coast in its passageway through the touristy town.

With an unprecedented spring in his step, Craig stepped down from the bus and took a deep breath, consuming the fresh ocean air. The taste of freedom was now more palatable than it was just a couple of days earlier. A new plan. A new town. Experiencing new hope. Exuding new energy. A new opportunity for a new life!

Craig waited on the bus attendant that was unloading the stored luggage from the storage compartment of his freedom bus. He anxiously approached as soon as the last *Samsonite* touched the hot blacktop of the depot lot.

"Excuse me, sir. Do you know if there's a coffee shop within walking distance?"

"Yes," the muscularly lean employee responded, wiping the sweat from his brow. He caught his breath before he continued. Then, pointing up State Street, he said, "There's a couple of them a few blocks up State Street."

Walking away toward State Street, before the young worker could finish his sentence, Craig raised his right hand in gratitude. "Thank you."

As the freed youth rushed up the street, he pushed past the foot-travelers strolling and window shopping with casual enjoyment. With his plan in place, his pace reflected his eagerness to put it into action, both fast and frantic. He grazed several tourists, bumping into some, nearly running over others, all the while repeating a quick, robotic apology.

"Excuse me. Excuse me," he repeated like a broken record, weaving in and out of pedestrians while his brisk walk transitioned into a slow jog.

As usual, there were a good number of tourists roaming State Street. Shopping bags in hand, chatting away, they roamed up and down the street, with no significant purpose other than leisure and frivolous spending. Meanwhile, Craig trotted up the retail and restaurant-lined thoroughfare with the ultimate purpose . . . a life-changing purpose!

After a couple of blocks, and across the street on the corner, he saw a coffee shop. The glass double doors projected at a forty-five-degree angle to the corner of the building. He gathered his thoughts. He gripped a clump of his shirt to accentuate the worn look. Looking disheveled was integral to his plan and clearly not a problem. Craig gave himself a quick look up and down. The transient preteen certainly looked the part. Heck, he was the part.

He reached out with his right hand for the door handle. He took a deep breath and slowly opened the door. Then, just as he was about to enter the coffee shop, he suddenly stopped.

"Oh God, that was close," he whispered aloud.

The backpack. He needed to get rid of his backpack. A boy toting a backpack stuffed with clothes and essentials would throw a giant wrench in his plan. An unimaginable opportunity to reverse the direction of his heartbreaking life almost vanished as quickly and unexpectedly as it had appeared.

Walking around the backside of the building, the alley had a dumpster, along with some cardboard boxes scattered around the trash bin. Immediately northeast of the alley, on East De la Guerra, to his right he saw some thick shrubs that outlined the landscaping of the adjacent business. Craig scanned his surroundings to see if he was being watched. The coast was clear. He quickly tossed his battered backpack behind the bushes. Once again, he swiftly looked around to ensure he was not seen. The coast remained clear, so he proceeded for re-entry.

Walking back toward the coffee shop front doors, Craig continued to pay particular attention to his surroundings. As had been the story of his life, no one seemed to pay any attention to him. For once, that was a good thing.

He reached the corner of the coffee shop. He grabbed the door, and once again taking a deep breath, he trudged in. The main counter was straight ahead, about eight paces from the door. Three patrons were waiting in line to order. A few small tables and chairs flanked the main counter. The employee area was behind the bar-height counter. A young lady, seemingly in her early twenties, with wavy brown hair and crimson lipstick, was taking orders, while two other employees, a female and a male scrambled around behind her, feverishly making drinks.

"I'll have a half-calf, double chocolate, mocha latte with a dash of cinnamon." The next-up patron ordered in her local coffee vernacular.

Craig took two steps in and one step to his left. Over his left shoulder was a cork bulletin board secured to the wall, about two feet tall by three feet in width. A dozen different business cards were pinned to the right side of the board, mostly by various real estate agents, who were notoriously cheap for their marketing efforts. Attached to the top center of the board was a piece of rustic barn wood, labeled "Our Community" that was burned into the wood in some sort of calligraphy-like font. More prominently displayed, the feature presentation of the bulletin board was the full-page flyer that occupied the majority of the left one-third of the information board, but it eluded Craig's sight line.

The rumpled young man slouched over and slowly looked around the establishment expressing sheer confusion. He continued to stand there with a look of bewilderment, determined to do so until someone noticed him. He had no intention of making a scene. That was not part of his plan. He continued to stand there, like a statue of disorientation personified.

With the next patron in line looking over the menu, the respectful cashier patiently waited. With a slight smile, she made eye contact with the young, puzzled, and ostensibly lost customer.

"Are you okay? Can I help you?" she politely offered, still waiting on the elderly customer who continued to peruse the extensive choices on the menu board overhead.

"I don't know. I think I need help," he responded. Rubbing his left palm up against the self-inflicted, egg-shaped lump that protruded from his forehead. "I have no idea who I am or why I'm here."

Overhearing his attention-grabbing statement, everyone turned to look at him. For a boy who had gone through his young life predominantly unnoticed, suddenly he had the attention of an entire room. At the drop of a hat, the coffee shop became totally silent. One moment, the weary runaway was barely a bleep on the radar; the next, he was the sole focus of a room full of strangers.

Both baristas stopped in the middle of completing their concoctions and stared at the boy. Then, as rapidly as the room became silent, the silence was broken.

The male barista hollered out, "It's him! He's alive!" He pointed to the flyer on the bulletin board. "You're the missing boy!"

***

A SIZABLE CROWD already had gathered outside the local coffee shop. Word traveled rapidly up and down State Street, and the lookie-loos congregated. The first responders arrived within minutes of the call placed by the barista. A couple of SBPD's finest stood outside the glass doors to keep the curious spectators from inundating the café-turned-instant-focal-point of State Street.

The boy's parents were on their way. Uniformed Officer Miguel Kusick, a tall, intimidating figure with a bald head and thick goatee to boot, stood guard inside to secure the paramedic's examination of the young boy and to provide a safe environment for the separated family to reunite. After checking his vitals, the emergency medical technician held an instant cold pack to the golf ball protruding from the boy's head.

One of the employees brought a water bottle over and handed it to the officer standing guard. "Here's some water for him."

"Thank you." Officer Kusick removed the plastic cap and handed the water bottle to the young boy. "Here you go, Tim."

"Tim?" The young boy responded to his cue for his first live performance and stepped into his role. He was now on stage. Act One, Scene One: Missing boy is found and suffers from amnesia.

The officer looked at the paramedic with curiosity and concern.

"It appears that he has amnesia," said the medical professional.

"Oh, I'm sorry," Officer Kusick said in a comforting tone. "That's your name, son. Timothy Schafer."

The boy took a gulp of water and expressed his gratitude. "Thank you, occifer."

Officer Kusick turned to the paramedic and raised his eyebrows. "Occifer?"

"Amnesia," the EMT responded, "and perhaps a concussion as well."

The doors to the coffee shop opened, drawing the crowd's attention. One of the uniformed officers parted the flock like the Red Sea, making way for the restless parents. Steven and Sandra Schafer took two steps in, stopped, looked at the familiar face, and broke down in tears.

"His parents." The door-guarding officer alerted the paramedic and Officer Kusick to the identity of the couple and gave them access to the boy.

"Oh my God!" the mother hollered, dropping her purse like a hot potato. Tears flowing down their cheeks, the euphoric couple rushed to the young boy, snugly wrapped their arms around him, and squeezed the breath out of him.

The boy looked shocked; his arms remained to his side. He stuck to his role. Act One, Scene Two: Missing boy with amnesia is reunited with his parents. For this scene, he was a natural. An Academy Award was sure to follow. His performance was flawless, as it should have been. After all, he had never seen these people before in his life!

After ninety seconds of nonstop sobbing and bear hugs, overjoyed that their son was alive, and wanting to keep it that way, they released their death grip.

"Thank God you're alive!" The mother clutched his hands and wept. Officer Kusick offered her a tissue, but she refused to let go of the boy.

"How is he?" the father asked the paramedic.

"He has a good-size contusion to his head, and some other scrapes and bruises. Otherwise, I see no other visible injuries and his vitals are fine." He paused and swallowed. "However, it appears he has a concussion—and amnesia."

The mother's grip on the young boy's hands tightened. "Amnesia? You mean—" She paused, and not allowing herself to finish her statement, she turned to the boy. "Do you recognize us?"

Somberly he replied, "No. I'm sorry, but I don't."

"Do you know who you are?" the father said hesitantly.

"No. The officer said my name is Tim, but that doesn't sound familiar to me."

Sandra Schafer completely lost it, bawling uncontrollably.

"Well, thank God you're alive and safely back with us," Steven Schafer said, easing the discomfort a bit. "That's the most im-

portant thing. I'm sure, after getting home to familiar surroundings, everything will start to come back to you."

Not yet willing to let loose of her grasp of the young boy, now
safe and sound in her care, Mrs. Schafer lifted his hands and
kissed them.

Then, gently releasing his hands to his lap, she noticed something. "Your bracelet is missing," she said, tenderly touching his
naked right wrist with her loving hand.

"Bracelet?"

"Shortly after you were born, we bought you a custom silver
bracelet, with a special engraving. Of course, you couldn't wear
it until you were much older. But as soon as you were old
enough to wear it, you never took it off. Except for getting a
link added here and there as you grew, that bracelet has been a
permanent fixture on your wrist. You always said it brought you
good luck."

The boy put on the best-disappointed face he could muster
up. It was a piece of cake. After all, disappointment came naturally to him, having been a foster child since birth.

"No worries," the comforting mother said. "The jeweler who
made it is a good friend of ours. We'll have him make you
another one, just like it."

"Although I seem to have a total loss of memory, I do know
this." The boy beamed. "You have no idea how good I feel to be
here with you both. What will be like back to normal for you
two, will seem like a whole new life for me."

"I'm sorry to interrupt," the ambulance attendant interjected. "But we need to take your son to the hospital for a check-up,

just to be safe. One of you can ride with us in the ambulance, the other can take your vehicle and meet us there."

Officer Kusick placed a hand on Mr. Schafer's left shoulder, leaned in, and whispered to him, "Detective Bob Brownstone will meet you at Village Hospital. He'll have some questions for your son."

"Okay," Mr. Schafer said. "I understand. Thank you."

The next morning, the front page of the *Santa Barbara Daily Press* contained a huge, heartwarming photo and only one story, with a headline that read: "LOCAL FAMILY PERKS UP AFTER THEIR MISSING BOY ENTERS COFFEE SHOP."

***

TWO WEEKS HAD passed quickly, but not without some touch-and-go moments that were too close for comfort. Fortunately, the boy was recovering nicely and had moved past the critical stage. The retired Navy vet had saved the boy's life, albeit after almost killing him. But that part of his secret he would take to his grave.

Carl explained to the youngster that he found him lying on the ground, unconscious on the side of a remote, private road, bleeding profusely, and knocking on death's door. He insisted that it was vital to the boy's health that he be treated immediately, with no time to spare, and that waiting for a paramedic team would have doomed his fate.

The victim had complete retrograde amnesia, so he was in no position to doubt what he was told. It made perfectly good sense to him. His rescuer had explained why he thought the boy must have been in foster care, perhaps a runaway from an abusive family. Carl had seen no reports of a missing child in the area, so foster care seemed like a logical deduction. And again, the boy was in no position to doubt what he was told. He was alive and being fed and cared for; and doubting his caregiver wouldn't do him any good anyway, so he went with the flow.

Carl had convinced the boy that he thought it best to get the youngster in stable condition before returning him back into a broken system that likely was the primary cause of his life-threatening predicament in the first place. Not having any other choice, the boy agreed.

First thing in the morning, while the boy was still asleep, Carl stepped out to grab them some fast-food breakfast and pick up the newspaper. When he returned home, the broken and bruised kid still was out like a light.

Carl sat at his kitchen table, sipped his coffee, and straightened out the newspaper to find out what was going on in the world around him. He was not much of a TV watcher and got most of his news from the *Ventura County Times*, which he picked up about once a week. With the Atlanta Olympic Park bombing still under investigation, the August 9, 1996 headline read: "PHONE AND COMPUTER DELAYS STALLED OLYMPIC PARK BOMB RESPONSE." He sipped the strong black coffee and read the newspaper until he heard his young patient wake up.

Carl entered his guest bedroom to assess the status of the young boy, who was sitting up in the bed. The room wasn't the Four Seasons, but it provided the patient with everything he needed. The five-year-old mattress was virtually new, only having been slept in a handful of times. Amenities included a soft pillow, fresh sheets, a comforter, and a chest at the foot of the bed that housed two Mexican blankets and an extra pillow. Beside the queen-size bed was a basic wood nightstand upon which Carl kept a clean glass and a full pitcher of fresh water.

"Good morning. How are you feeling today?"

"Good morning," the boy said. "Much better, sir."

"Please, I told you, you can call me Carl." The medic held up a thermometer. "I'm going to check your temperature to make sure your fever hasn't returned."

Carl took the boy's temperature, which came back ninety-eight point nine. He thoroughly examined his patient's wounds to ensure that no visible infections were sneaking up. The boy seemed to recover well, and with the speed only possible in a youthful body. And what astounded Carl most, the boy escaped without a single broken bone.

"Looking good young man," Carl said. "Oh, to be young again. Your speedy recovery has been nothing short of a miracle."

It was evident that his medical condition had stabilized, and the caregiver and his patient agreed that the time had come to pay a visit to the Department of Children and Family Services. After some breakfast, a shower, and throwing on clean clothes Carl had purchased at a local thrift shop, the patient would be discharged.

Carl drove the two of them twenty-plus miles southwest to the main DCFS office for Ventura County, located in the county seat of Ventura. They arrived when the office opened, entered the building, and Carl cut to the chase. He requested to speak with the person in charge, insisting that this was a most unusual situation, and everything he said would end up getting repeated up the food chain anyway, so why not just start there. It was a bold, direct approach, but it worked.

His persistence prevailed and the receptionist bypassed sending out the on-duty case worker, and instead dragged out her upset boss, who was a stickler for protocol. Carl wasted no time with pleasantries. The quicker he could explain the situation, the less the opportunity for an inquisition. He effectively conveyed his rehearsed statement to the department supervisor without a hitch. Following Carl's explanation, the supervisor confirmed it with the boy to the extent that his memory would allow, keeping the plan intact.

A copy of the missing child's file from the County of Los Angeles had been sent to all the offices of the neighboring counties' departments, anticipating that the runaway would flee the county in order to minimize getting caught. The DCFS Supervisor reviewed the file thoroughly and took a close look at the most recent photo of the missing boy. The boy in front of her clearly matched the photo and the description of the child, and who had been reported as a runaway from a Los Angeles County foster care family that was now under investigation for abuse.

With irrefutable visual evidence that the returned boy and the missing runaway foster child were one and the same, the boy was taken into the custody of the department. To further confirm the twelve-year-old boy's identity, Carl's timeline of events lined up with the date the Pacoima family reported that their foster son went missing.

Just like that, Carl was off the hook, and back to life as usual. Unfortunately, the same could not be said for the innocent adolescent.

Placed with a new foster care family, and with no memory of his past, the boy began a new life, and more so than he ever could have imagined.

Chapter Twenty-Seven

27

Depending on one's perspective, the week had gone by extremely fast for some and painfully slow for others. For Kendall, he resembled a chicken with his head cut off, trapped in a room on fire, with Colonel Sanders waiting by the door hovering over a commercial deep fryer with seasoned oil boiling over. Handling a double caseload for an entire week was no bucket-of-chicken picnic, but nothing he couldn't handle. He made it through without turning extra crispy.

Josh's week, on the other hand, dawdled at a turtle's pace. Fraught with worry over his best friend's survival, he struggled to focus. To add to his anguish, guilt riddled his conscience after his boss relegated him to desk duty while his partner did the heavy lifting. Josh felt useless numbing his butt, while Kendall worked his off. Not that Josh hadn't done the same for his partner in the past. That offered him a bit of relief.

When Kendall had been out for two weeks in the wake of his mother's death, Josh not only handled both caseloads, but he even tried one of Kendall's cases on short notice. At the last minute, a defendant refused to waive his right to a speedy trial, as was his right under the Sixth Amendment to the U.S. Constitution, the California Constitution, and California Penal Code section 1382. And with only two hours of trial preparation, a determined Josh scored a conviction. When the jury returned a verdict of guilty, a victorious Josh mumbled under his breath, "Be careful what you ask for."

For Kristen, after her second near brush with death in a matter of days, her week hit both ends of the spectrum. Now in stable condition, she remained confined to a hospital bed, with nothing to do when she was awake but stare at the walls, read or watch television. In that sense, it was sluggish. Conversely, sleeping upwards of sixteen hours a day, most with one eye open, it flew by rapidly.

Several days prior, the nefarious disconnection of various machines attached to Kristen had triggered the emergency P.A. announcement. It drove Village Hospital into a panic. Then, in a flash, the criminal culprit fled the scene.

After the uniformed rookie officer guarding Kristen's room had stepped away to use the restroom, an unidentified visitor appeared, completed his feat, and disappeared in a second. Evidently watching her room and waiting for a slight opening to slip in, the aspiring killer injected her with something, unplugged the life-support equipment, then snuck out undetected. Were it not for the quick response of Dr. Taggart and his staff, Kristen would've been dead in another second.

The disgraced officer earned himself a bag of adult diapers and a week of unpaid leave, and Kristen gained around-the-clock protection from two veteran officers, both with strong bladders.

Josh visited every day, but always less than thirty minutes before the end of visiting hours, and never without at least one other member of the happy hour gang. Sure, he had to work. But by no means did he race over to the hospital afterward. Trying to justify his actions, it boiled down to one main thing; he was avoiding telling Kristen how he felt.

But despite being a coward, he did have a good excuse. In his defense, he was burning the midnight oil, trying to solve the developing mystery in which he was unwittingly entangled; and particularly the newly added twist as to why Kristen was now a target.

After her near-death experience, and his second, followed by her second, at last, he appreciated how unpredictable life could be, and the importance of taking nothing and no one for granted. His entire life, Josh had felt invincible. Now, he knew differently.

Josh told himself, "Life is a gift, so be present in the present and treat it like a present." Yet despite this life-altering revelation, he still lacked the onions to open up to his best friend. Josh wasn't one to cower, but it was yellow-bellied, and he knew it.

With the work week coming to an end, and Kendall done with court for the day, Josh popped into his partner's office to pick his brain. The burden of his Leaving the Scene-DUI case weighed heavily on his mind and more heavily on his conscience. After all, the case was responsible for the death of Lee Davidson and the near-death of the love of his life.

He plopped himself down in one of Kendall's guest chairs, having dragged his leg over without his crutches. His armpits were bruised and raw from pressing his large, muscular frame on the hard rubber padding millions of times over the past several weeks, and they needed a break. Josh couldn't help but wonder—with all the advancements in science over the years, why hadn't someone invented crutches that help more than they hurt?

"What on your mind, my friend?" Kendall removed his reading glasses from his nose and tossed them down on his desk. From the looks of the twisted temples, hyper-extended hinges and scratched lenses on his glasses, assault victims were not the only recipients of abuse that had seen the inside of the District Attorney's Office.

"It's about the Knowles case," Josh said.

"No surprise. What an albatross that case has turned out to be. Have you been able to track down a copy of the missing report?"

"Nope," Josh muttered. "Without it, I'll have to dismiss the case. If Knowles retains a new attorney, I'm sure they'll file a motion to dismiss the charges on day one. And even if he continues to represent himself, at some point he'll figure out that he can file the motion and make his case go away."

"I can see the hamster running around on the wheel. So, what can I do to help?"

"I need to pick your brain, and your memory."

"Both have faded over the years, but I'll do my best. Fire away."

"I remember a long time ago you told me about the first case you had to dismiss for lack of evidence. And if I remember correctly, didn't you say the crux of that case hinged on a blood test as well?"

"Impressive Josh. I can't believe you remembered that."

"I remember because you prefaced your story with the saying, you never forget your first."

The partners chuckled briefly, then sighed. Kendall maintained his smile, while Josh flipped a switch to serious mode.

"Can you tell me more about that case?" Josh leaned over in the chair, hungry for some answers, or at least some direction.

"Wow, that was like twenty-five years ago. But, as you said, you never forget your first." Kendall hesitated, surveying the room as if looking for a transcript to assist his memory.

"Let me think. Well, like your case, it involved someone leaving the scene of an accident. But this was a hit-and-run with a victim and a possible kidnapping. Let's see . . . a vehicle hit a young boy, twelve years old I think, who was riding his bike over near the American Riviera Country Club."

Kendall stopped, again scanning the room in search of his archived memory bank to recall information from a quarter of a century earlier. "His mother reported him missing later that same day, and then drove the path he would have taken on his bike, looking for clues as to his whereabouts. Well, she found traces of an accident, so she called the police and they investigated; finding skid marks, broken pieces of a vehicle's headlights, and the boy's mangled bike in the bushes nearby . . . but no boy."

"The boy eventually turned up, right?" Josh asked.

"He sure did, a few days later, at a local coffee shop. I remember it well because the newspaper had a clever headline the next day." Kendall paused, undoubtedly trying to remember the headline. He drew a blank.

Josh prompted his partner, "So the boy turned up. And?"

"Sorry. Didn't mean to digress," Kendall said. "Yeah, the boy turned up, but he had total amnesia, so he couldn't provide any useful evidence." With his right hand, Kendall grabbed his reading glasses from his desk and began tapping them on his left palm. "Well, on the day of the accident, the police found blood on the boy's bike, as well as on some leaves in the bushes. They tested it and found two different blood types. One was O positive, which is the most common blood type in the world. The other was AB negative."

"What about DNA?" Josh interrupted.

"Remember, this was in 1996. So, this was a couple of years before DNA gained credibility in criminal investigations and in the courts."

"That's right! I forgot how old you are."

"You just couldn't resist, could you?" Kendall smirked, then continued.

"As it turned out, the blood types helped eliminate a key suspect, rather than incriminate him. Retired Police Chief Bob Brownstone was actually the investigating detective on that case. He thought that the perpetrator may have scraped and cut himself in the bushes to retrieve the boy. His theory was that one sample of blood was that of the boy, and the other likely was that of the perpetrator."

"So, remind me again what happened?"

Josh loved to hear Kendall tell stories of the good old days. They always involved something foreign in today's world of criminal prosecution, thanks in large part to the evolution of scientific evidence and technology. In twenty-five years, the world had changed more than in the previous hundred, and along with it, the way crimes were investigated and prosecuted.

"Well, the detective investigated further and gathered more evidence. Eventually, he amassed enough to garner a viable suspect. It was some guy seen in the area that same day, with damage to the front end of his vehicle, consistent with striking something smaller and lighter. A parking meter violation on State Street later that same day bleeped him on the detective's radar. There were also some other, less significant pieces of evidence pointing to this guy, but the details escape me."

"So, the police felt they had enough to arrest him?"

"Yep," Kendall responded, then resumed. "So, they arrested this guy on a slew of charges, the most significant being kidnapping. Well, the defendant agreed to submit to a blood test and his blood type was B positive, or something like that. I know it wasn't AB negative or O positive."

"How can you remember all of that?" Josh asked.

"I remember it so well because it turned out that the boy's blood type was AB negative, which is the rarest blood type in the world. I think less than one percent of people have that blood type." Kendall leaned back in his chair, flipping his glasses back onto his desk. "I remember thinking, before the boy and the suspect had been tested, that if the perpetrator had the rarest blood type, and the boy had the most common, it would provide strong evidence that we had the right suspect, and we could get a conviction. But unfortunately, for purposes of using the blood tests to help the case, the boy was the one with the rarest blood type. That left us with the perpetrator likely having the most common blood type in the world."

Kendall leaned back and raised his arms in the air in surrender. "What's more, it ruled out the initial suspect, whose blood type didn't match either sample. And unfortunately, the police never collected enough additional evidence to come up with any other feasible suspects, let alone find the culprit."

Josh peered at this partner with a contemplating look. He squinted and looked down and to his right. His partner recognized the look. Although the pondering prosecutor didn't say a word, he looked like he wanted to, but just didn't know what to say. Kendall noticed the puzzled look on Josh's face and decided to speak before his partner's head exploded.

"What is it?" Kendall chuckled. "Did I help solve your case?

"Actually," Josh said, then hesitated.

"You can't be serious?"

"No, it's not that," Josh said. "Well, not exactly. But you said that AB negative blood was rare, with less than one percent of people having that blood type, right?"

"Yeah, the rarest blood type in the world. And?"

"Well Grandpa," Josh joked. "As you know, in this century we use DNA to identify people."

"Okay, smartie. What are you getting at?"

"Well, as you know, the missing report in my case was a DNA report, and it matched that of Defendant Knowles to the DNA at the scene. But, in addition to the DNA profile, it also had the blood type listed on it, which just so happened to be AB negative."

"Hmm," Kendall voiced his curiosity. "That's interesting, but it's gotta be just a coincidence. Right?"

"Well, what would you say the odds of that are?"

"Statistically speaking, it would be like—well, less than one in a hundred, right?"

"You also said that your case, and may I remind you a case that was twenty-five years ago, involved a twelve-year-old boy, right?

"Yes, and?"

"That would make that boy around thirty-seven now, right?"

"Yes, and?" Kendall became increasingly inquisitive, eager to find out where his partner was headed with this line of questioning. Somehow, his partner, who was young enough to be his child, had transformed him into a defendant or hostile witness being cross-examined on the stand, being fired at from an ammunition belt of leading questions by an armed and dangerous prosecutor.

"Nicholas Knowles is thirty-seven years old," blurted Josh with conviction, "with AB negative blood!"

"Hmm. That's very interesting, but it's gotta be just another coincidence." Kendall hesitated and slightly tilted his head, no longer able to easily convince himself. "Right?"

"Humor me while I think out loud," Josh vocalized, whereby Kendall leaned in. "You have an unsolved case that involved a victim with AB negative blood. The victim was a twelve-year-old boy who got amnesia and never could recall anything from the incident. That boy would now be a thirty-seven-year-old man. My case involves a thirty-seven-year-old man who has AB negative blood, the report which has been deleted from the database of the Bureau of Forensic Sciences lab, stolen from two case files after a murder and attempted murder, and missing from the court file ever since."

"Josh, I have no idea how all of this equates, but when you say it out loud, I think you may be on to something." Kendall slid to the end of his seat.

"You and I both know there are never that many coincidences when trying to link a crime to a suspect. Too many coincidences are no longer coincidences, they are circumstantial evidence and vital pieces of the puzzle."

"Well Josh, I hate to throw a wrench in your theory or add more misfit pieces to the puzzle," Kendall lamented, "but the twelve-year-old boy in my cold case was named Tim Schafer. Your thirty-seven-year-old man is named Nicholas Knowles."

"To quote the famous eighties' love ballad—'True.' But—" Josh said, before being interrupted by his partner.

"True, but—" Kendall smiled and raised his pointer finger eager to point out a possible explanation when Josh anxiously reciprocated with his own interruption.

"Yes, there's a big ol' but!"

Chapter
Twenty-Eight

28

The undeveloped land several miles up the coast, north of Goleta, had remained untainted by human intervention for centuries. It consisted of a combination of several virgin parcels, a few owned by the state, more owned by the federal government, and one privately owned. Many parcels had restrictive covenants in place to preserve their unblemished status, but now they hung on the precipice of losing their virginity. Open to doubt, the rezoning of the prime and pristine terrain led to the approval for a massive development, one determined to devastate God's creation.

The future resort's journey started with tainted court battles, followed by bribery of committee members. Next came questionable eminent domain proceedings, falsified Environmental Impact Reports, and various less scrupulous tactics. When the fog cleared, the multi-billion-dollar development was well on its way. Now approved to ravish the land, the exclusive resort, casino, and high-dollar shopping promenade headlined the plans for the privileged getaway.

Nick followed Target X after he left his downtown Santa Barbara office for the day, all the way to a private region in the desolate, soon to be ruined, coastal oasis. But no *Mercedes* today for the uppity conspirator. Today, a plain four-door navy blue sedan was his vehicle of choice. His ride was so unassuming, its modesty spawned suspicion. Clearly, such a pretentious, self-absorbed professional not only would never own such a vehicle but even renting it if it was the only vehicle left on the lot would be a stretch.

The abandoned twenty-seven-acre ranch was in a prime location within the one hundred sixty-eight acres that would soon be spoiled forever. In a gamble that would pay dividends many times over, Target X had paid the owner well above its present value, just before word of the feasibility of the development became public knowledge. And once the development's approval was imminent and acquiring the final parcel of land was all that remained, he turned around and sold the property to the development's holding company for a nine-hundred percent return on his investment, wholly under the protection and anonymity of one of his shell corporations.

There was no visible mile marker on the highway and Nick would have missed the exit onto the dirt road if he hadn't seen the agitated dirt kick up from the speeding vehicle, whose tail he lost. Not fifty yards from the exit, a freshly painted wooden sign read "Future Site of Heaven's Vista Resort." He sped up, with his vehicle bouncing around like a rubber ball on the bumpy, private road. After a sharp turn up and around a hill overgrown with shrubbery, he spotted a small cabin roughly two hundred yards away coming into focus as the dirty air cleared. As the dust settled, Nick caught sight of taillights lit up, parked in front of the old wood cabin.

About thirty rocky, weed-infested yards off the dirt road, Nick pulled into a natural cove formed by an arrangement of massive natural rocks that had created a small hill. The peak was only two stories tall, but enough to shield him from the sight of the cabin, and the cabin's view of the ocean toward the west. He grabbed binoculars that he had placed on the passenger's seat and exited his new car rental, this time a white Chevy Impala. Courtesy of the dirt road, the white had turned to a dark beige. Peaking from around the corner of the natural shield, he leaned against the giant desert rock and made good use of his binoculars.

With the rubber coating of the black scopes pressed against his eyes, he aimed toward the cabin. The parking lights of the vehicle were still on, but when the air fully cleared, Nick saw that they were not that of the vehicle he had been following. Another vehicle was parked on the gravel driveway behind Target X's economy sedan. A few minutes prior, in the distance and dust separating the Impala from where the tailed sedan had exited Highway 101, another vehicle must have been following Target X as well.

Dusk was approaching, and a small but thick patch of clouds shaded the sun and diminished his visibility. Nick adjusted the center knob that controlled the binoculars' focus, trying to get a good, clear look at the driver of vehicle two, a newer model dark SUV with Nevada plates.

The driver closed his door and faced Target X, who was leaning up against the back of the economy sedan with the trunk open. The SUV driver wore a long-sleeved, black collared shirt and black pants, which stood out on a warm, sunny day. Another gentleman, professionally dressed in khaki slacks and a navy-blue blazer, exited the passenger's side of the SUV.

Nick stood as still as a sniper, intent on identifying Target X's mystery visitors. But not even with the aid of enhanced vision could he see the faces of the strangers, rather only the back of their heads, of whom the driver's seemed to be bobbing in anger in combination with his raised arms of rage.

"What the hell?" Feeling something bump his leg, Nick jumped back and dropped his binoculars on the dry, cracked ground.

A rabbit scooted across the desert floor, slightly disoriented from its unexpected encounter with the much larger creature. An armored tank firing at Nick's head would hardly faze him, but a tiny, harmless fuzzy hare had him screaming like a schoolgirl.

"Damn Bugs Bunny." Nick shook his head in disbelief, watching the furry local hop into some distant bushes. He took a deep sigh, then shook his head again.

Now composed, he meticulously looked around at his surroundings with the paranoia of someone feeling watched. Other than the rustling bushes in the wake of the waskly wabbit, no sounds could be heard, and no nearby dangers could be seen. Like its fate when encountering a magician's top hat, the rabbit had vanished. The rustling halted, and the air hushed. He took a deep breath, followed by a big exhale, but his newly acquired composure was short-lived.

"Bang!" A loud gunshot swept across the silent, dusty air.

Nick leaped to the side, scraping his arm on the jagged rock formation, then squatted to retrieve his binoculars. Blood began to drip down his arm. He grabbed the binoculars from the ground in a rush, not bothering to clean the dirty lenses, anxious to see what coincided with the gunshot. But before he could raise them, the rev of an approaching engine suddenly emerged from the dirt road behind him and rapidly grew louder as it drew closer.

He quickly stepped into the cove and ducked, then turned to see a dark-colored *Lincoln* SUV with Nevada plates race by in a cloud of dust, toward the sound of the gunshot. Immediately behind it, a Santa Barbara Sheriff's vehicle sped toward the cabin, but with no siren and no lights. It wasn't pursuing the SUV; it was accompanying it.

Nick hesitated to come out of his shelter, possibly waiting to see if more cars were to follow. When the coast seemed clear, he clutched the binoculars and returned to his sightseeing spot. He leaned against the giant rock to remain steady, then looked through the enhanced specs and saw nothing but a blur. He pulled them from his eyes and inspected them closely, only to find that the lenses had popped off. He scanned the ground like an eagle, desperately trying to find them before it was too late. But too late came too quickly.

Nick looked toward the cabin with his naked eyes, hoping to see something worth risking his life for, only to find that his life was further at risk. Emerging from the dirt-filled air, a *Polaris*

Ranger ATV rolled in his direction, occupied by two men; the driver, who had his right hand on the steering wheel while his left hand held a .44 Magnum, and a camouflage-dressed passenger pointing a shotgun out the side of the open-air vehicle. A welcome committee, they were not. Rather, the two hired goons looked to be more of the elimination committee variety; pissed-off, ugly as sin, and eager to shoot on sight.

The unwelcome intruder had to make a life-saving decision quickly. Try to hide, and roll the dice so that the versatile, highly mobile vehicle wouldn't make its way into his less-than-hidden hideaway or get the heck out of Dodge. If he hid, he might be able to find out more about the gunshot, but he also could find himself on the losing end of another one. If he fled, even if the *Polaris* were to spot him driving away, there was no way it could catch him. The worst-case outcome of each decision made it a no-brainer; getting out of Dodge was the only wise option.

The *Polaris Ranger* was still a good seventy-five yards away and zigzagging at a cautious pace of about ten mph to scope the area. The gun-toting redneck waved his shotgun side to side—likely bored without a Trump rally to attend or a Capitol building to storm—looking for something or someone to shoot. The giant wad of tobacco filled his pre-cancer-infected cheek, ready to burst. His face crinkled up, snorting and ready to fire, and he hocked a loogie. The driver maintained a slow, steady pace to ensure they secured the area from any uninvited guests.

If timed accurately, Nick possibly could use the natural rock formations and shrubs to shield himself from sight long enough to get down the dirt road, out of sight, and out of harm's way.

He pulled the *Impala* out of the confines of the cove and crept to the edge of the formation. He stopped and peeked around the corner. If he couldn't see them, they couldn't see him. He spotted the *Polaris* for a few seconds, then it disappeared out of sight. Clear! He stepped on the gas, heavy enough to get out of sight before being spotted, gentle enough so as not to cause a Middle Eastern sandstorm. He made it to the highway without being seen, or so he must have assumed.

Some forty yards from the cove Nick had used for cover, and in the direction of the highway, was a similar desert rock structure. It too concealed an unwelcome motor vehicle, occupied by two non-invitees. Unfortunately for the inhabitants, the location of this particular version of nature's hideaway did not have a view of the cabin. The rolling hills, large rock formations, and patches of shrubs and trees, through which the twisting dirt road ran, obstructed its sight line. It did, however, have a view of Nick's cove.

"My hunch was right," the passenger said. "Following Knowles proves that he knows something about what the heck is going on or is involved in something suspicious."

"True," the driver agreed. "But we can't stick around to find out more. It's too risky! From the sound of that gunshot and the manner in which he fled, we don't want to be seen by whatever, or whoever scared him away."

"I concur. We've gotta keep a low profile until we can find out more."

"Roger that!" The driver pulled out from hiding and edged along the rock formation toward the dirt road that led to Highway 101. He stopped to make sure they could escape undetected. "Especially if someone in law enforcement is on the take, which is entirely possible. Judging by the speed, that Sheriff's vehicle didn't look like it was out here on routine patrol."

"First of all, please don't call me Roger." The passenger laughed, flipping through his phone to examine the photos he took on the brief, impromptu stakeout. "Second, at least we got one question answered. Knowles knows something." He held up his phone, zoomed in on a photo of Knowles peeking around the edge, spying with binoculars, and showed it to his partner.

"Yep, we surely did. But one step forward, four steps back. Who was he following and why? What's with the Nevada plates? And, if law enforcement is involved, who can we trust?"

"As for the last question, you would know better than I, T-dub."

"Well for now Counselor, until we know who we can trust, surely we can't let this leave our tight-knit group." The soon-to-be detective grabbed his thirty-two-ounce mug from the cup holder and took a big slurp of his lukewarm cola, hydrating before scramming.

Josh nodded. "Copy that. And quit calling me Shirley."

TW erupted with laughter, spitting his drink all over the dashboard. "Son of a!"

TW grabbed a napkin from the center console to wipe the dashboard when the *Polaris* unexpectedly appeared in the distance, now unobstructed by nature's protection. Gunshots fired. Clearly, its occupants had spotted the two intruders as a bullet zoomed past the windshield and struck the rock barrier, about two feet above their vehicle.

"Son of a!" Josh hollered. "Floor it!"

Chapter
Twenty-Nine

29

A few of the underlying transactions connected with Heaven's Vista Resort had been on the FBI's radar for five months. The project was subject to an Environmental Impact Statement because it constituted major federal action, including the use of federal land, as well as the expenditure of some federal dollars. As such, it required the development to assess the impact of the proposed project on the physical, cultural, and human environments affected by the planned venture. A small red flag on one of the Environmental Impact Statements prompted an agent to contact the FBI in an abundance of caution.

A rookie FBI agent, ready to make her mark on the Bureau, spotted the minuscule bread crumb and followed the trail, which led to enough credible evidence to take to her partner. She had to be convinced. Barking up the wrong tree would've dug a hole for her too deep to crawl out of, and her partner would've harped on it every chance he got. The blowhard gave her a hard enough time without reason, so there was absolutely no need to supply him with more ammo.

Holly Hurley, the young, eager FBI newbie, was just nine months removed from graduating from "The Farm." Given the alliteration of her name, her parents must have been big Dr. Seuss fans.

Her poetic name rolled off the tongue, or so her parents must have said.

The ambitious Holly Hurley had grown and is now a badge-carrying fed.

Now they could see their child, dressed in a dark business suit,

catching Ponzi-scheming bad guys, who had their sights on stealing the loot.

Oh, how proud her parents must have been, of the achievements of their Holly Hurley.

> She had broken into the men's club, in a profession more tough than girly.

Placed with a thirty-two-year veteran agent who was contemplating his retirement, the new female suit was an annoying but much-needed thorn in his side. She had way too much energy for the old man, not to mention she was a woman. That latter fact alone took a little adjusting to for the sexist old fart. When he had attended the FBI Academy back in the day, it was a gigantic sausage factory that would've made Johnsonville jealous, comprising exactly zero women. Now, times had changed, forcing Holly's partner to do the same. The stubborn alpha male resisted for a couple of months, then came around overnight when his gentler-gender partner saved his life.

Agent Holly Hurley was a graduate of Cal Poly San Luis Obispo, about ninety-five scenic miles up the coast from Santa Barbara on Highway 101. Receiving her degree in Agricultural and Plant Sciences, she was adamant that her choice of study had nothing to do with her first name. A beer-guzzling party animal while attending Cal Poly SLO, as the locals called it, she was insistent that her college lifestyle had something to do with her last name. "It's my destiny," she would joke after drinking the men's rugby team under the table, then hurling her guts out.

At first, her senior partner brushed off the freshman agent's concerns. It sounded like a bunch of hogwash to him. Were it not for her Bachelor's degree in "plants and stuff," as her condescending partner called it, she never would have convinced him of the questionable findings of the Environmental Impact

Report for the planned posh resort. What he heard from her was "such-and-such causes air pollution, and air pollutants have a negative impact on plant growth, blah blah blah, certain indigenous plants would be impacted, blah blah blah, interfering with soil resource capture by the plant, blah blah blah, ultimately leading to the erosion of part of the coast."

"So, what you're saying is, if the resort is developed, California will fall into the ocean?" he mocked. Persistent and persuasive, the newbie persuaded her senior that it was worth digging deeper.

The two continued to investigate, hopping from one rabbit hole to another until the morsels created a meal, prompting the two feds to delve further, which spilled over into scrutinizing the financials of some of the major investors. Eventually, in addition to the investment group as a whole, they became fixated on a few in particular.

"I'm getting too old for this crap." The more-salt-than-pepper-haired man sat impatiently in the conference room at the Santa Barbara Police Department. He loosened his belt buckle one hole to ease the pressure building from his seasoned gut, and one that accurately reflected three decades of traveling around for the Bureau. "Why didn't you stop me from ordering that second cheeseburger at that burger joint?"

"I guess you stumbled upon the reason why they named that place Compulsion Burger. You revealed yours and overate."

"Maybe so." He patted his belly. "But at least I enjoy the finer things in life, Ms. Garden Salad. How can you function on ninety-percent rabbit food?"

"I have no choice," the slender, fit agent said, pointing to her partner's gut. "One of us has to be able to chase the bad guys."

"Ha, funny," he fake-chuckled. "Good to hear that you're past the awkward silence of our honeymoon period."

Holly grinned, refraining from further jabs at the easy target.

The two federal agents sat side by side on the hard, wooden chairs, waiting in the fourteen-by-eighteen-foot meeting room. The air-conditioner puffed at a low speed while a ceiling fan helped distribute the fresh air. Unfortunately for the feds, the comfort of the chilled air didn't make the chairs any less unpleasant. The senior agent squirmed side to side on his chair, trying to fend off the onset of hemorrhoids.

The suits had dropped into the Spanish-styled building on East Figueroa Street unannounced, so their level of patience was a little higher than usual, which was none. A few days prior, they had called the SBPD Captain to let him know they'd be in town within the week and would stop by in person to provide more details. In the interim, they only told him that they were looking into some possible financial improprieties of one or more of Santa Barbara's prominent citizens in connection with the massive resort development several miles up the coast. It was a minor attempt at professional courtesy, but coming from the feds, it was quite a bit.

The police headquarters, conveniently located one block from the historic courthouse, was an architectural compliment to the white stucco, red Spanish tile roof theme that ran abound in the American Riviera. A fitting atmosphere for the unexpected Spanish Inquisition the two feds were about to undergo.

The elder fed glanced at his *Citizen Men's Eco-Drive Pryzm Chronograph* watch. A gift he received on his thirtieth anniversary with the Bureau, his old school tendencies appreciated that it was powered by light and required no wires or plugs for charging. It had a stainless-steel case with an azure blue dial, a scratch resistant sapphire crystal, and silver tone luminescent hands and index hour markers, with Bluetooth compatibility and phone search capabilities adding icing to the cake.

But to this baby boomer, none of that mattered as much as the fact that the time piece did not need to be wound, nor did it need a battery to be replaced every couple years. A simple man with simple tastes. He liked plain, chocolate cake. No icing, no cute messages, no frills whatsoever. Just frickin' plain chocolate cake.

The door opened. A tall, thin clean-shaven man in his early sixties entered. The door swung closed behind him and he greeted his guests. "Hello, I'm Captain Stephen Weeks."

The two feds stood and extended their arms. Not surprisingly for a man with a wife and five daughters, he shook Agent Hurley's hand first. Before she could introduce herself, her partner spoke for her.

"Good afternoon, Captain Weeks. This is my partner, Agent Holly Hurley." He paused, waiting for his shake. "And I'm Agent Wayne Allenby. We spoke on the phone a couple days ago."

"Yes, of course. Welcome to our coastal paradise. Please, take a seat."

The three sat in unison, with the captain seated opposite the partners. Before the feds could provide any details of their visit, the door opened again, and two men entered. The older of the two spoke first. "Captain, you asked for us?"

"Yes, please take a seat." The boss pointed to the two seats to his right, then introduced his employees. "Agents Allenby and Hurley, I'm going to have a couple of my officers join us. This is Detective L. Morris Corsetti. We call him Elmo. And this is Officer Tom Wilkey, soon to be our newest detective on the force."

Heads nodded. The detective sat to the right of his boss; the officer sat to the right of his future partner.

"Captain, with all due respect," Agent Allenby said, "we need to keep this on a need-to-know basis."

"Understood. These are my two most trusted people on the streets. Corsetti is my senior detective, with over twenty-five years with the SBPD and Wilkey will likely be sitting behind my desk someday. If I need to know, they need to know. I trust them with my life."

"I can respect that. But we need to keep our circle tight; nobody outside this room until I say otherwise." Allenby gave a nod to his partner. She nodded back, looked down at a closed manila folder, then slid it to the captain in a dramatic fashion.

"The first two pages give a summation, to give you the gist," explained Hurley. She made eye contact with the captain giving him the okay. Weeks glanced down, reached for the file, slid it closer, then looked back at Agent Hurley. She continued. "It's a hefty file. You can review the rest of it when we're done here."

Captain Weeks looked Hurley in the eyes, then Allenby. Allenby nodded. Weeks opened the file and scanned the first page, then the second. His eyebrows raised. He turned back to page one, then ready the two pages in their entirety. He slid the file to his right. Corsetti mimicked his boss, then Wilkey did the same. After they all reviewed the synopsis, Captain Weeks spoke first.

"Wow, these are serious allegations."

Agent Allenby remarked, "We don't investigate jaywalking," demeaning the city personnel in the process.

"What he means is, yes, this *is* serious." Agent Hurley was new school, insisting on avoiding the jurisdictional pissing match between the feds and local law enforcement. He'd never admit it, but Allenby respected her for it.

Detective Corsetti threw in his feedback. "Serious allegations against leading members of our community, no less."

"So, here's where we are." More eloquent and organized, Hurley took over. "We're at the inception of our investigation and haven't quite broken this open. We're fairly certain that this may be just the tip of the iceberg. We're talking financial malfeasance via shady business operations, falsified legal documents, extortion, money laundering, and possibly more. And for one or more of the public figures, some of this may tie into some campaign financing violations. We also found a distant link between the primary investment group and a small chain of casinos in Vegas, rumored to have direct ties to the mob."

"Do you know if the whole group is in the know?" Tom asked. "Do you think they're all bad seeds?

"No, we don't." Agent Hurley fiddled with her dark shades on the tabletop. "We haven't been able to decipher who's in the know. It could be the entire group; it could be just one or two of them. Between the countless shell corporations and the global spread of offshore bank accounts, we're still trying to pinpoint the who. We're talking Cayman Islands' accounts, Swiss accounts, Bermuda accounts, even Belize; you name it."

"Do you know what local businesses might be involved? Do you know when this started? Do you know what the end game is? Do you know who is the top dog behind this? Do you know if any local law enforcement officers are on the take? Do you have any direct proof of any elected officials being involved? Are you going to request an injunction to put a halt on the development?" The three SBPD lawmen fired away with question after question, shouting over one another, giving no time for the feds to respond.

"Gentlemen, gentlemen," Agent Allenby broke in. "Please. Once we identify the whats and the hows, it should be a lot easier to narrow down all the who's. We've got to follow the money and see where it leads us. And given your first-hand knowledge of the potential suspects, we can expedite getting to the bottom of this with your help."

"Do you have a front-runner as to who your primary suspect is?" TW asked.

"Possibly," answered Agent Hurley. "But right now, it's just a working theory, and a weak one at that."

"Who is it?" Detective Corsetti waited anxiously for a response.

"Since it's just a working theory, we don't want to say," responded Agent Allenby. "We'd like to get your fresh perspective once you all have had a chance to look deeper into this. Your familiarity with these people can go a long way in narrowing our target. After that, we can share our theory with you."

Chapter Thirty

30

The building was quiet, dark, and secluded. For security, the outside exits to the building automatically locked anytime the doors were closed. Breaking in wouldn't be easy, but to a trained operative, it wouldn't be challenging. Downtown Santa Barbara was a dense, small area. Seeing a cop car or two on patrol within a ten-minute period was commonplace, and thus of major concern.

The plan was straightforward; cut the power to the building to make sure the cameras were inoperable, get in the office, open the safe, grab the contents and get out. That was the plan. Quick, simple, and succinct. Well, simple with a major hitch; he didn't know the code to the safe. He knew it was a digital entry safe, and he knew the code contained six numbers, but that was the extent of what he knew. The rest was a hunch.

Six numbers for the code meant the possibility of 720 combinations. With an average submission time of three seconds to enter a combination, that meant it could take 2,160 seconds; in other words, thirty-six minutes to open the safe.

Unfortunately, he didn't have the luxury of thirty-six minutes, or even six minutes, for that matter. When he cut the power, it would trigger the alarm. When the alarm was triggered, it alerted the police department. After the police department was alerted, they would send a unit. After a unit was dispatched, the closest unit would arrive at the scene. And statistically, the closest unit could be there in three to five minutes.

He dressed the part; dark jeans, black shoes, a black hoodie, and black leather gloves. He parked one block up and one block over from the target location, in a public parking spot with plenty of other cars so as not to draw unnecessary attention to his getaway vehicle.

He shut down the power at the outdoor breaker panel.

The prowler pulled a universal key tool from his back pocket and used it to enter through a back door, far from a street-eye view. He had to travel light to ensure his mobility and speed; a sports watch on his wrist set to stopwatch mode to track his time, a small military-grade flashlight, and a duffle bag to transport the contents of the safe. He had been in the building before and strode his route to get a workable estimate of how long it would take him to get in, get to the safe, and get out. But with all the planning in the world, he still couldn't account for all of his time. The wild card was the unknown variable—entering the correct code into the safe. If he guessed it correctly, it would take him three seconds to open the safe; but if the combination gods were against him, he'd leave in cuffs.

The office tenant had the commercial-grade electronic safe installed when no one else was present. The installer was brought in from out of town and paid a healthy installation fee to ensure discreetness and privacy. Strategically placed in the wall behind a large painting, the safe was further hidden and disguised by a hinged cabinet door designed to blend with the wall-papered wall, invisible to the naked eye, and of which only the owner and the installer knew of its existence.

The safe was powered by one 9V battery, with the battery compartment located below the keypad and accessible from the outside of the safe even when the safe was locked. The keypad had an illumination feature. This allowed the buttons to be seen even in complete darkness, and supported a stealth mode, allowing the operator to turn off all audible feedback for silent operation. To defend against pry attacks, the two-inch-thick door was equipped with a side locking bolt mechanism that engaged two large, one-and-a-half-inch cylindrical steel locking deadbolts, preventing door removal during a forced entry attempt. Simply put, the code was needed to open the safe.

His black sneakers didn't sneak so well. The rubber bottoms squeaked loudly with every step along the freshly waxed hallway floor. He scooted at a fast walker's pace. The main compartment of the canvas duffle bag swung from front to back underneath his swinging left arm, held up by the adjustable, detachable strap which crossed over his chest and pulled on his right shoulder. With his right hand, he pointed the military-grade tactical LED flashlight on the floor, about fifteen feet in front of his fast-paced strides.

Although he was moving at a much faster pace, the route seemed much longer than it had when he had practiced his trial run. The building was equipped with safety nightlights that ran along the hallway walls, about two feet up the wall and spaced every twenty feet. Backed up by a small generator, they shined directly onto the floor at a forty-five-degree angle.

He reached the office door without incident. It was time to assess his progress, A glance at his wristwatch aided by the flashlight verified his estimate; forty-two seconds. As he had expected, the office door was locked. He placed the flashlight in his mouth and bit down, then reached into his right rear pocket and pulled out a six-inch quick-pick knife, designed for a quick, easy, and non-destructive way to open the locked interior office door.

The hooded thief shoved the thin, flexible blade in the back of the molding stop and slid the blade to retract the latch. A successful click sounded. He replaced the handy tool back in his pocket with his right hand and grabbed the doorknob with his left. He slowly turned the knob, then froze.

In the distant outdoor air, the faint sound of a siren was heard, increasing in volume. It was approaching the building. He only breathed, and with his death grip squeezing the life out of the doorknob and his eyes now closed, he listened intently. Only ninety-seven seconds had passed since he cut the power that would have triggered the silent alarm. How bad could his luck be for the police to arrive in less than two minutes?

"No way!" he whispered to himself, ready to make a mad dash to exit the building.

The siren roared by the building and continued up the street, taking the reverberating ocean air with it. The good news for the intruder was that it was only an ambulance. The bad news was, he had wasted thirteen seconds frozen like an Otter Pop.

Focused and back on track, he entered the office and rushed to the picture on the wall. Time was of the essence. He glanced at his watch again, illuminated by the flashlight chipping away at his front teeth, making sure not to lose track of his time. Both hands reached around the picture on the wall with the makings of a bear hug. Slightly separating the framed artwork from the wall, he quickly felt for any trip wire. Clear.

The gloved hands removed the picture from the wall and placed it on the floor, leaning it up against a credenza positioned nearby. Absent the thirteen seconds squandered, he was making good time, with no hitches or glitches. Nothing but busy wallpaper covered the wall in front of him. As if omniscient, he quickly pressed the middle section of the wall of where the painting had hung, and a secret cabinet door magically popped open, revealing a safe.

With the keypad staring him in the face, the moment of truth was upon him; the moment that would make or break his plan, and with it, make or break his future. The mystery combination. The unknown variable. The wild card. The code. Six random digits stood between him and the rest of his life.

"Woo-woo-woo," a piercing siren resonated from the street and penetrated through the double-paned glass of the two office windows that flanked the wall safe, about two feet from each side.

The prowler snatched the flashlight from his mouth with his left hand, shined it on the floor, then leaned to his right to glance out the window. This time, it wasn't a false alarm. The cops had arrived. A marked unit parked in front of the building, with lights circling and flashing as if someone had escaped from Alcatraz. The two front doors opened, and uniformed legs swung out from the police car.

He straightened himself and stood face to face with the safe. He stared at the safe and the safe stared back at the burglar who was prepared to violate its privacy. He heard three car doors slam shut.

Even if the cops took their sweet time, they'd be checking that office in no more than three minutes. The thief had three seconds to decide. Whatever he opted to do would determine his fate forever. Leave without trying to crack the safe and leave behind with it any hope of securing the fruits of its content or leave in the back of a squad car? What was it going to be? It certainly didn't seem like much of a choice.

***

T-DUB AND HIS partner were on routine patrol in the downtown area when they received the dispatch. The closest unit near the location arrived within minutes of the call. TW parked his marked *Dodge Charger* out front on the street, and the occupants approached the building with pseudo-caution, for this was not the first time they had responded to a silent alarm at this location.

The older building was equipped with a newer alarm system after its most recent renovation, but it still didn't prevent it from sending out false alarms on a fairly routine basis. Most notably, the biggest flaw was that the alarm was designed to be triggered by a mere power outage. That was fine if a burglar tried to cut the power to the building to victimize it, but not so much so when the circuit breaker tripped on its own. All it took was a heavy storm or some other unsuspecting occurrence, and the

SBPD would continue to waste resources on the building that cried wolf.

"Derek," TW said to his partner, "you go around to the back entrance and clear from the first floor up, and I'll go in the front and clear from the top floor down."

TW walked up to the front of the building. Six strides from the entrance, he drew his weapon and a flashlight, then turned around to the civilian to his six. "You, stay behind me and don't make a sound after we enter. In the past, we've only had false alarms at this building, but you never know."

"This is pretty exciting. It looks like I picked a good night to have my first ride-along with you."

"Stay close to me," TW cautioned. "Remember, I'm the one with the badge and a gun."

"Don't worry," Josh replied, leaning on his crutches and holding up a badge with his left hand, and flexing his right bicep. "I have my D.A. badge and I'm always packing my guns."

TW looked at his friend, shook his head, and then stepped up to the door. "Your crutches can do more harm than your guns. So, just stay behind me, Rambo. I'm getting sick of visiting you in the hospital."

Other than the safety lights, no other lights were on. The officers tried the switches, but nothing worked. They would clear the building with the use of their flashlights, then check the breaker box. This had to have been the tenth time TW and his partner had responded to this building's alarm, so they had it down to a science.

Pacing deliberately down the hallways, led by his flashlight and trailed by his friend, TW checked each office door along the way. Closed and locked, closed and locked, closed and locked, closed and unlocked.

The future detective cracked open the door to uncover what was amiss. He entered with his gun and flashlight drawn. Now feeling warier in the dark empty hallway, Josh shuffled in and shadowed Officer Wilkey. Starting right to left, TW shined his flashlight around the room. Everything seemed to be in order; nothing unkempt nor did anything appear displaced.

The officer's flashlight focused on the artwork behind the desk and edged closer to get a better look as if something appeared off.

"What?" Josh said anxiously. "What is it?"

TW lifted his flashlight and used the back end of it to push up the bottom left end of the frame an inch, making it level and symmetrical with the two windows on each of its sides.

"Who are you," Josh snickered, "Detective Adrian Monk?"

"Who?" TW finished scanning the room.

"You know, *Monk*? The obsessive-compulsive, genius detective from the most brilliant TV show ever!"

"Sorry partner. You know how you hate to watch law shows because you're a lawyer? Well—"

"Got it," Josh gave a nod, understanding why TW had never given the show a chance. "But T-dub, seriously, you gotta check it out. Cop show or not, it's the best show ever! Hands down! Let me put it in sports terms I know you'll appreciate." Josh's volume increased, indicative of his passion for the show. "Your favorite TV show ever is like a good high school baseball team and *Monk* is like the '27 Yankees or the '75 Cincinnati Reds."

"Really?" TW conceded. "Okay, enough said. I'll check it out. Now, enough with the fake cop show. Can we get back to my real cop life?"

"Yes, of course. Sorry about the sidebar."

TW and his sidekick finished the sweep of their half of the building and met up with Officer Rodriguez. Officer Rodriguez found nothing suspicious. Same with Officer Wilkey. They checked the breaker box, and the main breaker was off. Same as it was on every other prior occasion. They double-checked the outside doors to the building to make sure they were closed, exited out the back door, and headed back to the squad car. Another false alarm.

A few steps from the back door, Josh heard a metal clank when his right shoe hit the walkway. He stopped, looked down, and lifted his foot.

"What is it?" TW zoomed his flashlight to the ground where Josh had stepped. Josh squatted down and picked up his discovery, a silver dollar.

"Sweet!" Josh smiled, flipped the coin, and placed it in his front pocket. "Who said crime doesn't pay?"

The joke was so cheesy, the three crime fighters couldn't help but laugh.

Now a dollar richer, Josh offered his two cents. "For such a prominent building, you'd think they'd get that alarm system fixed."

Chapter Thirty-One

31

J osh looked at his watch for the hundredth time that day. When he wasn't in court, time appeared to stand still during his working day. The fast-paced hustle and bustle of the criminal court system made desk work mind-numbing in comparison. Despite that, Josh made the most of his time. He painstakingly prepped cases all day long, until the last two hours. He specifically set aside that time to probe more into the world's most mysterious and dangerous misdemeanor case—*State v. Knowles*.

For a change of scenery, Josh moved himself to the office library. Not only did it have a computer workstation, but it also housed a plethora of reference books detailing the history of Santa Barbara County. He started by researching the area up the coast designated for the new resort development, and more particularly the parcel of land where he and TW looked a bullet square in the eye. There had to be a connection between it and the trail of violence shadowing Nick Knowles. Josh just had to figure out what that was before the trail ended at his doorstep.

The determined Deputy D.A. searched tirelessly on the computer. Punching in query after query, he took somewhat of a shotgun approach, hoping that something might jump out. His mind was leaping all over the place, hopping from one stream of thought to another, giving him a headache akin to motion sickness.

"Man," he said to himself, pinching his bottom lip. "Come on. Think! Who's behind this and how does it all tie together?"

Just then, Brenda Dyer hustled into the library. She was out of breath as if she just had completed a triathlon. "There you are! I've been looking all over the office for you."

"I've been walking with crutches so long; I move like a gazelle."

Brenda was one of three criminal investigators employed by the District Attorney, and the only female one. She was in her mid-fifties and single, had shoulder-length, auburn-colored hair, and was somewhat of a fashionista. She maintained a certain elegance and showcased her intellectually sophisticated style by wearing cat-eye-shaped *Prada* eyeglasses. The seasoned professional had dedicated the last sixteen years to the office, and her stellar research abilities set her apart from the other investigators for needle-in-a-haystack-related tasks. Josh knew it and made valuable use of her skill set.

"So, whatcha got for me?" said Josh, hopeful that she had something that could help him get over the hump.

"Here you go," Brenda said, handing a report to the prosecutor. "I'll give you the skinny, then you can go over the report more thoroughly and let me know if you have questions. So, it turns out that guy was in the system as a child. He bounced around from foster home to foster home. Seems as though he had a tough go of it. However, I came across several gaps in his history, probably because his time was before they started keeping digital records. And that Timothy Schafer, he shows every sign of having fallen off the face of the Earth."

Looking puzzled, Josh asked, "What do you mean?"

"All records of him suddenly ceased when he was in college in his early twenties, shortly after his parents died. It could be a situation of having some records under seal, or possibly in conjunction with being kept private by more questionable means. I asked some long-time residents around town who might've known his parents, but those that did had no idea what happened to him after his parents died when he was in college."

"Interesting. Thank you, Brenda," said Josh, opening the folder containing Brenda's report. "This definitely helps. Some more research, and a few phone calls, and perhaps I can get past this roadblock in our investigation."

Brenda drifted toward the doorway and said, "Let me know if you need anything else." Before Josh could thank her again, she closed the door behind her.

"Hmm, foster care," muttered Josh. "I wonder if, hmm. Or maybe—" Deep in thought, he wavered, then read about halfway down the first page of the report when his phone vibrated. He answered it. His friend-turned-investigative partner was on the other end.

"Hey J.R.," Being a man who lived by his initials, TW sometimes called Josh by his. "What time are you leaving work today? I've got some more info on the case, so we need to talk."

"I'm heading out around five. But Kristen is coming over. I told her I would cook dinner for her since she just got released from the hospital and is lacking in energy. I've gotta pick up some groceries on my way home, so I'll get enough for the three of us. Why don't you come over around six?"

"Are you sure?" asked TW. "I don't want to interrupt anything."

"Interrupt?" Josh said. "Dude, it's Kristen. Just one of the gang. I'll see you at six."

"Just Kristen," TW laughed. "Da Nile ain't just a river in Egypt. So, what can I bring?"

"How about some iced tea for Kristen, and some IPAs for you and me? And please don't say anything like that to Kristen."

"Done and done. And don't worry my friend, I've got your six, and I'll see you at six."

***

A FEW HOURS later, Josh was dicing some onions on a cutting board on his kitchen island, listening to jazz, and awaiting his guests. He loved to cook, following in the footsteps of one of his dad's greatest passions. Not near the top chef level of the late Jack Rizzetti, Josh's friends knew him to be able to whip up a tasty meal from time to time.

Josh's Mediterranean-style kitchen was appealing in that it both provided a relaxing ambiance for guests as well as an inspirational setting for the novice chef. Lively, bright colors on the textured walls were used for accents and set a nice contrast to the engineered hardwood floor, colored in a lighter shade. Looking up, the dark faux wood exposed beams on the vaulted ceiling capped the old-world vibe and combined with the smell of minced garlic, transported visitors to a charming little town in Sicily.

It was about five minutes to six when his doorbell rang. He looked at his watch. It must be Kristen, he thought, because T-dub was always right on time. Earlier, Josh had offered to pick her up, but she insisted on catching a ride-share so he could get started on their meal.

"Come in," he hollered. "Door's unlocked."

He was right and wrong. It was Kristen and TW. They opened the door.

"Hey guys, come in." Josh sounded surprised. "T-dub, I can't believe you're early."

"I stand by my policy," TW chuckled. "But I called Kristen and told her I'd pick her up on the way here. And you know her policy; if you're not early, you're late. So here we are, a little early."

"Please, have a seat," Josh said. TW placed the drinks on the island. A gallon of sweet, iced tea and a six-pack of State Street Brewery IPA. "Thanks for bringing the drinks."

TW had already made his way to the cabinet and was pouring a glass of tea for Kristen. Following in Josh's footsteps, Kristen now ambulated around on crutches thanks to a shattered foot. She took a seat in Josh's recliner, sinking into the oversized chair. TW handed a drink to her, grabbed a bottle opener, and popped open a beer for Josh, then for himself.

"Can I help?" asked Kristen.

"No, thank you," Josh said, pointing the knife at the recliner. "Kick your feet up. You guys relax. I got this."

TW smiled after a giant whiff. "Smells great. What's on the menu?"

"My dad's famous pasta sauce served over penne pasta, with a side of garlic bread."

"Oh, that ricotta and olive oil-based sauce. I love that!" Kristen raised her glass. "Jack it up!"

Josh and TW reciprocated, "Jack it up!"

"T-dub, you wanna grab that?" Josh pointed to a serving platter on the island, covered with baked bruschetta slices that were topped with olive oil, minced garlic, diced tomatoes, shredded Parmesan cheese, balsamic vinegar, and a sprinkle of basil. The smell was heavenly. TW served Kristen a piece before he placed the platter on a side table within her reach. Then, he shoved two in his mouth.

"So," Kristen snickered, "I guess we're carb loading to give our thought process a boost."

"Seriously," TW mumbled with his mouth full, swiveling on a bar stool in front of the granite island, facing Kristen, then Josh.

Josh cooked. The three laughed, ate, and drank. The food was delicious, if Josh did say so himself, and he did. "Your dad would be proud," Kristen complimented. And rather than voicing his compliments to the chef for the fine, home-cooked Italian meal, TW wore his. Comparable to the aftermath resulting from dripping mustard off a hot dog, TW had pasta sauce splattered over the front of his shirt from shoveling food faster than his mouth could chew. Josh knew that was his pal's way of saying kudos to the chef.

The conversation jumped back and forth between their topics of choice and the perplexing Knowles case. "That dreaded, baffling case," Josh kept repeating in his head. Officer Wilkey shared what he knew and divulged what information he could from what he had learned from the FBI. Josh shared what he knew. They both shared with Kristen what they both knew collectively. And from what Kristen lacked in factual knowledge of the case, she made up for with her thought-provoking questions.

"So, I take it you looked into the transactional history of that parcel of land purchased for the new development?" Kristen asked. "Where did it lead you?"

"I still haven't pinpointed that," Josh said. "I came across a couple of shell corporations but haven't yet figured out their true source. I was able to track down a phone number of the previous owner, you know, the great uncle of Doctor Overman's partner."

"Any luck?" Kristen asked.

"He's an older gentleman. He said he was confused and then pissed off by the whole process. Claimed that he got screwed in the deal. Although he sold to a corporation not knowing who owned it, he did remember meeting with a silver-tongued individual who convinced him to sell after the old man began to waffle right before the closing. Described him as a well-dressed professional, around forty, driving an expensive sedan. Sounds like every male real estate agent in town, so that wasn't much to go on. He insisted he wouldn't be able to point him out if he saw a photo. 'Looked like most middle-aged, rich white guys around here,' he said."

"Speaking of that land," TW stated, "the other day you were about to tell me about what you learned from Kendall about some old case. But before you could, we got sidetracked by that bullet sizzling past our heads."

Kristen yawned. "Fill us in, and then we gotta head out. I'm sorry, but I'm exhausted."

"That's right!" Josh said, responding to TW.

"Speaking of Kendall Jackson," Kristen interrupted, "I could go for a nice Merlot right now, but I can't 'cause of the meds they have me on." Kristen smiled. "I'm sorry. You were about to say—"

"I know you need the rest, so I'll cut to the chase." Josh continued. "So, Kendall had a kidnapping case about twenty-five years ago that he had to dismiss due to lack of evidence. A twelve-year-old boy went missing after apparently getting hit by a vehicle. Anyways, a key piece of evidence was blood found at the scene. This was before DNA came into play, so the evidence was based on blood type."

Josh took a breath, then a swig of beer.

"Okay," TW said anxiously. "We're listening."

"So, they found two blood types, one was a common blood type, the other was AB negative, which is the most uncommon blood type in the world. Less than one percent of people have it. Well, a couple of days after the accident, the boy turned up. He had total retrograde amnesia. Couldn't remember squat. Well, it turned out the boy was the one with the AB negative blood."

Kristen and TW looked at each other with confusion. Then they both looked at Josh.

"Okay, I'll bite," said Kristen. "What in God's creation does this have to do with your case?"

"Maybe nothing," Josh responded with a straight face, then held a long pause.

"Out with it," TW insisted. "You didn't tell us all of that for nothing. There's gotta be something more."

"Okay, so how's this for something?" Josh set his beer down and peered at his two friends. "That case was twenty-five years ago, involving a twelve-year-old boy with AB negative blood. Nicholas Knowles is thirty-seven years old—meaning twenty-five years ago he was twelve years old—and he has AB negative blood. Same as the blood type on the mysteriously missing blood report from my case."

"What the—" TW's jaw dropped.

"AB negative blood," Kristen mumbled, looking deep in thought. "Where did I see that? AB negative. Hmm, AB negative," she repeated softly, with her right-hand fingertips pressing up gently against her tilted forehead.

"Yes, AB negative," Josh answered. He stared at his best friend, recognizing that look. Her wheels were in motion, with her impeccable memory starting to process information. He knew just to wait, so he waited. TW was about to say something, then Josh held up his hand. They both sat tight. What seemed like minutes, was only a couple of seconds. Then, she spoke.

"OMG," she whooped. "I need to tell you something!" She paused and bit her right thumb. "But I can't!"

"What do you mean you can't?" TW cried. "If you know something important, you have to tell us. Josh's life depends on it. Heck, your life depends on it!"

"She can't!" blurted Josh, immediately understanding why. "I'm guessing it's attorney-client privileged information, isn't it?"

Kristen nodded. "Truer words have never been spoken, my friend."

"I don't suppose it falls within an exception?" Josh's voice faded, prepared for disappointment.

Kristen looked ready to burst but simply shook her head. Josh knew she wouldn't break a client's trust, nor did he expect her to. TW, however, was a little less empathetic.

"Okay, counselors. I get it. You're bound by your ethical code. I know that and respect the heck out of both of you for your high moral character. You are probably the two most ethical people I know. But you're also the two smartest people I know. So, no pressure; but figure something out."

TW looked back and forth at the two like he was watching a Wimbledon finals tennis match. His head bobbed back and forth, back and forth, hoping the volley would end in a game-winning, match-winning, grand slam-winning point. Unfortunately, at least from his perspective, the tournament favorite hit the ball into the net, resulting in a deuce point. The never-ending match continued.

"Sorry, my friend," Josh said to TW. "You understand. After all, you're a cop. You know that integrity is everything. Don't worry, at some point we'll solve this mystery."

"I get it," TW said. "And you're right, we'll figure this out eventually. I just hope when we do, we're all still alive to see it."

Kristen stood up and turned to her friends. "Joshua, thank you for an amazing meal. T-dub, shall we?"

TW looked bummed, but thankful, nonetheless. "Sure," he said, giving Josh a handshake combined with a left arm hug. "Thanks for dinner bro."

Kristen leaned over her crutches and gave Josh a hug as TW opened the front door and waited for Kristen.

Kristen labored to the doorway, then stopped and turned back to Josh.

"Hey Josh," Kristen said, "thanks again for cooking for me and Colonel Mustard. Lately, you've been working harder than a keyboard synthesizer in the 1980s. So, as soon as we close this door, go lay down and close your eyes, and then count from one to five, because you've had your senses working overtime." She gestured for TW to walk out first, then she winked at Josh and said, "Goodnight, Josh" and closed the door behind her.

"Goodnight." Josh hollered through the closed door, then waved to his friends even though they couldn't see him.

Josh was about to flip on the television to watch sports highlights when he realized he too was exhausted. Heeding Kristen's advice, he puttered to his bed, and with arms extended out, did a back flop onto the middle of his bed, bouncing up and down, with the back of his head sinking comfortably into his fluffy pillow. He closed his eyes, then thought about what Kristen had said.

He laughed out loud, "Colonel Mustard," picturing T-dub's stained shirt. "Huh," he said to himself, "Colonel Mustard. I love the game of *Clue*."

He felt more relaxed, but that was short-lived. He heard a car fly by in the night, blasting its horn. He smelled the garlic from his dad's pasta sauce as it still lingered in the air. He felt a sharp pain in his abs, still experiencing the aftereffects of his gunshot. Finally, in a flashback, he saw the SUV barreling toward his best friend.

Like flipping a switch, Josh immediately put his senses on hold and reflected. Kristen was right. He did have his senses working overtime. Obviously, she knew the stress he had been under and knew him well enough to know what he needed. So, realizing he couldn't go wrong by complying with her orders, he returned to relaxation mode. With his eyes still closed, Josh whispered to himself, "one two three four five." The counting reminded him of a song, which then instinctively prompted Mr. 1980s to start singing it in his head.

The music and lyrics played in his brain, putting a smile on his face. Then suddenly, the song was cut short. And as if powered by space shuttle boosters, Josh shot up like a rocket and yelled—from both pain and excitement, "Kristen, you're a genius!"

Chapter Thirty-Two

32

J udge Stricker's court had a typical docket of any other weekday in which no trial was scheduled. A variety of misdemeanors and felonies were set for possible settlement, a couple of procedural motions, and one dispositive motion. On paper, the court's calendar was mundane. In practice, it was momentous. It was the dispositive motion that was of particular note. The State of California was dismissing the matter of *State v. Nicholas Knowles*.

Despite persistent search efforts by the entire D.A. staff, the incriminating DNA report that decidedly placed Nicholas Knowles at the scene of the accident was nowhere to be found. Undeterred by Mr. Knowles's failure to file a motion to dismiss the charges, the integrity of the prosecuting Deputy D.A. prevailed. Joshua Rizzetti assured the court and the defendant that he would dismiss the case on behalf of the State knowing that he did not have the requisite evidence to link the named defendant to the charged offenses. To Josh, doing the right thing invariably took precedence over getting a conviction. He expressed that philosophy often, and he walked the walk.

By and large, the dismissal of a victimless criminal case was so far below newsworthy it wouldn't make the footnote of a footnote on a police blotter. But this case was far from normal. Not in the case itself, but from the unexplained path of destruction that rippled after the impact of the one car accident. In a town with minimal overall crime, disproportionately less violent crime, and where murders occurred as often as a total solar eclipse, the press capitalized on the dramatics. After all, the mystery behind the tragic events surrounding the Knowles case remained unknown. The whodunit was unsolved. The why was undetermined.

Two local news cameras were set up inside the courtroom as soon as Deputy Graham unlocked the door. He directed the camera crew where they could drop anchor and warned them to keep quiet or else the Honorable Judge Robert Stricker would kick them out faster than a streaker at the Super Bowl.

The reporters got the same warning, but with a little less vinegar and a touch of honey, mostly if not solely because they were young, female, smoking hot, and flirtatious. Deputy Graham was a single father whose life revolved around his job, his daughter, and her volleyball, so a wink or two from an attractive female, let alone two, softened him quicker than butter in a microwave. In fact, rumor had it that reporter Danielle Cadley from Channel Six News, with her camera-friendly image and sweet southern accent, had charmed the gun from his holster a time or two. Deputy Graham had joked that one couldn't have a Graham cracker without wanting s'more.

Josh and Kendall sat at the prosecutor's table, with four stacks of files piled in front of them and teetering on the brink of collapse. A couple of flat-fee criminal defense attorneys hovered over them, eager to be the first to talk to the prosecutors, hoping to resolve their cases, rather than play the sit and wait game. Quick settlements computed to higher hourly rates, while waiting equated to lawyers earning a lower hourly pay.

The peanut butter and jelly lawyers spread throughout the courtroom, and being new to the practice, they enticed clients with their locked flat fees, providing them comfort in the agreed-upon fixed cost. The steak and lobster attorneys, seasoned in the practice, buttered up clients with their experience and could more easily justify their high hourly rates, regardless of the undetermined overall cost.

The last attorney in line checked in with the judge's clerk and sat on one of the empty leather chairs that lined the front of the bar. A couple of old, portly, but sharply dressed surf and turf attorneys sat at the defense counsel's table, chatting with one another, inevitably sharing embellished stories of the good ol' days. Nicholas Knowles, still unrepresented, sat on the last bench located in the rear inside corner of the courtroom, likely preparing for the quickest possible exit after his case's dismissal.

Court Clerk Mary Kay looked at her watch, then sneaked a peek at Deputy Graham, who was preoccupied on the hidden door behind the bench, inexorably waiting for it to crack open so he could bellow his line, "All rise!" The time slipped past 8:45 a.m. Judge Stricker, like most judges, rarely started court at exactly 8:30 a.m., making everyone wait for no apparent reason other than to demonstrate his authority. Typically, he appeared from behind the hidden door around 8:40 a.m., give or take a couple of minutes.

The clerk looked at her watch again. It showed 8:52 a.m. Perhaps the judge received an important phone call and was stuck on the line. Maybe it was regarding the recent change of venue motion filed in his court, in which he needed to confer with a judge from another county to determine which court was the proper venue. Yep. That was probably it, so she gave it another five minutes.

Five more minutes passed. Still, no judge. Deputy Graham made eye contact with Mary Kay. With his right index finger, he tapped his watch twice and then pointed to the back hallway. The clerk gave a nod, picked up her handset, and buzzed the judge's office phone. Five rings, no answer. She shook her head at Graham, got up, and disappeared behind the hallway door used by the unelected common folks, located between the witness stand and the door to the inmate holding cell adjacent to the jury box.

Kendall tilted over to his partner and whispered, "I wonder what the holdup is."

Josh muttered back, "My gut tells me something is wrong."

As if on cue, the instant the last word fell from Josh's mouth, a high-pitched scream resonated throughout the entire courthouse. Crystal shattered and animals scattered all over Santa Barbara County.

"What the h–! How did you do that?" Kendall stated as he and his partner jumped from their seats and trailed behind the gun-drawn Deputy Graham, who bolted into the hallway.

Eleven minutes later, Judge Stricker's chambers was littered with law enforcement: two detectives, three uniformed officers inside and two standing guard outside, a forensic pathologist, three members of the forensic team, and FBI Agents Allenby and Hurley. Courthouse chatter spread faster than COVID at a 2020 Trump rally.

Four days earlier, the possibility of suicide would have been out of the question, almost unfathomable. Judge Stricker was young, wealthy, successful, and on his way to the federal bench. His work hours were reasonable, and his social life was enviable. Country Club. Yacht Club. And more golf than a PGA tour professional. People with that kind of a life don't kill themselves, rather people kill to have that kind of life.

However, three days earlier, a slow leak aired its way into the mainstream gossip, directing itself toward the courthouse and in a straight path to Judge Stricker's chambers. Rumor had it that the FBI was in town investigating some financial improprieties, some of which linked to possible disclosure violations stemming from campaign contributions to local elected officials. At the forefront of those allegations were donations made to the judge during his most recent election to the bench.

As soon as Judge Stricker got wind of the speculation, he was on high alert. Undisclosed contributions to his campaign were just the tip of the iceberg. This could open up the books to his entire financial profile, if it hadn't been already, including an investigation into his most lucrative investment, Heaven's Vista Resort. Undisclosed campaign contributions funneled to a Ponzi scheme routed to a fraudulent business operation riddled with money laundering. If everything came out, that's what he was facing.

Each additional day after the rumors broke, his stress level became more evident. Usually even-tempered in court, he was snapping at staff, yelling at counsel, berating defendants, and ruling irrationally. His erratic behavior culminated with him holding Salvatore Perricone in contempt the day before when the most admired attorney in town entered the courtroom simply to get a signature on a contract from another attorney who was holed up in court all day.

The local bar association was incensed, and its members were walking on eggshells trying to avoid being the next casualty of the judge's wrath. A cough in court could get you ten days in jail and a five-thousand-dollar fine. God forbid you had to sneeze; you could be looking at the death penalty!

Kendall loaded the wheeled cart with the State's files and walked them back to the District Attorney's Office. He was bombarded with questions before the office door hit him in the butt. He couldn't provide much more detail than the vanilla phone call from the clerk's office that preceded him five minutes earlier, but surely his partner would be back with a bigger scoop when he returned. Meanwhile, Josh lingered in the back hallway to find out more details firsthand, hopeful that his buddy TW would be on the scene. Sure enough, he was.

Josh approached Judge Sticker's office and flashed his badge to the two uniformed officers guarding the door, then stopped shy of the doorway. They looked in, seeking confirmation. TW hollered out, "He's okay."

He had seen dead bodies before. He had stood in on several autopsies before. He had even studied blood spatter evidence before, in painstaking detail at the National District Attorneys' Association at Northwestern University School of Law in Chicago. But this was different and much closer to home.

Josh knew what to expect, but it didn't lessen the blow any. He almost came to tears from the reality of what was in front of him. It wasn't his first rodeo, but it was the first time he knew the cowboy. This wasn't a stranger lying in the street, or a corpse laid out on a cold metal table. It was someone he knew, and someone he saw and spoke with almost every day for the past several years.

TW was busy taking pictures of everything, assisting one of the forensic team members with the photos while one of them assisted the medical examiner with the body, and the other bagged some evidence. With law enforcement still in the initial stages of gathering the evidence, it appeared to Josh that the body had not been moved.

Josh knew he would not be welcomed for long. With two feds in the room, he was certain to get the boot, and soon. He figured he had about ten to fifteen seconds before his butt was out the door. For now, he needed to flip on his high-speed processor, snap mental pictures of the scene, take it all in and store it on his hard drive. He scanned the room quickly, taking quick cerebral photos that he could develop and dissect further at some other time.

Josh's brain went to work. The body was hunched over on the floor with his chair at his feet, consistent with falling from the chair after the gunshot. Hole on the left side of his head and a gun in his left hand, consistent with Judge Stricker being left-handed. A pool of blood beneath his head, consistent with a gunshot wound to the head. Blood spatter on the wall, window, chair, and floor, consistent with the judge seated in his chair behind his desk when he pulled the trigger. The desk appeared to be in order, clean and organized as usual. The custom letter box was in its corner, with what looked to be a blank piece of paper in it, perhaps typed with a line or two. Sixteen seconds. Done. Those were the obvious clues and all he had time to observe. He'd have to explore the details of the less obvious ones at a later time, and in a different place; namely the evidence room that resided in his head.

Agent Allenby lifted his head from the desk drawers and spotted the new guest. "Who's he?"

"Deputy District Attorney Joshua Rizzetti," TW volunteered, speaking up for his friend.

"Is he necessary?" Agent Hurley jumped in without even looking at Josh, trying to score brownie points with her senior partner. After the words left her mouth, she caught a glimpse of the eye candy and retracted her position. She had read about him online on the *Daily Press'* website, and now seemed eager to take her own shot at J.R. "If so, let's put him to work."

"D.A. Rizzetti," Detective Corsetti intervened, "it looks like we have a suicide here, so I don't think we're gonna need your services on this one. So, would you mind steppin' out please?"

"No, sir," Josh said. "I don't mind. I understand."

TW was standing just inside the office door, taking some photos of the length of the office from the entrance perspective. Josh whispered on his way out, "I'll catch you later T-dub."

Officer Wilkey avoided any possibility of creating a reason for the feds to launch an inquisition of him if they were to find out that he and the snooping prosecutor were pals, so he stuck with formality and nodded, "Mr. Rizzetti."

***

EIGHT HOURS EARLIER, the night was darker than most. A thick cloud cover erased any glimpse of a moonlit night, and the cool chill of the fall evening created a Halloween-like ambiance.

From day one, he had managed to keep his hands clean from first-hand dirt, at least uncontaminated from the blue-collar violence he had orchestrated. As for the white-collar improprieties, his hands were dirtier than a coffee-drinking pig, suffering from intestinal flu, rolling in a pile of manure in the middle of a rainstorm. But keeping his hands clean from direct violence was an absolute priority in his master plan. When all was said and done, financial malfeasance would be much easier to pin on someone else; but direct violence, not so much.

His contingency plan was a last resort, to be implemented only if necessary. If executed, the elimination of the most problematic loose end would be two-fold in purpose: hammer the final nail in the coffin in framing the most obvious suspect, and extinguish the growing flame burning up the real offender's tail. And as much as he would've loved to outsource his next violent deed to a professional gun-for-hire, knowledge by anyone else beyond the mastermind himself potentially could create an easy opportunity for an endless cycle of blackmail, not only extorting his wealth but derailing his future along with it.

Certain deeds, no matter how dirty, are best done as do-it-yourself projects, ensuring two things: precision and privacy. No clue could be left behind and no person could have any knowledge of it. His philosophy was simple and indisputable—the more people in the know, the more likely you'll reap what you sow.

Following a months-long series of planted evidence that had been carefully contrived in the event that the most knowledgeable and potentially dangerous loose end would need to be eliminated, the foundation had been laid. Nonetheless, the contingency plan was strictly a safety-valve, intended never to come to fruition.

The two had planned for the last installment when completion of the payee's task was imminent, and the payer made sure all the bases were covered. Under the ruse of safety and secrecy, they both insisted on meeting in the middle of the night, in the dark, with no possibility of witnesses; where the payer could transport the cash without the risk of being mugged or killed, and the recipient could collect with the same security. The recipient's office, at a time long after business hours, was the perfect place. Dark, secure, equipped with a safe for the loot and a gun in his top right desk drawer for protection.

Well-orchestrated in advance, the pawn guaranteed the maestro he would be alone, and the building would be void of any witnesses for both of their protection. The money was packed, and the exchange set. The hour was late, and the building was empty. The alarm was disengaged, and the video surveillance was disabled.

Stuffed duffle bag in hand, the payer entered the building through an unlocked door as arranged by his expecting co-conspirator. Primed to complete the transaction, he entered the building and labored his way up the stairs and down the hall as his stretched arm lugged the hefty sack. He cracked the door and slowly entered the office. Unnerved, the dark figure sitting about three feet behind the desk leaned forward in his chair, opened the top drawer, and reached inside.

"Don't shoot. It's me."

Per the financier's instructions, no overhead lights were to be turned on. The dimly lit desk lamp provided only enough light to avoid walking into a wall, bumping into some foreign object, or upon closer proximity, shooting a familiar face. He ambled toward the rear of the office and addressed the man rooted behind the desk.

"As we agreed, here is your final half." He lifted up the bag to the light to show proof of payment.

"How do I know it's all here? I want this to be our last clandestine meeting. Scratch that. I *need* this to be our last covert meeting," he insisted. "As I told you before, this is it for me. I want out of this game."

"Trust me, I guarantee this will be our last secret meeting. You have my word. If you don't trust me, you can count it for yourself." Walking to his left and around to the side of the desk, he plummeted the heavy bag on the floor to the immediate right of the occupied desk chair. "Go ahead, count it."

The beneficiary swiveled a quarter-turn to his three o'clock and leaned forward a bit. He looked up at the man standing two feet in front of the bag, who casually leaned against the desk supported by his right hand on the corner.

"Take a look. I even threw in some extra cash for your troubles," he instructed, pointing to the bag. "I want this to be done just as much as you do."

The eager accomplice leaned over the canvas lump and reached for the zipper at the far end of the duffle bag. As he unzipped the bag, the right hand resting on his desk smoothly slithered over and down a few inches and into the open top drawer. Just enough to grab the 9mm pistol. Hunched over, the greedy judge reached into the bag with both hands and thumb-flipped through one of the many wads of paper-band-wrapped cash. But before he suspected a thing, like the green currency paper fanning in his hands, his days were numbered.

The human tool was unsuspecting, and the master carpenter was meticulous. Having been used to the fullest extent, the instrument served its purpose and became expendable. The craftsman was leaving nothing to chance and no trace of any suspicious or incriminating evidence. He even had dressed the part. Long pants, slip-on shoes, and a long-sleeved shirt. Leather gloves and a hair net on his head, hidden underneath a ball cap.

He placed the gun. He pulled a 9 x 12-inch envelope tucked into the back of his pants, slid out a piece of paper, and set it in the letter box. He grabbed the bag. He left the dupe for dead and fled the scene.

A few minutes later, a shadow in the night dressed in black from head to toe entered the office. The figure scurried up to the side of the desk and hovered over it for a few seconds, doing something. Next, the shadow leaned over the body, reached down momentarily, and then floated over the side of the desk briefly. Done. The hooded trespasser scampered to the door and stopped beside the bookcase. Four seconds later, he exited the office, hightailed out of the building, and faded into the night.

Chapter Thirty-Three

33

Before the crack of dawn, Josh sat patiently waiting for his friend. Josh waited at the door before the coffee shop opened at 5 a.m. One of the baristas let him in nearly five minutes early, presumably annoyed that he had been peering in the locked glass door for more than ten minutes. Josh was always early. TW always arrived on the dot.

Josh stirred a tablespoon of cream and sugar, flavored with a dash of cinnamon, into his large coffee cup. The robust aroma of freshly brewed coffee beans invigorated the air, and Josh cherished every hazelnut-scented whiff. It was a pleasant change from the musty body odor he endured daily when the court officers piled orange-jump-suited prisoners into the courtroom.

Josh glanced at his watch, and it was ten seconds past five. He skimmed the room. Two baristas were scrambling around, preparing for the morning rush of caffeine-addicted early birds. A cute college coed, who undoubtedly kept the young adult males returning regularly for overpriced lattes, filled two glass sugar pourers and checked the napkin dispensers on the granite top coffee-prep island. Then, looking toward the entrance, he saw the door closing behind his law enforcement pal. They made eye contact.

"Good morning, T-dub."

"Morning, Josh. Let me grab a quick coffee."

"One step ahead of you, my friend. I gotcha one here." Josh lifted a large cup next to his.

"Of course you did," said TW. "Always one step ahead of everyone. Or more accurately, I should say, at least one step ahead. Thanks, bro." TW sat down opposite Josh at the thirty-inch round, cold metal table and took a sip of his black coffee, straight up. Formerly a cream and sugar kind of guy, years on the force converted TW to leaded coffee and leaded beer.

"Since we both have to get to work in a couple of hours, let's get right to it. And as you obviously have a lot more information from yesterday than me, why don't you start? But, before you begin, were you able to test that item I gave you?"

"Yes," TW responded, handing an envelope to his crime-prosecuting turned crime-solving partner. "Here's the report."

Josh opened the large manila envelope and, leaving the tested item in the envelope, pulled out the report. "Hmm, not surprised. But we'll discuss that later. For now, let's hear what you've got."

"Well, I just got word from the medical examiner; and she is leaning toward ruling it a suicide. The judge is left-handed. The gun was his, the shot was to his left temple, and blood spatter was around his body, indicating that he was shot where he was found. And most notably, no pun intended, he left a suicide note. But she is hesitant in reaching a conclusion because of the very limited gunshot residue found on the judge's left hand."

Josh took notes on a small notepad he brought as he listened closely to TW, straining to hear him over the steam-blowing frothing machine that hissed in the background. TW paused for a few, waiting for Josh's law school shorthand to catch up with him and for the steamer to take a coffee break.

"I know you had less than a minute to examine the scene, but what did your photographic memory tell you? Did anything jump out to you as being fishy?"

"Blood spatter!" said Josh.

"What's suspicious about blood spatter? If there was no blood spatter; now, that would be fishy. Pardon the insensitivity of the expression, but he blew his brains out, so blood spatter was all around him."

Josh removed the lid from his tanned coffee, then casually took a sip. He then thumped his cup on the table; not quite a slam, but just enough for some to spill over, scattering random drops of coffee on the table. Then he tore a blank piece of paper from the back of his notepad and placed it on the table, smack dab in the middle of the spilled coffee droplets. "Or was it?"

***

KRISTEN'S TRANSITION TIME from recovery mode to work mode was short-lived. Like Josh, she insisted on getting back to the grindstone as quickly as possible, and against the doctor's orders. To ease her transition, Mr. Perricone insisted she sticks with paperwork for a couple of weeks and avoids any client meetings, which often came with added stress. Whether it was hard-earned or through the dumb luck of inheriting it—ready to squander it; wealthy, successful people tended to be overly demanding on the firm, rightfully cautious, and concerned with protecting their wealth.

The typical clients who visited the prestigious firm of Perricone, Pocino, and Salvatore were adorned in professional attire. If not wearing a suit, then a sport coat, collared shirt, and expensive slacks were par for the course for the men, and expensive, fashionable attire for the women. *Christian Louboutin* pumps strode the office's hallways almost as frequently as they did a Paris runway.

Giorgio Armani, he was not. A rugged-looking character entered the firm's lobby drawing no attention. He wore a navy-blue ball cap—with "UCSB" cap letters in white, trimmed in gold—Aviator sunglasses, and a thick, full nest of a beard that was recently cut back, but still could stand to lose another inch or two to rescue any remaining birds nesting in the heavy brush.

The receptionist was on the phone, with her head facing down as she chicken-scratched a message on the firm-logoed, fancy notepad on her desk. She sensed a body in front of her, but rather than take a peek, she just held up her pointer to signal the visitor to wait. This was a gutsy and rude move on behalf of the newest receptionist to the traditional and proper firm. Lucky for her, there were no partners around to see it, or her first week would've been her last.

She hung up the phone and finished her note. "How may I help you?"

She looked up, and shock overcame her. The notepad upon which she wrote probably cost more than his entire wardrobe. Expecting to see the likes of a Wall Street-type, she found herself faced with a weather-beaten Grizzly Adams-type. Apparently determined to get all of her rudeness out of the way, she offended some more. "I'm sorry. The pawn shop is the next building over."

Impervious to insult, the atypical, potential client responded, "Oh, I'm here to meet with one of your attorneys. I need to speak with Kristen Laney about representation."

"I'm sorry. Ms. Laney is not meeting with any clients this week." And rather than asking the expected "Can I see if one of our other attorneys is available to meet with you?" her seemingly endless supply of insolence continued. She said nothing further, expecting he'd go away, and hopefully take his scent of Aqua Velva with him.

"It's urgent that I meet with her, please. I just need a few minutes of her time."

The soon-to-be ex-receptionist threw out her ultimate affront to rid the firm of this transient. "Is it a matter of life or death? If not, she's not available."

In the most serious voice, he answered "Actually, yes, it is!" He stared at the young, now intimidated and increasingly frightened greeter.

She clearly had met her match, and undoubtedly, he wasn't going anywhere. She conceded, scrambled to find Kristen's extension on the laminated list that rested on the right side of the reception desk, then buzzed her office. "Ms. Laney. There is a," she said, then paused to clear her throat, "gentleman here to see you. I'm sorry to bother you, but he says it's urgent."

"Please, Kristen is fine. Who is it?"

"Let me check." The receptionist looked up at the visitor. "Your name sir?"

"It's confidential. I'll tell her when I sit down with her."

She pressed a button on the phone and talked into her head-set. "He won't say, Ms. Laney. I'm sorry, I mean Kristen. He says it's confidential, but he'll tell you when he sits down to talk with you."

Kristen paused and thought. She then responded, "Okay. Please show him to the fishbowl. I'll be right there."

"I'm sorry Ms. Laney. Fishbowl?"

"Yes. That's what we call the smaller conference room with all-glass walls and doors. It's extremely visible, you know, like a fishbowl." Gambling by allowing an impromptu meeting with an unnamed potential client, and recovering from an attempted murder by an unknown source; Kristen hedged her bet.

"Yes, ma'am."

Kristen grabbed a colored-sticky tab and marked her stopping point in the contract she had been reviewing. Even her organizational gadgets were well-organized and had a specific place on her desk. No time of hers was ever wasted trying to find something, thereby maximizing her time to bill clients, which the partners loved. She did it out of efficiency; they loved it out of greed. Either way, it kept everyone happy.

By the time Kristen reached the fishbowl, the unexpected visitor was seated in one of the middle chairs of the large, oval table, with his back to the hallway. His ball cap was pulled down so low, he could've been faceless for all Kristen knew.

The conference room was about twenty-two feet wide and fifteen feet deep. A gorgeous, Italian marble, oval-shaped conference table highlighted the space, centered left to right and front to back in the middle of the room. It was flanked by eight comfortable executive chairs, upholstered with Amber-colored Italian leather, styled with swiveled high-back support, and soothed with padded armrests and a retractable footrest. Three sat on each side of the length of the table, and one chair each at the head and foot of the artistically elegant furniture piece. The wall opposite the glass barrier was decorated with three brilliantly colored LeRoy Neiman paintings. The expressionist artwork of famous athletes reflected the personality of the firm; wealthy, yet down-to-earth.

The mystery man was nothing if not consistent. He was guarded, obviously not wanting to be recognized by anyone walking by, and perhaps wishing to remain a mystery forever to all but his new attorney. Unknown to most, the attorney-client privilege could extend to the identity of a client if he so chose. And being a stickler for the ethics and formalities of the legal profession, Kristen could respect and honor that.

But as to the cryptic nature of this meeting, she stood on guard. Still suffering from the aftermath of her untimely encounter with mortality, Kristen understandably walked into the meeting with one foot out the door and one hand on the manual emergency pull handle.

"Good morning." Leaving her crutches at her desk to avoid appearing weak, she dragged her plastered foot into the conference room. She sneaked around the table to sit opposite her visitor, and with a panoramic view of the hallway, to ease her discomfort a bit. "My name is Kristen Laney. But apparently, you already know that." There was a slight familiarity to his face, but Kristen couldn't place if and where she had seen it. She waited for him to introduce himself, but he did not.

The brilliant, young attorney got the clue and sat down.

He skipped the pleasantries and cut straight to the chase. "Is what I tell you confidential?"

"Excuse me?"

"I want to consult with you and retain you as my attorney. So, is what I tell you privileged? You know, attorney-client privilege."

"Well yes, even if you don't retain me. Even a consultation has the protection of the attorney-client privilege." Kristen raised her eyebrows. "So, how may I help you Misterrrrr?"

"Knowles. Nicholas Knowles. You can call me Nick."

"You mean?"

"Yes, that Nicholas Knowles. The one that your best friend is prosecuting. The one who's been all over the news because of an alleged link between *State v. Knowles* and the death of Lee Templeton, the near death of Deputy D.A. Rizzetti, twice . . . and the near death of . . . well, you."

"Oh my gosh!" She took a deep breath. "Wow!" Kristen stopped in total shock; her mouth wide open. Her prospective client said nothing.

She gathered her composure and said, "I'm sorry Mr. Knowles, but I'm not a criminal defense attorney. I'm a business attorney. You know, like contracts, business formations, asset protection, some estate planning, those sorts of things."

"Yes, I understand that."

"And isn't the prosecution dismissing your criminal case anyway? In fact, wasn't the dismissal set for yesterday, but got postponed pending reassignment due to the tragic death of Judge Stricker? So, I'm not sure what I can do for you."

"You're well-informed, Ms. Laney. And I understand you're one of the best attorneys in town."

"Well, as you stated, Deputy D.A. Rizzetti is a close friend. And I appreciate your kind words. But—"

"Those are precisely the two reasons why I am here."

Kristen tilted her head slightly. "I'm not sure I follow."

"I have very simple, but specific requests of you. I'd like to retain your services, tell you about some things in confidence, consult with you on a legal matter, and then set up a meeting with you, me, and Deputy District Attorney Rizzetti. Can you do that?"

"Without knowing what you need my services for, I can't say for sure. And as to meeting with Deputy D.A. Rizzetti, it would depend on what it's about, and whether it's relevant to your legal needs. If I represent you, I have to look out for your best interests. And I'm not sure how meeting with your prosecuting Deputy D.A., who's already going to dismiss your case, would serve your best interests. I'm sure you've heard the saying, let sleeping dogs lie."

"You'll understand how, when I explain it all to you. But for now, I need for you to trust me, even though you have absolutely no reason to do so."

"I guess I can see if Mr. Rizzetti is willing to meet. We can try to schedule something for next week."

"I can't wait that long. It has to be today."

"Today! Why the rush?"

"Any delay and someone could get away with murder!"

"Murder!" Kristen swallowed the jawbreaker that had instantly formed in her throat.

She regained her poise, and doing what she does best, Kristen buckled her full-attorney-mode helmet and prepared for the ride. "Please understand and acknowledge that if you communicate to me that you have the intention of committing or covering up a crime or fraud, it won't be protected by the attorney-client privilege."

"Yes ma'am, thank you," he said. "Copy that. I've done my homework." He persisted. "So, can we meet with Mr. Rizzetti today?"

"Well, as luck would have it, I'm supposed to go out to lunch with him today." Kristen looked at her watch. "He actually should be here in about thirty minutes."

"Perfect. I'm ready to sign a retainer agreement and pay you cash right now. So, can I get started?"

***

THIRTY MINUTES LATER, the conference room phone buzzed, then a voice said, "Ms. Laney, Mr. Rizzetti is here for you."

"Thank you, Mackenzie. Please send him to the fishbowl."

"Yes, ma'am."

Under the security blanket of attorney-client privilege, Nick Knowles had divulged a lot of information to Kristen known by only two people in the world, and some of it, by only one—him. In doing so, he was able to provide her with just enough so that she could advise him as to the possibility and legality of what he hoped to accomplish.

At the same time, Knowles walked a fine line between actual facts and hypotheticals, careful not to put his newly retained attorney in the precarious position where she might be obligated to disclose information falling within the exception of attorney-client privileged communications. If he crossed the line, his attorney could sing like a canary, his plan would be blown, and he'd be caged like a bird. With everything on the line, he tip-toed gingerly.

The last part of Nick's plan was an add-on and not part of his original blueprint. It was during the course of implementing his original strategy that he came across newfound data. The newly acquired information fashioned an opportunity for a significant bonus reward, or in legalese, a windfall.

Nick had opened up to his attorney while cautiously avoiding any hint of his intention of committing or covering up a crime or fraud. He had obtained the ingredients, written his recipe, baked his dessert, and now waited for it to be cooled before consumption. He was determined to have his cake and eat it too, including the freshly added icing.

When Josh entered the fishbowl, he saw the back of a stranger facing Kristen. Reluctant to walk in on a client meeting, he stopped at the door. Kristen waived him in. Josh entered and Kristen's client turned to him and greeted the stunned prosecutor, "Hello, Mr. Rizzetti."

"Mr. Knowles?" Josh was stunned. There he stood in the fishbowl, in pursuit of his white whale; now being confronted by the live bait who was meeting with his sea goddess.

"Josh," Kristen said, "obviously you've met my client."

"Client?!" snapped Josh. "You know I'm already going to dismiss his case, right?"

"That's not why he's retained me," Kristen explained. "It's so much more than that. So much bigger than that. He wants to talk to you. He has a plan, but he needs our help. And I know you have a lot of questions, and well . . . he's got almost all the answers. I'm not sure you'll believe it."

"You'd be surprised by what I'd believe." Josh pulled a silver dollar from his pocket, held it up to his eyes, and said, "1984, the year you were born," then gave it a flip. "And you'd be astonished by what I already know."

The client checked his wallet, then all of his pockets. No coin.

Kristen stared at her client. Her client stared at Josh. Josh stared at the silver dollar, then flipped it again.

Nick's jaw dropped. "How in the world?"

Kristen shifted her focus back to Josh, anxious to hear more.

"For now, let's just say that I picked up on some clues and started to put the pieces together. And by some clues, I mean all of them." Josh said, then glanced over at Kristen and gave her a wink. "Mr. Knowles, I'm pretty sure we want the same thing. So, you wanna talk? Let's talk."

Chapter Thirty-Four

34

County jail housed a sample of its usual suspects, including a few local habitual drunks, a frat boy being held on a DUI from a weekend binge, and a couple of retail shop thieves who couldn't make bond. On top of those customary detainees, it held a special guest visitor. A new tenant totally unfamiliar with the inside of a cell.

After the shock of his unexpected arrest, the newest captive played through every step, every minute, every second of the source of his confinement. He couldn't come up with anything. There was not a single glitch or speck of evidence that could have pointed a hint of suspicion in his direction. It made absolutely no sense. A well-respected judge, evidently willing to cut corners to reach the federal bench, was dead. And with nothing but signs of a tragic suicide, including a suicide note, somehow, this man found himself in the slammer.

Fear not, for he had the money to hire a dream team. It worked for O.J. Simpson, so why not him? Heck, O.J. had more evidence pointing to his guilt than the Cookie Monster videoed with his hand in the cookie jar, but his high-priced legal team still liberated his ass, at least until armed robbery and other charges gave his freedom the Heisman.

From what this jailbird could decipher, they had no evidence against him. He'd call his lawyer, have him hire the best private investigator and put together a dream team, fork out a couple of hundred grand, get them to file a motion to put an end to this blatant miscarriage of justice, and this nightmare would be ancient history. Innocent until proven guilty, and there was no proof. There couldn't be!

"You have a visitor," a deputy jailer said, breaking his thought process.

Shocked, he removed his burned backside from the cold bench. "A visitor?"

The announcement was odd. He hadn't called his lawyer yet, so how could he have a visitor? Perhaps his attorney got wind through the grapevine and took it upon himself to check on his client before he received "the call." Yep, that was likely it. The Santa Barbara rumor mill finally served a purpose. For the first time since his arrest, a slight sense of comfort settled over him, for the cavalry was on its way. Without yet having to lift a finger, or even having to push his pointer seven times on a phone, the wheels were in motion, and his freedom was imminent.

"Come with me," the deputy demanded, fumbling for the key to unlock the cell of the sole occupant. For his safety, the Sheriff ordered that this particular detainee not get mixed in with the general population of offenders.

The deputy slid open the cell door, cuffed his crook, and escorted him down the lengthy, frigid hallway, and opened the second door on the left into the visitation room. The cinder block-walled cave was centered with six sets of opposite-facing cubicles, all of them equipped with a phone handset and separated by clear, bullet-proof glass. Its bare walls stood naked, save for a round, black and white clock; perhaps symbolic to let half the entrants to the room know that their time was up. On the good side of the glass, another deputy guarded the visitors' door.

When the prisoner entered the room, it was only him, his deputy escort, and the stoic deputy on the freedom side of the room. Befuddled, he took two steps into the room, then stopped. Where was his visitor? Was this a ploy? Was the deputy going to rough him up in the absence of any witnesses? He had seen this before in a movie. He was about to get pummeled, and no one would be there to corroborate him. Was it payback for his recent, widely publicized lack of support for a proposed raise for local law enforcement?

His latest sense of comfort dwindled quickly until the robotic deputy opened the visitors' door and a man appeared. The man looked to be about six feet tall, approaching forty, wearing a Detroit Tigers baseball cap, dark, metal-framed sunglasses, and sporting a mustache that modeled the 1980s', *Ferrari*-driving television heartthrob. If ever there was a poster child for a private investigator, this guy was it. The jailbird's sense of solace was restored. He wasn't about to get his backside beaten to a pulp. His attorney must have sent a P.I. to gather what he needed to exonerate his client.

The inmate's guard uncuffed his prisoner and pointed him to a seat. The visitor's guard pointed to a seat for the guest under his watch on the liberated side of the room. Perfectly synchronized, the two sat facing each other. Likewise, in unison, they picked up their respective handsets.

"Hello," greeted the *Magnum P.I.* look-a-like.

"You must be the private investigator my attorney must have hired to help get me out of this hell hole. I'm so grateful you're here. I have so many questions. How can they charge me with the murder of Judge Stricker? What kind of evidence can they have against me? There's no way there's anything incriminating!"

"Please, please, slow down. I understand your angst. Unfortunately, they have the most incriminating evidence possible. Blood!"

"Blood?!"

"Yes, the judge's blood and—" The visitor was interrupted by the impatient client.

"Well, of course, the judge's blood was at the scene. There must have been blood everywhere, God rest his soul. But that still doesn't implicate me in any way!" The inmate was emphatic. "It's not possible!"

"You're right, the judge's blood was everywhere," the visitor agreed with a nod. He let it settle in for a few seconds with the suspect before he continued. "It's where his blood wasn't that stood out."

"What do you mean? I don't understand."

"There was blood spatter all over his desk, but none on the suicide note that was sitting atop his letterbox."

"So?"

"So, that means the suicide note had to have been placed there after the judge was shot, which means he couldn't have fired the shot to his head, then have placed the note afterwards. The medical examiner said he died instantly."

"Wow! Okay." He hesitated, carefully choosing his next words. "Well, that still doesn't implicate me in any way."

"True," the *Magnum P.I.* clone concurred, letting the inmate enjoy a brief ride back up his emotional roller coaster, then sat quietly for about ten seconds.

The jailbird couldn't tolerate the silence.

"Again, I'm glad you're here. But I still fail to see how they can charge me with the murder of one of my closest friends from what you've told me. You're not telling me anything that would justify them arresting me, let alone convict me of such a heinous crime. And while I'm sure you're good at what you do, I gotta be honest with you." The inmate smirked, as his free hand circled his face. "Don't you think that your Tom Selleck identical twin get-up is over-playing the P.I. role just a bit?"

"Very true. Just because the subsequently placed suicide note likely rules out suicide, it in no way implicates you for his murder." The visitor let the roller coaster reach its peak, then let it rest in the clouds for a bit. He patiently waited for several seconds, then gave it a nudge. "But there also was a piece of paper underneath the suicide note. Ironically, it was a DNA and blood test report. Unlike the fake suicide note, the report had blood on it. In addition to the judge's blood being on the report, there were a few drops of blood that weren't his."

He paused to let the inmate linger in anticipation and hang in agony. The normally dark complected, well-tanned Armani suit-wearing businessman was now a pale-faced, orange-jump-suit-wearing jailbird. The visitor turned around and gave a slight nod to his deputy. The deputy nodded back, opened the door, and in walked Deputy D.A. Joshua Rizzetti. Josh stood beside the deputy, easily within hearing distance of the visitor, and attentively listened.

Bewildered, the jailbird was speechless. The investigator had disclosed new information, but still nothing that implicated the accused. This waltzing around as to what evidence they had against him, if in fact they had any, tried the inmate's patience. And when the inmate couldn't stand the music any longer, Magnum saved the best dance for last.

"A DNA test confirmed who the other blood drops on the report came from, implicating the primary suspect."

"Who?" The jailbird waited for a response. Nothing. Then he clued-in. "Me?!"

"It's a one-hundred-percent match to your DNA."

"That's not possible. There is no way my blood was at the scene, not to mention that the state doesn't have my DNA on file. So, there's no way they could match anything to my DNA."

The inmate was emphatic. Almost every inch of his body was covered, and he had no cuts of any kind. He was sure of it. Not to mention the fact that his DNA profile was not in the system.

"Oh, I'm sorry. Did I forget to mention that the DNA report that was under the suicide note was yours—Mr. Mayor?"

The requirement for elected officials to have their DNA profile on file with the state was a referendum in the process of being placed on the ballot in the next election. But that hadn't happened yet, so clearly the investigator was mistaken. The mayor seemed certain of that.

"What? How? There's no way! That's not possible!" The Stanford-educated, wealthy, nine-figured, skyrocketing politician sat there stunned, mouth wide-open, catching flies like a mouth-breathing moron.

The visitor's smile hid beneath the rat resting above his upper lip as he sluggishly removed his ball cap, then pulled the sunglasses from his face in theatrical fashion. He lightly placed them on the cubicle countertop in front of him, and gazed ferociously like a prizefighter staring down his opponent after a weigh-in. Next, in slow motion he raised his hand to his face, pinched the corner of his mustache, and slowly peeled it from his face, revealing a smile the size of Texas.

On the other side of the glass, the mayor stared through the transparent shield. But the once-clear glass that separated them figuratively transposed into a mirror facing both of them. The prisoner studied the face in front of him, but no longer saw an investigator nor a savior. He saw a spitting image of himself!

Clean-shaven, and face unconcealed, Nick Knowles stared across the glass, through the eyes of Judas, and into the soul of the traitor. With his right hand, he reached behind his right ear, laying a finger on his faded childhood scar. "And I'm not Tom Selleck's identical twin, I'm yours."

Adopted as an infant, the once slender twelve-year-old boy had no idea that the only real parents he had ever known were not his biological parents. They felt that he was too young to know and decided to wait until he was older. And given his oddly coincidental resemblance to his adoptive parents, his looks provided him no clues. Like them, he was tall and thin, with light brown eyes and thick, wavy hair. They had planned to tell him someday; but given the unique circumstances of his adoption, including his heartbreaking separation from his identical twin, they were in no hurry to do so. However, after the boy's mysterious disappearance and miraculous return, they broke the news of the adoption to the imposter soon afterward; but kept the agonizing sibling separation a secret.

Fighting to the bitter end, the mayor refused to surrender his freedom. "You're lying to me. They can't pin this on me. There is no way my blood was at the scene!"

With the handset in his left hand, pressed against his ear, the Magnum-turned-Mayor-look-alike raised his right hand to eye-level, in front of the face of the only person on Earth who shared his exact DNA. He inched it closer to the glass, then pinched the tip of his index finger with his thumb and middle finger. Slowly, a drop of blood trickled down his finger.

The mayor was dumbstruck. Everything he had done since age twelve to acquire, maintain and protect the life to which he convinced himself he was entitled was vanishing before his eyes. The hope of one day living eight years in the White House abruptly transformed itself into the dread of spending life in the big house. In a last-ditch effort at self-preservation, he hollered, "It's not my blood! He framed me! I can prove it. Get a detective in here. Get my lawyer!"

The four other occupants in the room didn't move. They didn't wince. They didn't flinch. They didn't do anything. The mayor made eye contact with the Deputy D.A., ironically looking for some sort of twisted justice. Moving nothing else on his body, Josh merely shook his head which broadcasted his smug smile.

"You'll never get away with this," cried the mayor. "This will never stick. They don't have enough evidence on me, and I have the financial resources to make this go away."

The vindicated twin spoke. "Oh, did I forget to mention that the District Attorney's Office also received an anonymous letter revealing the location and code to your hidden safe? The police recovered your ledger, proof of falsified documents, tapes of incriminating conversations, and other evidence of your corrupt business dealings you were concealing in your safe."

Nick leaned toward the glass, whispering, "Of course, I took the liberty of keeping some of the documents for myself, like your Social Security Card and the bank information of your account in the Cayman Islands. That's quite a sizable nest egg you've accumulated there. I'm sure in large part with the help of your Vegas mob friends. It's certainly more than enough for *me* to retire in the lifestyle to which *you've* become accustomed. As you know, those assets are the property of Paul S. Dosteel III, who changed his name from Timothy Schafer. And since legally I'm Timothy Schafer, that all belongs to me."

The look of defeat snuck its way onto the mayor's face, but the entitled socialite refused defeat. "Whether or not that's true, I have more resources. Very substantial resources. So, as I said, I won't let you get away with this!" He slammed down his fist. Nobody in the room so much as blinked.

"Oh, that's right. I'm sure you're referring to the proceeds of your—I mean my inheritance. Remember, the inheritance went to Timothy Schafer. And like I said since legally I'm Timothy Schafer . . . well, let me put it this way. Your ass is mine, and now your assets are mine too."

The attitude of self-preservation quickly turned to an expression of total defeat. The mayor had met his match, literally and figuratively. And a smart man, hell-bent on revenge, and with a quarter of a century to plot his vengeance was not going to blow his opportunity for retribution. Obviously outsmarted, but ignorant as to how, the mayor was baffled, unable to figure out the answer to a couple of questions that had him stumped. He just sat there, thunderstruck.

Dismayed, finally the mayor found a few words and asked, "How did you know about the hidden safe?"

"Recently, I've had some faint memories as a toddler of hiding under my dad's desk, seeing him open a safe hidden behind a secret hinged cabinet door that was constructed to blend into the wall, and that was hidden behind a painting. I figured that if I could remember seeing that more than once, you must have seen it a thousand times."

Kicking himself while down, the mayor poured more salt on his own wound, asking, "How in the world could you break into my safe so quickly, without getting caught? The police response time is almost instant. And no one but me knows the code. And there's absolutely no way anybody could guess it."

"080196."

"But—how did you—," the mayor stuttered, and after a prolonged pause, choked out his final question. "How could you know such random numbers?" Shaking his head in complete disbelief, he stared into the eyes of his twin.

"August 1, 1996. The date you changed your life . . . and ruined mine."

Nick Knowles didn't crack a smile. He just sat there with perfect posture and stared through the transparent shield. As a decorated marksman, he had killed his fair share of enemies during wartime. A sniper rifle in his hand meant zero chance of survival for his marked target. But today, he needed no metal weapons or silver projectiles. Today, he needed no rifle. Today, he needed no bullets. If looks could kill. Well, looks accompanied by some bling.

Despite the jail's policy, the mayor had sweet-talked the collection clerk into violating the procedure, which mandated jewelry confiscation from inmates. In return, he guaranteed her a substantial raise when the wrongfully accused cleared his name. He assured her he was innocent, and that soon he would be back in power again. In exchange for his pledge, she let him keep his cherished bracelet.

Nick slowly returned the phone handset to its resting place and pointed to the jewelry that had adorned the prisoner's wrist for twenty-five years. The mayor looked to his bracelet, then back at his clone. Nick reached into his pocket and, with his fist tightly closed, pulled out a piece of metal more armed than a weapon, a piece of silver more deadly than a bullet.

He opened his clenched fist, and with both hands, he raised the original custom bracelet the Schafers had given to their son on his eighth birthday. He pressed it up against the glass, with the inscription carving deeply into the eyes of its captive reader, which read: "*Life is full of surprises. Some will change your life forever. Love, Mom & Dad.*"

Nick spoke softly, but carried a big stick, "Surprise! Have a nice life . . . sentence."

Mic dropped!

Chapter Thirty-Five

35

FIVE MINUTES LATER, Kristen waited patiently under the shade of a seventy-year-old oak tree, expecting her new client may need further consultation and also ready to step in if the plan went awry. He insisted on going in unescorted to intensify the impact and lower the boom. As part of the plan, Mr. Knowles was careful not to make his attorney complicit in any wrongdoing. All the while, his exceptional attorney provided him guidance on a strategy to lay claim to the ill-gotten gains the mayor inherited from his parents. An inheritance to which Nick Knowles was entitled.

The Schafers had died intestate, meaning they did not have a legal will in place when they died. So, under the laws of intestate succession, which determines the distribution of assets when one dies without a will, their entire estate went to their only son. Legally, the real Timothy Schafer was the beneficiary, not the Stanford-privileged imposter. Legally, it was Nick Knowles, not Paul Dosteel.

Kristen was prepared to file a civil suit on her client's behalf to seek damages under several tort theories. The suit's value would equal that of the Schafers' estate at the time of their passing, plus interest of seven percent per annum from the date of their death. Well over a decade and a half of interest would increase the total substantially.

After the Schafers' passing, the probate court assessed the value of their estate to determine the amount of their son's inheritance. Even after the probate fees reduced his take-home amount, the young man ran away with nearly twenty million dollars. In present-day dollars, the inheritance amount, plus interest, plus the lofty sum in the Cayman's account meant a massive payday for Kristen's client. His compensation stood to be the equivalent of him having earned tens of millions of dollars since the date of his parents' death.

Nick Knowles exited the police station and spotted his attorney under the cool canopy of the towering tree. He gave a thumbs up, and she smiled and reciprocated. He strode down the steps just beyond the door and nonchalantly walked by his attorney and said, "Thank you. I'll be in touch in a couple of weeks after I get back from my trip to The Caymans."

Kristen beamed and gave him an acknowledging nod. Nick walked up the street as Josh came out of the building. Nick continued around the corner and disappeared.

The law firm of Perricone, Pocino, and Salvatore had dumped the mayor as their client as soon as Kristen shared with Mr. Perricone her suspicions of the mayor's questionable business activities, even before confirmation of her skepticism. At first, Mr. Perricone was reluctant, given the financial impact, it would have on the firm. But he trusted his associate's intuition implicitly and deferred to her judgment. He was right about doing so. As it turned out, the firm stood to make substantially more money from their newly retained client than they would've from their old one; not to mention they didn't have to learn a new face.

In her typical generous fashion, Kristen insisted that her firm only receive twenty percent of the amount they recovered for Mr. Knowles, as opposed to the standard thirty-three percent. When all was said and done, Kristen's firm still would cash in over nine million dollars, of which Kristen would get half for bringing in the new client. And true to form, she had already earmarked one million dollars of her share to be donated to St. Jude's Children's Hospital.

And as for the van-struck, heavily beaten, home-bouncing, war-fighting, award-winning marksman; he finally hit his target and won the jackpot, and was looking forward to riding off into the sunset with almost fifty million dollars courtesy of a familiar stranger, Target X. After all, it was only fair that Nick takes most of the money from the man who had taken most of his life.

Josh approached Kristen, who was casually leaning against the great oak, glowing brightly as the sun while playing it as cool as the shaded grass on which she gracefully stood. Josh ogled, admiring, and loving everything about her.

"Thank you for doing the right thing," she said.

"Always," he replied. "Right back at ya!"

"Always."

"And thank you for remembering all of my random references to eighties' music over the years." Josh lit up with his biggest smile. "You always said it was useless, but it paid off. And for a non-litigator, you followed one of the key rules of being an effective litigator— know your audience."

"It was a long shot," Kristen said. "But I thought, hey, if great minds think alike. And speaking of, please humor me. Tell me what your thought process was."

"At first, when you referred to TW as Colonel Mustard, I didn't think much of it, other than the humorous reference you were making to the stains from the pasta sauce on his shirt. Then it made me think of the game *Clue*. But still, I didn't think anything more of it. It was when I closed my eyes and counted one two three four five, that made me think further. As I'm sure you expected, those numbers pulled the trigger and I started singing in my head the 1980s' song 'Senses Working Overtime.' That's when your wink and eighties' keyboard reference jumped out at me and, in conjunction with the game *Clue,* I realized you had given me a clue. I recalled that the 1980s' hit 'Senses Working Overtime' was sung by the band XTC. And, at least from what I liked, they had one other hit in the U.S., that being 'The Mayor of Simpleton.' And there it was, the final and most important piece of the puzzle that I hadn't figured out. The whodunit." Josh hung on a dramatic pause, then finished. "The mayor, that's who."

"Brilliant," Kristen exclaimed. "Do you know you are one of the few people on the face of the Earth that could have deciphered all of that from what little I said?"

"Kristen, my friend," Josh grinned, "you are the brilliant one! Do you know you are probably the only attorney on the face of the Earth that could've stayed well within the bounds of your ethical obligation to maintain client confidentiality, yet still convey a message necessary to save lives? Who else could say so much without really saying anything?"

"Hey. If there's anybody who knows a lot about saying so much without saying anything, you're the man." Kristen laughed. "I guess I learned from the best."

"Ha-ha, funny. Although, I do appreciate the backhanded compliment," Josh said, truly amused. "After your clue, I was fairly certain the mayor was the mastermind behind this mystery. But something else was the clincher."

"Really?" said Kristen, pulling her head back in shock. "What was the finishing touch?"

"The mayor's name—Paul S. Dosteel."

"Why was that the crowning blow? He changed his name from Timothy Schafer in college, right?"

"Exactly," responded Josh, followed by another dramatic pause before he revealed the capper. "In my research, I found out that Tim Schafer grew up on Puesta Del Sol, not far from the accident scene where the twelve-year-old boy went missing before his miraculous amnesiac return."

"And?"

"Well, if you rearrange the letters in Puesta Del Sol, it spells—," again in a staged pause, he held up his right pointer finger and titled his head, "that's right—Paul S. Dosteel. And I'm sure when he legally changed his name, he added 'the third' to turn aside potential suspicion."

"Wow! Impressive!" Kristen extended Josh a high-five. "Perhaps you should quit your day job and become a detective."

Flattered, but not interested, Josh replied, "Thanks, but no thanks. I'll leave that to TW. And speaking of T-dub, I've got some good news for you. He told me that among the many criminal enterprises of the mayor, it seems that Mr. Dosteel was involved in a pharmacy scam."

"Not sure why that's good news for me, but go on," Kristen said, pretending like she didn't sense where this might be headed.

"Well, he, along with two partners, owned and oversaw the operations of two local pharmacies. Both were 'closed door' pharmacies, meaning that they were not open to the public and only filled prescriptions for individuals associated with many senior care facilities."

"Is this going where I think it is?"

"Knowing your instincts, I'm sure it is," said Josh. "According to T-dub, the FBI believes he and his partners were engaged in a scheme to bill insurers MediStar, MediCo, and TheraMedic for approximately thirteen million dollars for medications that were never dispensed. Apparently, the fraud scheme was detected by MediStar, in part, because of a massive deficit between the pharmacies' documented inventories and the claims that each submitted for insurance reimbursement. As part of the conspiracy, they billed insurance companies for allegedly submitting claims for delivering over hundreds of medications to people who had died prior to the claimed date of delivery."

"Wow!"

"According to the FBI, proceeds of the fraud scheme were laundered by overpaying consulting and delivery companies owned by shell companies of the mayor and his two partners, one male and one female. To add to the mystery, apparently the male partner of one of the pharmacies is missing. They think he may have been killed for wanting out of the operation. And, as I'm sure you've guessed by now, one of those pharmacies happens to be the one next to Burrito Dynamite in Goleta."

Kristen's mouth dropped. "Unbelievable!"

"Agent Hurley thinks that Doctor Overman's partner, Doctor Bayle, learned that the mayor was the one who screwed his great uncle out of his land and got himself and his partner in too deep in the hopes of fetching some sort of revenge. They think he may have threatened to expose the mayor, and perhaps got whacked. Law enforcement is tearing up the old cabin where T-dub and I heard gunshots, thinking Bayle's body may turn up around there."

"Like the hit songs of Phil Collins, it sounds like Doctor Overman soon will be singing please 'Take Me Home' after she becomes an 'Easy Lover' in the sla-slaslammer, whoa oh," Kristen sang, attempting to mimic another Phil Collins hit, "Sussudio."

"And people say I can't sing," joshed Josh. He actually enjoyed her lovely singing voice. He added, "Profiting from the greed of Doctor Bayle, Doctor Overman is going to jail."

Kristen jabbed, "And to think, you were going to ask her out, in the hopes of some sort of 'Tainted Love,'" cushioning the blow with another 1980s' music reference.

"Well, I—a—no, but a—" Against the ropes, Josh stumbled to respond.

Too kind to let him sweat it, Kristen jumped in. "Don't beat yourself up. Heck, she's so hot, I was tempted to ask her out!"

"Seriously?"

"No, you idiot," Kristen said, giving him a soft punch on his toned bicep. "Although, if one could make another switch teams, she'd be the one. Those full lips were begging to be kissed." Sneaking in a faint snort, she laughed. "You know how you always say—at the end of your life, you'll regret more the things you didn't do, than the things you did?"

"Yeah."

"Well, I think this is one of the rare exceptions when you won't regret something you didn't do."

"Truer words have never been spoken, my friend. And following that train of thought, I have to give you something that I know I'll regret if I don't. I have an early birthday present for you."

Kristen lit up with excitement, as Josh pulled a blank white envelope from his back pocket, and not so much as handed it to her as much as she ripped it from his hands.

"Can I open it now?" She tore open the envelope like a kid on Christmas morning. "Who am I kidding, I'm opening it now!" She pulled out four tickets and shuffled through them.

"Are you serious? I love it. Two tickets to the Ole Miss-Alabama football game next season. And two plane tickets to get us there. Finally, I get to experience tailgating at The Grove." She caught herself and hesitated, before saying, "I'm assuming you want to go with me. They are for us, right?"

"That's totally up to you."

Kristen gave Josh a big smile, accompanied by a look he had never seen from her. Then she clued him in. "You know your friend's famous quote that you love to cite—women have choices, men only have chances? Well—"

With Kristen still speaking, Josh didn't hesitate a millisecond and planted a fiery kiss on her moving lips, the most passionate of which either had ever experienced.

When the prolonged kiss ended, they both sighed and laugh nervously. "Finally!" said Kristen.

"Hey," Mr. 1980s replied, "in my defense and in keeping with your Phil Collins-themed references, courtesy of his hit remake of The Supremes, 'You Can't Hurry Love.'"

"Touché."

Then Josh pulled a second envelope from his pocket and offered it to his companion, who now was giddy as a schoolgirl. Again, she snatched the surprise from his hand.

"There's more?" Tearing open her next gift, she screamed, "Two tickets to Vail!"

"Yep. I figured that, after all that we've been through in the past few months, we need a vacation. So, I thought we could go skiing in Vail. After we're both walking, of course."

Given a rare second opportunity, Josh had capitalized on his chance, finally having kissed Kristen for the first time. Now presented with her opportunity, Kristen made her choice and planted a big one on Josh.

Stay Tuned

Thank you for reading **_Murder in Santa Barbara_**. I truly hope you enjoyed it. If so, I have good news for you . . . there's more to follow!

But first, I want you to know that I welcome and appreciate online reviews, and I thank you in advance if you take the time to share your thoughts. Your support really does make a difference and I read all the reviews personally so I can get your feedback and make my next book even better.

Now, back to the good news! Book #2 of the Joshua Rizzetti thriller series, **_Murder in Vail_**, is now available. Get your copy today to see how the adventures of Deputy D.A. Joshua Rizzetti continue.

> Deputy D.A. Joshua Rizzetti and his best friend-turned-girlfriend Kristen Laney go on vacation to Vail, Colorado to ski, unwind and de-stress from their recent knock on death's door. But their ski escape unexpectedly gets derailed, as bloodshed once again crosses their path

and puts their lives on the line; turning their dream vacation into their worst nightmare.

To receive updates on the release of Book # 3 of the series, ***The Grove Conspiracy***, as well as other exciting news, content, and exclusive offers, please visit www.DeanCFerraro.com and sign up to join my email list.

—Dean C. Ferraro

About the Author

Dean earned his Bachelor's Degree from California State Polytechnic University, Pomona ("Cal Poly Pomona") and his Juris Doctor Degree from the University of Mississippi School of Law ("Ole Miss"). He is licensed to practice law in the State and Federal Courts in Colorado, Tennessee, and California.

Dean is a former Assistant District Attorney, where he worked for several years as one of the top prosecuting attorneys in the state of Tennessee. As a prosecutor, he tried seven first-degree murder trials, all resulting in convictions.

Today, Dean practices law in Colorado and continues to dedicate much of his time to pursue his lifelong passion for writing.

Dean lives with his lovely wife and their two amazing children. He enjoys skiing, kayaking, and coaching youth sports.

He is working on his third novel, ***The Grove Conspiracy.*** Go to www.deancferraro.com to stay updated on its release.

Social Media links:

Website: https://deancferraro.com/

Twitter: https://twitter.com/DeanCFerraro1

Facebook: https://www.facebook.com/DeanCFerraro/

Instagram: https://www.instagram.com/deancferraro/

Follow me on BookBub: https://www.bookbub.com/authors/dean-c-ferraro

Also By Dean C. Ferraro

Murder in Vail - Book #2 of the Joshua Rizzetti thriller series.

Deputy D.A. Joshua Rizzetti and his girlfriend go on vacation to Vail, Colorado to ski, relax and unwind from their recent knock on death's door. But their ski escape unexpectedly gets derailed, as murder once again crosses their path and puts their lives at risk. An innocent treasure hunt takes a deadly turn and if Josh can't solve a cryptic message quickly, his dream vacation will become his worst nightmare!

The Grove Conspiracy - Book #3 of the Joshua Rizzetti thriller series, coming in 2023.

Made in the USA
Middletown, DE
21 October 2022